CONFESSIONS OF A
Mother Inferior

First published in 2015 by:

Britain's Next Bestseller
An imprint of Live It Publishing
27 Old Gloucester Road
London, United Kingdom.
WC1N 3AX

www.britainsnextbestseller.co.uk

Copyright © 2015 by Ericka Waller

The moral right of Ericka Waller to be identified as the author of this work has been asserted by her in accordance with the Copyright, Designs and Patents Act 1988.

All rights reserved.

Except as permitted under current legislation, no part of this work may be photocopied, stored in a retrieval system, published, performed in public, adapted, broadcast, transmitted, recorded or reproduced in any form or by any means, without the prior permission of the copyright owners.

All enquiries should be addressed to Britain's Next Bestseller.

ISBN 978-1-910565-06-3 (pbk)
Also available as an ebook

Dedication

To Gracie, Daisy, Bliss and Sara

Acknowledgements

MASSIVE thanks to loads of people for making this dream real. John Jenkins for his editing and his faith. Murielle and Britain's Next Bestseller, for taking a chance on an unknown kid. Cornerstones, Katy Hill, Amanda Preston for your support. Jane-Ann-Cameron for the amazing illustrations. And most of all my brilliant family, mum, dad, John, Rachel, Michael, Jennifer and James. Without you this book could not have happened.

The Amazing Supporters That Made This Dream Come True

Shelley Brinkley, Diane Everitt, Jennie Broome, Meg Cooper, Skye, Abi Jacks, Marcia Hutchin, Christina Downs, Kate Burton, Hayley Bird, Andrea Taylor, Jade Evans, Caitlyn McCarthy, Lauren E Wickham, Larissa Lane, George Newton, Issi Doyle, Rebecca Greig, Alicya Eyo, Michelle Harding-Fleet, Becci Vale, Monika Dekany-Brown, Irenka Griffin, Paul (Nace) Furniss, Linda Broome, Natalie Bosher, Fleur Piddlesden, Karen Edwards, Georgia Richards, Sarah Allen, Corinna Kemp, Heather Ahearn, Rob Powell, Laila, Emily Tealady, Lucy Ridges, Caroline Simmons, Sallyj Scott, Dawn M. Swanton, Cat Blanchard, Tessa Marshall, JD, Jackie Laycock, Lynne Errington, Margaret Errington, Jay Kelly, Mark Oakley, Sara Merrett, Kelly W, Isabelle Foot, The Pmilitary Squad, Emma Collins, Fran & Jason Harling, Joanne Allan, Michelle Hardwick, Daniel Hansen, Lyndsey McCullough, Kelly Leighfield, Jo Hayes, Belle Howard, Louise Douris, Nicola Lee, Lynsey Summers, Caroline Rhodes, Helen Rourke-Hodson, Heather Speakman, Rivka Lipkowitz, Frankie, Carmen Schmitt, Jo Moss, Kerry van Wensveen, Hazel Carter, Alice Priday, Colin Scoggins, Joseph Halsall, Story of Mum, Michelle Garrett, Jill Roberts, Jen Raleigh, Chris Dell, Brian Ellis, Marylin Schlamkow, Amanda Hibbert, Marcia Hutchin, Craig Dallender, Jennifer Telling, Tim Swaby, Vikki Knight, Emma Durant, Violet & Roham, Pamela Robinson, Catherine Hughes, Sophie Alexander, Debbie Hutchin, Jacinta Fletcher, Aditi Scala,

Emma Shilton, Downs Side Up, Emma Cantrell, Josie Chapman, Kerry Steer, Clare Lewis, Lauren Curtis, Hayley Dormer-French, Alison Fisher, Kaleigh Daniels, Tall James, Louise George, Annette Wells, Mandy Hussey, Nicola Griffiths, Anna Webb, Chris Frost, Elle Hale, Jenny Parker, Steve Hicks, Wendy Marsh, Tessa Lowe Rawlings, Laura Duncan, Caroline Davis, Sharron Gurney, Philippa Gill, Crime Book Club, Lisa Jennings, Sarah Thomson, Christine Hern, Rebecca Greig, Alicya Eyo, Ed, Paula Haycock, Angels and Toads, Jemma, Jo Wright, Pippa Lilley, Ele Curtis, Kaye Sowden, Jackie Champniss, Michelle Frostick, R Woodman, Hannah-Leigh Brooker, Soraya Silarbi, Elizabeth McGivern, Emma Brough, Kay McAlister, Julie Timlin, Rachel Neal, Catherine Lee, Andrew Males, Rachel Castle, Teresa Brighton, Katie Turner, Reprobate mum, Victoria Fisher, Danielle Pickering, Adele Jarrett-Kerr, Rae Baker, Amanda Austin, Bill Hutchin, Rachel Paintain, Meagan Griffin, David McCaffrey, Olivier Thenard, Jacqui Wieksza, Pornanong Watts, Jenny & Daisy, Carey Vigor, Brandi Dennehy, Susanna Mare Rose Wildermuth, Vanessa Franklin, Noel O'Reilly, Lucy O'Gara, Rose O'Gara, Nicole Klein, Eric Hutchin, Natasha Hutchin, William J. Scott III.

Chapter One

"NO Rudy, you can't take your entire collection of Polly Pockets to school with you. Just GET IN THE CAR!"

Stupid school run. Will I ever learn a way to get through it without shrieking, forgetting something or someone or being late? I am crosser than normal because it's that day. The one I dread all year. It was a particularly bad morning already, without that on top.

Pip, aged two, refused to use the potty. She wanted to use the toilet like her big sister Rudy, aged five. She did not make it on time. Baby Juno, aged eighteen-months crawled through the puddle of wee and grinned at me. I had no time to bathe her; I rolled her in a pile of wet-wipes and hoped for the best.

While I was doing so, Pip and Rudy removed their shoes and pulled out their pig-tails.

Getting my daughters in the car is like one of those mathematical riddles about crossing a river with a wolf, a goat and a cabbage. This is not a simile for how I see my children. I (the boat) can only carry one passenger at a time. If I leave the wolf and the goat alone together, the wolf will eat the goat. If I leave the goat and the cabbage alone together, the goat will eat the cabbage and so on and so forth.

So instead, I'm a one-woman circus act. Balancing lunchboxes and ballet kits and school bags on my head. Running in and out the house, growing redder and angrier each time. All

I need is the Benny Hill theme tune playing in the background and a Charlie Chaplin moustache – which reminds me, I must remove my facial hair.

Even after driving like a maniac, we're late and all the other mums are not. As always. And they have removed their facial hair and their coats match their handbags. I look down to see what I'm wearing, nervous for a second that I'm still in my pyjamas. It's happened before.

I'm not, but I might as well be. They are cleaner than my toothpaste and snot-stained hoodie. I love it though. It's baggy and, when teamed with leggings worn very high on the waist, will hide the extra pocket of flesh I carry round my midriff, like a life-ring.

My mother-in-law loves to brag about delivering all 11lb of my husband without a single stretch-mark. I, on the other hand, have been left with what looks like a bowl of porridge strapped to my abdomen, until I bend over that is, then it looks like a pair of camel's testicles.

I do not own a handbag. I use a child's rucksack. My coat is bright red so the children can spot me from a distance, although normally they can hear me first anyway. Their coats are all red too. Jimmy hates them because it's 'Arsenal red'. I don't care. I stopped caring about fashion shortly after I started buying maternity clothes and have never looked back since. As for thongs, I stopped wearing them when I could not decide which side of my piles to have the string on.

I park badly, but no worse than any other mum. They might have neat hair and handbags, but they cannot parallel-park for Green and Blacks organic toffee. OK, I might have parked a bit worse than all the other mums. It took me ten attempts to pass my driving test. I know what you might be thinking but actually it's not because I was a bad driver. I simply had no confidence; having failed my Cycling Proficiency in middle school (I did not stop at a stop sign).

Luck was never on my side when I was learning to drive. A giant pigeon flew into the windscreen on one driving test and died. I could not see where to steer through all the blood and mounted the curb (narrowly missing a pedestrian). Then there was the time I tried wearing a sexy short skirt. My sweaty nervous legs got stuck to the leather seat and made farty noises when I changed gear. It put me off and I forgot to look in my blind spot before pulling away (and drove into a car).

The short skirt was my mum's idea. She said it worked for her. I don't know why I listened to her. When she took me out to practise my driving she would take me to Hemel Hempstead's 'magic roundabout' (in the pouring rain) claiming, "This is real life driving, Peta. None of those country lanes you have been practising on."

The magic roundabout, despite its name, is not actually a single roundabout. It was constructed in 1973 to reduce congestion at the original standard roundabout where seven roads intersected, and is the first and only bi-directional roundabout to be constructed in the UK.

Of course it was a disaster. I stalled on every one of the seven mini-roundabouts. People swore at me and beeped their horns. I kept getting the windscreen wipers mixed up with the indicators. My mum just sat smirking, as if she was giving me some life lesson I should be grateful for. My dad was no better. He used to take me to a giant disused waste-ground to practise my driving, having spent two hours beforehand making parking spaces out of cones that he bought specially.

"Right, Peta, its Saturday. You have driven to Watford to go shopping. You are in the Harlequin car park. This is the only free space and you have one attempt to get in it before lots of people start beeping their horns at you. If you don't reverse in quickly enough, someone else will drive in it before you. If you reverse too quickly, however, you will hit a cone. No big deal here in practise but in real life that cone is a brand new Audi

A4, 172 horse-power engine, with a new revised suspension system. Hurry up, time waits for no man."

"Alright, Dad, can I just get on and reverse? All this talk won't buy the baby a new bonnet."

"Hang on!"

"Why are you turning the radio up so loudly?"

"Because that's how loudly you will be playing it when you are driving alone, and you'll be singing along too."

"Seriously, I have to sing along as well?"

"If you want to pass your driving test you will."

"But I don't even like Take That"

"You do now, come on. I'll join in. You can be Gary, I'll be Robbie."

"I don't want to be Gary. He is the fat one."

"You look the most like him, now come one … *All I do is night is pray*"

"*PRAY!*"

"*Hoping that I'll be a part of you again someday!*"

"Pray!"

"*Surely we must be in sight, of the dream we long to liiiive, If you stop and close your eyes, you'll picture me inside I'm so cold and you're alive …*"

"It does not say that. It says, *'I'm so cold and all alone'*."

"No it does not."

"It does, I read the lyrics in the tape cover, and Gary sings that bit."

"I thought you didn't like them?"

"I don't. It's Mickey's tape. Mum bought it for him."

"Can you just reverse now?"

Of course I did not manage to reverse into the spot. It was half the size of the car. Dad was very cross. After getting out for the third time to set the cones up again, I locked the doors, opened the windows and sang Four Non Blondes 'What's going on?' very loudly in his face as I drove past him back home.

The sentence, "Be nice to your sister, she failed another driving test today," became an everyday one in my house. My eldest brother John delighted in my failings and campaigned furiously to the DVLA to employ a 'Three tries and you're out' approach to those attempting to obtain a licence. He found all my hidden test sheets which showed what I failed on to strengthen his case. He wrote lots of articles to the local gazette but they never got published.

I passed in the end though. Slowly, slowly, catchy monkey and all that. I was so nervous on my final test that when the driving instructor introduced himself as Nigel, and then asked what I would like to be called I said, "Nigel."

"Are you trying to be funny?" he said to me.

"No, God no. Sorry. I'm nervous."

"Please check your mirrors and when it's safe to do so, pull away from the curb."

"My dad is called Nigel."

"Pardon?"

"My dad, he's called Nigel. You look a bit like him, except he has more hair and a ginger beard."

"Do you want to pass your driving test?"

"Very, yes please" My tongue was so swollen with nerves I could not even speak.

"Then stop talking and drive the car."

Non-organic chocolate wrappers, high sugar drink-cartons and odd socks fall out of the car along with my squabbling children. I gather them up and toss them back in. (The litter that is, not my offspring). It's only after I have locked up that I notice the bin next to the car. But there is no time to do it now. Pip is refusing to go into pre-school.

"Roo, stand there with Juno and don't move. Pip, get off my leg. You know you will have a great time once you go in there sweetie." I try and prize her pincer-like fingers from my thigh as she hollers in despair.

A queue is forming behind me. I have no choice but to smile nicely and say good morning to everyone, then drag her through the door, still clinging stubbornly on to me. By the time her teacher comes to the rescue, my leggings are down by my knees.

"Faith, get her off me!"

Faith laughs as she peels Pip's fingers from my leg. "Ah Pip, I've been waiting for you. Someone needs to cut up the Play Doh. Will you help me?"

It works. Pip drops me like I'm hot and trots off behind Faith to the activity table. She does not even look back.

"Bye then!" I say as I hang up her coat and lunchbox.

"Bye, Peta. By the way, did you know your leggings are on inside out?" Faith yells at me through the closing door.

Shit. I wriggle the waistband of my leggings back up to bra-level, then race off to where the buggy lies empty and Roo and Juno are nowhere to be seen. It takes me five minutes of searching until I finally find my children in the disabled loo standing under the hand-drier.

"Mummy, look at my hair. I look just like you!" Roo admires herself in the mirror.

"That is not a good thing and you are going to be late. Why did you let Juno out the buggy, and Juno WHY HAVE YOU TAKEN YOUR SHOES OFF AGAIN?!"

The second bell is ringing by the time I've wrestled Juno back into her pushchair and frog marched Roo up the lane.

We stop outside her classroom and I pull her coat back onto her shoulders, then try and arrange her blonde hair into something resembling a style with the fluff-covered band I find in my pocket.

"Ow, you are hurting me, Mummy!"

"Sorry poppet. Here's your lunch. Marmite and cheese today. Love you, have fun, be good."

Her little lips are a butterfly kiss on mine. Her green eyes are shining. She has apple cheeks and a tiny nose. She smells of apricots and plimsolls as she wrestles free of my grasp, keen to get in and see her friends.

"Love you, Mamma, love you, June-bug!" she says, then turns and races across the playground, with feet slapping, pigtails flying and her lunch box dragging along the ground.

We stand and wave at her retreating back until she is out of sight, then I turn round and try to slip away before anyone notices my leggings.

It's too late. We get caught in a snare-up of mums with nothing better to do than stand around talking at the gate and I end up making eye contact with The-Iron-Curtain. My nemesis. I duck my head and pretend to be looking for something in my rucksack, hoping she will take the hint. Instead she looks down at Juno in the buggy and asks, "Is he eating crisps?" "At …" She pauses to look at the time, even though we both know it's only 9am, "9am?"

"No, no, *she* must have found some in the bottom of her buggy," I lie, red-face and flustered. I try to wrestle the Bacon Frazzles from Juno's grasp and wipe her nose on my sleeve at the same time. She shrieks indignantly and tries to bite my hand.

"I can't believe you give him crisps. They contain so much salt. He's still just a baby."

"SHE!" I say again, but The-Iron-Curtain does not seem to be listening.

"How is Rudy getting on at school?" she asks instead, falling into step beside me as we walk down the lane.

This is a trick question. She does not really care how Roo is settling into school. She just wants to start talking about her own daughter Poppy and how amazingly well she is doing. How she is already reading books for ten-year-olds and writing essays whilst spouting French. "Poppy love it. She already on blue-book. What colour Rudy on?"

I hate these sorts of questions. Competitive questions from competitive mums who brag about their children, but deeper down, are bragging about themselves. Last week I overheard The-Iron-Curtain and Cat (Competitive And Trivial) bragging about the books their kids were reading and how they spend all their time in the library these days, trying to keep up with the demands for more literature!

My children spend most of their spare time covering themselves with stickers or filling up plastic bags with dried flowers and ripped up bits of paper.

"I don't know what colour book Roo is on," I tell her honestly, then brace myself.

"You don't know?!" She screeches back at me. "Hooy na ny! Don't you check her reading log? You need look in it *every day* and pick book with her and read with her *every night*, and then write note in reading log. I write many notes because Poppy read many books."

I did not even realise Roo had a reading log. I'm guessing it's in her book bag which I lost in the first week of term. I must find it and make up books I've read with Roo. Hard ones. Blue sticker ones. I sneakily email myself as much while The-Iron-Curtain witters on all the way back to her car, which is parked much closer to the school than mine because she leaves an hour earlier than me.

She starts strapping children into car-seats with alarming efficiency. How does she do this? I can't get my children into their car seats without bribing them with Dolly Mixtures, and even then it's like trying to strap in octopi.

The-Iron-Curtain is a childminder and takes her career very seriously. She probably went on a 'strapping children into car seat' course. She wears a polo-shirt which has 'Registered Ofsted Childminder' sewn on the breast pocket. "I don't want people thinking these snotty badly behaved children are my children," she says to everyone who asks her why she feels the need to wear a badge.

She is still talking. "She read this one about a Tiger, and then she read this one about going to shops and then she read me this one about a lost dog and …"

"Oh dear, I think I Juno has done a poo," I interrupt, desperate for a chance to escape.

"NO!" Juno shouts at me. Ignoring her, I lean in and deeply inhale her nappy. "Uh oh, I think you have sausage. Nice chatting to you," I say vaguely in The-Iron-Curtain's direction. "Must dash!" Then I race off down the lane with Juno screeching all the way. I'll come back for my car later.

As soon as we are out of sight I give Juno back the Bacon Frazzles. She snatches them from me, giving me a kick for good measure in her bright blue trainers. We walk until we get to the village pond where we sit on the damp grass to watch ducks climb on the island and wade about in sticky mud.

"Rabbits," Juno says, pointing a crisp-dusted finger in their direction.

"That's right, poppet. Very clever," I say distractedly as I help myself to a Frazzle.

She smiles and looks pleased with herself.

Juno takes after Jimmy. It used to be just what I wanted. I was so infatuated with him, the thought of a mini-Jimmy had me taking my basal temperature and searching Amazon for ovulation kits.

Now I find the things that remind me of her father slightly irritating.

Jimmy was very shocked at the end of my first pregnancy when the midwife announced he had a 9 lb girl. He was convinced I was carrying a boy. So much so, he checked for himself. "But what about …?" he said pointing.

"That's the umbilical cord sir, would you like to cut it?" The midwife suppressed a smile.

He went squeamish and declined.

We both thought Pip was going to be a boy. My pregnancy was so different from the first. I felt sick as a pig and over-produced saliva.

"Oh, bloody hell. It's another pink one," he sighed as he passed her to me. "And she looks just like your mother."

"Should we not find out the sex at the scan?" I asked him nine months later when I was pregnant again. "Before we start buying lots of blue?"

"No. Third time lucky love, I feel it in my waters. This one is going to be a boy."

"Luck must be a lady," I said to him as I stroked Juno's newborn cheek, whilst simultaneously delivering the placenta. The first time something so large slipped out so easily I felt rather concerned, but by the third time it was no big deal.

They may not have been his first choice, but he is a great

father to our girls. Roo was so much bigger than the newborn clothes we had prepared. Jimmy went out to Debenhams and came back to the maternity ward with pink sleep suits, and snow white vests. They looked so small in his hands. "I picked them because they felt the softest. Is that right?"

He bundles with them as though they were boys, but he also sits patiently while they style his hair with sparkly clips and lets them colour his toenails in with felt-tip pens.

He has still not quite given up all his dreams though. Yesterday he took them to the park to play football, but all they wanted to do was rub mud over their pink scooters, and then go and clean them in a puddle. They came back an hour later hour covered in dirt and very cross with one another.

"You could have tried to kick it, Roo!"

"But every time I went to kick it, you moved it away, Daddy."

"That is the whole point of the game!!"

"Well it's a silly game isn't it, Mummy?"

"Sorry poppet?" I said, zoning back in.

"Looking at cooking books again?" Jimmy picked an apple from the fruit bowl and stood crunching it by my shoulder. "Why don't you just bloody write one?"

"It's not as easy as that," I said standing up, and shutting down the window I had open on the computer. "You don't just write cook books. You have to research them and think about them. For a long time." I took a quiche out the fridge and peeled off the cling film.

"Excuses, excuses," Jimmy said, patting my bum as I bent over to put lunch in the oven.

I slapped his hand away as I straightened up. "What is a silly game anyway, Roo?"

"Football. Daddy says we all have to learn how to play it, but I don't want to."

"Well you don't have to play football, my love" I gave Jimmy a stern look. "And you need to get over it. Honestly, you are like Brian Glover in Kes. Go and play with people your own age."

"All gone," Juno pulls me from my reverie to tell me there are no crisps left.

"Time to go then," I say, picking her up and holding her close "You little stinker." She giggles in delight, showing her orange-stained teeth from the crisps.

I suddenly realise she has never been to the dentist and feel a wave of mum-guilt. I still have not booked her in for her one year jabs and check-up either. I've not labelled Roo's school uniform or put her name down for gymnastics. I've not dropped Jimmy's suit into the dry cleaners, or changed the sheets.

I sigh as the weight of all the things I have not done settles over me.

"Say bye-bye to the ducks, June-bug."

"Rabbits!"

We get home and I see that the house has not been cleaned in my absence by some Disney mice and bluebirds wearing clothes.

"Seems I'll just have to do it myself then, Juno."

I put her down on the kitchen floor and find a selection of pots, wooden spoons, biscuits and wellies to keep her amused.

Then I look round at the upturned cereal bowls, piles of washing, abandoned toast and lumps of Play Doh, trying to work out where to start.

Then I put my head in my hands and cry.

I hate this day. I knew it was going to be hard, it's always hard, but I had sort of hoped it would get easier each time this day came around.

Today is the day I get a pain in my chest. Today is the four year anniversary. Four very long and yet short years, since I lost my best friend. I hate that term for it. I did not lose her. She died.

She died with no warning. No word of what was happening to her. One minute we were talking about the pink of her nail polish, and the next Sara was on the floor.

We were at work. She had just taken a sip of her Irn Bru. "Ye can take a girl outta Scotland …" she used to say each time she uncapped the lid for her morning sugar rush. I was nursing my first tea of the day when Des, the Sales Director came over.

"Sara, how many bids in the pipeline this week?"

Her cheeks flushed and I saw her hand shake slightly on the mouse as she opened the spreadsheet.

"Forty thou," she said quietly.

"You'll need to double that. Pronto," he said frowning at her, before turning on his heel to go and bully the production team.

Two seconds later she collapsed. Sara was a tiny size six, but the sound of her fall seemed to shake the foundations of our four-storey office. It rattled the floor around me, where she lay unconscious at my feet.

I wanted to believe she had just fainted, but I saw her body convulse, and the blood trickle from her mouth where she had bitten through her lip. Her face was lopsided when she finally came to. She looked like a stroke victim, slurring her words to me. "Wha' happened? My heed. My heed. Help."

I had no idea what to do or say. I shouted for someone to call 999 and then went and sat with her, stroking her hand and trying to keep her calm until they arrived.

She drifted in and out of consciousness.

"Make way, love," the ambulance man said as he crouched down next to us. "Now can you tell me your name, darling?"

He gently took her hand from me. I stepped back to grab her handbag and then started making calls.

Pat answered on the fifth ring.

"Pat? It's Peta."

"Hello, hen. How's ye? Ah was in the garden. Always so much to do."

I pictured her on her knees, tending to her beloved roses. Did she prick her finger in the same second that her daughter's blood ruptured? Did she feel the earth shake, miles away in Epsom? Or was she lost in the calm before the storm?

"Pat, it's Sara, she's had a fall. Collapsed. You need to get here. I think she … I don't know, does she have epilepsy?" I'm making no sense.

"Ye know she doesn't. Is she OK? Is she hurt?"

I couldn't bring myself to tell her about the stroke-face bit. "Pat, please. Just come."

The ambulance people were so kind. Looking back now, I see that they knew the inevitable outcome already. They talked about making her comfortable. They tried to calm her down. She was talking but it was making no sense. I could only make out one word in the muddle of Scottish vowels: "Bairns."

"Don't worry, Bird, I'm on it. I'll sort it. I'll get them picked up and we'll come to the hospital as soon as we can."

It was hard to look at her, laying awkwardly on the floor. The paramedic smiled at me sadly. I did not understand why. I didn't know she'd had an aneurysm. I didn't even know what they were. I thought it was nothing serious. Back then I was one of those people who thought horrible things only happened to other people in other lives, not you and the people in yours.

I kissed Sara's cold hand as she lay on the stretcher. I fought to stop the room from spinning as they wheeled her away, and then I sat down and carried on making phone calls.

They hoped to operate on her the next day. To stem the

bleeding before it did further damage. I was in my car on the way to go and see her when I got the call from Pat. "They ha' taken her down to theatre now. Scans showed damage 'at cannot wait. Don't come. I'll be in touch."

What do you do with your hands while your best friend's are full of tubes and drips to keep her alive? What do you do in the hours that she is being operated on and no one is calling you to tell you if she is going to be OK? The rest of the world keeps talking, eating, and sleeping. The rest of the world keeps living, whilst your life is on pause.

My brave best friend tried, but she had another bleed as they tried to work on the first one. It was too big. They stopped trying. Instead, they carefully stitched her head together and hooked her up onto life support. She never woke up. Her brilliant, beautiful brain died quietly and without fuss. And at her family's wishes, the machines were switched off and her body joined it.

She never got a chance to say goodbye to her children, her bairns. It would have been too much for them to see her at the hospital, weak and hooked up to monitors. To see her lopsided mouth and hear her slurred speech.

So their last memory of her is their goodbye kiss that morning, hastily planted amidst a flurry of "Have ye got yer coat an' book bag? HURRY! No time for teeth brushing. No you can't wear 'at to school!"

How could any of us have known it would be the last time they felt her lips on their forehead.

She never got to meet my Pip and Juno. How much she would have loved them.

Ignoring the mess and destruction indoors, I open the back patio and walk out onto the deck. Through the kitchen window I see Juno putting saucepans on her feet. The sight of her lifts my spirits slightly, as your child doing something adorably daft can.

I pull at the ivy growing through cracks in the brick wall and think about the first time I met Sara. She was taking notes in a production meeting where I was talking about ideas for the new website. No one could understand her Scottish accent. I thought she was German.

After the meeting she stopped by the photo of me and Roo on the beach.

"Whit a bonnie bairn. How auld is she?"

"Ich spreche German nicht" I said slowly. "J'aime English." I pointed at myself. "Oh shit, that's French, um …"

"D' ye think I am German? How rude are ye? Am fae Glasgae."

"Glascow?"

"Och aye, ye bapit hen!"

We were both part-time working parents, living in fear of being made redundant.

Our time together was always running out, right from the start. If only I had known. Our lunch breaks were snatched ten-minute affairs that we felt guilty for taking. We'd wolf down our tuna-melt bagels as we raced back to the office, laughing at our un-ladylike chomping and the mayonnaise round our mouths. Then we'd spend the afternoon sending one another hastily composed emails about our post-lunch slump and how much we hated the receptionist who made us feel like shite for leaving early to pick up our kids.

"It looks like she's been dunking for apples in a chip pan."

"I bet she has a fanny like a pub carpet."

"Her face looks like she has been set on fire and put out with a golf shoe!"

I'm still laughing at the memory when I walk back inside, where I spend twenty-minutes playing raucously loud drums with a wooden spoon on a Le Crueset pan I found at a car-boot sale, while Juno nods her head and stamps her feet.

When she looks tired enough, I hoist her into my arms and carry her warm weight up the stairs.

"Sleep, baby face." I lay her down in her cot with the duck Sara bought Roo as her christening gift. If I sniff really hard I can still smell Diptyque perfume. The posh one she could not afford but fell in love with.

I watch as Juno's eyelids lose their battle to stay open, then make my way back downstairs.

Later, I'll take flowers to Stanmer Park, where we planted Sara's ashes. Her children will be there with Pat. Nellie, Abi, Josh and I won't say anything as we solemnly weave roses and lilies round and through the wrought iron bench we buried her below. It takes a long time and no one bothers to wipe their tears by the end. When every inch is covered we will stand before our work in silence. Nothing left to say or do, but no one wanting to be the first to leave her behind again.

At her funeral we made everyone wear fuchsia pink nail varnish. And no one was allowed to cry in front of the children. We toasted her with her bloody Irn Bru. I tried to hold it all in, but back at home I fell apart. Each time the garage door slammed I heard the sound of her chair falling backwards as she collapsed in front of me. Each time the phone rang I thought it was going to be her telling me she was fine, that it was just a prank. Calling me hen. Making me laugh. I'd wake in the middle of the night, forgetting she had gone, and then, a sucker-punch in the gut as I'd remember it all over again.

Jimmy would find me sobbing as I watched Mamma Mia with the sound off at 3am, lost in memories of us dancing along, singing into wooden spoons.

He was the one who picked up my pieces and put me back together. He put me to bed, took my phone away and fed me Double-Decker bars. He took Roo to the park for hours on my worst days, so she did not see me crying. He listened to me tell him what happened over and over again as I tried to make sense of it in my own head. He cried with me, for my loss. For the death of someone so beautiful.

After a while the pain in my chest eased but I still could not face going back to work. To walk into our office and see her old desk with the tea stains, and the lip-balm that got passed back and forth between us. The Scottish to English translations board she made for me.

Instead I handed in my notice and took Roo out of nursery. I spent spring in my garden watching things that looked dead come back to life, trying to get my head round what it was all about. Pip came along that winter. We hadn't even been trying. She saved me, with her newborn demands for love and attention. She lifted my bell jar and connected me to the world again.

I'm staring into space when the phone rings. I assume it will be Jimmy, but Joe, his business partner's face shows up on the screen instead. Business partner and dear family friend.

Joe's son Jake is in the photo too.

Jake was a miracle baby. His mum was forty-six when she finally fell pregnant. 10lb of dark, Spanish beauty. "Too great for her to bear," Joe said. She never even got to hold her son. Complications in delivery meant Joe became a father and a widow in the same day.

"Hey, Joe."

"Hey, Guapa. How you doing today?"

"Oh, you know. Pretty shit."

"Yeah, I know. I still miss my Bonita every day."

"Does it ever get any easier?"

"Not really, but you learn to accept it."

"I don't think I ever will. I still don't understand it now." My voice breaks and I take a deep breath. "How's marvellous Jake?"

"Marvellous. He sang today in assembly. He sounded like an angel."

"I'd have liked to have heard him."

"Another time, Peta. Today you need a quiet day. Just be kind to yourself. Are you going to Stanmer Park later?"

"Yes, once the kids are in bed."

"You need their Grandpapi Joe to come over and read to them?"

"No. Jimmy should be home to help out. I hope. Thank you though."

"You not heard from him?"

"Nope." It comes out harsher than I intended. Joe picks up on it and immediately tries to pacify me. "I am sure he has not forgotten, Guapa. It is so busy here at work. Management reports and new staff documentation and …"

"It's OK, Joe," I force a smile into my voice. "I know he's busy working hard for us. And I always have you, my other man."

"You know it."

"Just don't you go dying on me OK, Joe? I really couldn't take it. I can't lose anyone else I love. It's just too bloody hard, this grieving business."

"OK, Guapa. I promise. Now wipe those tears."

I did not even realise I had been crying.

We say our goodbyes and he promises to bring Jake over to see me soon. When I have cut off the call I compose a text to Jimmy.

Stanmer Park tonight. Four years today.

I am matching melted Tupperware lids to Tupperware pots when my phone flashes twenty minutes later.

Shit, forgot. Sorry. You OK? In meeting. Call in a bit xx

He always seems to be in a meeting these days. I can't remember the last time he actually answered his phone to me.

I reply to his text, assuring him that I am fine. But I'm not, and I hate him in that second for his ability to forget Sara. Her absence has gone through me like thread through a needle. Everything I do is stitched with its colour.

Juno wakes up ten minutes later and I spend the rest of the morning cleaning the house absentmindedly whilst she messes it up again behind me. My thoughts flick between Sara and Jimmy. Last year on her anniversary he bought me a cup of tea in bed and a bunch of fuchsia pink Gerberas.

"These are not for her bench. These are for you. There is still beauty in life and all that."

When I got in from Stanmer Park the bath was run and there was a glass of chilled Bellina next to it. We toasted her in silence and I sat talking about how her children were growing up without her until my bath went cold.

This year it is so different. He seems so out of focus. Always distracted and his phone rings more than usual. The more I think about it, the crosser I feel. I slam un-rinsed plates into the dishwasher. I can't believe he forgot her.

I drink a cup of tea and try and calm down. Maybe it's his stupid diet that's made him forgetful I tell myself as I peel potatoes in the sink. Not that he will eat them. In the middle of January, with no warning and for no apparent reason, he told me he would be eating protein only as part of a 'Warrior' diet. He is forty this year. Could it be a midlife crisis? Is he going to buy a sports car and take up Pilates? God I hope not. I wish he would get over it.

I could really have done with him today. Instead I have to manage alone, putting on a big brave face as Roo tells me about her day and Pip and Juno demand sweets and jigsaws and dressing up clothes.

"So then me and Lily-Grace made chocolate land out of mud and leaves and Zac said that it was not chocolate land it was actually a poo-land and …"

"Choc choc," Juno has her hand out.

"No Juno, you are having your dinner in a minute."

"Mumma, help! I stuck!"

"That is because it is a build a bear cardigan, Pip. It's not going to fit you. You are not a bear."

"Mummy! You are not listening. I said to Zac it could be chocolate land if I wanted it to be. It could be, couldn't it?"

"Yes, Roo. Sorry, Pip, I am going to have to cut it off you."

"NOOOOOOO! It my best."

"Well, sorry. There is nothing else to be done. It's going to cut off your circulation."

"Choc choc."

"Zac always says things have to be a poo-land."

"CHOC CHOC!"

"Ow, Mumma, it hurts! You are hurting me!"

"Oh bloody hell, Jimmy, where the hell are you?" I sigh as I dole homemade meatballs and pasta into green plastic bowls and sprinkle parmesan cheese on top.

He gets home to do the girls' bath and bed so I won't be late to meet Pat, which is something. He has bought lilies for me to take along too, which softens my fury slightly.

"Thank you. They were her favourite. I'll see you later."

He steps forward to give me a hug but I know it will just make me cry again, so I push him away instead.

"They have had dinner. There is some left in the pan for you."

"Thank you but I can't eat pasta."

"You can eat pasta, Jimmy. It's easy. You just put it on a fork and put it in your mouth."

"Pete …"

"Sorry, sorry. I know. Warrior diet. Crap day. See you later."

I listen to 'Patience' by Guns and Roses in the car on the way. It was the song played at her funeral. I turn it up full blast, ignoring the people in cars next to me, who watch as I sing along in choking sobs as we wait for the lights to go green.

I get back after dark, my fingers full of rose thorns and my shirt stained yellow from the lilies. Jimmy is in his office, head bent over the desk, furiously typing away at his keyboard. He does not hear me come in.

"Hi," I say softly. I realise it's the first time I have spoken since I left the house earlier.

Jimmy quickly shuts down the window he had open on his screen and spins in his chair to face me.

"Hi."

"Everything OK?" I ask.

"Yes. Just, you know … work stuff." He waves his arm about vaguely, gesturing at nothing.

"Oh. Girls OK?"

"Out like lights."

"Good." An odd silence descends on us. I want to say, "Why did you close down your computer screen?" but it comes out as, "I am going to get in the bath then." The bath that you ran for me this time last year I think to myself.

"There might not be any hot water." Jimmy has the grace to look contrite.

"And you did not think to put the immersion on?" I'm pleased at the chance to let my anger at him show.

"Sorry, Peta, I've been busy." He does look genuinely sorry but I'm too cross to care.

"So have I Jimmy, laying flowers for my dead best friend," I snap out.

He says nothing but his face shows I have hurt him.

I don't feel like saying sorry though. Instead I storm out of the study and into the bedroom. He does not follow me.

I strip off my clothes and wash my tear-streaked face in the sink. I don't look at myself in the mirror, and I go to bed alone, missing Sara more than ever and wondering what my husband is up to.

Chapter Two

THE next morning when I wake up, Jimmy is still in his office, furiously typing away at his keyboard. He has shut the door so he can't hear the children wailing and fighting and demanding breakfast.

"I'll see to the kids then, shall I?" I mutter to myself, as I tie my dressing gown around me.

When I walk downstairs they are pushing and shoving to try and get closer to the screen where Peppa Pig is jumping in muddy puddles.

"Hey, move away from the TV. Pip can't see." I scoop her up and place her in the middle of the sofa, then grab the jungle print blanket off the floor and drape it over her knees.

My little bandy-legged Pip. How I love her. Seat-belts and highway codes do not apply to her. Sharing does not exist to her. Naughty-steps do not teach her. She is the mistress of mayhem, the queen of quarrels, empress of the eye-poke.

She is beautiful.

Pip is the middle-child and will do anything for attention. Pull hair. Scratch. Bite. Scream. Blame. Poo in baskets. Wee on high chairs. Shout. Stamp. Smash. Shriek.

But this is her too; standing sweetly on the side-lines, suspiciously watching. Clutching her Charlie-cloth comfort blanket. A limpet wrapped round my leg.

When she has been told off, I always know where she will be hiding. She will be behind her bedroom door, under her blankets, whispering. A little world she creates for herself when she does not feel welcome in mine.

And this is her too; the loudest one, the funniest one. The fastest one. The one who will wear a silly hat for a sad sister. The one who always pulls the happiest face for the camera as the flash goes off. The one who won't rest till we are all crammed on the sofa together holding hands.

She will turn my last hair grey, but there is a tiny piece of my heart carved out just for her. From the second I first saw her, blue and un-breathing (cord round her neck) she stole a bit of me that I'll never get back. She is my Achilles heel. It makes me too soft on her. Her temper is tiredness, I'll claim. Her biting is teething, poor thing. Her public defecating is 'sheer high spirits'. Jimmy calls her the-beast-from-the-east. I call her poppet.

"Mum! Pip was the one who started it!" Roo says, stamping her foot at me.

"Nonsense."

"Mumma," she nuzzles into me, and I rub my chin over her silky head. Roo and Juno gravitate towards me. It's all arms and legs but it's lovely, until the bickering starts.

"Hey, I wanted to sit on your lap, Mumma."

"Stop kicking me, Pip!"

"Mum, she called Juno a fat head again."

I sigh and stand up, detangling myself from them all. "Who wants a cup of tea?"

"Me!" Three hands shoot up in the air but no one says please.

I stir a pot of decaff for them, and put the espresso machine on for Jimmy. As I go to get milk I see the calendar pinned to the fridge and notice I have an appointment for a coil check-up. Oh joy. I always get seen by the doctor who has a child in Roo's class, so that's nice and embarrassing. There's nothing like bumping into the man who was measuring the length of your cervix in the morning, standing next you at school pick-up in the afternoon.

"Bollocks."

"Sorry, Mummy?"

"I said frolics. It's what horses do. Come on, let's be horses." I neigh and whinny my way over the table where I try and coax the girls to eat some Weetabix.

Jimmy stays upstairs whilst I get the girls ready. I make a point of shouting loudly and huffing and puffing, but he's obviously too absorbed in whatever he is doing to notice.

I slam the front door so hard it rattles the frame. "Can you hear that?!" I mutter as I strop down the drive with the kids.

I am walking across the playground after saying goodbye to Roo when the teacher runs out after me "Mrs Newton?"

Oh no. What have I forgotten?

"Have you forgotten our parent-teacher meeting this morning?"

I laugh nervously. "Nooo, of course not! I was just going to get my … um, notebook from the car."

"Oh, there is no need for that. It's only a quick catch up. Very informal." She barks out a laugh.

"Oh, righty-ho then. Lead the way!"

My orange trainers squeak on the floor as she leads me down a maze of corridors, before gesturing to a small breakout area with some tables and chairs dotted around. I park Juno up with a beaker of milk and a shortbread finger, then sit on a tiny plastic stool and look around me. Children's paintings are pinned on the walls. I spot one of Roo's and my chest swells with pride.

"Roo is quite the young artist," Mrs Peacock says, noticing. "So creative."

"Thank you." I am sensing a 'but'.

"She seems to enjoy drawing the most, which is fine, but it would be good if you could encourage her to do some reading and writing practice at home too, not just drawing."

I'm about to say that we already do, when Mrs Peacock hands me a green folder and says, "Here is Roo's reading folder. It would be great if you could …"

"Read a book with her ever night and write it down in the reading log." I finish for her, thinking back to my conversation with The-Iron-Curtain.

"Yes, perfect. Other than that, I have no concerns at all about Roo. She seems a very kind and caring child of God. She always tries to get people to be friends again if they have fallen out."

"Really? At home, her sole purpose seems to be seeing how quickly she can make her sisters cry."

Mrs Peacock looks at me strangely and says nothing.

"Ha ha ha, joke," I say weakly.

"Right, well, I think that is everything." She claps her hands together and stands up, all the while still looking at me as if I am some new species she has never met before. "Thank you for your time."

"No, no, thank you!" I say, in my best jolly posh-phone voice, hoping to salvage some dignity.

She smiles at me without it reaching her eyes. "Please don't forget to sign out as you leave." I refuse to tell her I have no idea where the exit is so my chances of leaving are slim to none.

Her sensible low-heeled shoes click on the tiled floor as she walks away. I stick my tongue out at her retreating back before remembering they probably have cameras all over the place, then squeak my way down four wrong corridors before I finally find reception again.

"Phew. Thank God for that," I say to Juno as I unstrap her from the buggy and dust crumbs off her coat. My phone rings just as I am opening the car door.

"Mrs Newton? Hello, it's the doctor's receptionist. You missed your appointment for a coil check-up."

"Good," I mouth to Juno.

"We have a space at two-thirty this afternoon, would you be able to pop along?"

"Oh. Um yes, that should be OK," I tell her, slumping in my seat.

As soon as I end the call, I ring Jimmy's mobile to see if he can pick Roo and Pip up. It rings three times and then sends me to voicemail. Thinking he meant to press answer instead of the ignore button, I ring again and the same thing happens. I leave him a message instead.

"Sod it, let's go to town" I say to Juno, driving past the turning for our road and down onto the seafront instead. I park up in Churchill Square and spend a blissful hour perusing the cookery section in Waterstones with a vanilla latte from Costa. I restrict myself to one book for me, and one for Juno.

Juno falls asleep on the way home. I lay her on the sofa and cover her with one of Pip's Charlie cloths. I'm just picking a lump of Play Doh off the carpet when my phone beeps. The screen tells me I have two new messages.

The first one is from my friend Heather who recently moved to Wales. It says: *Why the feck did you let me move to Wales? It's rained for two weeks. The kids have Trench-Foot and there are rats in the loft. Miss you and road signs in English. Kisses to girls. Text back xxx*. The text makes me smile. Then I read the second one. It's from Jimmy and says: *No can do. Sorry, treacle.*

When Roo comes out of her classroom, Mrs Peacock is with her. I try not to look nervous. The receptionist does not appreciate my late cancellation. I waffle through my excuses for not coming but I can tell she not listening.

"Hello." My smile feels wooden.

"Hello again, Mrs Newton. I was just thinking, maybe you would like to come in and do some reading with the class?"

"Oh." I was not expecting this. It must've been my posh phone voice. It obviously impressed her. Now I'm going to have to go and spend a morning listening to kids stuttering their way through dull books, and then I am going to have to have even duller conversations with their mums, who will corner me in the playground to ask how their little darling is getting on. Not just in reading either. They will ask me who they played with. If they ate their snack, wiped their bum, put their hand up. Did they scratch for nits? Do up their coat at break time?

It's going to be awful.

"Oh yes, I'd love to. Jolly Hockey-sticks. What fun!" I say in my best posh-phone voice.

"Marvellous, see you next week then."

I can almost hear Sara saying "An arse like a bag of washing" as I watch Mrs Peacock walk back indoors.

"Mummy, why are you talking in that funny voice?" Roo asks

"What funny voice?" I say

"This one – 'Whaaaat funnn'."

"I don't know what you are talking about. Kit-Kat?" I pull a bar of chocolate from my pocket and she drops her interrogation.

"How was school?"

"Fine."

"Who did you play with?"

"Lily-Grace."

"What did you learn about?"

"Can't remember."

"How much of your lunch did you eat?"

"Can't remember."

"Who went on the amber-traffic light for bad behaviour?"

"Zac," she replies instantly.

"Ah, so you remember something." I poke her gently in the ribs.

"Want to go swings," says Pip in a little voice next to me, with a tug on my hand. She does not like the chaos of pick-up.

"Rabbits!" shouts Juno from her buggy, spitting Kit Kat all over the place. It is grey and drizzling but they will not be perturbed.

We are the only people in the park. I'm getting soaked but I figure it's preferable to being bored to death by other mums and their boring mum-gossip. As the girls jump about in muddy puddles snorting like pigs, I compose a text back to Heather. *Raining here too. Only people at park. Kids not even wearing wellies. GASP! Been asked to do reading at school. Urgh.* I pause and wonder if I should mention Jimmy's distracted behaviour, but Heather has enough on her plate trying to settle her three boys into their new life in Wales and the rats in their derelict farmhouse, so I add: *All good here. Kiss to boys xxx* and press send.

As we squelch back home I worry about my commitment to Mrs Peacock. What have I started? It's just the kind of thing I was hoping to avoid. Getting too involved. Why can't I say no? Next I will be joining the Art Gallery Café Crew (AGCC), who meet up after drop-off to spend three hours drinking tea in the local café and have conversations like this:

"I am SO busy. I need to make dinner AND I have to get the girls' ballet kit ready for next week."

"Gosh you do sound busy. I have got to walk home and then walk back again four hours later to pick the kids up."

"Oh sod it. Take the 4X4. Let's have another cup of tea."

"Why not? We've earned it!"

We live in a very small, but very antiquated village. It has a 'historical' pond and 'gardens', complete with a croquet pitch and bowling green. It has a windmill and a park. It has a post office who will tell you what's in your parcel because they got so bored they opened it. But at the bottom of the village is a slope down to a beautiful and deserted patch of seafront that makes it all worth it. Even the AGCC mums.

I never thought we would end up in another village after growing up in Briar Wood, where ninety-five percent of the inhabitants are over eighty. As a child I used to pen obituaries for the people I thought were going to pop it next. I wrote a lot about how they would miss their geraniums. My dream was to be published in the local gazette. People told me I was mad: "You're crazy! You'll never make it that far!"

Briar Wood is full of beige raincoats and slightly senile residents. I think Jimmy and I were the only two people we know who ever left. When we go back people still ask us why we did it. They simply can't understand. To them Briar Wood is the end of the rainbow. Nothing has changed in the ten years that we have been away. Jimmy's uncle still talks about his crap campaign (Cobb Road Against Potholes), in-between going to open days at the local crematorium and giving tours of the crumbly castle whilst wearing a fez and his cricket whites.

Growing up we had a shop (owned by the exotic Patel family), a phone box and a bench. And we had a local pub, The George and Dragon, which is where I met Jimmy. I was a waitress and he was the manager of the local football team. It sounds a bit like a Human League song except the only time he ever noticed me was when I dropped his full English on his feet, which was frequently, because I fancied him too much to look up and see where I was going. (This is no longer the case. Now when I drop his breakfast on his feet it's because he left the toilet seat up.)

Jimmy lived three doors down from me. Other than the breakfast-dropping days, he did not notice I existed at all, even though I coated my hair in Happy Shopper wet-look gel to tame it and soaked myself in Impulse body spray before taking out his fry-up. It was the best version of me I could present at the time. He did not even look up from his formation planning.

After months of walking past his house in my snazziest outfit (for no reason other than the hope of him seeing me in my snazziest outfit), he finally shouted out "I get it. Stop walking past me in your snazzy outfit. You going down the town this Friday or what?"

'Down town' meant going into Briar Wood. A long cobbled high street full of pubs named after animals. The Goat. The Lamb. The Bull. The Dragon.

This trip down the town together did not seal the deal and secure me as his girlfriend as I hoped and prayed it might, however. He had also asked three other girls along too, being the local lothario that he was. We all sat together sipping our Martinis and lemonade while he played on the fruit machine and generally ignored us.

"Did you keep walking past him in a snazzy outfit too?" I asked one of them.

"No, I work behind the bar at the football club."

"Oh, you?" I said to the next one.

"I am his sister's best friend."

"Quite good then, lots of chances to impress, and you?"

"I work in Ici Patel's shop. I sell him the paper."

That was the total sum of our conversation. After that we sat in silence nursing our Martinis that none of us liked or got offered another one of.

I remember him inviting me back to his flat above a shop one night after the pub closed (the other three were green with envy). It was a bridal shop, so to me it felt like fate. I walked up the stairs all jelly-legged thinking "This is it! I am going to do it with Jimmy Newton in a flat above a shop like something out of a Pulp song and he will fall madly in love with me, dump all the other girls and ask me to marry him and I can have it announced in the local gazette."

I was just checking out the complete lack of interior design and unusual things they used for ash-trays, thinking about the changes I would make, when his phone rang.

"Stay there, sweet-cheeks," he said, blowing me a kiss before going out the room to answer it. When he failed to return an hour later, after which time I had put his CD collection in alphabetical order, straightened the tassels on the living room rug and pulled off all the dead leaves from his Yucca plant, I went to look for him.

His room was empty and his window was wide open. I did not know at the time, but later found out from one of my Martini-drinking companions that he'd jumped out of it to meet his 'real girlfriend' before she came in the flat and found me. He did not return until 7 am, by which time I'd cleaned out his oven, paired up his socks and de-scaled his kettle, before giving up and doing the long walk of shame back home.

I tried to play it cool. When he texted to apologise, and thank me for my housework I texted back, *No need. I always suspected you could go all night, and you did.* But inside my heart was broken. Everyone said I should give up. "One woman will never be enough for him."

I think about Jimmy's recent behaviour and wonder if they

were right. But he did change didn't he? The other girls were let go, and we started to go out every Sunday lunchtime for drinks in a country pub. Then he started inviting me to watch the football on a Saturday morning too. Before we knew it, we were a proper couple. Peta 'n' Jimmy.

"Let's get away from here," he said to me as we drove back home from the weekly pub quiz. "Before we both get old before our time and too scared to change."

"And go where?" I was not against the idea, but it seemed impossible at the time.

"Brighton. It's as different from this place as anywhere could be."

You'd have thought we were moving to Australia, the way everyone went on about it. "You'll be back. I give it a month," my mother said.

"What do you want to move there and be gay for?" said another.

But the second I saw the pier in all its gaudy neon glory, I knew I had not left home, I'd found it.

We both got pretty rubbish office jobs to start with. So lowly paid we both had to take weekend work as cleaners and waiting staff, but we didn't care. When our evening shifts were over we would share a bag of chips on the beach and talk about the crazy people we served, or about some tiny shop in the South Lanes and how it would never have been allowed back in Briar Wood.

Within a couple of years, Jimmy found himself on a career path that he enjoyed which meant we could afford to move from a rented flat, to our first home. I worked in marketing and gave up the waitressing, spending my evenings studying for a NCTJ in journalism instead. Jimmy tried to persuade me to do a cookery diploma but I worried it would take all my enjoyment out of it.

The decision to have Roo came after a girl at work announced she was pregnant and I felt jealous. Before then it was a plan we talked about, with no timeline. Suddenly having a baby was all I could think about.

We bought the pregnancy test at the Co-Op, slung in amongst our weekly shopping. "Probably not," I said to Jimmy as it went along the escalator. "I mean I'm not even late, but.. you know."

He was grating cheese when I came out the toilet, still holding the stick.

"Look!" I thrust the wee sodden stick in his face. His eyes welled up but he tried to remain practical. "It might just be a trick of the light. We must not get excited."

"You can't have false positives, only false negatives."

"Even so, let's do another one?"

Two litres of water and five pregnancy tests later Jimmy said, "I think you are pregnant, Pete."

We clicked empty Evian bottles together and sat staring at thin blue lines for the rest of the evening.

And now, five years later, Jimmy is all about work and emails and wearing suits and being the boss. I still feel like the same girl I was back then, but he seems so different. I don't like the way that thought makes me feel. There must be something going on he is not telling me. I decide to put my mind at rest by sneaking round the study but when I turn the handle, it's locked.

What work could be so private, I wonder? I am so distracted I don't notice the girls sneak into the kitchen, scoff a whole packet of Jammy Dodgers and therefore ruin their appetite for dinner. I cook it anyway. Cooking has always soothed my troubled mind. I decide to make chicken pie. I love the delicacy of pastry, the smoothness of the knife as it slides through buttery excess. Homemade chicken pie after a long day is the equivalent of a great big hug. The smell of it cooking in the oven lifts me. I hope it will work its magic on Jimmy. When the timer pings I carefully lift it out of the oven with the, keep calm and keep cooking, oven gloves that my mother-in-law bought me for

Christmas; the dish is heavy and satisfying to hold. I set it on the side then chop broccoli and string peas.

But they cook and cool and the kid's bath and bedtime comes and goes, and there is no word from Jimmy.

I mop the sopping wet bathroom floor and try and clear a space in the playroom to actually play in.

When I come back to the kitchen the pie sits mocking me on the counter top. It came out glorious, proud and risen. Now it has sunk into itself and the gravy is congealing round the edges. It looks ugly.

I think about the love and hope I'd folded into it, feeling stupid for believing the oven gloves. I pick off the heart I'd cut from pastry to decorate the top, and throw it in the bin.

Chapter Three

WHEN the phone rings at 10pm, I assume it's Jimmy with a reason for his absence, but it's Nellie, Sara's eldest daughter. I have hardly even said hello when she blurts out.

"Peta? I had the dream again."

I always get this call after the anniversary.

"Ah." I sit down next to the pile of washing I was folding, clearing a space amongst the bits of Duplo and Polly Pockets.

In Nellie's dream, Sara is in the school playground sitting down on the bench in the corner. Nellie sees her and immediately runs over, but the closer she gets, the further away Sara moves, until finally she disappears altogether and Nellie is alone calling her name, begging her to come back.

I hate this cruel dream for her.

After she first started having nightmares, Nellie and her siblings got sent to Foundlings for grief counselling. She hated it. "The people who talk to us, they treat us like babies. How can we be babies? We don't have a mum. We have to be grown-ups now."

She would ring me crying, begging me to tell her dad not to send them. He didn't listen; thinking counselling was the right thing to do. He remarried last year. It was so hard for the children. Although he and Sara had already separated years before, they were used to having him, and her all to themselves, depending on whose house they were in. Perhaps he thought he was giving them a mother by remarrying, but to them, they were losing theirs all over again.

Their step-mother Fleur, is lovely, but she can't hold a candle to Sara. She never met her, which is probably just as well. Those are not the kind of shoes you'd want to try and fill. I was her best friend and I still feel in awe of her most of the time.

Fleur tries not to ask too much about Sara. She looks forward, not backwards, which might be for the best, but Nellie struggles. She thinks Fleur wants to replace her mum and therefore hates her with all the determination of a fourteen-year-old girl.

"No one talks about my mum in this family. But I need to talk about her so I can remember what she was like."

So we talk about her. I tell Nellie little things. "Your mum loved the smell of hot tarmac. She could tell if the milk was put in first when someone made her tea. She always had flowers on her window sill. Even at the end of the month when money was tight. She used to buy chrysanthemums then so they would last the longest. She would put a two-pence piece in the bottom because someone told her it stopped the water going brown. She never put her bank card back in her wallet after she had used it, instead she would put it in one of the many pockets in her leather backpack and cause a long queue behind her in shops. People would tut until she turned round and gave them one of her smiles. She could disarm anyone with her smile."

"Thank you, Peta."

"Anytime, Nellie-girl."

"Jub jub." Her word for love you. Nellie could not pronounce it as a baby and it stuck.

"Jub jub."

When I hang up I see that Jimmy has texted me. *Be back*

soon. Sorry I'm late. I've had a shocker of a day. Hope kids went down OK. Can Joe and Jake come for dinner tomorrow night? I'll cook to give you a break xx

And when he finally walks through the door at 11 pm he looks so exhausted and weary that I cannot bring myself to be cross with him.

"Can I smell your chicken pie?" he asks hopefully.

Once upon a time I would have turned his comment into a double entendre and come back with something like, "Only if I can make your sausage roll." But those days seem a lifetime ago right now.

His suit is creased and the bags under his eyes make him look older than he is.

"Uh huh. Sit down and I'll dish up."

He slumps into the duck-egg blue chair at the head of the table. We all picked a different colour. Mine is yellow, Roo's is green. Pip's is pink and Juno's is one of those clear ghost ones so we can see what she is eating.

After I serve him, I go back to the kitchen and watch him discreetly while he eats.

"You okay, Jimmy?"

He looks up at me. I see a flash of something cross his face, but it has passed before I can work out what it was.

"Yeah. Just a really long day." He scrapes up the last of his food then brings the plate into the kitchen. "That was great, thanks."

He stands looking at his iPad while I load up the dishwasher and make him a coffee, then bite my lip when he walks up the stairs with it and shuts himself, once again, in his study.

He seems brighter the next day as he cooks his signature risotto. I whisk up double cream, lemons and white wine vinegar for a syllabub. I run out of time to make my homemade lemon shortbread which annoys me. I would have had time to make them if Roo had not decided get hold of Jimmy's shaving foam and spray it all over Pip's hair. Washing Pip's hair is near impossible on a good day, and that is with Johnsons Soft and Gentle, let alone with shaving foam which seemed to multiply the more times I rinsed it off and Pip screaming "MY EYES!! MY EYES!!" Repeatedly.

Getting them down to sleep took much longer than planned. It always does when I need it to be quick. I have no time to make myself look presentable, not that Joe is used to seeing me looking anything other than a mess. I spray some Clinique Happy on and hope for the best.

"Guapa, you look beautiful," Joe says, standing up to kiss me on both cheeks. I sit on the sofa next to him and Jimmy passes me a glass of Sancerre. I smile at him gratefully.

"What's going on?" I ask. "Why are you both looking at me like that?"

"Like what?" Jimmy looks puzzled and Joe looks away quickly.

"Peta!" Jake whizzes over and stops with a skid next to me. "Can me and Jimmy go and play cricket?"

"Hello to you too, Jake. Yes of course you can, but shall we have dinner first?"

After spending an hour and a half continuously stirring the risotto until the rice had the perfect crunch and flavour, Jimmy and Jake wolf it down as quickly as possible.

I talk about not exercising on a full stomach. They look at me as if I am from another planet. Joe sniggers and tells me to leave them to it.

"Go, have fun." I ruffle Jake's hair as he passes me. He ducks his head but grins at me.

I put a Tracy Chapman CD on and pour Joe and myself Limoncellos.

"That man needs a son," says Joe watching them from the back deck as they race one another to the cricket green. Jake looks like he might get there first so Jimmy trips him over. They sprawl onto the lawn laughing and shouting.

"Not you too! His mother is always on at me."

"Because he needs a son."

"I tried. Three times! Why do people always think it's my fault? It's the man who decides the sex of a baby anyway. Something to do with X and Y genes."

"In Spain, women keep going till they have produced a son."

"Well you have too much time on your hands, or not enough good stuff on the TV, plus he has a son. He has Jake. Anyway." I say, changing the subject in my usual unsubtle manner. "How's business? Jimmy seems to be working more than ever. Have you got a new project on?" I try and sound light and breezy but I can hear the tang of desperation in my voice.

Joe says nothing for a long time, and then instead of answering he asks, "How are you Peta?" Suddenly serious. "How are you feeling after Sara's anniversary?"

I shrug and pour us more Limoncello. "I feel the same as ever. Like part of me is missing."

Joe nods. "But are you coping?"

I don't really know if I am coping or not, but I don't say that to Joe. I punch him lightly on the arm instead and say, "You know me, I always cope, more or less, as much as my children try and send me insane."

"You are a good girl. Keep your strength, Guapa."

"What are you on about? You sound like a bad horoscope. No more Limoncello for you."

"No more for me." He laughs softly and says nothing more. I want to go back to asking about work but the moment has passed. We sit in companionable silence together instead, until Jimmy and Jake come home, covered in grass stains and grinning from ear to ear.

Later, when we are getting into bed I say to Jimmy, "Did you notice anything odd about Joe tonight?"

"No, why?" He has his back to me and his head in the wardrobe. "Where are my grey shorts?"

"Right in front of you. You are touching them right now."

"Oh yes. Ta." He pulls them out and sniffs them. I hate that.

"I hate it when you do that. He was saying some weird stuff. Asking if I was happy and telling me to keep strong."

"Did you give him Limoncello?" says Jimmy, his head still in the wardrobe, looking for a t-shirt. "Where …"

"On the pile to the left of you," I sigh.

"Oh yes."

"And in answer to your question, yes, I gave Joe Limoncello," I say.

"Well, there you go then," he says as he pulls his t-shirt over his head, before shutting the wardrobe door, and sliding into bed next to me.

"Urgh, you smell of sweat! Go and have a shower. I just changed the sheets."

"What will I get out of it if I do?" he looks at me hopefully. The sports session with Jake has put a twinkle in his eye that I have not seen for a long time. It's great to see but I'm exhausted.

"Jimmy, I'm knackered. I've been with the kids all day. Pip took her knickers off on the way to school. I didn't notice till we'd gotten to playgroup and she sat down to have the class photo

44

done. Juno refused to go down for a nap and Roo demanded we all go to the park after school again, where I got stuck with boring mums talking about sun-cream and the national curriculum. I am full of Limoncello and I am tired. I just want to go to sleep." I roll over and snuggle further down into my quilt.

Jimmy leans over and whispers in my ear, "It won't take long."

"Seriously. Give up. It's not going to happen."

"FINE," he harrumphs. "Then I am not going to have a shower."

"You're such a child."

"You're such a nag!"

I don't have it in me to answer back. I roll myself to the far-side of the bed instead and try and catch the worrying thoughts floating round my mind so I can make some sense of them. Jimmy's breathing changes next to me and I realise he is asleep already. I guess it really would not have taken long after all.

Jimmy thinks it's all fun and games being a stay-at-home mum. I've never worked so hard in all my life, but he just can't see it. My life was easier six years ago when I was working two jobs, seven days a week. At least when I fell into bed, I knew I was off duty for a few hours.

But as far as Jimmy is concerned, he goes out to 'work' because he has a 'job' and I don't. I stopped working and had kids and now I just sit around drinking tea all day.

Jimmy's day involves sitting round drinking tea not mine, I think spitefully to myself in the darkness.

After two rounds of racquetball in the gym, and then ten minutes in a Jacuzzi, that is.

Jimmy is an Operations Director for a commercial cleaning company. I still don't know what that means. All I know is that if you drive through London in the small hours of the night, you'll see his staff, lit up by street lights, headlights and billboards. They are industrious as drone bees; polishing and hoovering, putting high-rise offices back together, only to be taken apart again the next day by people who have jobs and go to work.

Admittedly, it's a tougher industry to make a living in than it used to be. Even I can see that. Companies are fighting to stay afloat and desperately slash budgets where they can. Jimmy is constantly being hauled into meetings and told to provide more, for less. I'm not saying it's not stressful, but it still sounds preferable to my morning. My non-working morning.

I stare at his back in the half-light, remembering when he used to sleep with one leg slung over mine.

There is no trip to the gym for me tomorrow morning, no soak in the hot tub. My day starts with a child demanding something from me at 5 am so loudly that it wakes the other two up within seconds. My day begins with children hanging off me like limpets on a rock.

My morning tea has to wait until I've put on Mr Tumble and changed a nappy or two. My day starts with fighting over who gets to sit on my lap.

While Jimmy serves a blinding backhander, I try and persuade the girls to eat some Weetabix and stop kicking one another's chairs. While he is stopping for a swig of water, mopping his face on the towel I washed for him, I am chasing our children round the living room with a hairbrush.

Jimmy will order scrambled eggs on wholemeal bread and a double espresso. I'll eat leftover Weetabix and reheated-in-the-microwave-tea.

Jimmy will sling his gym bag over his shoulder and walk languidly to his car, whilst I stagger down the drive with packed lunches, coats, hats, library books and drama kits.

I was so tired an hour ago, now I'm restless and irritable. I wriggle about and pump up my pillow, secretly wanting to wake up Jimmy. He will be cross if I do. He will tell me he needs to get up in the morning to go to work.

But it's not like he can be late, because he is the boss. I am always late. I wonder how this can be when we have been up since 4 am, but time does not only fly when you are having fun; it also flies when you have small children and need to be somewhere at 8.50 am.

Jimmy can cancel meetings with people he does not want to talk to, while I get cornered by The-Iron-Curtain, gleefully telling me how stressed-out I look, how late I am or if I've remembered something she knows I've obviously forgotten.

Jimmy sets budgets and signs off contracts, while I make beds, load the dishwasher and do four hundred loads of washing. He takes clients out to lunch at The Ginger Fox whilst I retrieve loo rolls Pip shoved down the toilet.

I imagine what it must be like to have something important to do. I imagine myself in a sharp suit saying "We need to get all our ducks in a line by the close of play or we are going to miss the low hanging fruit in the pipeline on this one," or "You will have to do it yourself. I don't have enough bandwidth for that."

I almost laugh out loud at the idea of it all. It's another world. A world where you go and do what you need to do, what you get paid to do, and then you come home and relax. Work done till the next day.

When Jimmy gets home, he bursts through the door full of beans and current events. "Hello gang. How was your day? Mine was productive. I've got some big meetings coming up in London next week. I might need to stay over in a hotel." He tries to make the last sentence sound like a hardship.

Then he'll swoop down to grab Pip and swing her high in the air, making her laugh hysterically. Roo and Juno will pile on him and cover him in kisses, the filthy turn-coats. He is not around all day and yet all he has to do is pick them up and he is immediately dad of the year.

I gave up my life, my figure and any fun I used to possess inside me for them and all they do is disobey me.

"Well, let me think," I reply in answer to his question. "I learned the sign language for lighthouse."

"What about that earthquake in Japan, eh? Awful." Jimmy responds.

I will not have heard about this earthquake in Japan. I will have had to watch Mr Tumble all morning, sing Disney classics all the way to and from nursery and can't hear the radio over the orchestra that is a Hoover, dishwasher, washing machine and tumble-drier all going at once, so I say

"What earthquake?", and Jimmy says "What do you mean what earthquake? It's all over the news. Everyone is talking about it. You are supposed to be a journalist. Don't you keep up with the news?"

"I *used* to be a journalist." I correct him. "Now I am a waitress."

"Excellent. I'd love a coffee." He's joking, but it rattles me. The only time someone makes me a drink is when Pip and Juno play tea parties. In my experience it normally involves un-flushed toddler wee out the toilet, however, so largely remains un-drunk, depending on how desperate I am.

How sad it is, when all you want from your day is a cup of tea not made by you. I really am fighting to not wake Jimmy up now and scream "You want to get lucky? Well I just want a frigging mug of Earl Grey and two minutes peace to drink it in!"

Sometimes being a mother feels like holding the cone while everyone else gets to lick the ice-cream, then finding a bin for the sticky tissue afterwards. Jimmy can't see it though, no matter what metaphor I use. He just hears "She is nagging me. I can't have done anything wrong." And we end up rowing, like we have tonight.

I try hard not to go to sleep on a row. But this is not a row. I assure myself. This is just two tired people. This is just being married with kids. This is happily ever after.

But my mind keeps going back to the computer screen he turned off too quickly for me to see, and the guilt on his face when he turned round.

Chapter Four

WHEN I wake up in the morning, Jimmy has already left, but the study door is open for once.

I sit down on the worn brown leather chair I found in a flea market when I was pregnant with Roo. When I log into the computer I see that mother has left a post on my Facebook page which reads: *How did your coil-check-up go? Did you get them to check on that hairy brown mole on your bottom? It's not normal. Love Mum, Dad and Fox*

I groan out loud.

Since they retired to France my mother has embraced the internet. To start with all she wanted to do was to download the Telegraph Crossword, but then she discovered Google. Before long she was watching Saddam Hussein get killed and signing up for Facebook (so she could share it with others). Most of her posts are about religion: "The most dangerous and destructive power tool of all time. Thank God I'm an atheist."

My dad hates 'Facefit'. He would prefer to be outside chopping down trees for no real reason. I dread seeing Mum has left me a comment. She is famous for embarrassing me. When I started my period (aged nine) she took us all to the pub to celebrate, announcing "My daughter has come a woman" over her Merrydown Cider. CHEERS!

Growing up, if I ever confided in her a friend was annoying

me, she never seemed to listen, let alone give me any advice. Then I would make up with my friend and it would turn out my mum had been listening after all, saying, "Oh, I'm surprised to see you round here, she's been calling you 'spotty-four-eyes' all week."

Mum really should just have stuck with horses, her first love. My dad hates them however. He was delighted when the horse meat scandal came out and rushed to show my mum the headline. My mother was so cross with his glee she did not speak to him for four days. He says it was the best week of his life.

She has French horses now. She has given them all French names that she pronounces in a very English accent. They have been there ten years and still can't speak the language. I once saw my dad try and order a jacket potato by taking his coat off and pointing at it.

I spend a fruitless half hour trying to delete her post and then end up replying lamely that it's a hearing test not a smear test and that I don't know what she is talking about regarding a mole.

"How was your appointment with the nurse?" people ask me as I make my way up the school lane.

I grit my teeth and say nothing, whilst in my head I call my mother every name under the sun. Roo and Pip go off without too much trouble for once, which is good because I need to get home and prepare for a Skype meeting.

In-between failing to be a good parent and a sexy wife, I write for an online mums' magazine called 'Tummy-to-Mummy'. It's awful, and not at all why I spent two years studying journalism, but it brings in some cash and it's an escape from the school gate banalities. I feel like if I do nothing at all my brain will rust completely.

When I get back, I put Juno in front of a mountain of raisins, then go and hunt out my suit jacket. I put it on over my pyjamas when we Skype. My boss, Michelle, does not need to know I am knicker-less underneath and wearing Roo's Hello Kitty slippers.

Michelle does not like me much and so always gives me the worst news stories to write about. Helen gets the highbrow ones like 'Is it right to outlaw independent midwives?' or 'What do the new cuts in child-benefit mean for the economy?' I get things like 'Top ten baby names' or 'How important is your baby's wardrobe?'

Helen hates me. She thinks I want her naff job. I don't. She is a full time member of staff. I am a free-lance contractor. She logs into my Wordpress blog and adds spelling errors into my posts then deletes any nice comments that I might have received from my small following of readers.

I never use my real name in my writing. God forbid the school-run mums find out what I do. Plus, I often use them as blog fodder. Not all the school mums, of course. Some of them are friends of mine.

The normal ones. The ones with Weetabix stains on their coats and a child's hairclip in their fringe. The ones desperately trying to grab abandoned wellies and reading bags as they run to stop their child from defecating on the playground. Those are the mums I like. They don't care about blue sticker books. They are just trying to survive another day.

I never thought I was going to be a mum like this. I thought I was going to be organised and fun. I remember my mum making fairy cakes with me as a kid but never letting me do more than watch, because it was quicker, easier and less messy that way.

She would whisk the butter icing in the mixer, cut the cake in half whilst it was still too hot. She'd swear as she scalded her fingers, then look at me as if it was my fault she was in a rush. The cream on the hot cake would melt, so the butterfly wings slipped pathetically down the sides of their paper cases. "At least it looks like you made them," she'd joke.

I'd sit watching in silence; licking my consolation prize spatula and vow I would never to be too busy for my children, or forget the child in me.

But this is the mum I am all these years later. Rushing just like she did. Desperate for a break. Resentful of my husband, suspicious even. God, what a cliché I am.

I did not find anything when I looked in the study but I am becoming convinced that he is hiding something from me. I decide to take action.

Morning, hope you have a good day. Shall I ask Faith to babysit tonight? x

I can't today. Working late. Give the girls a kiss from me Xx

I refuse to be put off.

Is everything OK at work? Feel like I never see you. Maybe we could do that thing that does not take long after …

Sorry Peta. Don't make me feel bad x

I was not trying to make him feel bad. I was trying to get his bloody attention! I want to text Joe and demand to know why Jimmy is to working all the time, but Jimmy would go nuts if I manipulated Joe into giving him a break.

My Skype is interrupted by a phone call from Pip's nursery, asking what she had for breakfast. When I nervously ask why I get told she has just poo'd out half a ton of raisins into her socks and shoes. Marvellous.

I can see Helen laughing on Skype. Bitch. Last week I was supposed to write about how great Shakira looked just five weeks after giving birth. I decided to change the brief slightly and Michelle got a load of hate mail, which Helen now takes great delight in reading out to me.

"You really have issues, Aunty. I guess you're just a fat-

grumpy-bitch with no job or social life, that is why you are too lazy to lose weight and so jealous of Shakira. P.S. You need a shrink and Jenny Craig."

"*I think you should find a counsellor to help work out your self-esteem issues, or failing that, a gym. Regards, a five foot nine, size eight, flat stomached mum of two whose youngest is little more than a year old.*"

"*You should not be allowed to work for Tummy-to-Mummy. You are a disgrace and very bad at your job. No one wants you here.*"

"Helen, I know you wrote the last one and your American accent is awful."

"Ha! Like I would bother reading the tripe you write, sorry Michelle. I know the 'fluffy' articles are important to the magazine." She does that finger thing round the words 'fluffy'.

I do it back while Michelle moves off screen, then flip her the bird at the end.

"Don't apologise, Helen dear. I cringe each time I read her articles too," says Michelle off-screen.

"Maybe if you would let me write something more substantial?" I say. "I have been working on a piece about women being made redundant while they are pregnant. I've interviewed the head of Maternity Action and a Solicitor who specialises in getting compensation for women who are unfairly treated. I've even sourced some women who are happy to name and shame their employers. I was thinking …"

"Great idea. Helen, get onto this at once. Peta, your article for next week is 'How to make mashed potato animals that will hide your kid's super greens'."

I'd love to stay online and row with her but I have to go and pick up Pip and her poo-splattered shoes.

As I drive down to pre-school I think back to how I am

changing into my mum. It worries me. My mum named me after a childhood friend she once knocked out with a prize turnip. To apologise, she vowed to name her first child after him. She forgot her promise when naming my two older brothers, but remembered just in time for me. I don't know how she remembered this trivial conversation from when she was fourteen, yet didn't remember vital information like collecting me from my first school trip, or which days I needed my ballet kit. Having two older brothers did not bode well for hand-me-down underwear. It was hard to feel like a ballerina in my brother's baggy He-man pants.

I am starting to feel as scatty as her these days. Maybe it's just what happens when you have three children so close together. My girls have the same age gaps between them as my brothers and me.

It was a conscious decision. My brothers and I are very close but very different. I wanted the same for my girls.

John, my eldest brother, is one of those geeky computer whizzes. I used to ring him up for advice when my laptop crashed but it was too soul destroying. He made me feel very thick. He made my mum feel even thicker. When he was first teaching her how to use a computer he said "Now right-click" and she did, at the top of a word document. "I have written the word click John. What do I do now?"

He is obsessed with cookery programs, mountain biking and red wine. He walks everywhere very quickly with his hands in his pockets and is slightly scared of my children.

Mickey is a landscape gardener. He lives in Tring with his girlfriend Jen. I am a bit jealous of her. She gets to see him all the time. I am two hours away.

Like Pip and Juno, there is fifteen months between us. We were more like twins growing up. We used do everything together. I'd build dirt tracks for his micro machine cars, and he'd practise double skipping with me. When he was six, Mum and Dad bought him a farm yard set for Christmas but forgot to buy any animals to go with it. In an act of love, I stole all the plastic sheep and horses and cows from school and took them home in my PE bag. I think deep down I knew it was wrong, but the look on Mickey's face made it all worthwhile.

We were playing with them behind the brown leather sofa when John found us. He was pretending to be Han Solo. He did a slow and measured forward roll over the settee wearing Mum's dressing gown and holding a wooden spoon for a lightsabre. "What have you got there?" he said,

"Nothing" we answered quickly, shifting our bottoms to cover the booty.

"Tell me," he demanded, in Obi-Wan Kenobe mode.

"No, these are not the toys you are looking for," we told him, but he would not give in.

"Come on, tell me, I promise I won't tell mum." The second the words "borrowed" and "school" were out my mouth he ran off shouting, "Mum, MUM! Peta is a thief!" When he got to the kitchen door he turned round, waving his wooden spoon at me. "You are going to get SOOOOOOO done," he said gleefully.

Growing up, not much has changed. John still dobs me into Mum all the time and Mickey and I still share a secret bond that winds everyone else up. I see this behaviour being replicated in my girls.

Roo seems slightly outside the circle at times, doing her own thing. Mostly she seems happy about it but sometimes I wonder if Pip and Juno push her out.

Roo is very imaginative. Give her a stick and some dead flowers and she can play all afternoon, making up other worlds and tall fairy tales. It's one of the million things I love about her, but the school doesn't seem to feel the same way, as I find out when I get collared by Mrs Peacock at pick-up.

It seems that at Christmas, whilst learning the nativity play,

Roo got Jesus confused with a donkey. In fact, the whole donkey part in general got a bit mixed-up in her head. So, according to Roo, Mary gave birth to a tired donkey, and then a flying donkey, on a ladder of donkeys, broke the news to the three wise men, who were all on micro-scooters.

"Surely that's harmless though?"

"Well no, Mrs Newton, it isn't. She has told this story to all the other children. It's going round the school like wildfire. She is denying Jesus. Your daughter is preaching atheism. This is a Church of England school!"

"She is five years old! She can't even say the word atheism! This is ridiculous. It's all just a silly misunderstanding."

"I think it would be very beneficial for Rudy," she pauses to look at me, "for all of you in fact, to attend Church more often. We used to see you there, during the application process …" she trailed off, leaving her implication to sink in and I blush with shame, remembering the short spate of church-going we partook in when it came to needing our forms signed. "But I've not seen your name on the attendance sheet for months and months now. Rudy could get involved in the Sunday school activities and gain a greater understanding of the Bible. In fact we need help with the flower arranging, polishing the pews and Sellotaping up the hymn books. Maybe it would be cleansing for you to do some of God's work too?"

She looks down her glasses at me. Her lips are thin and mean and painted in a hideous shade of peach that make them look like a bum-hole.

I decide right then that I hate this woman. This smug woman in her twinset and pearls with her bum-hole mouth who feels she has the right to judge me and my girl. I hate that I have to bring Roo to this woman's school five days a week.

It felt so wrong to turn round and leave her behind on her first day. She looked small and lost, as if a gust of the September wind could blow her away. Why do they have to grow up so fast in their black and white uniforms? Don't teachers know life should be colourful at this age? On non-uniform day I let Roo wear what she likes. How proudly she strides about in her wizard's cape, tutu and bow tie.

I hate that there is a top of the class and a bottom of the class and an average. Up until now, there has been nothing average about that girl of mine. Now I have to listen to someone I don't know and I don't like, with a bum-hole for a mouth, telling me stuff about my girl that I don't agree with. And I just have to take it.

I call Jimmy as I walk back the car. For once, he answers.

"What's up?"

I tell him about the donkey thing and he laughs.

"It's not funny!"

"It is a bit funny, Pete."

"I suppose you are right." I absentmindedly dust the dashboard with a wet wipe as he continues. "Who cares what she thinks? Roo has the best imagination ever. I much prefer the donkey story."

"But what if she gets in trouble about it?" I scrub at a stubborn stain. "You know what the mums are like round here. It's all about the church."

"Only because it gets them into the school. Chill out, Peta. This is not going to be a problem. Don't stress about it. Go for a run or something."

"I can't. I've got Juno."

"Want me to come home and have her for an hour?"

"Really? You are not too busy?"

"Well I am always busy but I'll come home for a bit if it helps."

"Thanks Jimmy. I appreciate it, but I've got a poxy article to do for Tummy-to-Mummy."

"Why don't you just leave? You hate it there."

"Yes, but it brings in money."

"Not much, and really, we can afford for you not to do it."

"But that just makes me feel useless. Like I don't contribute anything to the family."

"You raise the kids! You clean the house. Give yourself a break."

"I worry that if I don't keep writing I'll stop being able to do it."

"Nonsense, you are a great writer, and one day you are going to have a best-selling cookbook."

"Thanks, Jimmy." I mean it. It's the best conversation we have had in a long time. I am glowing as I drive home. I am so inspired I decide to make a Thai Green curry from scratch, which I have not done for ages.

Jimmy's good mood continues when he gets home. He takes his suit off and spends twenty minutes pushing the girls on the swings in the back garden. As it gets closer to bedtime I make them a beaker of tea each and call them in to watch Ben and Holly's Little Kingdom before getting in the bath.

When they are settled he comes and sits next to me.

"Here."

I look down and see a flyer about chickens. "What's this?"

"Chickens. I've just bought some."

"What?" I almost drop my cup of tea in surprise.

"We are going to get chickens," he announces slowly in his no-nonsense director's voice.

"But …why? Do you want to eat them?"

"No, why would we do that? The children would be heartbroken."

"I just don't understand where this has come from. Why on earth do you want to keep chickens?"

"Jake likes them."

"So what if Jake likes them?"

"Well, I thought if Jake liked them, then the girls might like them too."

"Jake is a ten-year-old boy. He likes completely different things to the girls. And don't we have enough on our plate? I struggle enough with the demented budgies that Roo wanted so much."

"I thought you loved the budgies. You're always walking round with them on your head."

"That is because I can't get them out my hair! They think it's a nest. I don't want chickens. No good will come of it. What about foxes?"

"Don't worry about foxes. I know how to deter them. All you need to do is piss round the cage. Foxes don't like that."

"I don't bloody like it either! And what about the neighbours?"

"Wojtek? He won't be able to see over his giant pile of fence panels.""

"Don't be rude about his summerhouse."

Wojtek is our Polish neighbour. He's one of the nicest people I've ever met, but his house and garden are crammed full of utter crap. He is incapable of throwing anything away. He even fishes through our rubbish to see what he can salvage. The other neighbours are always writing to the council and complaining but we love him. He comes and sits with the girls when I need to nip out and get milk or go for a run, and he looks after our budgies when we are away.

There is absolutely no way he would be bothered by our chickens. Before the Warrior diet thing, and the chicken thing, Jimmy's big thing was composting. He did not know that you are not supposed to put cooked vegetables or meat in composters, however. The smell was horrendous but Wojtek loved it. "This is quality!" he would say. He loved it so much he moved his BBQ next to it and invited his church group over to sniff it too. "Smell this quality," he would demand. We would watch from the safety of our house as they gagged and retched their way through their chargrilled kabanos.

"And that is not the point anyway, Jimmy. The point is that I don't want the bloody chickens."

"You won't need to get involved. I will handle the whole thing. Imagine all the lovely fresh eggs you will have every morning. The cakes, the omelettes, the soufflés"

It does sound good, but I can't just give in. "What about rats?"

"There won't be any rats. And if there are, we'll get a cat."

"I don't want a cat! Jimmy! Jesus. What is going on with you? Is this because of the Welsh holiday?"

"I don't know what you are talking about."

He so knows what I am talking about. I am talking about the farm we stayed on in Wales just before Christmas. As part of the package, the farmer gave us tour of his land. Unbeknown to me (and for no reason other than to show-off), Jimmy swotted up on poultry beforehand so he would know all the answers when the farmer asked, "Do you know which chicken this egg came from?" or "Does anyone know how old this breed of chicken is?"

The farmer was a bit annoyed with Jimmy stealing his chicken-thunder so he made him carry the pig feed. The pigs chased Jimmy. He dropped the feed and ran off screaming like a big girl. The farmer felt his sense of importance and manliness were suitably restored.

"This is about restoring your sense of importance and manliness after those pigs chased you and you ran off screaming like a big girl."

"No I didn't, and no it isn't. It's about the girls. Don't you remember how much they loved collecting the eggs?"

"No. Pip hated it. She kept demanding to go back in the car and watch Mr Tumble on the portable DVD player."

"Well Juno liked them."

"She did not even notice the poxy chickens! She was too busy trying to ride on that Jack Russell called Dora."

"The one whose foot you trod on?"

"Dog's don't have feet. They have paws. And I didn't mean to tread on it. I thought it was going to bite Juno."

"And it did, after you trod on its foot."

"Whatever, the point is no one except you liked the chickens."

"Roo did."

"Roo fell in chicken poo and it stained her hair green."

"So I'll get them hats. Chicken hats. Come on Bride, it will be fun."

I love this easy banter. It comes so naturally to us. It's what makes us work. I look into his earnest face, and warm at the word Bride. It's been a long time since he called me that.

Maybe these chickens will be soup for his soul. Maybe he will stop his silly Warrior diet and I can have the garage back; Jimmy turned it into a home gym, pulling out all the stops. He even installed a projector and bought all the Tour De France DVD's so he could pretend to be going up L'Alpe D'Huez in the yellow jersey with Sir Bradley Wiggins, when actually he peddled on a static bike going nowhere. Thinking about the Tour De France reminds me of the romantic holidays we used to go on before we had the girls.

The tour always goes through my parents' village and we would go each year to see them speed past. Jimmy would hold me in the crush of the crowd and kiss my sunburnt nose. Afterwards we would go to some local café for the plat du jour and drink thick treacly coffee. I miss those days. I miss us.

"Ok Jimmy. Fine. Let's get the chickens." He grins and kisses me quickly on the lips, before running off to tell the girls the good news, and getting them all excited before bed.

"I just hope you are around to look after them," I say quietly to myself.

Chapter Five

I HAVE my first reading session at Roo's school this morning. It was eye-opening to say the least.

Roo spent the whole time in 'cosy corner' looking far too cosy with a boy called Sonny. She's never once mentioned boys to me at home. I thought she played with Lily-Grace and Ava at school. I was so concerned I went and spoke to Mrs Peacock about it, after I'd dutifully listened to half the class stutter their way through 'Going to the Shops'.

"How long has this been going on, this cosy corner thing?"

"Since the donkey story. "

"Why didn't you tell me?"

"I did warn you of the catastrophic effects of atheism. I assumed you knew she was taking the path less travelled. You must have seen all the love cards she has been making."

"I thought they were for her father."

"Well, that's the other thing. She is significantly behind on her writing. Do you do any practice with her at home as we discussed??"

Bugger. If I lie and say yes they might think there is something wrong with Roo, but if I tell the truth I'll get done. I decide to use Jimmy's aversion technique.

"Never mind that! I want to know more about this boy and my Roo. What do they get up to?"

"Oh it's very harmless. Mostly, they pretend to be dogs."

"Sorry?"

"Well they crawl about and bark at one another and have races. Sometimes they lick puddles in the playground but that's as bad as it gets."

"Are you being serious?"

"Yes, Mrs Newton. She is in the 'Tortoise' group for development. They do more outside play while the brighter, I mean, other children read aloud and have spelling bees. Also, since the donkey story, Lily-Grace and Ava's mums, amongst others, have asked me to …" She stops at this point and makes a cutting action with her hand across her neck. "So Rudy has had to find some other friends, more suited to her, um, interests."

I can't believe what I am hearing. My bright, beautiful daughter is in the thick group at school, has a boyfriend and is a figurehead for atheism. Roo is the child that parents don't want their kids to play with. All because of a misunderstanding about a bloody donkey. How has this happened?

The thought of my baby being barred from playing with her best friends, and how rejected she must feel makes my eyes smart with anger and unfairness. Why didn't she tell me any of this?

Then another thought pops into my mind.

"You were not impressed with my posh-phone voice at all were you?"

"I beg your pardon?"

"My posh-phone voice. That's not why you wanted me to come in and read with the children is it? You wanted me in here so you could surreptitiously make notes about me and my girl in your little red log book."

"Mrs Newton, please calm down. We encourage all the

parents to come in and spend time with the class. It's always eye-opening to see how their children behave outside the home environment and it's a good way for them to see where their child ranks amongst their peers."

"I could not care less where she ranks amongst these kids. She knocks the ironed socks off any kid you'll ever meet. Why can't she be praised for her donkey story? Encouraged to continue exploring her amazing imagination."

"I agree, Mrs Newton. It just needs channelling into something more productive than pretending to be a dog." We both look over just in time to see Roo roll on her back with her hands and feet in the air shouting, "I'm rolling in a cow pat! WOOF WOOF!"

"Making love cards for who?"

I have Jimmy's full attention.

"Sonny. He's nice. Honestly, Jimmy, that's not the bit we need to focus on. We need to focus on the fact she is not sharing stuff with us."

"I disagree. That is exactly why we need to focus on the Sonny bit. What else have they been up to that she is keeping from us?"

"Jimmy, you are blowing it all out of proportion. She is FIVE! I am more bothered about the fact that her friends have been told they are not allowed to play with her. She must be so hurt. Can you imagine how confused and rejected she is feeling?"

"And she turned to Sonny to comfort her. Not me. Her dad. I am feeling pretty rejected myself right now."

"Oh for God's sake, Jimmy, would you take it seriously! It's not all about you all the bloody time. Anyway, you have not been around much recently. You have not done the school run for weeks. You know how Roo loves it when you drop her off."

He says nothing but his gaze burns me. I can tell I've upset him but it needed to be said.

I turn back to the sink and start rinsing dried yoghurt out of kids' lunchboxes with unnecessary force. I hear the back door slam and then the sound of a shovel cutting through chalk. Oh no, not this again. He always does this when he is cross. I race outside.

"If you are going to start digging, don't go mad and hurt your back. You are nearly forty now, remember."

"Leave me alone!"

"Well I'm going out tonight, remember. I promised Nellie I'd take her to Sara's bench."

"Fine." He stabs at the ground with his spade and I know there is no point talking to him. The garden is his man cave. His retreat in bad times. He is ridiculously precious about it.

I once caught him creeping outside at midnight, wearing nothing but his pants and a head torch. I then watched in horrified fascination as he bent over each and every one of his tomato plants, lovingly tracing his fingers up and down their dainty stems, before shouting, "ha ha! caught you, you bastard," and then, five seconds later, I heard the small, sad noise of a snail landing over the far side of the road.

He has even passed his dislike of snails onto the children. I heard him asking Roo who made all the holes in his sweet peas and her replying: "It was that bloody Mr Snail, Daddy."

"It was! It was my girl," he said, offering her a muddy hand for a high-five.

She used to be so fond of them as well, picking up the dead ones and saying, "Look, this one has gone out."

He used to be so much fun to live with. Sure, we had our fall outs now and again, but most of the time we were just, well, us. We have exactly the same sense of humour. He is the only person other than Sara who gets me. Well, he was. Now he acts like a stranger most of the time. I know something is going on, but I don't know what. And whenever I resolve to find out, something always gets in the way. I know when he has retreated to his garden that there is no point anyway. He will communicate with grunts and 'make me tea' signals and that is all.

I sigh and go back inside. His phone has lit up. A message from an unsaved number is on his screen. I tell myself I am not going to look as I walk past to load the dishwasher, nor am I going to look at it as I stand next to it to rearrange the cereal boxes on the shelf directly above it. Nor am I ... oh bollocks, I think, and read it.

GR8 to meet u 2day. Thanks for the chat. Really helped. Lk forward 2 next week. M xx

And that is what happens when you read someone's text messages. You end up feeling worse than you did before, and wishing you had not done it. Who is M? What chat? Is she someone at work? What are they doing next week? Why don't I just go and ask Jimmy? Oh yeah, because I will look like a psychopath jealous wife who reads other people's text messages.

Instead I go over and over it in my head as I read to the girls after their bath. They have probably already been asleep for ages before I finally notice, and then I see the time and realise I am going to be late to meet Nellie.

I force my worries to the back of my mind as I park the car. The next hour is not about Jimmy and I. It's about her.

Nellie is very quiet to start with. Her too-big-trainers scuffed in the dirt as she swung her legs back and forth on the bench. I sat with my collar upturned into the late evening breeze and waited.

"Abi says she can't remember what Mum looks like, but Fleur does not like having photos up all over the place. It's because Mum was so much prettier than her."

She pulls a dog-eared photo out of her back pocket and passes it to me. "I think I look like Mum here, do you?" Looking at photos of Sara always makes my breath catch in my throat. I have them all around me at home, but I've gotten used to those ones. This one hurts to see. Sara is leaning against some railings. She is frowning at something or someone. I imagine Jeremy was taking the photo.

She's wearing white Converse trainers, black skinny jeans and her scarf has butterflies all over it. Nellie does look just like Sara in this photo, not just because she is sat next to me wearing the exact outfit. It's the fact that it almost fits her now. She looks like such a young lady and Sara can't be here to see her. I bite the inside of my cheek and remind myself my pain is nothing compared to hers.

"Just like Sara," I say softly, stroking my thumb over her face in the photo before handing it back. Nellie sits staring at it for a long time before standing up to put it away.

"I'd better go. I can see Fleur's car coming. She wants us to have a 'family dinner' together. She does that two-finger thing over the word family, but it does not wind me up when she does it. We walk back hand in hand. I love that she still lets me do this.

"Hey Pete, you are not much bigger than me. Want me to sort out some of Mum's clothes for you? Her green jumper would look great on you."

The kindness of this girl astonishes me. The few possessions of Sara's that I asked for are too precious to be used or worn, apart from her red dotty mug. I like drinking out of that. I feel like I am raising my glass to her each time I take a sip. Jimmy knows never to put it in the dishwasher, never to use it or let the kids near it.

"You wear her clothes, Nellie girl. They look better on you."

I get home and walk straight upstairs to check on the

children. I look out Roo's window and see Jimmy is still out in the garden, but now he is wearing the head torch and something is beeping somewhere.

"What are you doing?"

"Nothing. Go indoors. I'll be in soon."

"What is that? What are you doing? Is that a metal detector?"

"No. It's a spirit level. I am just checking the foundations."

"Liar. You've lost your wedding ring, haven't you? I told you time and time again to get it re-sized since your stupid he-man diet."

"I'll find it. I promise and it's not a he-man diet, it's a Warrior diet."

"You don't have a hope in hell of finding it. I can't believe you lost the ring I bought you. I bet you did it on purpose. You didn't want to wear it anymore did you? … hello wojtek, lovely evening!" I shriek at him as he watches us over the fence, and then I stomp across the deck and open the patio door with so much force it bangs on its hinges.

"Peta, wait …"

But I don't. Instead I go to bed and cry myself into an exhausted, angry sleep. Hours later, I, and all the children, are woken by a loud cry of, "GET IN THERE!" – coming from the garden. I stumble downstairs and open the patio door to find Jimmy on his knees in a chalk pit, kissing his dirt encrusted wedding ring before holding it up to the approaching dawn. Next to him, Wojtek is standing in his dressing gown holding a torch.

I look at the clock. It's 4am.

"You've been looking for it all night?"

"So I lost a night's sleep. What's that compared to you losing your best friend?"

"You really did not mean to lose it?"

"I really did not mean to lose it."

I think back to the text message and decide M can't be anyone worth worrying about if he spent all night looking for his wedding ring.

I pluck it from him and slip it back on his finger. We sit together in the dirt with our foreheads touching.

"I really bloody miss her, Jim."

"I know, baby, I know."

"I'll go now," says Wojtek, and turns the torch off.

Jimmy still leaves the house early the next morning, but last night feels like a sticking plaster, papering some cracks for now. I spend the next morning baking gingerbread and cutting red hearts from the softest felt I can find and stitching them onto the inside of Roo's school cardigans. I imagine her face when she notices and hope that she will feel the love I sewed them on with.

Chapter Six

JIMMY says he has work to do on Sunday so I decide to take the girls to a car boot sale at the race course. I want to see if I can find any more le Crueset pans. I give the girls a pound each.

Roo immediately drops hers and Pip offers up her own. I reimburse Pip. With it, she carefully chooses a little dolly in a wooden crib. Her chubby hand opens like a flower to display her sweaty pound.

"Fank- you for mine dolly," she says shyly to the seller's shoes.

When we get back and see Jimmy out in the garden I decide to try and make a family day of it. I put together a picnic lunch and the girls sit under their trampoline eating ham and salad-cream sandwiches, washed down with pink-milk and slices of apple. I make James a bowl of cous cous and tuna which he accepts gratefully.

After lunch I start digging a hole to plant a red Acer tree in. I don't enjoy gardening but I saw the tree at the boot sale and it made me think of Sara. She loved seeing the change of seasons.

Jimmy was busy working on the chicken run. We dug in companionable silence to the background noise of Jarvis Cocker's Sunday afternoon BBC Radio Six playlist.

The children bounced on their trampoline and went into their cubby house. I was busy swearing at ivy roots my spade would not cut through. Jimmy was busy making sure the foundations were flat for the run.

I did not notice Pip get off the trampoline and go wandering. Round and round the garden. Did she stop to pick up a snail or a dying daffodil head before she found the weed killer? She appeared by Jimmy's side with the nozzle in her mouth. Her little chubby hand, that so recently held her pound, was now on the trigger.

We dropped to our knees, trying to make eye contact and stay calm. "Did you spray it in your mouth baby? Tell us," I asked gently.

"No" she said, her eyes as big as saucers.

"You can tell us Pip," said Jimmy, holding her by the shoulders. "We won't be cross with you." She carried on shaking her head, and seemed to be fine for about ten minutes or so, but then the sickness came, again and again and again. Her little body shuddering and shivering.

"I'll take her to A&E. You stay here," Jimmy ordered, scooping her floppy body up into his arms. I appreciated him taking control. My limbs would not seem to work.

We stood on the drive and watched him roar off.

I spent the next hour pacing, obsessively cleaning and waiting for my phone to ring. Roo and Juno seemed to realise that something was wrong. They sat quietly on the sofa watching TV.

At last my phone rang.

"She is going to be OK. We'll be here for a while yet though said Jimmy." I crumpled into a pile of her dressing-up clothes.

"What happened?"

"She has been given an anti-sickness jab and they are treating for dehydration. When they asked her to open wide so they could put the lolly-stick in her mouth she asked 'Where's the lolly?' She is going to be OK Peta."

"Is her throat badly burned?"

"No, not too badly at all. We will be home tonight."

The relief soon gave way to guilt over who left the weed-killer out, which in turn caused a row.

"It does not matter who left it out, Peta. The point is she is fine!"

"But we can't let this happen again."

"And it won't! I have put it somewhere safe."

"I think you should chuck it out. What if you forget again?"

"I am not going to."

"But you are a bit all over the place at the minute Jimmy."

"What?"

I wish I had not said anything. It's the worst way to approach Jimmy.

"Nothing. I'm tired. You're tired. Pip's going to be okay and that's the main thing."

I can't settle in our bed. I decide to go and sleep with Pip in case she wakes up with a sore throat and wants a drink. It used to drive me mad to sleep with the kids, but after such a long time of Jimmy and I sleeping with our backs to one another, and no part of us touching, I welcome Pip's spaghetti arms and legs all over me.

Pip sleeps for thirteen hours straight then wolfs down two bowls of Weetabix. I decide to keep her off school for the week anyway, so I have both her and Juno with me when I get summoned into Roo's school again that afternoon.

"What now?" I ask warily.

"Rudy got moved to amber on the behaviour-related traffic light for barking her way through the feelings register. When I asked her why, she said she 'felt like a dog'. She pauses and looks at me. "Are there problems at home, Mrs Newton?"

"No. What problems? Why do you ask?"

"Well, we're concerned about Roo saying she feels like a dog. A child's most formative years are from birth to age five you know. Ninety percent of a child's brain develops in that time. And eighty-five percent of a child's intellect, personality and social skills too. It's a critical time for a child to build the foundation for literacy, which is really about the early relationship a child develops with a parent. I can't stress the importance of this. If Roo is being told that she behaves like a dog, or maybe is hearing her mother being told she is like a dog, it can cause unrepairable damage."

"What on earth are you going on about? Of course we don't tell her she is like a dog! And of course she does not hear me getting told I am like one! Where do you get this stuff from? Roo is just playing. Having fun. Acting out. Maybe she really does feel like being a dog today. Sometimes she feels like dressing up as the tin man from The Wizard of Oz. Does that mean she's going to become an axe-murderer?"

"Have you considered, Mrs Newton, that she may be feeling insecure because of the 'weed killer incident'." She does those two finger things round the word incident which I hate.

"You heard about that?"

"Roo drew a very graphic picture this morning. When Mrs Shoe asked her about it, the story came out. We think Roo is traumatised after seeing her little sister get poisoned."

"She did not get poisoned, she poisoned herself! And who is Mrs Shoe?"

"She is the school counsellor."

"Why is Roo seeing the school counsellor? How long has she been seeing her for? Don't you have to ask me before you refer my child for counselling?"

"She has been seeing her since the donkey story. Mrs Shoe is really very good. She coaxes children to work through their issues by painting and drawing. She is particularly interested in Roo."

I spend a fruitless half hour trying to persuade the teacher that Roo does not have any issues and not to read too much into her drawings, but I can tell my words are falling on deaf ears. I need to prove to her that we are a nice, normal family. I decide to corner Jimmy that evening before he can lock himself into his study for the night.

"Forget it. I am not doing it and you can't make me."

"Come on Jimmy. It's not for me, it's for Roo."

"No it isn't. It's for you. You do it."

"I can't. They need a man."

"I'm not joining Morris' neighbourhood watch scheme and that's the end of it."

I'm surprised at his vehemence. I thought he would be up for it.

"Why? Why would I be up for it?"

"Because I'm making a pig's ear of everything and I need you. Roo is going to get kicked out of school."

"How is me joining Morris's Nazi party going to help?"

"He is not a Nazi! It will show we are a nice, normal family. You can wear the 'I'm a friendly neighbour' arm band to drop off."

"I don't have time to do the school drop off and I am NOT BLOODY DOING IT!"

Morris is our other neighbour. An ex-army man who runs the neighbourhood watch scheme with military-like precision and spends his weekends drawing round the tools in his garage with chalk, whilst secretly fitting surveillance cameras.

When the Sunday football league play on the field next to our house he goes over with his own whistle and red cards to use if they swear. When they then swear at him, he calls the police and tries to get them arrested. He phones the council about Wojtek's mess and the RSPCA about his barking dogs at least once a week. He knows everything about everyone, yet his own wife is rarely seen. I've only met her once.

It was at our housewarming party. We had dutifully invited the neighbours, trying to make a good impression. Morris' desire to have a nose around our security measures was so great he let her out for the night. She got very drunk very quickly, while Morris was busy checking out our smoke alarms, and then spent the rest of the evening hitting on us. She kept stroking my bum and trying to do slow sexy dancing with Jimmy.

Morris finally stopped trying to see if he could fit through our cat flap and noticed what she was up to. He carried her home in a fireman's lift. Her kicking protests showed her lack of knickers.

We've tried to avoid both of them ever since.

"I am not going round there. I won't get out alive. Plus, I am busy that night."

"Busy doing what?"

"Work, Peta. To support you lot."

"Hey. That's not fair. I work too. Sort of."

"Speaking of which, I have a function at London Zoo on Saturday. A work family thing, you don't need to come."

"Why would we not come? The kids will love it. I will love it. Remember how you used to take me to the zoo? We fed the bear Black Jacks and snogged a lot."

"Not really, no. Why don't you just stay here and we'll take the kids to the Sea life Centre on Sunday instead. I am sure there will be 'things with big heads on' at the zoo. You know how Roo hates them. They like the Sea life centre. No big heads there, just big fish."

"I am sure she is over that by now. It was months ago."

"Well on your head be it."

"Excuse the pun"

"Sorry?"

"Nothing." He did not seem in the mood for jokes.

"Don't you want me to come?"

"Why would I not want you to come?"

"I don't know. You are acting funny."

"What are you on about? It's a boring work do. I'm trying to save you from having a boring time and Roo from being scared."

"I think we'll risk it. I really fancy a trip up town."

"Don't call it up town. Call it London."

Well. I soon found out why Jimmy did not want me to go to the work do. And now I know what the locked study door has been about and now I know who M is.

God it was awful. There were so many people there I did not notice at first. I was too busy being a dutiful wife and trying to get round everyone to say hello. That takes a long time with all the staff, and their wives and kids and the very strong Bulgarian accents. All Jimmy's staff seem to be Bulgarian or African. I spent an hour politely saying 'pardon' a lot and grinning like a goon before I finally gave up.

I first noticed M whilst saying hello to Joe. He looked tired and his shirt was all creased, a far cry from his normal impeccable demeanour.

"You OK Joe?" I kiss his stubby cheek and smell Issey Miyake

"Si."

"You look crumpled, and tired."

"I'm just hot. I don't like this zoo. It's noisy. Why can't we be by the seaside?"

It's not like Joe to moan like this. I study him for a moment. He looks agitated so I don't push it, instead I ask, "Where's Jake?"

"In the Aquarium. He loves the sharks."

"Sharps, sharps!" Pip and Juno chant, pulling me away. I turn to go and that's when I spot her. I spin back, I'd love to say on my high-heels, but I am wearing flip flops.

"Who's that, Joe?"

"Who is who?"

"That blonde girl talking to Jimmy."

Joe looks hideously awkward. He pales under his Spanish tan.

"That's Meg."

"Who's Meg?"

"His new PA, didn't he tell you?" Is it me or does he go a bit red as he says it?

Something was definitely not right with Joe. He was acting suspiciously. As far as I knew he had not had any Limoncello yet.

I sensed that now, with all his staff around him, was not the time to get into it, so I let the girls pull me away. While they pressed their faces up against the giant tanks and tried to lick fish as they swam past, I hid behind a giant cut-out of Steve Irwin and watched Jimmy and Meg.

Meg is stunning. She's wearing a floaty white dress that stops on the knee. Pretty, but not tarty. Her skin is shiny and tanned and her blonde hair shimmers in the sun like in that old Timotei advert. A perfect French polish peeks out between the gaps in her on-trend gladiator sandals. When she laughs, it sounds like a trickling stream.

I look down at my own hastily put together outfit. Cut-off jeans displaying corned beef coloured legs. Flip flops (no French polish) and a black t-shirt which Pip smeared chocolate on within seconds of us arriving.

I should go over there and introduce myself. Be funny and fabulous. Outshine her obvious vacant beauty with my wit and intelligence. "I'm funny, right Steve?" I say to the crocodile wrestling cut-out. But something in the way Jimmy is looking at her stops me. He used to look at me like that.

Suddenly it all makes sense. The dieting. The weight-loss. The absence.

It's for her. What a bloody cliché. My husband is shagging his PA.

Winded, I turn and walk over to Roo, who has moved away and is sitting alone eating a lolly in the shade. She looks pensive as she licks strawberry drips from her star-shaped hands.

"Alright, Pops?"

"Who is that lady, Mummy?"

"That is Daddy's new, um, helper."

"She is very pretty, isn't she Mummy? Her dress is like a wedding dress."

"Hmmm."

"I wish you wore dresses like that Mummy. She looks like a princess."

I want to cry, but I don't. Instead I say, "But if I had that posh old frock on, I would not be able to do this!" Then I pick her up and throw us both onto the bouncy castle.

"Mummy, Mummy, let's be doggies!"

"Ok woof woof!"

Pip and Juno dive on too. I watch Jimmy and Meg deep in conversation, and clench my pelvic floor so I don't leave a wet patch.

I spend the rest of the day being dragged round by the kids and keeping as far away from Jimmy and Meg as possible. The kids have never had as much fun with me. I have never felt as stupid and insufficient.

In the car on the way home, I finally bring it up.

"So, you have a new PA, huh?"

"Who Meg? She is not just my PA, she is Joe's too," he says defensively. Joe never mentioned she was his PA too. He just went red and looked awkward. Was he protecting Jimmy? Surely not. Joe loves me. There is no way he would be an advocate in any of this.

"You never mentioned it to me."

"Why would I?"

"I don't know. I just thought you might have told me."

"What's to tell?"

"Meg is very pretty."

"Is she?"

"You know she is, Jim."

"What do you fancy for dinner?"

"I'm not hungry. I …"

I want to ask more questions, but a squirmy feeling in my tummy stops me. I realise it's fear.

Instead we drive through the London streets in silence, as the girls sleep in the back. When Jimmy brakes at the traffic lights, their heads knock gently together. I remember a photo of me and my brothers asleep like that. I imagine my mum turning round in her seat to take the shot. The winding noise of the camera. I wonder where we had been, why she wanted to capture that moment. It's a moment I should probably capture too, but I don't want any memories of this day.

I sneak a look at Jimmy. He looks the same to me as he ever did. High handsome forehead. Straight nose and big brown eyes. A generous mouth with a dimple in the side of his cheek that deepens when he smiles and annoyingly still makes me feel like I went over a hump-backed bridge. Dark brown hair (no grey, bastard) pushed into an effortlessly messy side quiff. He could be twenty-three not forty. I find him as fine as I ever did.

Then I pull down the sun-visor and look at my own reflection. I've changed so much in the last few years. My face looks older and it's gotten gaunt. My make-up sweated off at some point and the hollows under my eyes look like bruises. My lips are chapped. I have a blob of ketchup on the side of my cheek. My hair got wet in the playground pool (we were doggy-paddling) and has dried in the style of Lady Di. Up until today I did not take the time to notice how bad I was looking, I did not care. Did not realise I needed to. Never for a second thought that Jimmy might be looking elsewhere. We used to joke about people who 'took a lover'. It was a game we would play. When we went out for a meal we would both have to pick someone from each table in the restaurant 'as a lover'. We used to end up crying with laughter.

It does not seem quite so funny anymore though, nor does it feel so far-fetched. Jimmy and I have always rowed. We both enjoy the drama of it all. The sulking and door slamming. The silent fuming. The sound of the kettle boiling for sorry tea and biscuits, and then the sorry sex afterwards.

But it's not like that anymore. Our rows are not games we are playing. There is no sorry tea or sorry sex afterwards. The words we throw at one another these days land like stones and leave bruises, yet we still toss them out so casually. It's now become normal to go to sleep on an argument. On the rare nights I am not in Pip's bed, I tuck the quilt round me tightly, a cocoon which shrieks don't touch.

How did it get to this? We've even rowed in front of the girls. Something I'd never thought I'd lower myself to. I grew up hiding in home-made trenches to avoid my parents' marital wars. Their insults and swear words felt like bombs falling around me, blowing my safe place to pieces.

Mickey and I would huddle together behind the brown leather sofa and make up worlds where we were kings and queens with superpowers. John would sit close to the TV watching Star Wars turned up loudly so that he could not hear anything else. I suppose that was his made-up world to escape to.

I feel hopelessly inadequate and I have no idea what to do. If only Sara was here to talk to. I imagine her saying "Jimmy loves ye! What ye greetin' over that Skinny Malink for? Away an boil ye heed" or some other overly Scottish nonsense, just to make me laugh.

Jimmy is overly attentive when we get home. I am suspicious when he offers me tea and to run a bath. I decline both and pretend to be absorbed in my book – 'How to talk so your children will listen'.

Chapter Seven

I'M almost grateful to the children for being such hard work the next morning. It's far easier to deal with than working out a way to ask Jimmy if he is having an affair. It's getting harder and harder to avoid though, and I end being a little too harsh with them, and they all end up sobbing as I strap them into their car seats.

I pull a bag of Haribo out the glove box, and as if by magic, no more crying. If only Haribo could do the same for me.

"Sorry for shouting so much, Pops," I tell Roo as she wipes her eyes on the sleeve of my coat, "the morning lost its legs."

"That's OK, Mummy. Shall we share a fizzy cola bottle?"

"Why not? Just hide if you see The-Iron-Curtain." We chew in companionable silence for a couple of minutes and then she says, "You did do my boot, didn't you, Mummy?"

"What boot, treacle?"

"The one I bought home from school last week. With the note about decorating it."

Somewhere inside the frazzled recesses of my mind, a bell rings. It sounds like a death toll.

"What kind of decorating?" Please be something easy, please be something easy.

"Anything we like, Mummy. Ava's mum has sewn pearl

buttons all over hers. Lily-Grace's mum glued sparkles all over hers. Daisy's mum had hers dipped in gold. Steven's mummy would not touch the shoe he got given though. She said it smelt disgusting and was un, unhun …"

"Unhygienic?"

"Yes, Mummy, that word. What does it mean?"

"It means when something is covered in germs."

"Like Daddy's sports kit? You always say that smells disgusting. Is that *unhungenic* too?"

"Very." I wonder if Meg would still look at him like he'd hung the moon after she'd had to wash his sweaty cycling shorts. "When does this shoe have to be done by?"

"Today, Mummy."

"Today?"

"Yes, look!"

Stuck in traffic, I gaze through the windscreen to see a procession of children walking to school, proudly holding their decorated shoes and boots. Cat and The-Iron-Curtain are leading the cavalcade, their offerings perched on plump velvet pillows.

I don't even know where Roo's poxy boot is. I have a horrible feeling I threw it away. I am very good at throwing important documents away. It is a skill of mine. "So where is my boot mummy?"

I can't tell her I threw it away, she will be so upset. She is still cross about being the only girl in school in uniform on non-uniform day.

"Remind mummy again what colour it was?"

"It was a big purple boot with yellow stitching round the sole. Everyone else wished they'd been given it."

Brilliant. A Doc Martin. How the feck am I going to find one of them, and then decorate it before the end of today?

"Oh yes, silly me. I remember now. I left it in the um, err, garage to um, dry. I'll bring it in later."

"Phew! Thanks mummy. For a minute I thought you had forgotten, like the time you forgot it was non uniform day and I was the only girl in school in uniform. Or the time you forgot it was red nose day and I was the only …"

"Another fizzy cola bottle Roo?"

"Yes please mummy."

Walking up the school lane, we are the only people not carrying a highly adorned shoe or boot that would give Jimmy Choo a run for his money.

"Where your shoe?"

Shit. The-Iron-Curtain has materialised beside me. How does she always manage to do that? Maybe Russians are taught silent stealthy walking in school. They are certainly not taught any social skills.

Poppy is with her looking like a smug mini-replica of her mother. The shoe on Poppy's cushion has been covered with *papier mâché* and made into a perfect replica of the Winter Palace. It even has tiny Russian dolls in the window.

"You had the big Doctor Martian boot, yes? I remember this boot. It a good boot. Why they waste the boots on this project I don't know. Still, they say decorate a shoe, so we decorate the shoe? It funny English thing, is it? In my country, we lucky to have shoe, let alone pair. Here, you English have so many shoes you decorate for fun. This crazy country I move to, heh?"

She knows. She knows I lost the shoe. I must look guilty. I try and re-arrange my face to look happy and carefree. I probably just look constipated.

"The boot is in the garage drying off actually," I say airily, tossing my head in a casual but surprisingly painful way.

"Why you not have it dry and ready like everyone else?"

"Because it's extra special." What? No it isn't. I don't even have the bloody boot. Why can't I just shut up?

"I can't wait to see this extra special boot." She narrows her eyes at me briefly, before poking Poppy in the back and saying, "Come Poppy, we go in school now, drop off our poor no special boot."

I throw Roo into school and run shouting "Be right back with the boot!" across the playground over my shoulder. Then I get in the car and bang my head on my steering wheel ten times. When I look up The-Iron-Curtain is standing in front of my windscreen, smiling.

I finally find a Doc Martin boot in a charity shop after two hours trawling round the Lanes in town. They are not purple, and I'm pretty sure someone died wearing them, but it's the best I can do. I look up at the clock and see I have two hours left to decorate one of them and get it to school. I've never felt more uninspired. I'm not very good at arts and crafts. I don't cope well with messy play. As a child my favourite game was lining all my toys up in size order neatly, then dusting them.

I could put lots of Peppa Pig stickers on it? Go Lady GaGa style and cover the boot in strips of bacon? Blue-tack my leg hairs onto it and make it into a hedgehog?

No, no, no.

I look through the kitchen cupboards frantically. Jimmy's whole-wheat quinoa falls out and spills all over the floor, then I spot some icing sugar, and inspiration hits.

Roo races out of the school gate, her coat flapping like a cape. "Mummy, Mummy! Everyone is talking about my cake-boot. They love it. They wish they had a cake-boot too. You are so clever mummy." I glow with achievement.

"It was nothing, Pops, nothing at all."

"I especially loved the strawberry laces and the jelly beans you stuck to the icing."

"Good. I am so pleased. Sorry it was late, treacle."

"That's OK, Mummy. It was worth waiting for. It's a very big cake, isn't it, Mummy? It must have used up lots of cake-mix. Did you save me the spoon to lick?" I pull the cake-mix-coated spoon (Clingfilm covered) from my pocket and pass it over to her as we walk down the lane. Pip has already licked hers. I let Juno have the cake-coated bowl. She put it over her head and I got an hour of peace.

"I think we are going to win the competition," she says happily, skipping along beside me.

The-Iron-Curtain is waiting for me as we pass the school gate. She says nothing and I try my best not to smirk.

"Have a nice evening!" I trot out in a jolly fashion.

"Yes. You too," she says, looking like she wants to stab me.

I am preparing dinner back at home when Roo wanders into the kitchen looking pensive. "What's up, Pops?"

"Nothing." She lifts her arms to be sat on the worktop. I plonk her next to the sink and wait.

"Why doesn't Daddy ever pick me up anymore?"

"Well he is very busy at work, my love." I reach over her for a grater to turn potatoes into rosti.

"But he always used to pick me up on a Tuesday and Friday. I do like that you picked me up and that you made me such a good cake-boot but I do miss Daddy. Lily-Grace's dad picks her up on a Tuesday too and her daddy and my daddy used to play football. Even Zack thought daddy was great at football." I wipe my hands on a tea-towel and think about what to say. "He used to take me to the seaside on Fridays and let me order the fish and chips for dinner," Roo carries on, picking at a dried lump of icing on the worktop. I can see she is going to eat it so I quickly pass her a raw carrot.

"Eat this instead."

While she crunches I tell how her daddy is really busy at the moment and how he needs to work hard to bring in the pennies for us and that really he would much prefer to be at home with us. It sounds a bit lame to my own ears, but it seems to pacify her, or maybe it's that she hears the theme tune to Jake And The Neverland Pirates. "Thanks, Mum!" She grabs a couple more carrot sticks and jumps down to watch TV with her sisters.

I wait until they are engrossed then call Jimmy. He ignores my phone call on his mobile so I ring the office.

"Good afternoon, JPA cleaning, how can I help you?" a voice I don't recognise trills at me in a sing-song voice. It catches me off-guard and I stumble over my words.

"Oh hi, hello. It's Peta, Jimmy's wife. Is he around?"

"Oh hi, Peta. Yes, he is right here next to me, I'll just pass you over."

Suddenly I recognise the voice. It's Meg's. I hear a muffled conversation between them and then finally Jimmy comes on the line. He sounds cross.

"What's up?"

I can tell by his tone of voice that he is expecting an emergency situation. My conversation with Roo suddenly seems trivial. Don't be a wimp, I tell myself. His children miss him. He should be at home with them instead of nestled in his office with his secretary.

"Roo is very upset you did not pick her up from school today."

He sighs down the phone. "Peta, I'm snowed under, could this not have waited?"

"Not really. She was really gutted not to see you. I don't know what to tell her. She misses you." There is a silence at the end of the phone. I imagine him rolling his eyes at Meg and mouthing 'nagging'. My vivid imagination then pictures Meg brushing her heaving breasts against his arm as she looks up at him sympathetically.

"You are still their dad, Jimmy. They still need you."

"I know, Peta. But now is not the time to talk about it." He punctuates each word so it comes out in staccato. He is furious with me for embarrassing him. I don't care.

"Be home for their bedtime," I staccato back at him then put the phone down before he can.

I am still shaking as I tidy up the debris from my cake-boot-making frenzy. I wipe the kitchen sides and try to calm down. I'm hosting the pre-school committee meeting tonight. I can't cancel because I'm the chairperson. I don't know how I get roped into these things. I fully intended to say no when I was asked, but yes came out instead.

The manager, Pamela, can't stand me. I see her face fall each time mine appears in the glass door when I ring the bell.

Pamela despises all children. She can't bear their smells in the toilet, spilt sand, Play Doh colours that have been mixed together or role play. When the children bring cakes in for their birthdays she makes sure she cuts herself a huge bit first before she serves it to them, so it won't have snot on it.

They have been using the same toys and resources for the last twenty years and refuse to replace anything when it's broken. I'm desperate to get them some new jigsaws and colouring pencils but they won't let me. Tonight we are discussing the pre-school sports day.

Jimmy walks through the door at 6.10 pm just as I've put the girls in the bath.

"I'll take over." He drops his suit jacket on the floor and sits down on the toilet seat to push his sleeves up "Hello, girls. What did you get up today?" His light tone does not match his cross expression but the kids don't notice.

"Hi, Daddy!" Roo beams up at him from under the afro she has fashioned out of bubbles. "Do you like my hat?" It's as if her conversation with me a mere two hours ago never happened. Jimmy looks at me with an eyebrow raised but says nothing.

It's not the time to get into it. People will be arriving any second. I pass him some mango shampoo and leave him to it.

Twenty minutes later I am handing round some hastily made mini courgette and bacon muffins. "Tell me again why we can't have sports day outside?" I ask.

"It's much easier indoors," says Pamela, then "this muffin is delicious."

"Thank you. They are very easy to make. I could come in and cook them with the children if you like?"

"God no, imagine the mess!"

"Right, I see. I forgot about the mess. Back to the organised fun that is sports day then. The hall really is too tiny. The children might crash into the wall at the end and hurt themselves."

"Yes, but if we have it indoors we can sell tea and coffee and cake. I love cake."

I dutifully push her over the banana and blueberry loaf I had in the freezer.

"Ooh, cake, thank you!" I don't bother telling her that it is very easy to make and I would be very happy to cook it with the children at pre-school." Instead I say, "But it will be in the summer. If we do it outside, we can serve cold drinks and ice lollies."

"I like having it indoors. Now, who is doing the price list and who is going to make cakes? Will you make more of this cake? And those muffins? I'll serve them so I can make sure no children get anywhere near them. I'll need the stereo too."

"But we normally use it to play party music," says Faith, who has been desperately trying to get a word in edgeways.

"I like to have The Archers on while I serve tea."

She has a negative answer for every suggestion we make.

"Should we award prizes?"

"No, too expensive. They can have a sticker. Faith, you can make lots of stickers out of the laser labels that got donated once."

"The ones that are not at all sticky, hence why they got donated to us? Terrific. Thanks," mutters Faith, draining her wine glass and hastily filling it up again.

"Will we do a beanbag race?"

"No. We don't have any."

"We could buy some. How much money do we have in the kitty, Kate?" Kate is the treasurer. She did not realise how much was involved in the job and gets flustered under pressure. By the time she finds the page in her accounts book, Pamela has moved on. "No, no need for them. We'll put an orange in a sock and they can use that, and then eat it at snack-time."

The meeting finally ends with Pamela somehow getting all her own way, as usual. We all pretend to say goodbye, then once Pamela has driven away, Kate and Faith come out of the Wendy house where they were hiding and we crack open more wine and indulge in some Pamela-Tourettes, as usual.

"Miserable, tight arsed, odd-sock wearing wanker!" That was from Faith.

"You really don't want to do those labels do you?"

"No I don't. At least she is going to allow us to do new ones. For a moment I thought she was going to say we would have to reuse the ones we made them peel off last year."

"She didn't?"

"She did. Cake eating, limp-haired, high-pitched harpie!"

"Very good, Kate. I did not know you had it in you." I toast her with my Chablis.

"Thank you." She blushes and helps herself to more cake.

This is the other reason why I help on the school committee. It's not just that I can't say no. Somewhere amongst all the do's and don'ts and fundraising, we always manage to have a good laugh. Jimmy is asleep by the time I finally say goodbye to Faith and Kate, both of whom are slightly worse for wear as they stagger their way down the drive slurring. "I'm going to tell her to shove her orange up her arse."

"I'm going to make her a sticker which says …" Kate pauses. "I'm *not* here to help".

I snort as I make my way upstairs. Then I see Jimmy and the events from earlier come flooding back. For the first time, I start to consider the genuine possibility of him having an affair. Is he washing more or wearing more aftershave. When did we last have sex? My final thought is that I must check his trousers for receipts before falling into a slightly drunken sleep.

Chapter Eight

I OFFER to take his suit to the dry cleaners and find there are no receipts in his trousers. I raid the glove box of his car but there is nothing more sinister than some out of date turkey slices. His clothes smell of my washing powder and his aftershave. I don't know the password to his email account. I would give up but I know there is something going on. Things feel weird. He is keeping something from me, and I have a horrible feeling it's got large breasts, blond hair and goes by the name of Meg.

After two weeks of worrying but not having the guts to confront him, I go to the doctor for pills to knock me out. I'm desperate for some oblivion. The doctor is reluctant to just hand them over though. He wants to talk to me first.

"You seem on edge. Are you getting enough help at home, Mrs Newton?" He peers over his glasses, trying not to look like he is assessing me.

"Not really. I have three children under six and a mostly absent husband. Please may I have the pills now?" I hold my hand out and smile in what I hope is a winning fashion.

He ignores me.

"What about friends? Do you have anyone who could help you out, anyone you could talk to?"

In my head my friends are all lined up like the board game of Who's Who. Do I have someone who I feel I can really talk to? Do they wear glasses? No. Not them, or them. I flick their faces downwards quickly in my mind. I have Heather but she has so much on her plate with the move, and I know she would feel helpless being so far away and unable to help. As always, Sara's face flashes up and my heart skips a beat. I lay her down gently.

"Not really, no."

"How long have you been having trouble sleeping?"

"A couple of weeks"

"And before then?"

"Better, if the kids let me."

"Nightmares?"

"God, yes. I don't know why I kept having them."

"I mean, are you having nightmares in your sleep, Mrs Newton?"

"Oh yes. Them too." I watch him make a note on his pad and kick myself under the table.

"Does your husband know you are here?"

I look down at my hands and twirl my rings around my finger. My gorgeous engagement ring. The one I saw in a jeweller's shop in the Lanes and instantly fell in love with. I didn't even mention it to Jimmy. He just knew somehow it was the one for me.

I never knew why he was so nervous that night, or why he rushed our dinner. In the car on the way home 'our song' kept playing over and over on repeat. We pulled up on the drive. "Oh the iPod must be stuck. It's in the glove box. Please may you reset it?" And there was the velvet lined box, lid open, diamond glinting, waiting for me. Fitting perfectly first time.

"Oh yes, and will you marry me please?" he said casually, but his voice went up at the end and his hands shook as he slipped the ring onto my finger.

Then my wedding band, the one he said 'I do' with. The one we picked together, giddy on love and sparkling stones. Diamonds that were supposed to be forever.

Where has that boy gone? The one who would write 'You have a lovely bum' on the loo roll for me to find. The one who used to bring me home whatever book he noticed being most read on the train, hoping I'd enjoy it too. The boy who carried me with words when I was exhausted in labour. "Beautiful, brave, amazing girl. Your strength is astounding. I know you can do this."

We used to sit up all night talking. The massive phone bills we have paid over our years. Now I can't ask him five simple words. "Do you still love me?"

Faith's husband told her he was leaving her on New Year's Eve. They were taking down the Christmas decorations. She vividly remembers climbing on the arm of the sofa to reach the star at the top of the tree as she asked, "What shall we plan now, Roger? Shall we go on holiday?" When he did not answer her, she turned to look at him, clutching on to the tree for support.

He was wringing their son's gaudy stocking in his hands. He did not look at her. "Faith, you must know I'm leaving." She wobbled and dropped the star. He left later that day. She never saw it coming. Never noticed anything was wrong. When she first told me, I didn't believe her. "How could you not have known?" I asked her. "I was just so busy trying to cope with Ben and the house and commuting to London everyday. I couldn't keep on top of everything, literally."

I understand now. I thought once we'd said 'I do' that love and happily-ever-after was sorted. I could tick it off my to-do list and crack on to the next project. I was wrong. A marriage is a living breathing thing. It needs feeding and watering. It's like my middle child, an attention-seeker that can't be ignored.

"Mrs Newton?"

I zone back in and realise I am still sitting staring into space at the doctor's surgery.

"No, I've not told him how I feel. He is very busy at work. He doesn't need to be bothered with my problems." This is easier to say than trying to explain that he *is* the problem.

"I think you might be suffering from post-natal-depression. Would you like me to refer you for counselling? I'd be happy to, and I can write out a prescription of beta-blockers for your anxiety."

"What? No, I don't need counselling or beta-blockers. I'm not depressed, I'm just tired. I just need some sleeping pills. Please."

He looks at me for a long minute. Finally, he consents. "OK." Then he writes something else down on his pad. "I'll give you one week's worth, but I'd like to run some blood tests too, just to see if anything else is going on. You look underweight."

"Thank you. That's the nicest thing anyone has said to me in months."

"This won't be. While you are here, shall we do your missed coil-check-up? You never turned up last time."

"Sod it. Why not?"

"I'll just ring for a nurse. How's Rudy getting on at school?" he asks, as I strip off behind the see-through blue curtain.

"Yes, very well thanks. We must do a play date with Amber soon."

I trip over in my haste to get my trousers off and the awful test done and fall through the curtain at his feet. He tries not to laugh.

"Oh yes, Amber would like that. Let's ask them about it at pick-up. Ah hello, Jeanette." The nurse shuts the door and the curtain opens. "Now hop up onto the couch, pop your ankles together and flop your knees apart. Lovely."

I sleep better that night thanks to the pills, and the night after. It fills me with a positivity I have been lacking and I decide that I cannot carry on like this any longer. I need to make an effort and save my marriage! It can't be that hard. Jimmy and I just need to spend some quality time together where we can re-bond and then have a good time and have good, noisy sex and all will be well.

"Morning, can you have Juno for an hour while I go for a run please?" I struggle to hold both Juno and the still hot chocolate muffins I've made to bribe Wojtek with.

"Yes, of course. Come in, Juno. We will go and see if we can find that book you like."

"Love you." I kiss them both, then go and dig out my running kit.

Running is my sanctuary. It's the only time I feel like I am doing something for myself and no one else. I always feel guilty to start with, my head still full of all other people's needs that I should be facilitating. But the further I run, the smaller everything gets in my mind, until I am a muted version of myself.

For a brief hour, nothing matters. Just for a short time, all that I have to do is land one foot down solidly and then the other. Over and over, like an eraser on a blackboard, wiping it clean. I never feel more alive than when I'm running. Blood sings in my veins, roars in my ears, and makes my heart pound. It's the only time I ever feel bigger than the challenges I face.

My running playlist is like a secret family recipe, handed down through generations to create the perfect soufflé. Only I don't share it with anyone. Like my running time, it's mine alone. It even got me through labour. The midwife thought I was listening to whale music or Hypnobirthing. As she got closer she heard the Ramones singing 'Twenty-twenty-twenty-four hours go-ho-ho. I wanna be sedated.'

I run past the pond and the shops that litter the tiny cobbled high-street of my village. I don't look up until I hit the seafront.

The sea is a foreboding grey and the warning flags are up. I love the sea like this. When it's sparkling and blue, we are clogged with tourists and traffic, litter and noise. Hen-do's and hooliganism. But when the sea is angry and swirling, when the rain lashes against the cliffs and the seagulls fly sideways in the wind, everyone goes home. No one wants to be here for that, so the seafront is mine alone.

My feet pound out a rhythm as they land on the concrete underpass. "What is going on? What is going on?" I ride it out all the way along to the pier, then turn back and head home. When I reach my estate, I stop and clutch my side, leaning over to take in deep lungful's of air.

Everything aches. My legs are wobbly, my feet are swollen in my shoes, yet I feel stronger than I have in a long time. I'm still in me somewhere. I had thought that maybe I had gotten lost.

"Jimmy?" I am still panting slightly from my run.

"You okay?"

"Yes, I've been running. I booked Faith to babysit tonight and booked a table at Fishy Fishy? We've not been out for ages."

"Oh, um, can we do it another time?"

My heart sinks but I try to keep my voice bright. "Why? You are working too hard. Joe needs to give you a break. You are going to make yourself ill at this rate." I remember when Jimmy first got made a director. I used to call him a 'very important business lad', which soon got shortened to 'Vibl'. It was a joke back then. Whenever he started to take himself too seriously I'd call him it and he would immediately grin and say, "Sorry." I have a feeling if I used it now it would not have the same effect. Instead I say, "You deserve to have some fun."

"I can't go tonight, Peta. I'm sorry."

"Why not? Where are you going?"

"I'm out with Joe"

"And Meg?"

"Yes."

"Where?"

"We are looking at a building."

"Why?"

"Peta! Stop it. I do not have to explain myself to you!"

The conversation has turned into a row again. I feel all my good intentions slip away. "I assume this means you will not be picking Roo up from school again either?"

"That's low, Peta. Plus she did not seem too bothered last time."

"Well she was bothered! The kids never see you. I never see you." I am shouting and my voice has gone all squeaky. I am being everything I promised I would never be, but then, so is he.

"Hang on." I hear Jimmy talking to someone in the soft voice he normally saves for the girls and I have a pretty good idea who it is. I hang up without waiting for him to come back on the line.

Juno and Wojtek are in the front garden collecting woodlice when I arrive. "Thank you for having her." "No problem. She is a good girl," he says fondly.

I turn to go but the hand on my arm stops me. "You OK, Peta?" I realise I am shivering and digging my nails into my palms.

"Yes, just a bit cold. Come on, June-bug" I pull her into my arms and make my way past the traffic cones and bags of building sand littering their drive.

When we get home I pull on some warm trousers and a fleece lined hoody, then throw some stuff into a change bag. Juno is too sleepy to argue about being strapped into her buggy, and sleeps as I march to Stanmer Park, the wind in our face.

When we arrive, I wipe the rain from Sara's bench and plonk a still sleepy Juno in the middle of it where she chases yoghurt covered raisins around her plastic lunchbox.

Hoping she is distracted enough not to notice, I put my head in my hands and cry hot bitter tears. They are gone as quickly as they came, and I feel no better for them.

I rest my head on the silver plaque which reads "Sara Williams – forever in our hearts." It's cold against my skin.

"Rabbits!" says Juno, temporarily distracted from her snack.

I look and see a squirrel running through the mulch of dead leaves on the green in front of us. The copper of its bushy tail shines in the weak sun, which is trying to find a way round the black cloud in front of it.

"Is that what I should do, Sara?" I ask her plaque. "Keep going and hope I can chase the black clouds away?"

As if in answer a single shaft of sun cracks like egg yolk in the sky. Juno skips off to chase squirrels and kick leaves in her blue wellies. The wind dances across my face and the sun shines in and out as I sit, wishing desperately that Sara was sat on the bench next to me, not reduced to ashes below my feet.

On the way home I try and come up with a plan. It's Pip's birthday next week and I desperately don't want to tarnish her special day with rows and awkward atmospheres. She has done nothing wrong.

My anger at and distrust of Jimmy needs to be put on hold, just for a few days. He may be being a shitty husband at the moment, but he is a wonderful dad. The girls adore him and that is what is stopping me from confronting him about Meg.

What if the answer is yes? He is having an affair. Then I have to kick him out. Then I have to cope with three children alone. The idea of taking on more than I am already makes my head swim and I have to stop for a moment to compose myself.

Back at home I feel better for making a decision, even if the decision is to do nothing. I cancel Faith and prepare a Superfood Stir-fry which can be made in minutes. Jimmy gets home at 9.30pm. As soon as I hear the car pull up I drop veg into the hot oil. By the time he has walked in and hung his jacket up, dinner is almost ready.

He looks at it and the glass of chilled Albarino next to it with a frown. I know he is surprised and probably suspicious.

I've already practised what I am going to say enough times that it doesn't sound too forced. "Shall we call a truce?" Before he can answer, I race on to the next part of my carefully constructed speech. "I thought it might be a good time to discuss Pip's party."

Jimmy looks relieved. His shoulders drop visibly. I gabble on. "Do we cater for veggies? Vegans? Coeliacs, or screw them all and have a hog roast with white baps?"

"I don't think we will be allowed to roast a pig on the leisure centre basketball court," Jimmy says. I smile at him and we spend the next hour hunched over my notebook making plans and food lists. The wine is crisp and PJ Harvey sings to us quietly on the radio. It's the closest we have been in a long time.

It's the first year that Pip is aware she is having a birthday. She's been counting down the sleeps for weeks and keeps going through the invite list on a daily basis to make sure I have not forgotten anyone.

"Let's go through mine party list, Mumma"

"Now? It's 4am, Poppet."

"Yes please." Her sweet little face presses against mine.

She rubs my nose in an Eskimo kiss, smelling of milk and sleep. How can I say no?

"Oh go on then, but whisper." I point to the top bunk where Roo is snoring gently.

She sits up and says, "Is Sammy coming to mine party?"

I prop myself up on the pillow next to her and stroke down her crazy morning hair.

"Yes, Pops."

"Ned?"

"Yes, lovey."

"Darrie?"

"Is he the boy who runs around shouting THUNDER!!?"

"Yes, Mumma."

"I think he is busy that day."

"But he is my BEST friend, Mummy. I lush him."

"Fine. I'll see what I can do."

"Fank you, Mummy."

Just then Roo wakes up and starts giving me all her party demands. Or maybe she was never asleep.

"Don't forget you said I could invite people too, and that there would be a real dog at the party."

"I never said there would be a real dog at the party, unless there are any blind people coming. Are there any blind people coming?"

"No."

"No dogs then."

"How about a dog cake?"

"It's Pip's birthday, she should pick the cake, don't you think?" I turn to look at her. "What cake would you like, princess?"

"A pirate one with lots of treasure please, Mumma." Her eyes are as big as saucers at the idea.

Bloody hell. How am I going to make one of those?

"Pirates huh? Are you sure?"

"Very yes, Mumma."

I try to persuade her to go with something easier, but she's having none of it. Then Juno wakes up from her bedroom opposite demanding "MULK!!" and "CAKE!!" so we all stumble out of bed to go and see her and watch Mr Tumble.

I invite Ava and Lily-Grace to the party for Roo to play with but they all decline with piss-poor excuses. My poor Roo. I must adopt a dog for her. It's a poor consolation prize, but it's something. I write it on my to-do list, underline it twice then promptly forget about it again.

For the first time, we are not hosting the birthday party at home. I loved hanging the birthday bunting and setting the table with paper plates, but Pip has invited twenty boys, all under the age of four. I fear it is more than my beloved house can handle.

My house is used to little girls who like to drink tea and tuck dollies in bed. I said we should have it in the garden but Jimmy was too worried about something happening to the bloody chickens. "The boys will let them out, a fox will eat them and that will be the end of them."

"Good. They have not laid a single egg between them yet and we've had them a month!"

Jimmy sighs heavily and says, "You can have it in the garden if you like."

"No, no, God forbid anything happens to your chickens. Wojtek would be devastated anyway. He is obsessed with them."

"I thought you loved Wojtek. He is always helping you out."

"I know, and I do, but I'd prefer to pay him in cash, rather than free-range eggs. It would be far less smelly. You never told me how much chickens stink."

"What are you talking about?" He opens the patio door and shouts, "Smell this quality!" very loudly.

It breaks the tension and we both grin.

He even takes a rare day off work so we can take Pip into Brighton and buy her a new dress, a tradition handed down from my family.

My mum and dad used to buy me a frilly frock each year at the Thame show. It was one of those Game Fayre and County events held in a muddy field. Family tickets were always for two adults and two kids though, so to save more money for cider I'd either have to hide in the boot when we went through the entrance, or my parents would drop me off by the hedgerows outside and tell me to meet them at the beer tent. Not all of the tradition has been passed on.

Within two minutes of walking into Churchill Square shopping centre, Jimmy's phone starts beeping.

"I need to take this." He points at the Costa Coffee next to Debenhams. "I'll be in there."

I am instantly filled with rage. He is supposed to be off work. If that's Meg on the phone she can just bloody well wait and speak to him later. This is our daughter's special day. There cannot be anything more important than that, especially not bloody Meg.

"NO!" I shout, louder than I mean to. "What can be more important than her?" I gesture to Pip who is stood holding onto my leg shyly, with her Charlie cloth blanket out. Crowded places scare her.

"It's the head of the Home Office, Peta. Turns out over two

thirds of the cleaning staff do not have up-to-date passports. If I don't get this sorted ASAP there will be no one to fulfil the contract. Then there will be no contract, no money, no mortgage, no home, no birthday parties and no frilly bloody dresses."

It does sound pretty serious. I think quickly. "Ok, take the call, but can you take Pip with you? I need to get her P.R.E.S.E.N.T."

"Fine, but she will have to be quiet."

"She will be good as gold, won't you, sweetie?"

Pip looks nervously at all the legs passing her by. It reminds me of a Doctor Suess story where a giant pair of pale green pants with nobody inside them goes round the town scaring everyone.

I bend down so I am on her level. She puts her Charlie cloth over our heads and murmurs in her secret little language. Through the crocheted holes, the legs seem far less intimidating and the bright lights and noisy chatter is dimmed. I see why she loves being under here so much. "Ok, baby?"

"MMMmm." She is unsure.

"We are here to buy you a pretty party dress, remember?"

"Ok." She cheers up slightly.

"But first Mumma just needs to go and get something, and I'll be right back. Daddy is going to take you to Costa. Would you like a cup of tea?"

She nods. I kiss the end of her button nose, slide out from under the blanket and then pick her up so her head is still beneath it until we are in the softer lighting of Costa, then I pull the blanket off her and tuck it round her shoulders.

Jimmy is already sat in the corner jabbering away on his phone. I buy him a double espresso, Pip a Babychino and a cupcake then take her over to Jimmy.

"Right. You eat that and I'll be right back, OK poppet?" I smile brightly. She is distracted by the sprinkles on her cupcake.

I stand, feeling worried about leaving, until Jimmy waves me away but carries on talking. I walk quickly out of Costa and go to find Mothercare.

I'm going to have to buy Pip a baby doll for her birthday. She is dolly mad. It's very sweet that Pip can be so caring, but I already have a real life baby to wrestle with. I don't want to have to dress a plastic baby each morning as well, change its nappy and feed it breakfast or give it a bath and put it in a buggy or sing to it as I feed it 'nickle-milk'. I feel like I am back at NCT classes.

I stand in front of a row of Baby Annabels and think back to the one and only session I attended.

"Hello and welcome," said the lady running it. "Namaste." As she bowed I decided I hated her. She was wearing Birkenstocks which pretty much sealed the deal. I hate Birkenstocks. I have no idea why the middle class find them so classy. The inside soles are always black from sweaty-foot-dirt. What is classy about that?

She explained that they were working on some Hypnobirthing techniques. "It helps relax the cervix if you imagine it opening like the sun." She opened her legs and pointed at her fanny as if we did not know where babies came from. The rest of the class who were all sat in-between one another's legs, nodding beatifically.

"Don't worry about me", I said smiling nicely. "I'm planning on an epidural. Namaste.' I did a long, exaggerated bow.

When I sat back up there was a loud, audible gasp from my audience. Things had not started on the right Birkenstock.

I laugh out loud at the memory and a heavily pregnant woman picking Babygro's next to me waddles away looking alarmed.

Jimmy shares my hatred for NCT groups. He got dropped as best man at best-friend-Lyndon's wedding due to his new

NCT pal being picked instead. "But you have only known him FIVE months Lyndon! We've been friends since we were seven."

"I know man, but you have to understand. Jez and I, we've been through things together in the last five months that have brought us closer than I ever thought I could be to another man."

"What about the time Lindsey dumped you and you drove your car all over her front lawn and then ripped up her flowers and posted them through her letterbox. Who paid your bail and collected you from the station?"

"I know man, but …"

"Or the time you tried to write your Citroen Dolly off for the insurance money but were too calm to do it having just been to hot yoga? Who drove it into a tree for you?"

"I know dude, but Jez and I … we've watched each other's wives in labour on video together. We've cleaned out birthing pools together. We are in a different place."

"But you were the best man at my bloody wedding!"

"I am sorry you are feeling hurt man. Let's spend some time together. You are coming on the stag do, right?"

"Depends. Who is going?"

"Jez. Felix. Big-bear. Paddy. Rupert."

"Who are they? What is it? A teddy-bear's fucking picnic?"

"They are NCT boys. You will love them."

"No chance. You can all piss off. Call me when you've stopped injecting oestrogen or whatever it is you hippies do."

I find a dolly with a large plastic nappy attached to it. You feed it with a plastic milk bottle and then it wees or poos and cries. Pip will be in toilet heaven.

I race back to Costa. The sugar has picked Pip up and she is jabbering away to herself as Jimmy frantically stabs out emails and messages on his iPhone, looking cross.

We spend the next hour trailing round Debenhams finding Pip a dress which is 'twirly' enough for her. Jimmy is on the phone the whole time, completely disengaged.

Pip keeps going up to him in different outfits and twirling round for his approval. He barely nods. I am seething with rage but I'm determined to make Pip have a nice day so remain pleasant.

"I've just thought, we must do food for the grown-ups. I hate lurking about hoping the kids will leave a soggy sandwich I can eat. And we must not clear up till everyone has left, but then again if we don't start clearing up, no one will leave," I stop to look at a jumper with a dog on that Roo would love. "But then we don't want to be like Phoenix's dad," I waffle on. "He got out a penknife and started stabbing all the balloons bang on 3 pm. Remember when we took Roo to Phoenix's second birthday party and when she gave him his present he gave her a punch in the eye, and then his dad said, "Do you want to punch me back to make it fair? I still don't know why you didn't.""

I turn round and realise I am talking to thin air. Jimmy is sitting on one of the sofas in the homeware section muttering urgently into his phone, and Pip is twirling in a mirror, lost in the frills of her skirt.

When I make my way over, Jimmy walks off. Following him feels too weird so I sit and wait till he gets back.

"Everything OK?" I ask when he finally reappears.

"Not really, no. I could really do with not being here."

Pip is wearing three dresses on top of one another and grinning from ear to ear.

"But look at how much fun she is having. This means so much to her, Jim. Shall we get these and then go and have some lunch? What do you fancy? We could go to the café here, but it's never very good. There is a Zizzi just outside but I bet they have long queues. Shall we go down to Jamie Oliver's along the road? It's not far, just up the road and turn right." I am aware I am babbling and sound like a tour guide.

"Whatever, let's let Pip pick."

"Great idea!" I gush. "Where would you like to eat poppet?" I ask. "Zizzi? Jamie's?"

"Dinner in the window."

Jimmy rolls his eyes. "I am not eating at McDonald's."

"Oh look at her," I say to him. "So proud in her twirly dresses. Come on, let's have nice day, please?" I look at him imploringly and link my arm through his. "Hey, what's that?" I notice he's holding a water pistol.

"I thought we could get it for Jake."

"Is it his birthday?"

"No, I just thought it would be nice."

How lovely that even amongst all his work woes he still thinks about Jake. This is the Jimmy I know and love. My anger melts and I smile properly for the first time all day.

"You are so thoughtful," I tell him, standing on my tip-toes to give his wrinkled brow a kiss.

McDonalds is down the Marina. Jimmy gets back on his phone again the second we sit down, wincing in disgust at the coffee.

"FOUL," he mouths at me.

Pip eats her chicken nuggets and promptly breaks the cheap plastic toy that came in the Happy Meal.

"Going to M&S," I mouth at back at Jimmy. "To get food." I do that gesture where you raise each hand alternatively to your mouth, which you open and close at the same time. No one actually eats like that really, but he seems to get the idea or does not really care.

This time I take Pip with me. She sits in the trolley as we whizz up and down the aisle, squeezing tomatoes and searching for the perfect bananas. I make her laugh by pretending I can't stop the trolley and keep crashing into everything. She looks at me as if I am the most fun mum in the whole world ever. If only it were so easy to win back Jimmy's affections I muse as I break off a piece of French bread for us to share on the way round.

I fill up my trolley with Wotsits, grapes, strawberries, cucumber and Wagon Wheels. Standard party food. I plan to make pizza and hot dogs. I even bought Quorn ones for the vegetarians. For the adults I'll make a lemon drizzle cake and some homemade loaves of bread, which I will serve with a selection of cheeses and cold meats. We can't serve alcohol so I buy some Schloer and elderflower cordial.

Feeling very pleased with myself, I make my way over to the car. Jimmy is leaning on the bonnet. "I hate McDonalds," he tells my grumpily.

When I get home I tick things off my hastily written to-do list. Book the hall? Tick. Hire a bouncy castle? Tick. Pip's present? Tick.

I spend the evening working on her cake. After three failed attempts, I finally crack it. I baked a chocolate cake, then on the top I fashioned a treasure chest out of ready to roll icing which I dye yellow. I even use edible gold paint to make a latch and hook. Then I fill the chest with chocolate coins and wine gums till they spill over the top of the cake and down the sides. I cover the silver cake base with sugar dyed yellow for sand. A flag poking out the top announces 'Happy Birthday Pirate Pip'. I am very pleased with myself as I take photos of it.

Next morning, the house is filled with the delicious smell of home-made bread baking. The children are beside themselves with excitement. They've been up and dressed since 5 am so of course they are filthy by 9am but I don't care.

I spend the morning chopping, baking, and arranging things prettily on foil trays, singing along badly to the Foo Fighters on the radio.

The party is at 2.30pm. I finally sit down at 1 pm for a cup of tea and to cast a final eye over the to-do list.

Tick, tick, tick, I sing in my head, tapping my toe along to the music.

Then I see the last item. Party bags.

Shit. I had forgotten the bloody party bags.

"Argh, I've not remembered poxy party-bags. Do people still expect them?"

"Of course they do, Mummy!" Roo said. When I went to Ava's party her party bags were actually little wicker baskets, and they were full of brilliant toys. There were miniature Wizard of Oz finger puppets, and some red glittery slippers. I'll go and get it, hang on!" She races upstairs, petticoats flying.

"What am I going to do?" I wail to Jimmy when he comes in from cleaning out the chickens.

"I'll go and sort something out."

"Really?" I am so surprised I almost fall off the chair.

"That is very helpful of you."

"Yes. Well, I need to nip into town anyway. How many am I catering for."

"Um, about forty," I say, trying to make it sound like a small number by saying it very quickly.

"You've invited forty kids to the party?"

"Plus siblings." You can't say that quickly. It's impossible. Too many syllables.

"Tell me you are joking. Pip does not even play with anyone at nursery. She spends the whole time on Faith's lap hidden under her Charlie Cloth. Is Faith even coming?"

"Um, no. She is busy. Just stop talking and go and get the bags, then get back so I can put them together and load the food into the car. Please."

"OK, OK, Jesus calm down, Peta."

"I can't! I *need* this party to be a success. I've worked so hard. I knew it was all going too well, I bloody knew it."

"It will be a success. Just stop panicking and get changed."

Oh yes. I had forgotten that part too. I spend the next hour trying on every outfit in my wardrobe to work out what best says 'I am a good mother and very happily married'. None of them say that so I make do with some black Harem pants and a grey t-shirt with a lace pattern on the back. I look in the mirror and sigh, then slap on some under-eye concealer and spray myself liberally with Clinique Happy, wishing it did what it said on the bottle.

Jimmy is still not back so I spend ten minutes trying to persuade my curly hair to fall into something resembling a hairstyle, not a bird's nest. I fail and shove one of Roo's sparkly clips in it instead.

I expected Jimmy to walk through the door any second but he rang instead.

"Where are you?" I hiss.

"I've had a break down."

"What? It's only the 99p shop for God's sake. Pull yourself together."

"Not me, the car, Peta. The car has broken down."

He makes it back with twenty minutes to spare before kick-off. The car had to be abandoned.

I throw cheap plastic tat that would no doubt break within seconds into party bags and load up the children like packhorses.

It takes fifteen trips to get all the food and bags there. Food which I had lovingly arranged. Food which Juno has already demolished half of.

We are still blowing up balloons when people arrive, my iPod refuses to find any service to play my painstakingly prepared playlist, but all in all things are going well.

The children are running round shrieking. Parents are chatting to one another. Roo is having so much fun on the trampoline she has not noticed that Lily-Grace and Ava are not here.

Everyone loves the food which makes me glow inside.

"This lemon drizzle cake is amazing!"

"Wow! Did you make the pirate cake? Incredible."

We've pulled the party out the bag. I didn't think it was all going to come together but it has. Even Jimmy seems to have a nice time. He organised a five-a-side game of football on the other side of the gym and his team are winning. I know this because he pulled his t-shirt over his head then skidded across the court on his knees.

But most importantly, our little Pip is having a ball, just like I wanted her to. She spends the whole time jumping up and down on the bouncy castle, giggling with delight as her twirly skirt rises up round her middle with each leap.

Jimmy comes to find me towards the end and rests his sweaty chin on top of my head. I love that we fit together like this, like a jigsaw. We stand together watching our girl and smiling. This is what it's all about, I think. This is one of those precious moments to take a mental snap-shot of and remember forever.

Then Pip does her highest leap yet and I notice she is not wearing any knickers.

Chapter Nine

"I REALLY don't feel comfortable writing about having an orgasm in labour, Michelle."

"It's the new thing to do, since that article in the Guardian. That famous midwife wrote about having one, and now everyone is trying it."

"Come again?"

"Don't be funny, Peta."

I look down at the article in front of me. "I felt brilliant. I was in utter ecstasy," I read aloud.

"Apparently women in labour need darkness, privacy and comfort to zone into the sexual side of birth, to move and groan and moo while their partner gently stimulates their nipples and clitoris to get the oxytocin flowing," Michelle reads out.

"You can't expect me to write this stuff, Michelle. It's pornographic! In my labour I got told to 'strain like I needed a big poo'. How could anyone have an orgasm whilst straining to do a big poo, or even a little poo? Why would anyone want to try and give someone an orgasm whilst they were doing a big or little poo?"

"You are missing the point. This is exactly the sort of trend our readers want to know about."

"Having an orgasm is not a trend! Neither is giving birth!

I'd prefer to eat my own placenta than have someone try and arouse me in labour. The only part of birth I salivated over was when the midwives brought me tea and toast afterwards. Men are always asleep in labour anyway, the midwife would have to do it. ARGH! Why are you making me think about this? It's so wrong."

"Yes, well no one wants to know about what you think, Peta."

"Thanks, Helen" God I hate her. I hate both of them. Neither of them have ever given birth, so they have absolutely no idea what it's like. I try and appeal to them.

"Look. I had a natural labour. I'll write about it if you like. It was a defining moment for me. It really was. I gave birth to a 9lb baby without so much as a sip of water. Now I know I can get through anything. Mountains of washing, hideous school singing concerts, shopping trips to ASDA …"

"Do you have a point?"

"Yes, Helen. I do actually, which I was just getting to. I achieved it using deep breathing, and a TENS machine, NOT through having my nipples nuzzled and my, urgh, I can't even say it. You can't have an orgasm whilst giving birth. End of story."

"Well, you must have been doing something wrong."

Oh my God. I don't want to be writing about this stuff. I want to be writing about making the perfect roast chicken, or how to make sure your meringue is sticky in the middle.

I don't know why I don't get out of this contract and cut ties with Tummy-to-Mummy. Fear I suppose. If you never attempt the things you really want to achieve, you can always pretend you would be amazing at them if you did. I have a similar attitude to making an effort with my appearance. If I don't try to make myself look good, I can always fool myself that I would look like a knock-out if I did.

I'm going to stop working for Michelle. I have to. It's soul destroying. I'll write the stupid article but as soon as I can, I'm off. I still have some contacts at The Argus. I know they do a food supplement each month. I'll ask about it and send in some recipes.

Meanwhile I need to tell my readers about the benefits of nipple tweaking. I sigh and start typing.

Don't forget Jake's concert tonight, Jimmy texts that afternoon. Jake is performing at St Aubens School in their adaption of Oliver. I love seeing him perform. He lights up the stage when he is on it, outshining everyone else around him. It's the first time Jimmy and I have been out together in ages. I pull on a navy shift dress with thick black tights, short Ugg boots and wrap a light blue scarf with feathers on it round my neck. The dress feels loose and I realise I must have lost some weight.

We are late getting there, as usual. Roo is a master at working out that we plan to leave her with a babysitter once she and her sister have gone to sleep, and therefore stays awake much later than normal. Even after all this time and honing of technique.

I read to them with my huge dressing gown on so they cannot spot my 'going out clothes' underneath. I don't put any perfume or make-up on until we are in the car and on our way (and by then I am normally so exhausted by the act of going out I don't usually bother), yet still they work it out.

Everything will be going well. They will be in the bath on time and to schedule and then suddenly out of nowhere Roo will say, "You know what I don't like, Mummy? Babysitters."

Then Pip will say "Noooo, Mummy. No sitter." And they all start crying and try their best not to fall asleep. Jimmy has to go and wait on the drive to make sure Faith is utterly silent as she enters the house.

"Take all your bracelets off. They will give you away. And your high heels."

The tickets are waiting for us at the collecting office. Joe had ordered them for all of us. I was surprised to see his was still there unclaimed.

"I'll text him to make sure everything is OK. It's not like him to be late," I say to Jimmy, hastily composing a message.

Joe responds to say he won't be able to make it, but to please clap extra loudly for him.

"I can't believe he would not come to his own son's play. He has never ever missed a play in all the years we have known him," I whisper as we sit down in the darkened wings.

Jimmy is distracted by the terrible rendition of 'Gangnam Style' we are being subjected to before the play kicks off.

"We are still in hot water over the passport stuff. Joe is desperately trying to get it sorted."

"Even so, it's not like Joe."

"Jesus, Pete, stop being so judgemental. We can't all be perfect like you, attending every single one of our children's concerts and lord knows what else. Joe would love to be here, OK? But he can't be. HE CAN'T! You need to live in the real world and understand that sometimes you can't just wave a wand and make everything better."

Wow. Where did that come from?

"Sorry" I mutter. I never knew he felt guilty about missing so much. "I always film all the concerts, and they are mostly rubbish anyway. Pip does not even join in any of hers. At the last music concert, she was the only one without an instrument."

"How come?"

"She got given a drumstick when she wanted a triangle. She threw it over her shoulder in a temper and it hit Pamela on the forehead. Pamela has now banned her from playing anything. She claims she could have been killed. You don't need a triangle to make the noise anyway. You can just make the noise with your mouth. Like this. TING."

The old Jimmy would have smiled at my joke, but the new Jimmy just frowns slightly and turns back to the stage.

Jake is dazzling, wonderful, amazing. We stand shouting and whooping and cheering for ages after everyone else has sat down. I can see that he not Jake is looking for Joe through the glare of the spotlights. No matter how much we whoop and cheer, we can't compensate for his dad not being there.

"Your blood tests show you have low iron levels," the doctor tells me.

"OK.. Are there tablets for that?"

"Yes."

"Excellent." I stand up and hold out my hand for the prescription.

"Please sit back down, Mrs Newton."

Oh.

"I wanted to ask you a couple of questions on this form I have here."

"What kind of questions?" I ask suspiciously.

"Well, you seem very anxious."

"I have three children under six, what do you expect?" I know I am being defensive but I can't help it.

"I don't expect anything. I am just trying to help you," he says slowly. Then, "I think you might be suffering from post-natal depression."

"What? No, I am not. PIP! Stop touching things. Juno, get off her hair!"

"OK, well would you mind answering a series of questions for me anyway?"

"Fine," I sigh loudly and sit back down. Juno climbs on my lap in a rare show of affection. It's almost as if she knows I need the moral support. Her head smells of marmite. I inhale her deeply and prepare myself.

"Have you been feeling anxious in the last two weeks?"

"No," I lie quickly.

"Have you had trouble sleeping?" He raises an eyebrow at me. I can't lie about this answer because he gave me the sleeping tablets.

"A bit, but it's fine now."

"Do you often feel overwhelmed or unable to cope?"

"Nope." Yes! My head shouts at me. All the bloody time.

"Do you cry often?"

"Not very often, no." Liar liar liar.

"When was the last time you cried?" He is not going to give up easily.

"Well, last week." He goes to write something down. "But listen." I try and explain. "It was Roo's turn to bring the school snails home, and chickens really love eating snails. It's their favourite, second only to slugs, so Jimmy told the girls to feed any snails they find to Rosie, Charlie and Jude."

The doctor looks confused. "Who are Rosie, Charlie and Jude?"

"The chickens. It's awful really. Jimmy pokes snails through the bars of the run and the chickens jump up and peck at them. Anyway …" I witter on, seeing the doctor looking more and more confused, "Roo asked if she could play with Shelly after dinner. And that's when I realised they were missing."

"Shelly being a snail or a chicken?"

"A snail, hence the name."

"Ah."

"Yes. Pip and Juno had fed the class snails to the chickens, who ate them. All that was left of them were their giant orange shells. Roo was so worried she was going to get in trouble, even more trouble, since the donkey trouble ... that I did the only thing I could think of."

"Which was?" The doctor has given up on his form now.

"I found normal garden snails and fitted them into the shells of the dead Giant African Snails." I look down ashamed, remembering my conversation with Roo on the way to school.

"Mummy, am I going to get in trouble for this?"

"No sweetie, of course not."

"But the teacher says we must never tell lies."

"And we are *not* lying, treacle. We are just *not* telling something, that is very different from lying."

Roo still looked scared and confused when we parked the car, where The-Iron-Curtain was waiting for us.

"It my turn to take these snails home," she sneered at me.

Oh shit.

"Right! Well, here they are then, um ..." Fuck, what is The-Iron-Curtain's real name?

"You not know my name?"

"Of course I know your name ...Oh Nikita." It's the first Russian name that pops into my head.

"Ha, You will never know. My name not Nikita. We not all named after Elton John song."

"Um, Olga then?"

"No, not Olga." Beads of sweat start to trickle down my forehead. I just wanted to hand over the ordinary garden snails masquerading as Giant African Land Snails and get the hell out of there. "Regina, my name Regina, like you English Lizabet Queen name." She snatches the snails from me and storms off muttering, "What is this bloody country where people not even know name of other people? In my country we all know names, but then we have nice normal names. None of this Jay-Z rubbish. Boys named after girls."

The doctor looks up at the clock on the wall. "I have other patients to see and a lot of questions to get through. I'll just tick that you cry a lot. Do you feel stressed often?"

"No." I decide to go back to lying.

"Do you feel stressed right now?"

"Yes."

He leans forward. "About what?"

"You wanting to see my coil again?"

"Relax. I don't. Honestly." I feel there was no need for the 'honestly' remark and feel slightly rejected.

He carries on asking me a series of questions then we sit in agonising silence save for Pip and Juno munching on Wotsits, while he tots up my score.

"Well, you are borderline. I think your biggest problem is that you are exhausted. You might have a dash of post-natal depression. I'll start you on a course of iron tablets and put you on the waiting list for counselling. No arguments," he says, seeing I am about to argue.

I nod and hang my head, feeling like I have let everyone down.

"Lots of people go to counselling, Mrs Newton. It is nothing to be ashamed of." I nod again but I feel ashamed, and cross. If Sara were here I would not need to go to some Birkenstock wearing counsellor because I could talk to her, and if Jimmy wasn't so busy trying to get into his secretary's knickers I could talk to him.

By this point Juno is bored of sitting on my knee and starts to trash the room. She and Pip get hold of the see-through and therefore pointless tracing paper that you spread over your knees when you have examinations and wrap one another in it like mummies. They think this is hilarious. I think it might get me out before I lose it and end up confessing all to the doctor who will probably commit me to the funny farm and have my children put up for adoption, so I let them carry on.

The doctor is no match for my girls. He quickly types up my prescription for iron tablets and I unravel Pip and Juno, like giant toilet rolls, out the door.

When we get in the car, Pip turns to me and asks, "You sick, Mamma?" I am amazed at her perceptiveness. How can she go from being a poo-obsessed-fiend to this amazing, caring girl in an instant? But then, look at her father. He switches between Jekyll and Hyde fifty times a day. She must get it from him.

"No, baby, I'm not sick."

"Why you have pills like Miss dolly?"

"Sorry?"

"Miss Polly dolly had pills."

"Ah," I see.

I assure her that I don't need to be put to bed quick quick quick and we drive home singing about Miss Polly and her dolly and hope that I don't have to go back to the doctor again for a while.

The next day all three girls woke up with chicken-'pops' as Pip called them and Jimmy told me he had to go to London for two days on a conference.

The time drags. I thought chicken pox might make them sleepy. I was wrong.

"Does anyone want a wee or a poo?"

"No, Mamma."

"A drink, a snack or some magic cream?"

"No thank you, Mumma."

"You sure?"

"Yes, Mamma."

"I am going to sit down now and drink this nice cup of tea then, OK?" I sink into the sofa cushion. My neck cricks loudly as I take a sip from my tea. I am exhausted. My eyelids feel heavier than my heart.

"Mamma, can we all have a cup of tea too?"

And just like that, I am back on duty.

The day passes in a blur of demands and cream applications and attempts to distract them from itching.

Pip wants a plaster on her spots, all thirty-two of them. I didn't have any so give her a tic-tac for each one instead, just to silence her for ten minutes. When she eats them it looks like she is chomping on teeth.

Pip and Juno do not feel unattractive covered in chickenpox. Instead they seem rather proud, and keep standing naked before the mirror to admire themselves. Roo is not finding it so easy though. I hear her upstairs shouting, "Go away, I hate you. LEAVE ME ALONE!" Slightly alarmed as she is on her own up there I call out, "Who are you talking to baby?"

"My chicken-pops," she replies sadly.

I offer to douse her in lotion but she says she hates the coldness. I offer her medication but she hates the taste.

After two days of them driving me insane some of the spots looking like they are getting infected so I take them, en-masse, back to the doctors.

I am delighted not to see the same doctor as last time, but my happiness does not last long.

This new doctor says that all the children's chickenpox are fine and not infected but that Juno is overweight.

"It does not mention here that she has had her one-year check-up," she says, tapping away at her computer.

"Doesn't it? I ask, trying to sound surprised.

"Has she had it then?"

"Um, no."

"Why not?"

"I've been busy …" I trail off, casting my hand over the children's spotty heads.

"Busy feeding her from the looks of things," she mutters as she makes notes.

Juno refuses to go on the scales.

"NO! Choc choc," she demands, holding out her hand.

"I don't know what you are saying, my poppet. Just get on the scales, there's a good girl."

"Choc!" she says, louder and clearer than ever.

"I don't know what you mean," I say, pulling a confused face and looking at the doctor.

"Kid's eh? What can you do with them?" I say in what I hope is conspiratorial fashion.

"She said CHOC CHOC, Mummy," pipes up Roo from the back of the room. "She wants one of the chocolate drops you keep in your coat pocket for her, to make her do what she is told."

I shoot Roo a look which quite obviously means, "Shut up and stop talking," yet she carries on "Shall I get them for you, Mummy? Why don't we all have one?"

The doctor sits watching this exchange with a look of horrified wonderment on her face.

After six buttons, we finally get Juno on the scales.

In order to achieve this, I have to get on holding her, then deduce my own weight after. It turns out that she is half a stone overweight and I am half a stone underweight.

"Perhaps you should be the one eating the chocolate drops," the doctor says, handing me a diet plan for Juno. Her tone is slightly spiteful. Her physique is slightly rounded.

Fat people hate thin people. No one is horrible to a fat person, in case it hurts their fat feelings. When fat people lose a bit of weight everyone applauds and marvels at how well they have done. Thin people don't get such support. They get told, "You look awful. You need to put some weight on. Eat something," as if it's that simple. Imagine going up to a fat person and saying "You look awful. Eat less." It would never happen. Unless you were my mother. She would have no problem saying that to someone. I think she has actually.

"I'd like to see Juno in a month's time for another weigh in. I expect to see a significant reduction in her weight by then. Please make an appointment with the reception staff. Good day."

She goes back to her computer and I assume we have been dismissed.

We stand at the check-in-desk knowing there is 'fat chance' of us getting an appointment in advance. Doctor's receptionists are the most unfriendly, unhelpful people on the customer care spectrum. I swear they are employed to be nosy rather than efficient. Maybe they get commission for each appointment they manage not to book.

We wait for half an hour while the receptionist ignores both me and the phones ringing off the hook to tap her nails on the keyboard and chat about other patients in far too much detail.

I stop trying to stop the girls from doing a loud rendition of the hokey-cokey and, finally, she deigns to look up.

"Hello! I need to make an appointment with the doctor, please." I smile nicely.

"When for?" she scowls back.

"Four weeks today, please," I sing-song back at her.

"We don't do advance bookings. You have to book on the day." She looks triumphant.

"What if it's an emergency?" I counter back at her. Around me, other patients cock their ears, wondering where this is going. One of them shakes her head sadly as if to say, "You might as well give up now."

"Is it an emergency?" she says in the same tone you might use to say, "Yes, of course father Christmas is real."

"No." I admit. She smiles like a lion that has spotted it's prey.

Patients go back to their ten-years-out-of-date magazines, thinking I've lost.

"Well then. Please ring closer to the time. Four weeks closer." She goes to turn around in her swivel chair, but I'm not done. Maybe I cannot ask my husband if he is shagging his secretary, but I can stand up to this old witch.

"Why can't I just book it now? The doctor says not urgent, but important none-the-less."

"What is it about?' she snaps.

"Sorry?" I'm confused. I thought she was the receptionist. Not the doctor.

"What is the appointment about?" she repeats, as if she is speaking to a very simple person.

In my head I say, "Are you a qualified GP then?" and she looks red and contrite, then the waiting room burst into a round of applause and cheer, "For she's a jolly good fellow ..." and we all do high-fives, Mexican waves, and an energetic bout of the hokey-cokey, which is really what life should be all about, but what actually comes out my mouth is, "It's a weight check-up."

The fat receptionist looks at me.

"For you?" she says. But from the look she gives me she might as well have said, "You skinny time-wasting bitch."

"No, it's for my daughter."

"You can't make appointments for other people. She will have to make her own." I can tell she is desperate to high-five the other receptionist who has stopped answering phones and checking people in to watch the exchange.

I hold Juno up so she is eye-level with her.

"She can't make an appointment. She is twenty-months old."

"Is she? She looks much bigger."

"I know. Hence the appointment."

We go back and forth until she finally books Juno in with the nurse for a weigh-in in six weeks time. It's a small triumph but I get the odd "well done" from people waiting. One man asks me to book his prostrate check up with the nurse. I hurry the children out the door quickly.

The nurse appointment will not go well. My children all hate the nurse since their injections. "Noooo, not the pinchers!" Pip shrieks, each time she sees someone in a white coat.

Roo and Pip spend the car journey home arguing over which of them are going to check if the chickens had laid an egg. Juno was suspiciously quiet. When we pulled up on the drive and I unstrapped her from the car-seat I saw why. She had been busy eating the diet plan leaflet. It did have photos of food on after all.

When we get back we find Wojtek on his knees in the garden feeding the chickens. He has the grace to look slightly guilty, but not for long.

"The chickens were hungry. They made hungry noises at me."

"What does a hungry chicken noise sound like?" Roo asks, immediately interested.

"Like this ... Bwooooorky bwooork. BwoRK BWORK!" Wojtek says.

"Oh, I thought that meant they had laid an egg," Roo said.

"No, when they have laid egg they say 'bwoooooooooooooooork'."

"Have they laid any eggs today?" Roo asks, as if she is having a normal conversation with a normal person.

"No, no, none today," Wojtek says, shifting slightly on his haunches and going red.

"That's odd. They normally lay at least one," I say, pulling open the side tray of the Eglu and peering in.

No eggs. Just loads of stinking chicken poo.

"Anyway, I go now. Must do my jobs," say Wojtek, and scurries off.

Jimmy arrives home at 4 pm. He has bought the girls some new build-a-bear outfits and they run off immediately to play.

"Was it hell?"

"Yes."

"Sorry."

"What for?" I turn on him, wondering if he is going to fess up.

"For leaving you with them, when they were ill. I had no choice. This passport thing is a nightmare. We have all had to go through HR training and have our licences checked and procedures put in place for new starters. Half the bloody staff can't speak English, and hardly anyone turned up to have their passports done. We've lost a massive number of staff. If word gets out about this in the industry, we are fucked. I don't know what I am going to do. No staff means no people to do the contract." He pulls his tie off and throws his suit jacket over the back of the chair before sinking into it and resting his head on the table. I walk over and rub the back of his shoulders.

"Nice," he mumbles into the tabletop.

"Why don't you buy a recruitment company and use their staff? No one will have to know what made you do it. Hopefully all the agency staff have their papers if they work for a recruitment agency."

He sits up suddenly, knocking my hands from his neck and turning to look at me.

"You are a genius, Peta!" I swell with pride and pucker up for a kiss, but he is out the chair like a shot and spends the next two hours on the phone frantically talking through ideas.

The girls go to sleep easily thanks to a dose of Piriton. Once they are down and most of the chaos of the day is tidied up, I make a ham and mushroom omelette assuming Jimmy will want to eat it in his study, so I'm pleased when he says "I'll come and eat with you."

"Wojtek has been stealing our eggs again," I say after our plates are empty.

"What makes you think that?" Jimmy goes to the fridge and brings over a Double Decker for me and some Greek Yoghurt for him, then puts it back and pulls out two beers instead.

"Well he was in the garden with them when we got home, and he looked guilty when there were no eggs in the nesting box." I pause to look out of our kitchen window which faces his. "And he is having a giant omelette for dinner."

We both look out to see Wojtek stuffing a too hot omelette down in record time, then racing to wash his plate and fork in the sink before spraying deodorant round the kitchen and opening all the windows.

We duck under the counter.

"Something fishy is going on," I whisper.

"Why are you whispering? He can't hear you. Hey, remember when your mum kept chickens? And how she decided to kill them, but before she took them to the farmer she gave them a last supper, of haddock?"

"Yep."

"And remember how your dad kept saying the chicken tasted weirdly fishy?"

"Yep."

"Your mum is mental."

He is so close to me. I want to sit here and soak him up. I am just tracing my finger down the side of his cheek, when there is a knock at the door. "Who can that be?" I ask as I climb out and walk down the stairs to the door. Jimmy mutters something behind me but I don't hear him.

When I open it Meg is standing outside under the sensor lights.

Its yellow beam make her hair shine like strands of gold. She is wearing a white blouse under a long grey cashmere cardigan, a navy skirt that stops on her knee and a pair of nude coloured ballet slippers. She looks amazing. I am wearing a pair of creased harem pants, Jimmy's odd football socks and a t-shirt which says 'Team Edward' which Heather sent me as a joke.

"Hi, Peta. Nice to see you again." She smiles at me as if we are friends.

I stutter out a hello in reply. I am just about to woman up and ask her what she could possibly need to speak to Jimmy about at 9.30pm at night when he brushes past me and says, "Meg, hi. Thanks for coming over. Follow me. Would you like a coffee, or tea?"

I stand in the porch, my mouth opening and closing like a goldfish as she wafts past me in a wave of Marc Jacob's perfume. "Have you got any herbal tea?" she asks as they climb the stairs to the study.

"Pete?" he yells at me. "Have we got any herbal tea?"

"No," I shout back. I want to add that herbal tea is for NCT hippies but it seems childish.

"Don't worry," I hear her reply to him. "I've some water in my bag."

I can't believe she came here. I can't believe he brought her here. I am so angry I don't know what to do with myself. I stand doing nothing for five minutes then hear Sara's voice in my head saying, "Listen in ye feckless tart!"

I press my ear to the study door, noticing as I do so that Roo has drawn the figures from the Wizard of Oz on it and the tin man's axe looks phallic.

Suddenly the door opens and I fall into the study. "Everything okay?" Jimmy asks me in surprise.

"What is she doing here?" I hiss at Jimmy.

"She is helping me!" he snaps back then shuts the door in my face.

She stays till 11.30pm. By that time I have scrubbed the dining table and the kitchen sides, Hoovered the kitchen floor and cleaned the fridge out. I am just about to de-grout the bathroom tiles when I finally hear the study door open and the sound of their muffled voices.

"Night, Peta," Meg says to the bathroom door.

I am too surprised to say anything back. When I hear the front door slam I open the bathroom, rush out and charge into the study. It smells of her perfume. Jimmy is sitting at his desk filling out some forms. I see a solicitor's name on the top of one of them. Why does he have solicitors' forms? Surely he can't have been in here with Meg filling out forms to divorce me whilst I was next door cleaning the loo.

"What's up, Peta?"

The forms have knocked the wind out of my sails. He does not look like someone who has just been having a fumble. He looks calm and composed and resolved. He's never looked more handsome. Fear trickles down my spine and I physically back away from him. "Nothing. Night then."

I hold onto the banister for support as I go downstairs, then make a cup of hot chocolate just to give my hands something to do. I take my time, heating the milk up in the milk frothing machine and melting in marshmallows. I sprinkle a crushed up Cadbury flake on the top, then pour in a slosh of brandy, overestimating the quantities.

I wish Sara was here to share the excess with. She was the one who helped me perfect this recipe. She loved it when I experimented with a new version. As the night wore on we'd move to rum and dance round the kitchen to Michael Bublé.

Missing her comes out of nowhere, like a dam that keeps bursting.

It's cold outside. Round the trees, white fairy lights glimmer like tiny stars. I wrap one of Pip's Charlie cloths round me and sit on the deck, tucking my knees under my chin and watching the clouds move quietly across the sky. I don't know how long I sit there, breathing in the steam from the top of my cup and thinking about Sara and Jimmy and Joe and Meg and the cracks in my heart that only ever seem to get bigger.

I am just about to make another brandy hot chocolate, minus the hot chocolate when the phone rings. Only one person would ring this late.

"Hi, Mum."

"Who's that?"

"It's Peta. Your daughter. Your only daughter. And you phoned me."

"Oh, yes. Shall we Skype instead?" I sigh but do as I am asked. It's easier. It takes three attempts before she answers and when she finally does accept my call I can see nothing but a black screen on the computer.

"Mum, are you there? I can't really see you."

"Good. I've got the lights off."

"Why?"

"I don't feel like being seen,"

"So why did you ask to Skype then?"

"Well I wanted to see you. You look too thin. Eat something."

She asks how the girls are and I give her the update on chickenpox and Juno being overweight.

"Rubbish," she scoffs. "This is why I never took you to the doctors when you were children."

"Or the dentist," I say.

"There was no need. Everyone knows cloves are all you need for a toothache." We chat for a while about her horses. I ask how Dad is. "Who knows? she says "He got himself a bike off The Madman and has not been seen since. He did not think to get me one so we could go together."

The madman is their name for the French man who runs the local sports bar. He is not at all mad. He is slow and old and quiet and would not say boo to a French goose.

"I thought you didn't like cycling?"

"What are you talking about? I love it. Love it! We used to take you cycling all the time."

"I don't remember going once."

"Well you were very small. You used to go on the back of your father's bike."

"I do remember the fold-up bike you stole from the back garden of the pub once."

"Yes, well, that was a long time ago as well."

"And how it folded up on you while you were cycling it."

"Alright, stop now."

"Hang on, it's all coming back to me now. I remember the time we were all cycling back from The Plough and one minute you were there and the next minute you were in a bush."

"The path was full of potholes."

"You were full of cider."

"Well at least I did not fail my cycling proficiency test."

"How come you can remember that but not what my first word was, or to pack my ballet kit?"

"Well it was taken very seriously by the school. They phoned me up and I actually answered. No one had ever failed before. They said you were a danger on the road."

"Is that why I had to stay behind with you on bike rides along the canal, while the boys were allowed to go far enough ahead that people might not think they were out on a bike ride with their parents?"

"Yes. And just as well we did. The one time I let you go ahead you fell in."

"I did not! Mickey pushed me."

"Why would he do that?"

"Because he is not the perfect son you think he is, believe it or not!"

"He is a genius. He made a brick wall at work last week. It's amazing. You have never seen anything like it. I've put some photos up of it on Facebook. You must go and like them." I grit my teeth. "He is so talented. He has really inherited my creative gene." My mum dabbles in oil paintings, but the way she talks about it, you'd think she was the next Picasso.

"I'm not sure how creative you need to be to build a wall."

"That is because you do not share our vision. I hope that girlfriend of his realises what a good thing she is on to there."

Mum witters on about how when she last Skyped Mickey she noticed some ready meal packages on the side in the kitchen and how she is worried her little prince is not being looked after properly."

"Can I say hi to Dad, please? I interrupt.

She sits and thinks about it for a moment, relishing the power she has over me.

"Fine," she says finally. "If I can find him."

After a long wait, a light comes on and I see Dad facing me.

"Is Mum nearby?"

"No. She has gone to make dinner for tomorrow night."

"Oh my God, Dad. Why did you marry her?"

"Oh, you know. Any port in a storm and all that." My dad and I try to get as many sayings as possible into our conversations. We don't understand most of them.

"People as annoying as her are as rare as hen's teeth."

"Come on now, this won't buy the baby a new bonnet."

"I don't care. Throw the baby out with the bathwater."

"If you kick a stone in anger, you will hurt your foot."

Suddenly I say, "Da, turn the light out again."

"Why?" he asks.

"Just do it."

When the screen goes black I blurt out. "Da, Roo is being bullied at school because of a donkey story. None of her friends are allowed to play with her. The headmistress thinks she is a figure-head for atheism. I think Jimmy is having an affair with his PA. Juno has been classed as obese. Pip is obsessed with pooing in public places. The doctors think I might have post natal depression and are sending me to counselling. I'm too scared to confront Jimmy. I'm screwing it all up."

He does not try and comfort me with pointless platitudes. He does not promise me everything is going to be OK. He does not tell me I am just tired. Instead, he sits quietly in the dark while I fill him in on the last few months and then he says, "Right, what are we going to do about it?"

"What can we do about it?" I wipe my nose on Pip's Charlie cloth.

"Plenty. I'm coming over for a visit." I cheer instantly and then say, "Are you bringing Mum with you?"

"Yes, but I promise she will behave."

"If 'ifs' and 'buts' were candy and nuts, we'd all have a merry Christmas."

"Yes well, half a loaf is better than no bread, eh?"

"I love yo, Da"

"Love you too, Pete."

Signing off, I feel better than I have in a long time.

Jimmy is up and gone by 5.30am. I spend the morning trying to cajole Roo to play her part in the drama production.

"But, Mummy, I don't want to be Goldilocks."

"Why not poppet? It's the best part. You get to wear a lovely pretty dress and carry a basket. Doesn't that sound fun? You love baskets."

"No. I don't want to be Goldilocks. And it's Little Red Riding Hood that carries a basket anyway."

"Well what do you want to be then, mummy bear, or baby bear?"

"I want to be the porridge." She looks at me and stamps her foot.

"The porridge? You can't be the porridge though. It's not a part in the play."

"Yes it is. It's a ginormous part. There is a big porridge, a medium porridge, a little porridge, a hot porridge, a salty porridge, and a sweet porridge. I want to be the sweet porridge."

"You want to be the bowl of sweet porridge in the play, not Goldilocks. Or baby bear, or mummy bear?" I smear homemade blackberry and apple jam on toast and hand it to Juno and Pip who have wandered into the kitchen in search of breakfast. We picked the blackberries as a family last year, when life was normal. Jimmy got himself scratched as he tramped heroically through brambles to get the juicy fruit at the back. I sat in the bath with him that night plucking splinters from his back. Then we had sex, twice.

"Yes, Mummy, I've been practising." I shake my head to erase the image of him kissing me and turn to look at Roo.

"Practising what?"

"How to be a sweet porridge. Watch."

Rudy lies down with her back on the floor with her arms and legs up in the air.

"See, Mummy, I'm a bowl."

"So you are. Sort of, but where is the porridge?"

"Well you have to make it Mummy, and pour it on me. Here in my tummy. I'm not allowed to make porridge. You said if I touch the microwave it will shrink me to the size of a pea and Juno will eat me."

"Oh yes, so I did." I make up so many white lies it's hard to keep track of them.

Roo thinks charity shops are 'repair' shops. A place for run-down, or broken toys to recuperate, and we have a small troll who lives down our loo. I told the girls he is called the poo troll and that if little hands don't wipe little bottoms he will climb out the cistern and chase them round the house. I got my inspiration from the film The Ring. Jimmy says this is probably the reason Pip refuses to use the toilet and will only poo in public. He is probably right.

The rain is God's tears, I told Roo. He gets sad when she is naughty and picks on Pip. I am especially proud of this one as it makes me feel I am following the school's ethos. When we go out, there will always be someone with a beige coat on. They are policemen, I tell the girls, who come out especially to keep an eye on them and no one else. If they are naughty he or she will come over and tell them off. If I can't see a 'beige coat' I pretend to ring one up instead.

"I really don't think you can be a bowl of porridge in the play, poppet. I am sorry," I say, trying to sound kind but firm.

"If I can't be the porridge, I am not doing the play." She sticks her bottom lip out and stamps her foot again.

"Rudy, please. Be reasonable. We are going to be late for school. Again. Please, please can we be on time for school once? Just once." I get on my knees, clasp my hands together and beg, hoping to appeal to her better nature. She completely ignores me and says instead,

"What does raisin-nibble mean?"

Her mispronunciation makes my eyes well up. Jimmy is missing so much precious time with our girls. Soon they will be all grown up and stop calling picnics '*picmicks*' or bracelets '*nicelets*' and looking for '*dog cracks*' the pavement.

Jimmy used to actively encourage them to get the words wrong. He'd drive them to school, singing loudly with the window down, "This old man, that old bum, he played nicky-nacky on my mum," or "Head, shoulders, cheese and clothes, cheese and clothes." I used to argue that we should be correcting them. "Nonsense!" He would look at me in horror and then say "Now who's seen the muffling man recently?"

I realise we are already far too late for school to bother rushing anymore. I sit down and decide I might as well brush her hair so when she does finally turn up she looks half-decent.

"Raisin-nibble means not being a bowl of porridge."

"Well then I don't want to be a raisin-nibbler."

"I thought you might say that."

Later at drama I explain my predicament to the very lovely teacher, Soraya. She wrings her hands and pats her purple hair and finally says, "I am very sorry, Mrs Newton, but I really don't think that Rudy can be a bowl of porridge in the play. For health and safety reasons as much as anything else."

"Of course. I completely understand. Have fun explaining that to her," I say, then dash off before she can involve me in the discussion or Pip has time to poo in the corner. I can see her eyeing up a pot plant.

As promised, my dad booked some flights and they arrive the next week. I ask Jimmy if he can take some time off to spend with them. He trots out his usual nonsense about being busy, but that he will try and sort something out.

I spend a lot of my parents' visit being asked annoying questions like, "Can you straighten my hair?" or "Will you go and get me the Telegraph, I forget which side of the road to drive on," by my mother.

Without asking first, or thinking how she would fit them in, she also invited my brothers, and Mickey's new girlfriend to come and stay with us as a lovely surprise. For her, not for me.

John is a very good cook. A very messy and bossy cook, but a good one. I will never admit this to him though and he will never admit that I am either.

I wander into the kitchen to see he is making chicken jalfrezi for dinner.

"Want some help?"

"No, like you would know what to do."

"Like you do either?"

"Um, I am not even using a recipe."

"Is that supposed to be a good thing?"

"Um, what starts with 'P' and looks like a twat?"

"Um, who cried when he got lost on the sand dunes … aged fifteen?"

"Just keep Mum out of the kitchen, OK?"

The kids are stir crazy anyway so I decide to take them out to Middle Farm. They produce their own cider so mum and dad are raring to go. Jimmy said he had to work when I asked him, even though it's a Sunday.

I am not as suspicious when he says this as I have been all the other times he has said it recently. He always runs off to work when my parents are visiting. He claims to be allergic to my mother's perfume. "That is not perfume," I tell him. "It's just her."

My mother spends the first half of the trip to the farm trying to persuade the girls to stroke a horse. They are petrified.

"What is wrong with them?" my mother asks.

"Nothing mum! And don't say stuff like that when they are listening. We live in Brighton. It's full of gays and art students. This is only the second time they have ever seen a horse."

"You should get them riding now, like I did with you." I bite my fist as hard as I can to stop me from responding. My mum has a wonderful talent for changing the past to suit her. To stop me from punching her, I send her off to the farm shop while Dad and I push the girls on the swing.

"So, how do you think Jimmy is being?"

"I think he is being the same as ever."

"Really? You don't think he is acting strange?"

"No, but then I have hardly seen him. He left early yesterday to get netting for the chickens and today he is going to work."

"Hmmm."

"What? You don't believe him?"

"I don't know what I believe anymore."

We are interrupted by my mother shouting, "Look! Look at this beauty! Isn't she gorgeous?"

I am expecting her to be holding a rabbit, or a duckling, or maybe even a glass of her favourite cider, but she isn't. She is holding a cabbage.

I go to respond. My dad, knowing me as well as he does, puts his hand on my arm and stops me.

"Now Pete, a tongue weighs practically nothing, but so few people can hold it."

"The narrower a man's mind, the broader his statements," I retort.

"Shush, she is coming over. Don't say anything please. It's not worth it."

"Fine. For you and you alone, I will dutifully admire a cabbage."

"That is no way to speak about your mother," he says.

I am still snorting with laughter when she approaches.

"What are you two whispering about?" she says, coming to stand with us.

"Nothing," we say in unison. The girls have wandered off to see the sheep and cows. Pip is looking at the cow pats in fascination.

"I can't wait to cook this cabbage later," Mum says.

"Do you have cabbage with curry?" Dad asks innocently.

"What are you talking about, Nigel? This is going to be the centrepiece of the meal. John is going to be so pleased I got this. Come on, let's get it home while it is still fresh."

I go and retrieve the girls from the hay bale soft play.

"But I don't want to go yet, Mummy. I am having fun."

"I know my love and we will come back again soon."

"With Daddy?"

"Yes, my girl." I send up a silent prayer this is true. Looking round I see a lot of weekend fathers keeping one eye on their kids and one on their smartphone. Jimmy can't want that surely? And what about Meg? The thought of them here with my children makes me feel sick.

"Come on, let's go." I lift Juno up and chivvy the other two out with promises of Percy Pig sweets in the car.

Mum carries on admiring the cabbage all the way home and talking about how all it needs is a small knob of butter to enhance its flavour.

"She tells more than she knows," I whisper to my dad.

"Even a stopped clock is right twice a day," he whispers back.

We finally get home and out of the car. The children dispatch themselves immediately and trot up the drive. I think they are as fed up with the cabbage as I am.

Mum gets out last, holding it in her arms as if it's the crown jewels.

Dad and I are sitting down to do some LEGO with the kids when John calls me from the kitchen.

"Seriously. Get that cabbage out of the kitchen or I am going home."

"John! That is no way to speak about your mother!" I admonish.

Dad and I then giggle like school children, while Mickey the creep says, "I think the cabbage looks delicious, Mum. I can't wait to try it."

"Twat," John and I whisper to him.

"Piss off," he says back.

"Mum, Michael told me to piss off," says John with the same petulant look on his face as he wore when he was a little boy.

"Oh grow up John!" Mum snaps at him, going over to pinch Mickey's cheeks. "He would never say something like that, would you, my handsome little prince?"

"No Mumma," he purrs back at her while John makes very rude gestures at him from behind the kitchen door.

Mickey's girlfriend looks very uncomfortable with it all. I am not surprised. Mum has taken to going into the bedroom they are staying in each morning, drawing the curtains and sitting on the end of the bed so she can watch Mickey waking up.

By the time we finally sit down to eat everyone is hungry and fed up. John and Mum are not speaking to one another. The cabbage is annoyingly and surprisingly tasty but no one except Mickey will admit it.

"Hey Jimmy, did you manage to get that extra netting for the chickens? I'll help you fit it tomorrow if you like," says dad, loading up some flatbread with Jalfrezi and yoghurt.

"Have some cabbage, Nige," says Mum, pushing the dish at him.

"No. They were out of stock. I'll have to go back tomorrow," Jimmy says, then fills his mouth full of curry before we can ask him anything else. He gets an extra hot bit of chilli in it and his eyes go red and start streaming. Good, I think to myself.

"Water …" he mouths. "Must … have … water."

"Nonsense," Mum says. "All you need is a bit of this lovely fresh cabbage." She drops a big dollop on his plate and says, "Eat up."

"Mum," I say suddenly. "I love you."

She looks very pleased and goes a bit red and silly.

Dad and I share a look over Jimmy, but say nothing.

He is up by 6.30am the next morning and looks awful. He was tossing and turning all night long and muttering in his sleep.

"Are you OK, Jimmy?"

"No. I've got a disciplinary at work today and I'm dreading it."

"Is it Meg?" I ask hopefully.

"No? Why would it be? Meg is the best employee I've ever had. I simply could not cope without her."

I bet she bloody is, and I bet he bloody can't. In my head I make a voodoo doll of Meg and then poke pins in her eyes and rip her shapely legs off.

"It's Andrew," Jimmy continues, oblivious to my mental spell casting. He's been caught working at another firm in the day, and his van has been spotted visiting a notorious car park off the M23 on more than one occasion."

"How do you know?"

"We have trackers on all the company vehicles."

"What do you think Andrew has been doing at these car parks then?" I ask innocently as I get out of bed and immediately begin to make it.

He stops trying to get his cufflink on and looks at me like I am an idiot. "What else do you do in a car park in the middle of nowhere at 3am? DOGGING OF COURSE!"

"Jesus Christ. Dogging. I can't believe it." I sink onto my freshly primped up pillows. I really can't. Is this the kind of thing the people at his firm get up to? Is this what him and Meg get up to?

"How do you know about this car park and this, this dogging?" I ask.

"Pete, everyone knows about the car park except you."

"Oh."

"You never leave the village."

"Yes I do, sometimes."

"Anyway, it's going to be bloody hideous, and it's going to be a long day, so don't wait up." He finally manages to get his cufflink through the hole. "I'd better run. Have fun with your folks." And just like that, he is gone again, without even a kiss goodbye. I stand in the space he left, and miss him.

The slam of the front door wakes my mother up.

"What's the time?"

"6.45am"

"Why didn't you get me up? I need to get the dinner on for tonight!"

"No Mum, you don't. There are two meals to go before then."

"Yes, but I like to be organised. You could learn a thing or two from me. Now where is that leftover cabbage?"

"You can help me be more organised by getting the girls ready for school."

"No, no. You made your bed. You lie in it. If I start helping you will become dependent on me and struggle even more when I leave. Plus, I want to make sure Mickey has some proper meals in him while I can. I don't know why he does not move to France where I can look after him."

I bite my tongue and leave her to it. Getting the girls ready for school is even more of a palaver than normal. They play up as they have an audience. Roo wants a French plait in her like Ava has. Pip won't take her night time nappy off. Juno senses I am not on the ball and eats all the leftovers out the bin. John and Mickey are still asleep. Da is outside chopping down trees that we have not asked him to. Jimmy will probably be too busy dogging with Meg to notice anyway.

"Cut them all down, Dad!" I holler out the window, then shut it quickly before the budgies escape.

I finally get the girls out of the house. It's not till I get to the school gate that I realise I am wearing my slippers.

"What wrong with these snails?"

Shit. I forgot about the snails. I should have known this was coming. I turn round slowly to face The-Iron-Curtain.

"What do you mean, REGINA?!" I practically shout at her, half out of fear and half out of pride that I remembered it.

"I had them three days. They not come out once."

Fuck. I have to find a way to make it seem like her fault.

"Oh dear, that does not sound good. Let me think." I panic. "Have you been feeding them?" I ask, trying to sound knowledgeable.

"Of course I feed them! Who you think I am? I give them delicious *khodlets* and *oladyi*. Good food for everyone."

"Is that Russian for cucumber and banana?"

"No."

"Oh dear," I say sorrowfully whilst thinking YES! I have been saved! I am so happy I almost want to kiss her.

"Oh dear what. What you mean, oh dear? Why you say this 'oh dear'?"

"Well, I *think* you might have killed them." I try and look troubled, surprised and helpful. I probably just look constipated.

"Chatzo za huy. This can't be my fault. This your fault." Her eyes narrow at me. "This must be your fault."

"I don't think so. If you look in the snail diary you will see them out and about having a lovely time with us. Anyway, must dash. I do hope you sort it out. Bye REGINA!" I skip out the playground feeling fantastic. This is the best news since the dog died, which is what my mum said when we told her me and Jimmy were engaged. (I don't think she liked the old dog much.) I am not going to be blamed for killing the snails. One less thing for the school to hold against Roo. Things are definitely looking up.

I will make sure that Jimmy has a delicious dinner tonight after his hard day. I'll run him a nice bath and sit and talk to him about the disciplinary. Maybe I can even offer to type up the minutes of the meeting. I bet I can type much quicker that Meg. I have a certificate in typing. Maybe I should get mum to babysit and we can go to the infamous dogging site after we have finished. I don't particularly want to get my white, wobbly bum out in the moonlight, but if it will save my marriage, I'm game. "I'll prove to him I am not one of these village people," I say to myself, then I do the YMCA all the way back to the car.

When I get home my mum is looking in the washing machine.

"Do you want to do a load of washing, Mum?"

"No, of course not. I have lost the leftover cabbage. What did you do with it?"

"I didn't do anything with it. I didn't clear the table. Ask the boys or Dad."

"I already did. They say the last time they saw it was on the side. Where is it?"

"I'm pretty sure it's not in the breadbin, Mum."

"Well where is it?! I need it."

"Really? You need it this second?"

"Yes. Maybe Jimmy knows where it is. You'll have to ring him."

"Mum, Jimmy is in a disciplinary. It's very serious. I am not going to ring him up to ask him where he hid a cabbage."

"FINE!! Don't blame me when the dinner is ruined!" she shouts, then storms off. She is in a bad mood for the rest of the day, until Mickey asks her to go and pick some flowers on the downs with him.

"I think I am going to have to break up with him," his girlfriend Jen says as she watches them go off down the road hand in hand. "I really like him, and he is a demon in the sack …"

"URGH!" John and I say, while dad looks a bit proud.

"But this is too much," she laments sadly.

"Don't chuck him because of Mum." I say. "That is what she wants. She is not normally as bad as this." I am jealous of Jen too, but I don't want Mickey to get dumped and be miserable. Plus my Mum's delight would be too much to bear.

"She will be going back to France soon and you won't have to see her again for ages."

"I suppose so," Jen says looking at me. A bad smell fills the air. "I think she bought that cabbage just to make me windy. Excuse me. I'll be in the bathroom."

When Jimmy finally gets home at 9.30 pm he looks exhausted.

"How did it go?" I ask

"Awful. He claims he did not get the evidence we posted him. He is trying to make it as difficult as possible for us."

"Oh Jimmy. I'm so sorry, is there anything I can do?" I stand behind him and massage the back of his neck. He shakes me off.

"No, Pete. But thanks. When are you parents leaving? That would help"

"Tomorrow."

"Thank God. Can we have Joe and Jake over for dinner on Friday?"

"Of course we can. It will be lovely to see them. It's been too long since we had a catch up. It's July already. Christmas is going to be here before we know it. I wanted to talk to Joe about hiring a cottage for New Year like we did last year."

"No!" he bakes at me.

"Why not?"

"It's too soon to make plans like that!"

"What do you mean?"

"NOTHING!" he shouts. "Just stop pressuring me, OK? I'm going back to work. I'll see you later." He holds his hand up to stop me. "No, No I don't want any fucking dinner."

As he walks down the stairs I hear his phone ring. "Hi, everything alright? I'm on my way," he says in a voice that used to be for the children, but is now for Meg alone.

I sit down on the chair and try and make sense of what just happened. Why did he get so cross with me? Why can't I make plans for New Year? What if he is planning to leave me in the New Year? For her. For Meg. My head spins. I put it on the table. Why is he going back to work again? What is happening to my marriage?

A couple of minutes later, I hear a cup of tea being placed in front of me. A Double Decker rests on top of it.

Without looking up I say, "Thanks, Dad."

"No problem. That did not go too well, eh?"

"You heard that? What do you think?"

"I don't know what to think. Maybe he is just stressed at work. I don't think us being here is helping. Why don't you make him a nice dinner for tomorrow night after we have gone and try and talk to him, properly, with no distractions."

"Do you think he is shagging her, Dad?"

"Honestly? No I don't. I've known him a long time and I just don't think he is capable of it. His work does sound busy. Maybe she is really helping him?"

"I could help him." I bite a chunk out of the chocolate and spray crumbs all over the place.

"You do help him, by being a fantastic mother." I snort at this but he continues. "And an understanding wife. Peta, if I thought for one second he was messing you around, I'd rip him from ear to ear."

I chew a large lump of nougat and ponder on Dad's words. They make sense, and more importantly, they make me feel better.

"So you don't think I should confront him and ask him if he is having it off with Meg?"

"I think if you do, it shows an enormous loss of trust. She might be a bit mad," he says as he gestures upstairs to where mum is in the bedroom. "But I trust her."

"Thanks, Dad." I offer him the last bit of the Double Decker but he declines, so I shove it in my mouth and say, "What's Mum doing up there anyway?"

"Reading some story about a donkey that she found."

"Oh shit." I race up the stairs but it is too late.

Mum is in raptures about the story. "Amazing, why didn't you tell me that Roo shares my view of religion?"

"Because she doesn't, Mum. She is just a slightly confused five-year-old girl who got Jesus and a donkey confused."

"I disagree, I think she is a genius. She knows exactly what she is doing. Her portrayal of the nativity story demonstrates just how farcical the whole system is. If people believe that a virgin can have a baby, then they might as well believe in flying donkeys. Plus, factually the nativity story is all wrong, you know. In the early translations of the bible, the word virgin got confused with the word 'unmarried'. The virgin Mary was actually just the local bike."

I try and cut in. "Please Mum, not this story again. I know what you are going to say. This is why you did not ..."

"YES! Yes, Peta. This is why I did not let you play the role of Mary in the nativity play at school. No daughter of mine is going to play the role of a local prostitute."

"If you are such a heathen, why did you send me to a C of E school?"

"It was within walking distance."

"Oh my God."

"NO, Peta!! There is no God. When are you going to get it?"

"ARGH!!!" I walk down the stairs with my hands over my ears.

"Mickey!" I shout. "Do something with Mum before I kill her. Are you OK, Jen?" I say to his girlfriend as she speeds past me to the toilet.

"No. No, I'm not. I think your mother has poisoned me," she groans as she slams the door behind her.

I spend the next day doing jobs for my mother. It's easier than listening to her lectures. Juno and Dad clean out the chickens and tidy up in the garden. I take lots of photos and wish they could be around more often.

The children are very upset the visitors are leaving. They loved all the dangerous things that my family left casually lying around. Razors, cigarette lighters, gin and tonics.

We stand on the drive and wave as they load up the car. I have a lump in my throat. "Silly girl," I tell myself. It does not help.

Dad holds me closely before he goes.

"I've lost so much, Da. I don't want to lose Jimmy too." My voice against his chest comes out muffled.

"A blind person who sees is better than a seeing person who is blind," he muses.

"What are you on about?" I whisper back.

"No idea. A dripping June sets all in tune."

"Dad, that is so bad it's made me feel sick."

"I'm sorry."

I sob in my dad's arms instead of answering, while Mum sobs in Mickey's and Jen stands round looking green. John already left last night. I think he was missing his computer.

"Bye Peta," he said as he left. "Your kids are weird, and I think your husband might be cheating on you."

"Wow. Thanks John. Nice to see you too." He gave me a dead arm and drove off.

I keep thinking about what Dad said for the rest of the day. I suppose without realising it, I have been working myself up to ask Jimmy if he is sleeping with Meg. Dad has made me realise that if I do that, it shows I have lost my faith in him. I need to be really sure I have before I rip our family apart. I try and look at things rationally. Yes he is being weird and losing weight, and keeps sneaking off somewhere, but here and there I can still see flashes of my boy.

He feels distant but not lost. If I ask him if he is cheating on me, I will be changing the landscape of our life together as we have known it. Am I prepared to deal with the fall out of my actions? Am I prepared for the answer to be yes?

I look at Sara's photo, willing some of her Scottish rubbish to come through the paper and help me The phone rings instead and it's Nellie.

As she gets older, Nellie sounds more and more like her mum. Like new photos of her, it takes my breath away. The last phone call I had with Sara ended far too soon. We never took the time to stand still when we were talking. I was chatting to her and cleaning the dining table at the same time. I remember she was just telling me about how we must get together the next weekend as I knocked a vase over and it smashed into a million pieces.

Roo was a crawling baby back then, and I was petrified she would cut herself on the glass, so cut Sara off mid-sentence with "Smashed glass, got to run, Jub jub."

As always, I never know whether to mention her mum to Nellie or not. I am torn between trying to keep her in the present, or leaving her in the past. I don't know which hurts the least. I know for me trying to forget is harder than letting myself remember.

Nellie does not seem to have called to talk about Sara. Instead she talks about school, and friends, and make-up and films. Her brother Josh is in a band and they played at the school concert.

"Mum is so proud of him." The mention of Sara in the present tense makes me feel winded and I have to sit down.

"She sent him down a feather, it landed on his guitar. Has she sent you any recently?" I stop and think. Has she? Have I even noticed? "I bet she has. You just need to look for them." Leaving me floored, she switches back to talking about her forthcoming school trip to Wales and how boring it will be. I am still trying to catch my breath when she says "Uh oh, teacher coming. Gotta go. Jub jub."

After we have hung up I sit holding the phone, still warm from her voice, and think how cruel it is that I can ring Nellie up any time for a chat when her mother, the person she really wants to be talking to, can't.

My problems suddenly seem so trivial. So what that Juno is overweight? She is alive. Roo can always be moved to another school if things get worse. Pip may be naughty but she is full of life. Her cup overflows with it.

I don't know what's going on with Jimmy but at least he is here to work it out with. When will I learn that life is too short? I've seen life end in front of my eyes and I am still running away from what's left of mine instead of embracing it. If Sara had somehow miraculously been saved that day, I am pretty sure her life would have changed forever after being so close to death. I let myself image that she did not die, that she survived and went back into work the next day and called the bitch on reception a bitch and snogged her crush Roger from the floor upstairs in front of everyone and went and picked her kids up from school early, refusing to take no for an answer.

I go to my wardrobe and take out Sara's blue cardigan. We bought it together in All Saints and it cost so much we had to cross our fingers that her credit card would work. I treasure it too much to wear. I thought it too good to get ruined by snot and yoghurt stains. I slip it on. It feels like a hug from her. My life is snot and yoghurt stains I tell myself. There may never be a day for me when it isn't so.

Sara did not let herself get bogged down by these things. Her house was always untidy. When I went round there I itched to clean it. "Why, you bappit hen? Sit yerself and drink tea," she would say. And I'd try, but while she was chatting I would surreptitiously fold clothes and plump pillows. She would laugh at me. "Ye can tidy your life as much as you like hen, but ye'll never be in control."

She knew me so well.

I ignore the Hoovering I was supposed to do and the mountain of washing, taller than me, that I left in the middle of the kitchen floor.

Instead I sit on the nursing chair in Juno's bedroom and watch my baby sleep. Her mouth is a perfect rosebud. Her dream makes her sigh, her chubby fists clench, and her long eyelashes flutter. I wish I knew what she was dreaming about that was making her so happy. I lean over the cot and I breathe her in, watching until she wakes. She is surprised and delighted to see me when her eyes sticky-open. I should be there when she opens them more, I think to myself. Every day while I have her home with me I should take the time to watch her.

I pick her up and put my nose in her neck for as long as she will let me.

"Shall we have a bath, my baby?" I ask her. She giggles. Her hands hot on my face.

I never bathe in the daytime. I never use the luxurious bubble soak that Jimmy buys me each Christmas. I never try to stop time, instead I am always running to catch up with it, but today I will. I'll try anyway. Gently I wash Juno's hair. The golden strands are warm and soft in my hands. I remember helping Sara bathe Nellie once. I was heavily pregnant at the time and my bump got soaked in the process. I remember Nellie kissing it and Sara and I both welling up. She was so excited about me becoming a mum and all the joy that came with it.

When Pip and Roo get back from nursery and playgroup, I have homemade banana loaf, pear upside down cake and cheese straws waiting.

"Is it my birthday?" Roo asks, delighted and yet confused.

"No baby, it's just a day."

I don't clean up the baking debris. I sit on the sofa with the girls instead. Mess can't hurt, I tell myself, repeating it like a mantra. "Dust if you must," I tell the girls. "But the world's out there, with the sun in your eyes and the wind in your hair." I struggle to think of the rest of the poem. "Dust if you must, but bear in mind, old age will come and it's not kind." I pat Juno on the head and hold Roo's hand. "And when you go, and go you must, you yourself will make more dust." They don't understand the words, but they sit quietly anyway.

It wasn't mess that killed my best friend. It was stress and pressure and no time to relax. To stop. To soak in a luxurious bath. She made time to drink tea with me, but I know the guilt she would have felt afterwards for not spending that time doing something for her children. I know she would be up half the night trying to get organised for the next day.

I must learn from her tragic loss. I must keep seeing the hole she has left and use it as a reminder of what is important. It's not setting up the wooden cake-stand in the right order each night, or worrying about the sour-milk smell coming from the car. I'd drive round with that smell forever if I could just have one more conversation with my best friend. To tell her how great she was. How much I miss her. But I can't do that. All I can do is honour her by looking after myself and my family a little bit better.

"Wow, what have I done to deserve this?" Jimmy asks when he finally comes home and smells lasagne cooking.

"Nothing," I tell him, reaching up on my tip-toes to give him a kiss. He is so surprised he jerks backwards and I get his cheek instead. Resolved to not care, I go back to cutting the homemade garlic bread up. "I know you are on your Warrior diet," I tell him, "And this is probably not allowed …" I point to the garlic bread. "But you've had a hell of a week and you deserve a treat."

"No arguments from me. New cardigan?" I've still not taken it off.

"No, I've had it ages," I tell him. "It was Sara's,"

"Well it really suits you. You should wear it more often," he says, snatching a slice of garlic bread and wandering out to the deck to look at his chickens in the back garden.

We eat outside with the sparkly lights round us. I open a bottle of Sancerre. "Sure there is no special occasion happening?" he teases me. "You've been saving this bottle for ages." Suddenly his face drains of colour.

"Fuck, you are not pregnant, are you?" he says. He looks horrified.

"No, I am not pregnant," I say, my anger instantly ignited.

"Thank God for that," he says.

"Why did you look so horrified?" I ask, trying to be calm.

"Because it's the last thing we need. It would be awful."

I think of the day I've had with the girls. Watching Juno sleep. The bathing and the banana bread. The jigsaws we did and the camp we made. The bear hunt we went on. It was the best day

I've had in a long time. I think of the fact I could not possibly be pregnant as we have not had sex since Christmas. No longer hungry, I push my plate away.

"Hey, what's up Pete?" Jimmy asks, his mouth is full of hot lasagne, no idea how cross I am. "This is amazing. Did you use chicken livers?" He shovels in another mouthful. "You really should do your book."

"I'm not hungry," I snap, picking up my plate and going back indoors, adding over my shoulder. "You know how it is when you've been cooking all day." I don't want to fall out with him, but I'm tired and emotional and don't think I can do bright and breezy right now. "I'm going to get in the bath."

My ears are under the water when he comes up to find me. He is carrying a cup of hot chocolate, made in a hurry with lumps of un-dissolved powder floating on the top.

"What is going on, Peta?" He puts the mug down on the table next to the bath. I am working out what say when he continues. "I'm sorry if I upset you about the baby thing. You don't want another baby do you?" He looks down at me. " I mean, you seem to be so tired as it is. The kids are such a handful, and you have your work and all your other stuff. Do you really think we could manage another child? Do we have the space even? We'd have to convert the garage."

What? One minute he is horrified that I might be pregnant and in the next breath he is planning for it as if I am.

"What are you going on about?" I ask him, sitting up and sploshing water all over the tiles. "I'm not pregnant. Tonight was not about being pregnant. I just wanted to have a nice bloody dinner together, for once." I reach for the towel and wipe my sweaty face.

"So you don't want another child?" He looks upset.

"Are you even listening to me?" I ask him, standing up

and wrapping the towel round me quickly, feeling exposed and vulnerable in the bright light of the bathroom. "I'M NOT PREGNANT! We've not even had sex in months."

"Well, we can rectify that, eh?" he says winking at me.

"Oh Jimmy, just leave me alone." I clamber ungracefully out the bath and push past him into the bedroom. As if we can just have sex after all these months of not having sex. Well, I've not been having sex anyway. I don't know if he has. The thought makes me gag. I clutch the top of my towel to my chest and take a deep breath.

I am stood behind my wardrobe door so he cannot see me naked when he comes in. I pause midway through my rifle for a clean-t-shirt to hear him say, "I'm trying, Peta. I know I'm not doing it the way you think it should be done, or saying what you think I should be saying, but I am trying. It's not easy for me either. I've got stuff going on too, you know." I hear him swallow. "In fact there is something I've been wanting to talk to you about."

My heart beats erratically, the sound seems to whoosh in my ears. Is he about to confess to having an affair? With Meg? Now it's finally happening, I desperately don't want to hear it. Like a child, I want to cover my ears and loudly LA-LA-LA away his next words. I don't want to do this on my own. In that second, I do not care if he is sleeping with someone else, I don't want to be on my own. I wrench the t-shirt over my head and step into the first knickers that come to hand.

"No, Jimmy," I practically shout at him as I shut the wardrobe door and run into to bed. "Not now, OK. It's been a really long day. A really long week. I need to sleep, please. Please let me sleep. Can we do this tomorrow?" I am breathless. Desperate.

I feel him sag on the bed beside me. He goes to say something but sees the tears on my cheeks and stops. He looks like he might cry too.

The words I know I should ask sink like stones in my tummy and settle there. I wish I could find my voice to let them out, but I am so tired. I can't do this right now. I don't know if I can ever do this. I think I'd prefer to live in this horrible in-between land than have my boy leave me. I've already lost one person I love. I cannot bear to lose Jimmy too. If he is going to confess, it can't be tonight.

"Can you just hold me Jimmy? Please."

He puts his arms round me, but it feels wooden and awkward, the way it always does when you try and force intimacy that is not really there.

I lie with him until I hear the sound of his breathing change, then I take my pillow and climb the stairs to the girls' room. I slip into the bottom bunk next to Pip, and pull her hot little body against mine. I find her feet in the darkness and hold their small shape in my hands. Where will these take you?, I wonder.

Jimmy and I spend the next couple of days awkwardly avoiding one another and when we do start talking again, it's through the medium of the children. "Have you kissed Daddy goodbye?" "Does mummy need some help with her bags down to the car?"

Something has changed between us. Another link in our chain has broken. He seems further removed from me each day. I should have let him say what he needed to, now the moment has gone and I'm too scared to try and get it back again.

As if she knew, my work assignment from Michelle this week is 'How to keep your sex life spicy after children.' Helen laughs at me as it gets read out. "What is so funny?" I ask her. "Nothing," she says, with a look that tells me she knows there is nothing spicy about my sex life.

If we had had sex the other night it might have bought us closer, but I can't sleep with Jimmy while there is even the vaguest chance that he is sleeping with someone else. But then, if we don't have sex soon, I fear things are only going to get worse.

Sex has always glued us together. We have a spark. The first time he kissed me, on a lock by the canal one freezing November night I knew, right then I never wanted to kiss another person again. We kissed in the cold until I could not feel my hands on his face, then he bundled me up in his jacket and walked me home.

He makes me feel attractive, even with my camel-testicle tummy and ski-slope breasts. Or he used to make me feel attractive, but then for so many years he has had no one else to compare me too. The thought that he might have seen Meg naked makes my toes curl in shame at the state of my naked self. There is no way she has a camel-testicle tummy. Hers is probably brown and toned and adorned with a cute belly button piercing.

I stand in front of the full length mirror in our bedroom, pull up my top and brace myself. The skin on my stomach is as puckered as ever. It sags over the waistband of my jeans. I lift it up and then let it flop back down again. This is why no matter how many times people tell me how thin I am, I don't believe it. How can I be thin when I have this skin hanging off me? How can I have a good figure when my tummy is so terrible crinkled and saggy? What was it I did wrong?

"Mummy, where are you?"

I pull my top down hastily. "I'm in my room, my love." The door opens and the girls pile in to sit on my bed. "Can you do our makeup? What is this cream for? Why don't you ever wear nail varnish?"

"Wow, one question at a time girls." I pull out my sparse make up bag and dust their noses with powder, then let them rub some cocoa butter on themselves. "Lovely, now you look like three princesses." I tell them, screwing the lid back on firmly, and smoothing the bed after they have jumped off it.

"Mummy, did you ask Lily-Grace's mummy if Lily-Grace can come to tea?" Roo asks, stopping to look at herself in the hall mirror.

I realise I have still not called her. I don't want to let Roo down, but I don't want to promise her a play date with Lily-Grace, that probably will not happen. I tell her I'll organise something and start firing off text messages.

Anna's mum Rachel replies to say they are free and would love to come and see us. Roo and Anna went to pre-school together and used to get on really well together. They bonded over a love of playing sleepovers and eating Play Doh.

It seems starting different schools has changed things though.

Within ten minutes of Anna arriving, Roo comes over to tell me she is bored in a very loud voice.

"Roo! Of course you're not bored. Anna is here to play with you. She is lots of fun! Why don't you go and do a drawing in the playroom?"

"I like drawing!" says Anna brightly. "At school today we had to draw what we did at the weekend. I drew going to the seaside. I drew a big seashell and lots of sandcastles."

"But there is no sand on our beach," says Roo who usually lives in her own la-la land and never notices if beaches are pebbles or sand.

"It was a pretend seaside."

"Sounds boring," says Roo. I blush with embarrassment. "I'm so sorry," I say to Rachel. "I think she's tired, it's been a long term."

"No need to apologise," she replies with no warmth in her voice whatsoever.

"Another muffin?" I offer. "I made them this morning." Rachel takes one and says, "They are truly delicious. How do you get them to rise so well?" I keep the conversation steered on muffins and the merits of baking powder over bi-carb. It all seems to be going well when all of a sudden there is a shriek from upstairs and Anna comes racing down in tears.

"Mummy, Mummy, Roo says I am not a big girl because my uniform is blue not green."

"Of course you are a big girl, my darling. You just have a different coloured uniform that's all."

"She has a weird uniform," says Roo, stomping down the stairs with a frown on her face. "Why does she have so many clothes on?"

I have to suppress my smile at this. I noticed how many layers Anna was wearing when she arrived too. Leggings, socks, long-sleeved top, dress, cardigan, hair-band, bunches.

"Don't be rude, Roo. If everybody wore the same clothes it *would* be boring. Now …" I clap my hands together in the style of a kids' TV presenter. "Who would like some pizza for dinner? It's homemade," I assure her mother. "I'm trying a new recipe which substitutes olive oil for honey. Let's all go and pick some toppings." Roo makes sure to pick none of the same as Anna.

At the dining table, there is a breaking of garlic bread and peace descends save for chomping noises.

Roo swallows a piece of pizza, looks over the table at Anna and says, "Swings or slides?"

"Slides," says Anna firmly.

"Ice cream or cake?"

"What kind of cake?"

"Pink fairy cakes with sprinkles."

"Cake."

"Wrong answer. Chips or chocolate?" she fires back.

"Chips?"

"Snow or sand?"

"Snow! No, sand. No, snow. Yes, snow," says Anna looking nervous.

Roo looks at me, shrugs her shoulders and rolls her eyes.

"Cats or dogs?"

"CATS!" Anna shouts. "I love cats! I have my own one called Thumbelina. She is so pretty."

"I hate cats. I like dogs. If I had a dog it would eat your cat," Roo sniffs.

"That is enough!" I shout. "I don't know what has gotten into you young lady, but pack it in right now. Poor Anna has come to have a nice time with you and you have been nothing but mean to her. You used to be the best of friends at pre-school."

"That was when we were babies," Roo shouts back at me. "I am not a baby anymore and I don't want my baby friend here with all her weird baby clothes on!"

When I turn around her mother is ushering Anna into her coat, raincoat, hat, gloves, earmuffs and scarf.

"I think it's time we left," she said. "Thank you for the, um, muffin."

"I am so sorry. Again. Would you like to take some home with you?" I ask to her back as it heads down the drive. She doesn't answer.

"I'll email you the recipe then!" I holler as she picks Anna up and straps her in a car seat that even Juno has grown out of.

When I get back indoors Roo is sitting on the sofa sulking. I give her five minutes to think and then sit down next to her and pass her a beaker of tea, before taking a sip of my own.

"Want to tell me what that was all about?"

"I don't like her."

"Why not? She's a lovely girl."

"She smells of soup. When she draws people she forgets to put on their eye-lashes. She loves cats. She's, she's ..." there is a pause and a snivel.

"Not Lily-Grace?" I finish for her. Roo nods sadly. I pull her into the crook of my arm. "I know what it feels like to miss a friend," I tell her.

"Do you?" she asks, turning to look at me

"Very much so," I say. "I had a very dear friend once."

"Do you mean Sara, the lady in all the photos?"

"Uh-huh." Roo fiddles with my necklace. Its silver and it has five disks on it with each of our initials on. Jimmy bought it for me on the first Christmas after Juno was born and I've never taken it off since. "Tell me about her, Mumma."

And so I do. I tell Roo how beautiful Sara was, and how she had a scarf to go with every outfit and how she always knew when it was going to rain because she could smell it in the air. I told her about her messy house full of treasures, the old tree in her back garden where she hung mirrors and old bits of string and brightly coloured wool for the birds to build their nests with.

"She sounds lovely, Mummy."

"She was, my darling."

"Where is she now then?"

"She's in heaven." I try and smile as I say this.

"I know about heaven! Mr Fitzpatrick's dog is in heaven. In heaven he chases balls all day and digs bones up from the clouds. What does Sara do in heaven?"

"I think she watches over her children."

"Oh, they must miss her."

"They do." Roo sees Nellie, Abi and Josh now and again, but she does not know they are Sara's children. It seemed too hard to explain at the time.

"I miss Lily-Grace, Mummy."

"I know poppet."

"I've tried everything I can think of to make her be my friend again. I found her a pebble with a hole all the way through, which I know she has wanted for ages. I even offered her my worry dolls that I keep in my pocket to play with in church. She said she is not allowed them though. Not even the pebble. Why isn't she allowed to play with me, Mummy? What did I do wrong? If you tell me and I say sorry, will she be allowed to be my friend again?" Big fat tears roll down Roo's face. She turns to bury her head in my chest. My own tears fall too. What can I say to her? How can I explain small-mindedness to a five year old?

Instead I say nothing. I just hold her in my arms and stroke her golden hair, crying for lost friends and the unfairness of it all.

After she has gone to bed, clutching her bedtime bunny, I down two Limoncellos and I call up Lily-Grace's mum.

"Hi Wendy, its Peta, Rudy's mum."

"Oh hello, Peta." Wendy does not sound pleased to hear from me. "How can I help you?"

I neck another Limoncello and stammer, "I just wanted to … that is I … Roo really misses Lily-Grace." I burst out, "Are you and her free this week for a play date?"

"I am afraid not. Lily-Grace is very busy with all her after-school clubs."

"Of course, I understand. Are there any days she is free?"

"The devil makes work for idle hands, Peta. I like to keep my children busy and stimulated."

"It would mean so much to Roo." My argument sounds weak to my own ears.

"I am afraid it is simply out of the question."

"Right. It's just … that donkey story, it was just a joke. Please don't let it stop Rudy from spending time with her best friend. And the dog thing …well …"

"You do not have to explain yourself to me. Now I must go. I promised Father Matthew I would help at Sunday school. I have lots of Noah's arks to cut out. This week the children are also learning about Judas. Maybe you could read the story to Rudy. Oh, I forgot, you don't do reading practice, do you?"

I stare at the phone in disbelief after she has hung up. How could someone who thinks themselves so religious be such a bitch?

"Roo is missing Lily-Grace so much," I say to Jimmy over dinner that night. He does not get home till 9 pm so the enchiladas are dry from being reheated. "We had Anna round but it did not go well." I tell him about the disastrous play-date. "I really want to cheer her up, but I don't know how."

"Maybe we should have Jake over for the weekend? They seem to get on well?"

"Maybe," I say doubtfully. "I'm not sure a ten-year-old boy is going to be a good replacement for a five-year-old-girl but it is worth a shot. Are you sure Jake will want to come? Does he not have his own friends he wants to spend time with at the weekend?"

"Jake is a bit of a weird kid too. I think he finds it hard to make friends. He is very shy."

"Shall I pick him up?"

"NO!" Jimmy practically shouts at me. "I will get him on my way home from work."

"Won't Joe be lonely without his boy? They are normally inseparable?"

"It will be doing him a favour. We have loads of work on. I know Joe plans to spend all weekend at the office preparing for an audit."

Joe never used to work at the weekends. Poor Jake.

"Do you need to help him?" I offer. "Sounds like a pretty rubbish weekend on his own with all that work to do."

Jimmy looks relieved. I guess it's because he won't have to make a lame excuse now. "Would you mind? Will you be OK with the four of them?" he asks me, hopefully.

"I suppose so. Jake is a good kid, and I'm already outnumbered. Might as well add another one into the mayhem."

"Thanks, Peta," he says suddenly. He sounds like he means it. It's so unexpected. My eyes immediately fill up and a lump comes into my throat. I swallow awkwardly. I've not cried so much since Sara first died.

"S'OK," I say, wishing I had the confidence to say more while we are having a *moment*. I look down and fiddle with my kitchen roll, building up some confidence, but when I look up Jimmy is already walking towards the door with his car keys in his hand.

"Gotta run, see you later. Don't ..."

"I know, I know, don't wait up."

The door shuts. I put my head on the table for five minutes, then I finish the Limoncello and fall asleep on the sofa.

Jake arrives on Saturday mid-morning with his overnight bag, and his special night-time dog. Roo notices it immediately. "What's that?" He is defensive, thinking she is going to laugh at him. "It's nothing." He tries to look tough. His too long black hair is unruly round his face, which is flecked with freckles. He is wearing hi-tops, skinny jeans and a Superman t-shirt. He looks adorable.

"I like dogs," she says shyly. "I want one as a pet but Daddy is allergic." This is not true.

"I'd like a dog too, but Dad says it would not be fair as we are not home all day so there would be no one to walk it," Jake says from under his fringe.

"If you had a dog what would you call it?"

"Well, I have a pretend dog and he's called Spike."

"Ooh." Roo is aglow with excitement. "Is he here now?"

"Yeah."

"Where?"

"He is sitting on the doormat, waiting till I tell him he can come upstairs."

"I can see him! I can see him!" shouts Roo joyously and claps her hands together. "Here boy! Here Spike!" she calls. There is silence for a moment and then she adds, "Oh, he is not coming." Her face falls.

"That is because I have not told him he is allowed to move. He only answers to me … Come boy," he says in a stern voice. I feel a sudden rush of love for him.

Three seconds later they start patting the air and scratching imaginary ears. It looks like they are doing some kind of Tai Chi. Pip and Juno stand watching them puzzled, then join in anyway. I have to go into the kitchen and shove my fist in my mouth so I don't laugh out loud. I'm delighted they are getting on so well. I wish Jimmy and Joe could be here to see this. I record them on my phone instead to show them later.

"Does he want to go on the trampoline?" asks Roo.

"Oh. I don't know. He has never been on a trampoline before." Jake kneels down and whispers into the air for a second or two. "He says yes, please."

"Woo-hoo," Roo shouts and opens the back patio door so the two of them and one imaginary dog can run off up the garden. Pip and Juno are still lost in their Tai Chi.

I stand and watch from the kitchen as they bounce up and down, before pushing an imaginary dog on the swing and then taking it for a walk round the garden. Roo runs off with the bamboo stick as if she is being pulled on a lead. Jake then stops and tells off the patch of grass next to her.

"Crazy kid," I say to myself. "He fits right in."

After half an hour I call them back in for a snack. They take their plates dutifully and then Roo holds her hand out for another one.

"Your sisters are napping. You only need two."

"It's not for them," she says, in a voice that suggests I am an idiot. "It's for Spike."

"Oh, silly me. Sorry Spike," I say to the floor, then hastily put another plate together. Cheese straws. Cucumber, strawberries. Carrot sticks. That will do for an imaginary dog.

"Silly Mummy," Roo says as she takes the plate. "Dogs don't eat cucumber."

"Well, go and give it to the chickens then," I say.

"Ok, Mummy. Come on Jake, come on Spike." Roo is loving her new play-pals.

When Pip and Juno wake up they are still very confused by the pretend dog. Pip spends the afternoon calling his name and looking round the garden while Jake and Roo laugh at her from the tree-house. Juno keeps herself busy eating the extra snack I made. Jimmy gets home at about 5 pm. When he walks in we are all sat on the sofa together watching Homeward Bound. Juno is on Jake's lap and Pip is holding his hand. Roo is resting her head on his shoulder. Jake looks torn between hating it and loving it.

"How did it today go?" Jimmy asks me, taking a bite from a too-hard pear out of the fruit bowl. "Pretty well from the look of things." He nods his head towards the sofa, where Jake is mouthing along to the lines from the film. "I'm too pooped to poop!" he says in an awful American accent. Roo looks at him adoringly.

"Really well, actually. How about you? There is chilli con carne cooking if you are hungry, with turkey mince so it's healthier."

"Thank you. It was quite good, got a lot done." He kicks his shoes off and sits down at the dining table.

"Don't leave your shoes there. Someone might trip over them," I say automatically.

"Bloody hell, Pete. Can you lay off for five minutes?" he snaps, standing up and throwing his shoes by the front door with a loud clatter.

"Sorry."

"I am shattered."

"So am I actually. I've had four kids to look after all day!"

"I thought you said it went well?"

"That does not mean I am not knackered Jimmy. Jimmy? Where are you going?"

He is walking up the stairs to our bedroom.

"I'm going out on my bike for half an hour. I need some fresh air."

"But dinner is almost ready."

"I'm not hungry."

"Oh, so a pear fills you up now, does it?" I say, opening cupboards and slamming kids plates down on the counter.

"Would you ever just back off?" he says, barging past me and heading for the front door. It slams behind him.

Well that did not go as planned. I rest my head on the worktop.

Why did I have to open my big mouth and ruin everything?

"Shhh," says Roo to the sofa cushion next her. "There there. It was just a door banging. Go back to sleep, Spike."

I go to sit with them. Sometimes I think I am the only sane person in the house.

Jimmy comes home two hours later covered in mud. "I'll read to Jake while you do the girls," he says. It's not an apology but neither is it the beginning of another row. Jimmy falls asleep on the rug next to Jake's bed. He looks peaceful enough so I dig out a duvet from the airing cupboard and drape it over him. He stirs but does not wake.

The next morning I ring Joe.

"Hey, old man."

"Hello, Guapa," I can hear him panting down the phone.

"You OK, Joe, you sound a bit breathless?"

"Si, Si, I just ran for the phone. I was in the garden. What can I do for you?" He sounds strained and a bit put out at being disturbed.

"I wondered if you wanted to come over for a barbeque later? I bought some ribs and I'll make my secret special sauce."

"Not tonight, Guapa. I've got lots of work to do."

"Oh. OK. I just thought you might like to see Jake. I guess he is at school all week."

"And I would, but while he is not here, I can get things sorted. How is he getting on? Is he having fun?"

I tell him Jake is having loads of fun and how he and Roo have bonded over the imaginary dog. I tell him about the hand-holding on the sofa and how he fits right in here as if he is already part of the gang.

"He smells fabulous. I might not give him back," I say.

There is a long pause.

"Joe? Are you OK?"

"Si Si, I go now." He says something in Spanish and puts the phone down.

I stand holding it after he has hung up. Something felt wrong about the conversation. It niggles me as I marinate the meat and squeeze lemons for the salad dressing. I've bought hot dogs for the kids and fish for Jimmy and Juno. I cover the salad and put it in the fridge. Suddenly I realise what is bothering me. Joe said he was in the garden, not at work. What plans would he be making if he was not at work?

Later, as Jake chases the girls round our garden, I try to ask Jimmy about him. "Is Joe OK? He sounded breathless on the phone and said he was in the garden. Why wasn't he at work?"

"He is working on some stuff at home this week. It's too noisy in the office."

"Oh." Something still does not feel right. "Have you got a big project on then?"

"Very."

"Is Meg helping?" I try to say her name without scowling.

"Very much so."

He pauses for a moment as if he is going to tell me something important, but then seems to change his mind. Instead he says, "Pete. It's been a long, hard week. I really don't want to talk about work, and I really, really don't want to argue with you. Not tonight please. Jake is here for a break, let's give him one." He bats a fly away with his hand, lays back on the deck chair and closes his eyes.

"Okay, no more questions," I say, sitting quietly next to him, trying to relax.

Shrieks of joy are coming from the trampoline, where Jake

is lying while Roo, Pip and Juno take it in turns to jump up and down round him. Suddenly, and without warning, Jake shoots an arm out and grabs Pip's leg. They all tumble down on him in a hysterical pile.

"Argghhh! I'm going to get you!" he roars at them. Then he leaps up and chases them round and round the trampoline.

Jimmy watches them and looks happy for the first time in days. Months even.

I go inside to get the ice cream out the freezer and see that Joe has text me.

Sorry about earlier. I was in the middle of something. Hope is OK for Jake overnight again? J said OK, but don't want him to outstay his welcome Got to take car to garage early tomorrow. Will collect him on way back.

I text back that I would be delighted to and that I hope he gets his work sorted, then pick up the desserts and make my way back out onto the deck.

"ICE-CREAM!" I holler up the garden. Four pairs of legs in various sizes and shades of summer tan come charging down the path to greet me. As I pass around cones with vanilla ice cream and sprinkles for Jake and the girls (frozen yoghurt and no sprinkles for Juno), I ask Jake, "Do you fancy sleeping over here again tonight? Your dad text to say he has stuff to do tomorrow morning and will get you later."

"YES PLEASE!" he says to me, then immediately turns to Jimmy. "Can we watch the boxing together tonight on Sky Sports? There is a big fight on." He starts jabbing at Jimmy playfully. Jimmy immediately starts jabbing him back, and then stops when he sees my disapproving face.

"Careful. The fun police are watching," he says to Jake.

I frown and say "I don't know. It's not on till 11pm. That is pretty late, he is only ten." They both look at me and roll their eyes.

"Mummy, what is boxing?" asks Pip.

"It's another word for punching," Roo tells her.

"Can I watch punching?" Pip asks.

"NO!" we all reply at once.

"Fine, you can stay up Jake, but don't tell your dad, OK? I am supposed to be looking after you."

"You do look after me, Guapa," he says, coming over and giving me a cuddle. He has his father's charm. I try and stay stern but I can't. The kid smells amazing. I go to walk off but he refuses to let me go. "Alright, alright. Let go. Let go I need to clear up," I say laughing.

"Hang on, just a second longer," he begs.

I almost fall for it, but then I hear a wet licking sound from behind me. I wrench myself out of him arms in time to see Juno licking the last dregs of ice cream out the tub she went and got off the kitchen counter. She has sugar sprinkles on her nose and devilment in her eye.

"You were in on this?" I ask Jake. "All of you were in on this?!" I look at Jimmy who is pretending to be asleep. "She is supposed to be on a diet!"

"NO RABBITS!" shouts Juno.

Chapter Ten

I'M just walking through the door after another frantic school run when the phone rings.

"Peta? I need to see you NOW." Nellie is crying. Really crying.

"Calm down, sweetie. I can hardly make out what you're saying. Are you OK?"

"No, I'm not. She's pregnant. Fleur is pregnant."

Oh shit. I knew this was going to come at some point, but I hoped it would not come yet. The kids just need a little bit more time, especially Nellie.

"Where are you, I'm coming to get you."

As I drive to meet her I think about how hard it must be for Nellie to accept that life is moving on and there is nothing she or I can do to stop it. I wonder the best way to approach things, and realise I have no idea.

"Give me a sign, bird," I say to the skies, but it seems Sara has no idea either.

We sit in McDonald's car park. Pip and Juno are asleep in the back. I've bought Nellie a hot chocolate but she is crying too much to drink it.

"She's going to have her own baby now. She's not going to want us around."

"That's not true." Her drink is steaming up the car. I wind down the window to let some air in.

"It is! You should see her, Pete. She's happy. It's horrible. She's already planning where the baby is going to sleep and it's not even been born yet. It's all 'the baby this' and 'the baby that', makes me sick."

"How do Josh and Abi feel?"

"Josh is happy because they are going to convert the garage for him. His band can practise in there. All he cares about is being in his stupid band and being cool and impressing Biba in the year above."

"And Abi?"

"Abi is excited. She can't wait to have a baby to play with. I'm not going to play with it though. I'm not going to touch it. I hate babies, except yours," she says quickly. I smile at her so she knows I am not cross.

"Babies are quite fun sometimes," I say, nodding to the girls in the back. They look so sweet.

"This one won't be, not if Fleur made it. It will scream all the time and keep me awake and poo all over the place. Fleur is getting fat. People keep telling her she is glowing. I want to tell her she is fat, not glowing. A big fat cow."

I shoot her a look. "I know, I know." She sighs at me. "What would Mum do? That is what you are going to say, isn't it?"

"Yes, and what would your mum do?" I finish my Coke and squash the cup.

"Kill her with kindness."

"You've made that sound slightly menacing, but yes, that is exactly what your mum would do. Make her proud, Nellie girl. I know it's hard and it hurts, but pushing that hurt onto other people is only going to cause more pain in the end."

"S'pose so." She is an adorable sulky teenager but I can't tell her this. My job is to be her friend, to be someone who she can confide in without judgement. She changed overnight after Sara died, wearing a dress to the funeral that she'd picked herself.

It was awful, and it fitted her so badly. Sara would never have let her wear it, but I had no energy to intervene. It wasn't really important, was it? The point was she was burying her mum and if that dress helped her in the smallest way to get through it, then it was worth every penny.

Nellie often tries to be tough but I see the little girl beneath the scowl. An angry, scared girl who feels all at sea without her anchor. I understand that because I often feel exactly the same.

"How about we kill her with sugar instead, and take everyone back home a doughnut?" I offer.

She looks at me and rolls her eyes, but lets me buy them all one anyway.

Juno's weight check-up does not go well. She has not lost anything at all. When I tell Jimmy about it, he does not seem too bothered.

"Are you worried about her weight?" he asks me, looking over to where Juno is watching TV.

"No, I don't think I am." I put the lid on a beaker of milky tea and take it over to her. She smiles up at me. "I think she is perfect."

"So why are you going along with it then?" he asks looking confused, then opens the patio door to go and put the chickens to bed. I pour myself a tea and ponder on what Jimmy said. Why am I going along with this diet if I don't agree with it? I decide then and there to stop caring about it. I'm just writing 'learn to say no' on my to-do list, when Jimmy comes in with some muddy eggs. "We can go swimming this weekend if you like?"

he says over the noise of the tap. "That's exercise. The triangle in Burgess Hill is great for kids. They have slides and all sorts there. The kids will love it. Let's take Jake too."

I am surprised and delighted that he wants to spend the weekend as a family. "Sounds like a brilliant idea." I rub his back as I walk past him.

"That's sorted then. Now make me an omelette, wench."

They are all ridiculously excited by the time we pull up and park at the Triangle. It takes a long time to wrestle Juno into her bathing suit (aged 3-4) but finally we make it down to the pool, and it all seems to be going well. The children splash about and go down the little slide. Jimmy goes off to the adult pool with Jake to do some laps and I sit on the slope of the baby pool watching the girls and thinking how nice it is to all be together as a family doing nice normal family things.

I'm determined to do this more often. I scoop water through my hands and think about what to make for lunch. Swimming always makes everyone hungry. Sighing with contentment, I lie back and let the water lap over me. Out the corner of my eye I can see Pip and Juno huddled together giggling. Jimmy is having a nice time, Jake is having a nice time, and the girls are having a nice time. I've even found time to shave my legs. I lift one up to inspect my handiwork and it rides in on the wave I create.

I don't know if all mothers can recognise their own child's poo, or whether it's a specific talent of mine, but the second I saw it, I knew.

I fight off the panic that washes over me and force myself to stay calm. I need to get the kids out the pool before anyone notices us, or the poo, but each movement I make brings it ever closer. I wonder if I can direct it into one of the holes cut out in the side of the pool wall without drawing attention to myself. No, that's madness, I need to get out the water, get

Jimmy and Jake and the girls far away, and then go and tell the lifeguard I've noticed a poo but have no idea where it came from. Without looking guilty.

It comes closer still. Oh my God, is that blue crayon in it? What is wrong with her?

I sidle out of the pool and make my way over to the girls.

"GET OUT!" I hiss at them.

They completely ignore me.

"Get out NOW! I know what you have done," I say through gritted teeth.

They carry on splashing about, pretending they have never seen me before in their lives.

"I SAID GET OUT NOW!" I end up hollering at them.

Everyone turns to look at us. The motion causes a mini tsunami that sends the blue poo out into the middle of the pool.

Juno spots it at once.

"Poo!" she shouts. "Poo, Mamma, poo! Pip poo."

"URGH!!" comes a voice from behind me. "There is a poo in the pool."

Everywhere, people start panicking and shouting, "Poo! Poo! Get out, there is a poo in the pool," snatching up children and holding them above their heads. There's no etiquette in their escape attempts from the pool. Women and children are not going first, it's every man for himself out there.

"Why is it blue?" I hear one horrified child ask as they are being hoisted out.

I'm so embarrassed I think I might die. The news has spread to the adult pool. I see Jimmy and Jake making their way over.

"Is it?" Jimmy says into my ear as he picks up Juno.

"Of course it bloody is."

"I thought you were watching them," he says as he lifts Pip out and ushers her away from the side.

"Watching to make sure they were not drowning. How was I supposed to know she was going to do a giant blue poo!" I shout at him.

People tut and sneer at us as we do the walk of shame back to the changing room. An angry looking dad turns to Jimmy and says, "I only get to see my kids every other weekend. I've been looking forward to taking them swimming for a fortnight and you've ruined it. Wanker."

All around us children are crying because their session has been cut short. The lifeguards are arguing over who is going to go in and catch the blue poo as it's too far away to reach from the edge with the net.

We get dressed while we are still sopping wet, making it impossible to do up trousers or pull up socks. Finally we get to the car, lock the doors and collapse in our seats.

"I am NEVER going swimming again," Jimmy announces as he starts the engine.

Jake says, "I am never going swimming again with Pip."

The girls sing "Going on a bear hunt" all the way home, but instead of looking for a bear, they change the words to 'poo'. They find this hysterically funny. Even after the eighth time of singing "We're going on a poo hunt, we're gonna catch a BIG ONE! What a blue poo, we're NOT SCARED!", Jake tries not to find it funny, but in the end he can't stop himself from smiling. He looks ten-years-old when he does it and it suits him.

Jimmy turns on Talk Sport Radio to try and drown them all out. I shut my eyes and try and work out the exact second it all went wrong.

I seemed to take to parenting so naturally initially. Despite my mother-in-law's protests that I would not be able to breastfeed with my 'little chest', I proved to be a champion lactator. Living in Brighton, if you don't breastfeed your kid till they are five you are not doing it right, of course, but I just steered clear of playgroups and people who looked like judgemental hippies. Quite hard round these parts but I managed.

Even after Pip came along, I was still doing pretty well. Life was busier, but I felt semi-in-control. I still remembered to shave my armpits once a week and Jimmy still kissed me goodbye each morning and tried to get me into bed twice a week, or on the sofa.

Was it Juno who tipped the scales or would we have gotten to this point anyway? In this day and age, can you have children and stay happily married? It seems more or less impossible right now.

"You're quiet," Jimmy says, during a break in the football results.

"Just thinking."

"Sounds dangerous." I know he is trying to make friends after blaming me but I can't muster up much of a response. Meg's face keeps popping into my mind and I can't shake her off.

The next day, I wake up no happier after dreaming that I was watching my wedding video, but Jimmy was marrying Meg instead of me. I was the bridesmaid, holding her dress. It's quite funny really, because in our actual wedding video, Jimmy's mad uncle positioned the camera so it looks like Jimmy is marrying his sister instead of me.

I spend the morning feeling furious with Jimmy. How dare he go off and fall in love with someone else while I was not looking? How dare he make me feel so worthless, so replaceable, so insecure? I feel like I am seventeen again. I remember asking him, full of confidence after an energetic bout of sex, "Are you only with me because I wore you down?"

"I'm with you because I want to be with you." He lent up on one elbow and looked down at me. "I didn't rush into a relationship with you because I wanted to sow my wild oats first."

"Well you certainly did that," I said, thinking about my Martini-drinking buddies.

"You wanted more from me than I had to give, Peta. I knew if we got together that would be it forever. I always knew you were the one, but I was not ready to be with the one. Does that make any sense?" "Not really." I replied. From the second I met Jimmy I felt ready, ready for forever to start.

"Yes but that's you, Pete. Always racing at a hundred miles an hour – and that is one of the things I love about you," he adds quickly, before I can turn it into a criticism. He pulled the cover over his head and wriggled down the bed. "And I also love these pants with cherries on, let's have a closer look shall we."

Where has that boy gone? I don't want to get over him. I don't want to be a single mum. I want my husband back. I could not bear the shame of a divorce. I'd feel such a failure, and how would it change my girls? Three daughters growing up without a dad around? I shudder at the thought. It can't happen. I have to keep this family together.

After I've done the school drop, I ask Wojtek if he will have Juno for an hour. "Of course. We will clean out the chickens."

I run to Stanmer Park and try and get my thoughts in order. I remember how last time I ran to "What is going on?" This time I chant "Save my marriage" as I pound along the dusty road and then up through the trees. I stop and fill Sara in on my decision, wiping her plaque as I do so before pulling up weeds round the legs of the bench.

Juno splashes in the bottom of the shower as I wash my run away. Afterwards I am re-energised and ready to tackle the world. "I am a happily married woman." I tell myself. "And I am going to take control of my life."

I decide to start with loading the dishwasher. It seems as good a place as any. Then I move onto the washing. I've not seen the bottom of the basket in a long time. I dread reaching it. I have a horrible feeling Pip might have left me a present there.

Gingerly I sort through the colours and whites saying which category they fall into for the sake of Juno who sits on the floor eating a slice of homemade flapjack. I sound like a racist version of Carol Vorderman when she selects consonants and vowels for people on Countdown. "Colours, whites, colours, whites. Whites, whites, whites, whites, colours. Colours. Whites, whites, colours."

As predicted, there is a poo in the bottom of the washing basket. What is wrong with my middle daughter? How did we cock up potty training so badly? Juno is keen to stop wearing nappies now but Jimmy is not having any of it. On one of the rare evenings he was home I asked him about it.

"I think we are very bad at it. Look at Pip."

"She is good at some bits of toilet-training. She can premeditate whether she is going to do a big poo or a little poo, that's pretty clever."

"Yes, but she never does them in the toilet. Last week I found one in my work shoe."

"You know she has abandonment issues."

"And on the middle of the trampoline."

"She was probably just excited, I bet she did not even realise she'd done it."

"And in a pot of Play Doh."

"Thrifty!"

"Stop defending her. She does not poo all over the place because she is a middle child. She poos all over the place because she is insane. What about the time we took her to the Tring stuffed animal museum."

"Ok. I'll give you that one. That one was bad. It was only 2pm. I did not know to look out for the 5 pm poo."

"I thought it was a croissant on the floor till I looked closer."

"It's lucky we were in the café."

"Not for everyone else eating their lunch it wasn't!"

I know I should bite the bullet and put Juno in pants. She can't be any worse than Pip, but I'll miss nappies. I'm a fan. Nappies mean not stopping every two minutes on a car journey, or having to go and pat children on the head to 'help it come out'.

Nappies are my friend. Initially, it took me a while to get to grips with them, and I don't like it when they explode and leave weird crystals everywhere but that does not happen much. Over the last five and a half years I've become a master of judging how much wee each brand can hold. It's a skill of mine. Not one I'd put on my CV, but a skill nonetheless.

Nappies are a great way to get you out of awkward situations or boring conversations. "Oh, I think she has done a poo, I'd best go and change her bum."

Nappies mean you have a baby, and Juno is my last one. I don't have any left after her. I don't want life without a baby in it. I don't know why people brag about their kids being advanced. I hated it when Juno took her first steps at nine months, and said her first word on her first birthday. I wanted to press pause. I don't want her to walk and talk and poo on the toilet. I want her to be a tiny baby, who smells nice and falls asleep in my arms. I'll miss the all-in-ones and the sleeping bags I zip her up in at night-time. I'll miss pushing a buggy and having people smile at me, because that is what happens when you walk round with a buggy. So long as it has a baby in it, otherwise you just look weird and people do not smile at you. They cross the street and try and avoid you instead.

"No nappies for you yet, Pops," I tell her as we hang a load of washing on the line.

When I get back in Jimmy has text to ask if we can have Jake again. I happily agree. When Jake is around Jimmy and I call a truce and get on. There is nothing like having an audience to make you pretend you are happily married, or another mum around to make you pretend to be a good parent.

This will be the third Saturday Jake has been with us. Joe and Jimmy work all day and then when he comes home we spend the evening together, and it's good.

I take all the kids to Nymans Gardens. It's beautiful. There are lots of big wide open spaces, with brightly coloured flowers to pick and trees with holes in, a kid's heaven. It's also nice and quiet for Pip. Even the beach in our village is getting filled up now it's the peak of summer. Her little face gets anxious at all the people, packed together like sardines lying in the sun. I can see she can't relax. Everyone else is wearing as little as possible, whilst my little Pip sits there with a blanket over her head.

But she loves Nyman's. She grins all the way there. I park up, open the door and say, "Run, be wild," and off they go, shouting, and laughing. Once they have got bored of throwing sticks for Spike, we go for a cream tea in the National Trust cafe. When I walk in with my three blond beauties and then dark Spanish Jake, I see all the posh middle-aged people turn to one another and whisper about me.

It probably does look like I had some holiday romance with a Spaniard and came back home with more than just a nice tan. The kids are oblivious to these looks. It's one of the many things I love about kids. They are so accepting. The girls don't ask why Jake is with us all the time and, all of a sudden, they just adjust to it. Jake seems to have adjusted to spending all his spare time with us too. I am completely in love with him. I can't help it. I have no will power. I can't stop touching him and telling him how handsome he is.

When we get back from Nymans we have a brilliant evening. Jimmy does not check his phone once. I manage not to say anything nagging like an old fishwife. Instead we go over to the field with scooters and balls and imaginary dogs and spend a happy hour in the late afternoon sun playing cricket.

The children are all exhausted by the time it comes to bedtime. I've moved Juno's cot in where Roo and Pip sleep and made Jake his own room. He loves it. The girls call it 'Jake's room' now, not Juno's. When he is with us they knock on the door and shyly ask to come in, but when he is not there they guard it like dogs. "No Juno! That is not your room anymore, it's Jake's!"

I check on him before I go to bed, leaving a glass of water and a glass of milk next to his bed in case he wakes up and is thirsty. I would never do this for my girls, it's water or it's nothing. Already the room is beginning to smell like boys. I like it. I tuck him in and see he is clutching his night-time dog tightly.

The rest of the week is happily uneventful. I even manage to be on time twice. Annoyingly, The-Iron-Curtain has gone on holiday to Russia so is not around to witness it.

"So how is it going?" I ask Nellie on one of our ever frequent phone chats about Fleur.

"Awful. Fleur is getting fatter and fatter. Abi is always kissing and stroking her tummy. It's disgusting. Dad wants to get our old baby stuff down from the loft. I told him if he dares put anything Mum bought for us on HER baby, I'll run away and never come back."

"Is she going to find out what she is having?"

"No, she wants it to be a surprise. Abi is desperate for it to be a girl. She wants to dress it up and play with it."

"How about Josh?"

"He does not care. All he cares about is his band and impressing Biba from the year above. They have signed up for Battle of the Bands next month. Will you come and watch?"

"Of course, I'd love to."

"She'll be there."

"Fleur?"

"Yes. I've told her she isn't welcome and that no one wants her there, but she didn't listen. Dad still told me off anyway and sent me to my room and took away my laptop for a week. It's so unfair."

"It was a bit of a mean thing to say. It's not Fleur's fault that …" I don't finish my sentence and we sit in silence for a bit.

"Peta," she says, turning to me. "Can I come and live with you?"

"Oh Nellie, you know you can't, my lovely."

"But they won't even notice I am gone! All they do is tell me off all the time." I picture her looking at me with her mother's eyes.

"If I lived with you everything would be so much better," she implores. "And when the baby comes, I won't have to listen to it scream and cry all the time. I mean, lord knows what it will mean for my schoolwork."

"Nice try, Nellie pops, but you know I have to say no. I know it's hard for you right now and I understand you are angry and lost, but you can't direct that at Fleur and her baby. It won't help anything. We might not like it but the world still spins without your mum, and we have to spin with it."

"She wants me to help pick the name."

"Well see, that's nice, she's trying. It must be hard for her too. Imagine how she feels. She is having a baby with someone who has already done it three times before. Twins at that! She has no idea what she's doing. She is also a lot older than your mum was when she had you lot. She knows nothing that she does for you will ever compare to what your mum did." Nellie does not reply, but I know she is listening. "Giving Fleur a chance does not mean you are betraying your mum or trying to replace her. It does not mean you are moving on and leaving her behind either. She will always be your mum, even if you do pick baby names with Fleur, or get involved in the pregnancy."

"She says I can call it whatever I like."

"Wow. I take back what I said. Fleur is a crazy woman!" Nellie giggles. It's one of my favourite noises. "And you are going to say no to that?"

"Abi wants to call the baby Tinkerbell."

We spend ten minutes thinking of ridiculous baby names.

"My Mum was the best mum in the whole world, but if she had not been my mum then I wish that you had been instead."

"Thank you Nellie." I pinch myself so I don't cry.

I put the phone down, still smiling and walk into the kitchen. Jimmy is standing by the sink drinking an espresso.

"That was Nellie," I tell him. "I told you Fleur was pregnant right?"

"No. Poor Nellie, it must be hard for her."

"It is," I say, walking over to the kettle and thinking how much I'd like to sit down over a pot of Earl Grey and chat to him about it all. I've no idea if I am saying the right stuff to Nellie and I'd value his opinion, but he is swinging his keys and looking awkward.

"Joe just called, he wants me to meet him at the office to go through some stuff."

I make my voice light. "No problem, will you want any dinner later?"

"No ta, we will probably get a Nando's or something."

"Right. I called Joe earlier but it went to answer machine. We've not had a catch up in ages. I wanted him to come round and see how well Jake gets on with the girls, and Jake wants to show him his room."

"I'll ask him about it." Jimmy drains his espresso then turns and drops the cup into the sink instead of the dishwasher, where it lands with a clang. "See you later then."

I drink my cup of tea and wonder if Jimmy has anything planned for my birthday tomorrow. He normally comes up trumps. He blows up balloons for me and puts up a 'Birthday Girl' banner to greet me when I come downstairs. I pretend I am too old for it, of course, but I love it. I love the thought of him getting all out of puff blowing up balloons just for me. He gets the girls to make me cards at school, and he always buys me vouchers for the spa up the road and something from Not On The High Street. Last year he bought me a bottle of Dipytique perfume too and said it was from Sara. 'Wear it. Don't bloody treasure it' said the label. It's exactly what she would have written.

We always have lunch at The Coach House in the Lanes which is where we had our wedding reception and which does the most amazing Roast Turbot with a herb and parmesan crust. Afterwards we go down to the beach and have a contest to see who can skim pebbles the furthest. The kids are rubbish at skimming. They just throw them in. It does not sound the most exciting of days but it's perfect for me.

I'm not really surprised when there are no balloons or banners to greet me when I come downstairs the next morning and Jimmy tells me he will not be able to take the day off work.

"Sorry, Pete. We have so much work on."

"But you have been working so much, it's crazy. You can't keep going like this. It's ridiculous. You are the boss! Can't you take one day off? You will make yourself ill at this rate."

He laughs as if I'd make a joke.

"I'm not joking, Jimmy."

"I know. Sorry. I've got a day booked off for Roo's drama play next week. That is all I can manage right now."

It's right that if he can only have limited time off that he should save it for the girls' special things, even if this time it means watching his eldest daughter not join in because she cannot be a bowl of porridge, but I still feel ridiculously jealous.

"I'll make it up to you, OK?"

"OK." I've still not had my present. I try not to look like I am hanging about waiting for it.

"Oh shit, Peta, I forgot to get your present … and a card. Here …" He grabs his wallet and pulls out some notes. "Go into town and get yourself something nice. I've gotta run."

He does not even give me a birthday kiss as he brushes past me.

I stand holding the money and feeling very cheap indeed.

I get the girls ready for school and nursery. They seem to have picked up on my sombre mood and for once don't make too much of a fuss when I brush their hair and teeth and spray them with Cath Kidston fabric spray.

"Why you sad, Mamma?" Pip asks me as I zip up her yellow hoodie.

"I'm not baby, I am just a bit tired today."

"Was I naughty?" she asks me, her little face peering into mine, as if she is trying to read my eyes.

"No, sweetheart."

"Did I do a naughty poo?"

"No, baby."

"Lush you. "

"Lush you too, baby."

I decide as it's my birthday we are all allowed to eat sweets on the way to school, even Juno. The fact that The-Iron-Curtain is not around means we don't even have to do it in secret. It's slightly less fun than when we do it illicitly.

While we are waiting for the gates to open, I call Wojtek and ask if he will have Juno for me. It's not till I queue for parking in Churchill Square that I wonder what I am doing. There is nothing I feel like buying. I never go shopping, not for me. I only ever come into town when I need something for the kids.

I finally find a space and head straight to Starbucks for a coffee. I don't really like coffee, but I find it very hard to get a good cup of tea when I am out and about. People have no idea about the perfect tea to milk ratio. Sara understood this. Fuck I miss her.

I sit on a high stool in the window, sipping my peppermint latte and watch people coming and going. Brighton is very good for people watching. You never know what you are going to see next. I love the anything-goes attitude here. No one bats an eyelid at the old queens mincing along in full regalia at 10 am, ordering a double espresso in their gravelly voices and flirting with the baristas.

Then there are the art students. Brighton is riddled with them. They wear velvet jackets and carry large plastic folders to show off their (crap) drawings. Everyone here is an artist or a musician. I eavesdrop on the conversation happening on a table next to me. A young couple are having a heated row about politics. Brighton was the first place to vote in the Green Party, and now the bin men are always on strike and the streets are riddled with litter. The girl next to me is on the side of the bin men, but the boy disagrees. I imagine that later their self-righteous angst will tip over into heated passion and they will spend the afternoon in a cramped bedsit making love to some alternative indie band, dust from their un-Hoovered carpet sparkling like magic dust in the late afternoon sunshine. Lucky so and so's.

I remember when Jimmy and I could not be alone together for more than five minutes without ripping our clothes off.

I finish my coffee and march across the road to Debenhams where I spend an hour looking at clothes for the girls, LEGO for Jake and a new tie for Jimmy. I pause by the make-up counter to check the time and the girl behind it beams at me in what I think she thinks is a winning fashion, but in actuality makes her look like a clown.

"Can I help you today?" she says in a sing song voice.

"I'm um …" No! my head says. No, walk away. Instead my finger betrays me, pointing like E.T. at the pots of potions and lotions spread out in front of me.

"I have no idea what all this stuff is," I tell her honestly.

She looks at me for a long minute and says nothing but I know she is thinking, 'Obviously, or you would not walk around looking like you fell out of a bin.'

"What are you looking for *specifically*?"

"I have no idea. I just don't want to look like this." I peer into the magnified mirror in front of me and recoil in horror. Things are worse than I thought.

"Sit down here, madam," she says kindly, and patronisingly, whipping a paper cloth out and placing it round my neck.

"What are you going to do?" I ask, suspiciously.

"I am going to give you a full make-over, of course," she announces, studying my face for a second then going off to gather lots of pots and sticks and powders. She comes back, looks at me again and goes to gather more.

"What here? Now?" I look at around at the shoppers milling about. "In front of everyone?"

"Yes. Don't worry, you will look lovely," she says absentmindedly, busy reading the label on a bottle.

"I don't want to look like a clown," I tell her.

"Why would you look like a clown?" she says, looking up at me, her painted on eye-brow arching upwards making the layers of orange face powder crease on her forehead.

"Um, no reason." I blush.

"Just sit back and close your eyes," she says. I do as I'm told and a few seconds later I feel a brush sweep softly over my flushed cheek. It feels ridiculously nice to have someone touching my face.

"It's my birthday today," I tell her. I have no idea why.

"Oh, happy birthday!" she trills. Now she has a smaller brush out and is painting something under my eyes. She goes over it a few times. Then she stands back to look before doing it all over again.

"My husband forgot. He didn't blow up the balloons this year." I can tell she feels awkward and slightly worried that I am a psycho, babbling about balloons but I can't seem to close my mouth.

"Um, sorry?" she asks, like it's a question.

"Guess how old I am?" As soon as I say the words I regret them.

"Oh I couldn't."

"Yes, you can." I have no idea why I am pushing this.

"Um, thirty-nine?" she says.

My eyes ping open.

"Thirty-nine? You think I'm thirty-nine?"

"Sorry. Is that wrong?"

"YES IT'S WRONG!" I bark at her. "I'm thirty-two, today, and no one is being nice to me or wants to spend time with me, except you, and that is only because you want me to buy all this gunk you are slapping on my face."

Around us people go quiet. I did not realise how loud I was being.

"Happy birthday, dear" an old lady says as she passes me by.

"Thank you," I say graciously.

The make-up girl does not say anything. She paints and smoothes and plucks and sweeps that lovely brush over me a few more times, before she finally announces, "Finished, would you like to take a look?"

"Wow," I say to the person looking back at me in the mirror.

"I know. Don't you look lovely?" the make-up girl says proudly. "Oh no! Don't cry!" She quickly snatches up a tissue and dabs under my eyelids to try and stem the flow of tears that have sprung out of nowhere.

"Sorry, it's just …" I trail off again, speechless. Who is that girl in the mirror? I keep looking at her in amazement.

"Whatever you used, I'll buy it. All of it, and tell me what you did."

And that is how I spend my birthday, having a make-up

lesson from Belinda. Behind the painted smile is a very nice girl just trying to get herself through art college.

"Well I think you are going to do very well," I tell her.

She has worked wonders with me. My green eyes are sparkling. The grey eyeliner she has smudged around the edges brings out the yellow stripes round my pupils. "Like sunflowers," Jimmy once said. The bags under my eyes have gone. My cheeks are pink, making me look brighter and younger. My lips are a slightly darker shade of the same pink. I'd never normally wear lipstick, but this looks good. I look young. I look, well, pretty. I actually look pretty.

By the time Belinda and I part we have swapped numbers and are friends on Facebook.

"Have a great day, you deserve it. Jimmy will break up with Meg the second he sees you."

I hug her tightly. "Bless you, Belinda."

I walk out of Debenhams with my head held high, and my arms full of shopping bags. To go with my new face I bought a pair of new skinny jeans and three jersey jumpers from Topshop, all in different pastel shades, not the normal grey marl I have favoured for so long. I even ventured into La Senza and had a bra fitting. It was not as bad as I thought.

"Like ski slopes, aren't they?" I sadly lament to the old lady measuring me.

"You've had babies, yes? she asks.

"Three of them."

"Then they are not ski slopes, they are just tired. You need better support. Feel this."

She offers her ample chest in my direction.

"Touch it."

"I'm not sure."

"Do it!" she commands.

"OK." Gingerly I reach out with one finger and poke the side of her left breast.

"Not like that, you need to cup them, like this …" She grabs my hands and places them on her chest. It's ridiculously firm.

"Wow."

"I know. They are not going anywhere. I had three babies too. Would you know?"

"No. You look amazing."

"You are a 32B," she announces, looking down at the measuring tape. "Not much to work with, but we can do something."

Who knew there were so many bras on the market? Underwired, uplifting, t-shirt, padded, non-padded, extra-padded, gel-inserts, ultimate cleavage, balcony. I try them all on in various sizes and colours until finally she announces she is happy with me.

"Stand straight! Be proud of your chest. Push it out."

I thrust my modest bosom forward and tilt my head. Not bad. There is a slight curve pushing out my Smashing Pumpkins t-shirt."

"Not bad, eh?"

"Thank you," I say honestly.

"Pleasure. Be proud of yourself, pretty girl. Now have a great birthday. I am sure Jimmy will stop sleeping with Meg the second he sees you in this bra."

I promise to come back in a month to give her an update, then go to Waterstones and spend the last of the cash on cooking books.

As I walk towards my car I check my phone. Four people have said happy birthday to me via Facebook. My mother is one of them.

Heather has text me: *HAPPY BIRTHDAY. NOT POSTING PRESENT. THEN YOU HAVE TO COME AND SEE ME. LOTS OF LOVE XXXX*

I must catch up with her, I tell myself.

Joe has text me: *Happy birthday Guapa, spoil yourself with the cash, you deserve it xxxx*

I guess Jimmy told him how he forgot it was my birthday. At least he felt guilty enough to mention it.

I have half an hour left before I need to go and pick the girls up so I leave town and drive to Sara's bench.

"Hi, I got you this," I place a hot chocolate on the seat next to me, then take a sip from my own.

"So I guess you hardly recognise me, huh? It's crazy what a bit of make-up and a push up bra can do. I swear the chap who sold me the hot chocolates was flirting with me. I went all red, you would have loved it."

Sara used to fancy Roger on the fourth floor in production. When he spoke to her, she would go so red her ears throbbed. I'd be sat in my office mindlessly adding sales leads to the database when she would charge in, and flop into the chair next to me. "Roger was in th' planning meeting, he asked me to pass him a biscuit. Ah went so red ah almost passed out. Am ah still red now?"

"Yes."

"Fuck. Make it go quick hen! I've told them I was going for a wee. I have to go back in there in a minute."

I fanned her with my to-do pile and poured cold water on her socks.

"Do ye think that it will work?"

"Who knows? Worth a try."

"Pour more on then. Quick!"

Just then the intercom went ping and the bitch on reception said, "Can Sara Williams please return to the planning meeting in MR2, as *soon* as possible," in her most smug voice.

"Bitch," we said in unison.

"I wonder what you would have gotten me for my birthday," I muse out-loud. Sara always used to get me great presents. Space NK candles or cashmere throws, ridiculously soft to the touch.

"Silly. You can't afford this," I would say to her. "But I love it, so I am not giving it back."

"Jimmy did not put the balloons up for me this year," I tell her. I know if she was here she would be surprised. She loved Jimmy. "Cow. He's gorgeous," she said when she first met him. He thought the same about her.

After I had Roo we made our will. I remember saying to Jimmy, "If I die, you *must* remarry and give my girl a mum." "Ok, I'll marry Sara." He said, quick as a flash.

They were both excellent at pub quizzes. When she would come over for dinner on Friday nights I'd read out trivial pursuit questions and they would desperately try to outdo one another. I'd serve my latest recipes, loving that the two most important people in my life got along so well.

I tell her about Roo and the dog and donkey thing. As I said it out-loud it sounded pretty funny. "Nellie is good," I told her. "I know she comes to see you anyway, but in case you are worried it's a front, it's not. She is an amazing girl. You did so well. Abi and Josh are busy all the time. I hardly see them, but Nellie tells me they are doing well too. They are all on the young and gifted register at school, but I guess you know that. I hear

Josh's band sound great. He does a cover of Snow Patrol for you. He says that's as Scottish as he gets, better than nothing hey?"

I run out of news to update her with, so just sit for a while instead until I remember the time and panic.

"Shit, gotta go. It's pick up time. Oh, I almost forgot. I bought you this." I pull out a pale pink silk scarf covered in white feathers and wind it round and round her bench. "It looks beautiful on you," I say, bending down to kiss her plaque.

I walk back to the car, and then turn to wave at her like I always do. The ends of the scarf are being lifted at the corners by the breeze; it's almost like she is waving back at me.

"Wow, Mummy, you look so pretty," says Roo when she skips out of school.

"Thank you, poppet," I say, leaning down to give her a kiss.

"And your face smells lovely." She sniffs my cheeks and nose, then licks it like a dog. I take her hand and turn to walk off when a voice from behind me says,

"Ah, Mrs Newton. I'm glad you are here. Have you got time for a quick chat?"

"What have we done wrong now?" I hiss at Roo as her teacher waits for us to walk over.

"Nothing, Mummy," she replies automatically.

"Hello!" I smile brightly. "How can I help you today?" I sound a bit like Belinda.

"Could you follow me please?" she asks, leading us through the lurking parents and abandoned coats back into the classroom. Juno escapes from her buggy and chases Pip down the corridor to the classroom.

Mrs Peacock sits down at her desk then says, "Rudy is getting worse." Next to me Roo looks down at her shoes, her cheeks darkening.

"Wait." I turn to Roo and say, "Pops, why don't you go and show your sisters the decorated shoes?" then wait until she is out of earshot before turning back to the teacher. "You want to talk about my girl? You wait until she is not listening, you hear me?"

The teacher blanches slightly and then composes herself. "Rudy has been disturbing the class again. She has developed an imaginary dog called Smike."

"Spike," I interrupt.

"Sorry?"

"The dog is called Spike, not Smike."

"The dog is not real, Mrs Newton! Yet she has half the class saving it their crusts and chasing it round the classroom in the middle of reading time."

"Oh, I see". I bite the insides of my cheeks to stop myself from laughing and picture Sara next to me snorting. "Do you find this funny, Mrs Newton?"

"No. Well, a bit."

"You find disrupting the education of children who have been put into our trust amusing, do you? What if Ofsted were visiting?"

"They would probably admire your creativity, Mrs …" Fuck. Why can I never remember anyone's name?

"Peacock! My name is Mrs Peacock."

"Sorry, of course, Mrs Peacock. The thing is, this is reception class. I thought the children learnt through play and all that?"

"As long as the playing adheres to the syllabus, Mrs Newton, and let me assure you that there are no imaginary dogs called Smike in the syllabus."

"Spike."

"Whatever! There are no dogs called Spike in it either! There is mathematics, and reading, and writing."

"But they have so much time for all that. They are only five. Why can't they just be children for as long as possible?"

"This is not Sweden, Mrs Newton, where people run round milking cows all day and not going to school till they are seven. This is a very reputable school and I am not going to have its success jeopardised by your daughter's behaviour."

I see there is no appealing to her better nature. She simply does not have one. So I smile my pretty new smile and say, "OK, I understand. I'll ask Roo to leave Spike at home."

"He is not real! Tell her he is not real!!"

I gather up my children and bags and make my way to the door. Before leaving I turn back to face her.

"God is real." I pause for dramatic effect. "But you can't see him, can you?" I'm so pleased with myself I don't look where I am going and trip over the shoe and boot collection by the glass door as I leave.

Picking myself up, I say, "And by the way, why did we have to have the shoes back so bloody quickly if the competition is not for ages?"

"Because the children have filled each of them with soil and seeds, and we need to wait until they grow before we can judge them." She smiles without it reaching her eyes. "We can't put soil and seeds in yours, of course, because you cooked yours inside a giant cake and then iced it."

Damn, I should have shut up while I was winning.

"Come on girls," I say, "We are going." Then just to piss her off I say, "Come on Spike, there's a good boy."

"You sure told her, Mummy," Roo says as we walk across the playground.

"Hmm." I don't really know how to handle it from here. It's one thing for me to argue back with the teacher but the last thing I want to do is make Roo's life any harder, or make her anymore unpopular than she already is.

"Do I really have to leave Spike at home?" she asks me. "He really likes it at school and Jake gets to have him at the weekend so I hardly get to see him."

"I think it would be best if you did. I'll look after him for you, and so will Juno, won't you poppet?" Juno's head nods up and down in her buggy.

"Do you promise, Mummy?"

"Yes."

"Will you give him a bone and a bowl of water?"

"Yup, sure will!"

"And walk him?"

"You bet."

"And pick up his poop before Juno eats it?"

"Most definitely." I hold my hand up for a high-five. She ignores it.

"Ok. You tell him then."

"Sorry?"

"Kneel down and tell Spike that you are going to look after him and do all those things."

"What now?" I drop my hand.

"Yes, Mummy."

"Here?"

"Yes."

Sighing, I kneel down and say to the space in front of me, "Hello Spike. I'm afraid you can't go to school with Roo anymore. You are too simply too much fun for Peacocks. You are going to stay at home with me instead." I go to stand up but Roo stops me.

"Tell him all the things you are going to do for him."

I go to tell her off, then think again of Sara and how she would do all this for her children if she could just have one more day with them, and kneel back down again. "I promise to buy you a bone and give you water and walk you, and pick up your poo before Juno eats it. There, I said it. Can I stand up now please?"

"Yes. Spike is actually over there …" She points towards the tree in the far corner of the playground. "But I'll be sure to tell him what you said."

I grit my teeth. "Thank you, that is very kind of you. Now let's get out of here."

"OK. COME ON SPIKE!" she hollers across the playground. "Remember when Mrs Peacock thought he was called Smike instead of Spike, Mummy?"

"Uh huh."

"It was a bit funny but I was very good and I did not do any laughing."

"Well done indeed." I smile at her.

"Can I laugh now?"

"Go for it."

She stands in the middle of the playground, throws her head back and laughs. She laughs so much tears roll down from her eyes. She stamps her feet and waves her arm and twirls round laughing. Pip joins in although she still does not get the Spike thing. I wait patiently watching them, and think how much I love my crazy kids.

When Jimmy gets home that night he has bought me a bunch of flowers. There is something sad about cheap flowers laying sideways on a table. I almost can't bear to look at them. I have to force myself to peel off the cellophane and chop their stems, before arranging them in a vase, which they droop over the sides of. In the spirit of not treasuring things, I use one of Sara's vases. Even that does not make them look pretty.

"Thank you," I say, when he hands them over, not meaning it. He does not look up from the paperwork he is absorbed in anyway.

"Jimmy?" I ask.

"What?" He still does not look up.

"Can you just look at me, please, for one second?" He sighs deeply, then puts the paper down and looks up.

"Yes? What is it? Is this about your birthday again? I'm sorry, OK? Please don't give me any grief tonight. I really don't need it."

I don't say anything. He glares at me.

"Well? Do you have something to tell me or can I get back to my work?" He looks angry. I see lines that did not used to be there under the glow of the spot light. I think back to the zoo day. Is it Megan who has aged him?

"You can get back to your work" I say softly, sliding off the chair next to him and taking my drink outside.

I sit on the bench and rest my back against the railway sleepers we used to form a wall of the deck years ago when we did things like home projects together. I watch flies get stuck on chicken shit and smell other people's summer barbeques. I stay outside until it gets dark. He does not come and get me. He does not make me a hot chocolate.

He never noticed my make-over.

The next morning he comes out as I am pegging out the washing. Roo passes me the wet clothes and Pip passes the pegs. They make me hang things in size order. Juno tries to pull on her still damp t-shirt and I fight to get it off her.

"Do you want to go back to Briar Wood at the weekend?" I ask him as he feeds the chickens.

"What, this weekend?" He picks up Rosie and tickles her under the chin. Lucky fucky chicken I think to myself.

"Yes. That's what I just said."

"No, I don't think so. I am pretty busy." Now he is checking her all over for fleas. I don't think most chickens purr, but I am sure our one just did.

"All weekend?"

"Yes."

"Doing what?"

"Work stuff. With Joe"

"OK, well maybe I'll go back with the girls." I'm determined not to row. I had hoped he would come with me and we could spend some quality time together but that is not going to happen. Maybe I can make him miss me instead. "I can catch up with Mickey. He wants to show me some of the jobs he has been working on and if your mum will have the girls for an hour, then maybe we will go fishing for a bit."

"I was sort of hoping you could help out with Jake." He has finished inspecting the chicken and is now changing her hay.

"Again?"

"I thought you liked having him."

"I do. I love having him, but I have things I need to do too."

"Sorry, Peta. We'll go soon I promise. Why don't you invite Mickey down here and we can all go sea fishing. Jake can come along."

"And Joe? I've not seen him for ages."

Jimmy looks distracted for a moment. Something flashes across his face, and then an instant later it is gone.

"Sure, maybe Joe too."

It's not warm at the weekend so the beach is deserted. Like all children, after finding a patch of sand they spend a long time burying one another in it. I remember doing the same thing with my brothers when I was little. I also remember them doing it so well I could not move, and John putting a bucket over my little pinhead and them both leaving me, for dead.

After they get bored, Jake and Roo throw sticks for Spike in the shallow of the waves. Pip is as confused as ever, cross that she cannot see him too. She sees lots of other dogs on the beach, but none of them are called Spike. We sit against the rocks bundled up in jumpers and coats for lunch. Juno eats a lot of sand with her tri-coloured stuffed ciabatta I made. The mum of the only other family mad enough to be on the beach comes over to ask me where I got it from.

"I made it," I told her. "It's dead easy."

"It looks amazing, how did you do it? "I give her the recipe and she copies it down. "You should write a food blog," she says. "I'd read it." I smile and say thank you but dismiss the idea immediately. I already have too much to do without starting a blog as well, but I can't stop myself thinking about how the blog might look. The photos I would use and the explanations I'd write about why I picked each recipe. The names I would give each dish. I could use photos of the people they were dedicated to. I could …

"Mumma, can we have a cuppa-tea?" Pip asks me. I zone back in and see that Juno has fallen asleep clutching the last of her ciabatta, and Jake and Roo are making a sandcastle out of stones. Pip's face is pale and her hands are cold on my face. I'd love a cup of tea too but we will have to take all the stuff with us to go and get one and it seems like too much hassle.

"I can carry the pushchair over the sand, Peta," says Jake, flexing his muscles at Roo and making her laugh.

"Really? It's pretty heavy." Jake is at the age where he is desperate to prove himself as a man, not a boy. It only demonstrates how much of a boy he still is. For some reason, seeing him try and drag the pushchair over the pebbles brings a tear to my eye. Fucking useless tear ducts, I think.

Sara and I were forever swearing at the bits of our bodies we did not like. "Shitting little diddies," we'd lament to one another's breasts. "Shagging useless stomach," she would screech at it on the beach in the summer. She was the only person I knew with a tummy like mine. We were the only two people sunbathing in t-shirts.

When we got too pissed, our tummies would have very racist conversations to one another, us making mouths of the loose skin with our hands. I remember her telling my tummy it was a 'fookin doolie fud face' (fucking idiotic fanny face). Remembering this is not making me want to cry any less.

I get us all takeaway mugs of tea and chocolate and we snuggle up on a bench with Pip's Charlie cloth over our knees, before finally trudging home via the windmill and the mini golf course. It leads up to the Downs, and through the wood at the back of the park where I once lost Roo. This is the first time I have been back in it since and I hold onto her tightly, remembering how scared I was.

I'd been pushing Pip and Roo on the swings with Juno strapped to my chest in a Baby Bjorn. The weight of her always made me need a wee. Roo did not want to stop swinging. A mum in the park offered to keep an eye on her while I whizzed to the toilet with Pip. It was a sunny day and there was a queue. When I finally came out I bumped into one of Roo's friends from pre-school. "Where is she?" Bliss asked. "She is in the park," I said "on the swing." "I want to show her my fairy tattoo sticker." Bliss ran ahead, calling for her mum to hurry up. Pip then decided she wanted a wee too. I was holding her while she weed on my flip flops when I saw Bliss and her mum stop and turn to look at me. I knew from the looks on their faces that Roo was not in the park and I realised, as I felt it slide down my back, that I had never known real fear till that moment.

I scanned my eyes round the park and the fields surrounding it but I could not see my little Roo anywhere. She was missing. I remember how the atmosphere became uneasy. Pip and Juno started screaming. Roo's friends leapt on scooters to hunt for her while their mums stood, hand-to-mouth, and looked aghast. Horrified and yet relieved it was not their baby missing.

I screamed her name into the summer air until my throat bled. I ran stumbling, with Juno pressed against my chest and Pip round my legs, calling her name again and again, like a prayer.

Then, finally, after what seemed like hours, people started shouting and pointing. Roo had appeared. She had been in the little wood at the back of the field, where we are stood now. Her glittery-pink vest sparkled in the sun and she was skipping. I remember how she fell asleep in seconds that night, worn out from the summer sun and the constant attention I bestowed on her all afternoon. But I could not switch off. I sat up all night to watch her sleep, kissing her knees and the space between her fingers. I whispered sorry into the folds of her nightie, dampening it with my tears.

"Mummy! We've been calling you for aaaages!" Roo says, peering into my face. "Can we go on a Gruffalo hunt please?" Jake tries to pretend he is too grown up to join in such silly games, but he can't help singing along, and soon he and Roo are skipping along singing, "A mouse took a stroll through the deep dark wood ..."

I love seeing how he and Roo get on. Pip and Juno are so

close in age they might as well be twins. Much like Mickey and I did, they have a way of closing in together, like petals of a flower, and not letting anyone else in. I worry sometimes that Roo feels left out. She never seems to mind. She has her own world which she lives in half the time, but still I worry. It's great how her and Jake seem to be on the same wavelength.

I'm starting to forget what weekends were like before Jake was with us all the time. He is such a good helper that I am able to take the children to places I avoided before. I'm enjoying him so much I have almost stopped wondering what Jimmy is up to in all the extra work hours. The fact that I have Jake makes me more confident that Joe is with Jimmy, and it is not just Jimmy and Meg. I don't even know if Meg works the weekend. I cannot bring myself to ask. I hate her regardless and the fact it might be unjust only feeds my fury.

Sara had a lodger once to help bring in some much needed cash. To start with she quite liked having a man about, but within months her good intentions turned to abhorrence. "Ah just have to smell his shagging patchouli aftershave as he walks through th' door and ah am furious before he has even opened his mouth. Who knew ye could loathe someone based on the pattern their feet make walking down th' stairs?"

I don't know any personal details about Meg, and I don't want to. I don't think they are going to help me. I know that I hate how pretty she is and how much younger she is. I know that I hate how much time she spends with my husband. What more is there to find out, it's only going to get worse from there surely?

As I hide in the bushes ready to slither out as the snake, I realise what a wimp I am. Other women would not live like this, scared to know the truth. But if the truth is that Jimmy is having an affair, then I'm not ready for the truth. I do not want to be a single mum. Weekends are one thing but I don't want to be like this forever. Am I turning a blind eye and hoping he will get this fling out his system and come back to me? Maybe. Can I stay with him, however, while there are seeds of doubt about his fidelity towards me? Maybe not. Sara would tell me to pull myself together and ask him, but she is not here, and when she died she took a large slice of me with her. I'm not whole enough to be alone.

Could I ever love someone else? I try to picture myself meeting another man. Going on a date. What would I wear? Clothes paid for from mine and Jimmy's joint account? The sea blue dress I always fall back on when I can't think of anything else to wear? The one Jimmy bought me in a little shop on a cobbled street on one of our French holidays? No I can't wear that.

I hate first dates. I hate the nerves and the not knowing what dish to order in a restaurant in case you spill it down yourself or worrying it costs more than the date was planning to pay. I hate the whole 'do I shave my legs or not thing?' and wondering if they are going to try and kiss me, whether I want them to, who pays the bill, who makes the first move.

Sara only went on one date after her and Jeremy split up. It had been a long week at work and the kids had all been fighting like mad. The date was with a man who worked as a freelancer in our office. He had asked her to go out straight after work, and without thinking too much about it she said yes.

We'd missed our rushed bagel lunch-break as she was working on a deadline. Sara got very drunk very quickly on an empty stomach and ended up having to be escorted home by her date, who confessed on the way that he was only twenty-five. Sara did not remember this bit until the morning after. All she remembers is waking up in her makeshift living-room bedroom, as she had rented out her actual bedroom to the lodger, and realising what it must have looked like.

"He must have thought I had set it up t' seduce him. The bed on the floor, the scatter cushion, the underwear all over the place. God it was awful!"

"Did you snog him?"

"I don't know. Ah have a horrible feeling I tried to."

"Oh dear. Never mind, at least his contract has ended so you never have to see him again," I tell her soothingly.

Sara's project did not get finished in time, however, and had to be extended by another three months, meaning all the freelancers were brought back on another temporary contract.

She had to sit opposite him every day for twelve weeks. He did everything he could to avoid her, and if they were forced to speak to one another he got so nervous he trembled.

"I am never ever going on a date again. I am just going to acquire lots of cats and drink tinned Gin and Tonic."

"Urgh, why would you do that?"

"Because that is what people who have cats do. They are disgusting. They eat off plates that cats have licked. They cook on sides that cats have sat licking their bums on. They talk to their cats as if they were people, and put up photos of them all over the place. They call them stupid names and get those awful desk calendars with 'What your cat is thinking today' jokes on them."

"I bet the bitch receptionist has a cat."

"Then cats are for cunts." Sara swore beautifully.

"Good name for a club."

"Ooh yes. Definitely. Let's do it."

"No one would want to join apart from us."

"Then they are all cuddie toleys."

I check the translator. "Donkey shit. Nice."

"Mummy?" Roo interrupts my reverie. "We are not playing Gruffalo anymore. Spike won't come out the bushes."

"What poppet?"

"Spike is refusing to come out of the bushes. I've tried offering him Juno's chocolate drops and everything. He still won't come."

"Oh, why not?"

"He's seen a cat up a tree."

"Ah." I nod knowingly "Does he want to chase it?"

"No, he is scared of it."

"But it's up a tree, it won't be able to get to him?"

"I know, Mummy, I've tried telling him that, but he won't listen to me."

"Well, get Jake to explain it to him." I'm losing interest in this conversation. I want to get home.

"Jake has. Spike is not listening to him either."

"What do you want me to do about it then?" Pip and Juno are just a tiny bit too far ahead for my liking now. "I really think we should just carry on, I am sure he will catch up with us."

"No, Mummy! I am NOT leaving without him. You have to tell him." Oh no, not this again. I hate talking to the poxy pretend dog.

"Roo, please." I look at her and her bottom lip wobbles on cue.

I turn to Jake to try and appeal to him, but his bottom lip is wobbling too.

"Oh for God's sake. Hang on." I run and grab Pip and Juno who are hiding in the ferns, wooing them back with the last of the chocolate drops and some fluffy sweets from the bottom of my rucksack.

"Right then, where is he?"

"He is over there. Can't you see him?"

"Oh yes, silly me. He merged in so well with that tree I didn't spot him. Hello, Spike," I call out to the tree. "It's time to go now."

"Tell him the cat is not going to hurt him," Jake says.

"The cat won't hurt you," I repeat.

"Tell him that there is a big juicy pig's ear waiting at home for him."

"There is a big …hang on, why do I have to say all this stuff?" Jake and Roo start giggling. "He isn't there, is he?"

"No, Mummy." Roo laughs even more. Jake has tears running down his face and is holding his sides.

"He is over there." Jake points to a patch of grass in the distance then they both fall about laughing again.

"Who ever heard of a dog who is scared of cats? Silly, Mummy."

"Ho ho yes, silly old me."

They spend the afternoon in the garden chasing imaginary dogs to give them imaginary baths, then I let them all help me make homemade pizza for dinner. The honey in the dough is a winner.

I write down the recipe and send a photo of it to Heather on my phone. A couple of minutes later my phone beeps and I see that she has sent me back a picture of a packet of Birds Eye frozen fish fingers. I am guessing she's knee deep in troubles with the new house.

I've just put the girls to bed and Jake in front of The Goonies when the phone rings. "Hang on," I tell him. "Don't start without me and don't eat all that popcorn!" I know Roo wanted to stay up with us but she could not keep her eyes open as Jake read Robin Hood stories to her.

I love having Jake to myself. I let him melt the caramel and add the salt to pour over the popcorn. He held the lid over the pan and counted the pings with excitement.

"I love it here, Peta."

"Good. I'm glad."

"Will I always be allowed here all the time?"

What do I say to that?

"Well, your dad and Jimmy are really busy at work right now, sweetie, which is why we are seeing so much of you. NOT that I am complaining." I lean in and ruffle his hair "But you know you will always have a home here with us anytime you want it."

"I never see Dad anymore," Jake says. "And when I do it's not the same."

"What do you mean, love?" I ask, putting the popcorn pan in the sink where it sizzles under the cold tap.

The phone rings before he can answer. I wipe my hands on a tea towel, search under the sofa cushions and finally locate it.

"How are things. Has the eagle landed?"

"Hi Dad, what do you mean?"

"I am not sure. I've always wanted to say it."

I smile at Jake and point at the phone, mouthing that I won't be long, then walk outside.

"No, no new developments. He is still being weird, and disappearing all the time. *She* even came round one night."

"What happened?"

"They went into the study?"

"Did you listen at the door?"

"Yes."

"And?"

"Um. I could not hear anything."

"Hmm. Any more trips to the garden centre?" He says it in a voice which I know means he does not believe they are actual trips to the garden centre any more than I do.

"Lots."

"Ever come home with anything?"

"Nope."

"Odd."

"Very."

"Going to do anything about it?"

"Maybe. Sometimes, then I change my mind again."

"If you do, remember you'll catch more flies with honey than vinegar."

"Interesting. What do you suggest?"

"Woo him, Peta. Woo him back from this pop singer."

"She is not a pop singer and we don't actually know he is having it off with her."

"Well whatever he is doing, he is not spending time at home with his wife and family, is he?" Dad sounds cross.

"No he is not."

"If I'm honest I'd like to come and punch him on the nose." He sounds even crosser, and slightly drunk.

"That would be the vinegar approach."

"True. Oh Pete," he sighs. "What a tangled web we weave, when we practise to deceive."

"You can say that again."

"What a tan …"

"Alright. I was only joking. You've changed your tune though, I thought you said it was all innocent."

"I know, and it probably is. I'm having a bad week. Your mother has bought herself a bike and insists on coming out with me everywhere. She cycles very slowly and keeps wanting to stop and buy vegetables."

"Stupid is as stupid does."

"An empty vessel makes most noise."

"Ha! Do remember though, that a man is known by the company he keeps."

"What can I do? You can't polish a turd."

I'm trying to think of a comeback when he hisses, "Gotta go. She's coming. I can hear her on the stairs, She wants me to put up a gazebo to impress the new English people in the village. I've told her a bragging woman and a crowing hen, always comes to no good in the end, but she never bloody listens."

"Tell her to do it herself. We saddle our own horses round here."

I hear my mother shouting, "NIGEL! NIGEL WHERE ARE YOU?"

"Love you. Chin up."

"Love you, Da" I say, but he has already gone.

Chapter Eleven

"PETA, we need to talk. You have missed the last two Skype meetings and both your articles have been late."

"I'm sorry, Michelle. I've got a lot going on this end and …"

"Spare me. Please. You signed a contract promising us two articles a month. Are you saying you can no longer honour this?"

"No, if you would just let me explain."

"There is no time and I don't want to hear it. This month I want you to write, 'Ten top hospital bag essentials'.

Terrific. Brilliant. I did not even open my hospital bag. I might have well as taken a box of spanners along with me. Nor did I stick to my birth plan which is the other article she wants me to write about.

Roo was two weeks late so her labour coincided with England's first game of the World Cup, which did not coincide with my birth plan at all. I'd tried everything to get her to come out beforehand, a cervical sweep (I think a broom was used but still did not work), acupuncture, pineapples, curry (not all at the same time) but Roo being Roo was determined to dance to her own tune, even back then.

I ended up being induced, which I think was the last time I waxed my fandango. Well, Jimmy did actually. I could not see it by that point.

I can't believe she is going to be six this year. I still remember how the umbilical cord thrashed when she finally slipped out, the smell of her newborn head and the extra hairs she had on her shoulders that Jimmy and I both noticed but refused to mention until they had fallen out. Then he blurted out, "Thank Christ those weird long shoulder hairs have gone."

"I know, what were they about? She looked like one of those people from a Channel 4 documentary."

Pip's labour was the birthing ball and TENS machine one, and that was only because I had a bitch of a midwife who told me I was not allowed an epidural as I was too far gone. I am sure it was a lie, but it worked I suppose.

I did not even take a hospital bag to Juno's labour, I didn't have time to pack one. She came like a cannonball. Her labour lasted an hour and I was home an hour after that. Jimmy almost missed it. By the third time round he had decided he was a bit of an expert on the workings of my birthing canal. "Nothing happening tonight, Peta," he said. "I'll go home and get some sleep, relieve Faith," (who was babysitting the other two.) I could tell he had his mouth full of kebab (this was pre-Warrior diet) when I called him and told him to get back as soon as possible.

He had not been in the door five minutes before she shot out, pink, perfect, alert. Ready to go.

I Google the ten top things that people should take in their labour bag and make up an article from that. It's not very good but I don't really care. I care less and less about Tummy-to-Mummy on a daily basis. I spend an hour reading food blogs and thinking about what mine would look like. I get as far as setting up a Wordpress account and then lose my nerve. Who is going to read it, for God's sake, there are a million of them out there.

Juno wakes moments later and sits on the Hoover while I try and go over the floor with it. I pick her up and plonk her in front of some grated cheese, laughing to myself as her chubby fingers miss the tiny strands. I need to make the most of our time together. Roo breaks up for the summer holidays next week. Where the hell did time go, and how am I going to get through six weeks with them and no help? Normally Jimmy takes a couple of weeks off and we go away somewhere, but something tells me that is not going to happen this time.

We got an au pair to help us out last year, but she told us she was leaving on the first day of the summer holidays. I was not too bothered anyway. I thought that as she was German she would be very efficient. Like an Audi, or a Bosch dishwasher. Instead, it was like living with a ginormous dormouse. Every time I turned around she was curled up under a blanket fast asleep. There was always something wrong with her which required a hot water bottle, but none of the ailments affected her appetite. No matter how bad the headache, earache, suspected 'blown sinus' she managed to force down two huge bowls of cereal each morning while the bread was toasting. The only time she missed a meal was when a seagull stole her doughnut on the pier.

I snigger at the memory. Jimmy used to have to wear a dressing gown round the house because he felt weird in his pants. On the day she left he threw it away with great delight and spent the rest of the day naked. He tried to get me to join in but I refused. I once made breakfast in bed for him naked and shut the loose skin of my tummy in the dishwasher. It put me right off.

Before Meg and the secret-life stuff, I could have text him: *I've got a hot water bottle strapped to my my head, who am I?* And we'd enjoy banter about it all day. We used to text all the time.

Just spun Pip on yellow thing in the park. She got off, walked into slide and told me her boots were dizzy x

Lesbian at work refuses to make me a coffee unless I put

my shoes on. Says I am exposing feet to show dominance. Shall I sack her? x

Roo refusing to get in the car, says driving will melt the ice and the polar bears will have nothing to stand on x

Faith booked on Friday night. Shave your legs, please x

How I miss us.

Instead I text him: *Will you be home for the kids dinner?* like a nagging old fishwife. I feel I have no choice though, the girls hardly see him. Plus I'm exhausted and I bloody hate dinner time. I'm sure if I were clever enough I could work out a mathematical equation that works out the percentage ratio between how much effort has been put into making a meal for the children and how much of it actually gets eaten.

I'll try.

As usual, dinner time starts with a ten minute argument over who is going to sit in 'the birthday chair'. The birthday chair is not as special as it sounds. It's just a white chair, with a red leather cushion on it that spins round. It used to be called the 'turny' chair. They all wanted to sit in it and it caused no end of rows. I got so sick of them crying and shrieking over it that I told them it was a special chair that could only be sat on when it was someone's birthday. They did not get the point and now they row over whose birthday is coming up *next*.

Dinnertime is at 5.30 pm. By then I've already been up for twelve hours and my eyes ache. The children announce they don't like the dinner before I've even walked out the kitchen with it.

"Yuck, cold peas," Pip says, pushing her plate away and making them spill everywhere.

"Pip peed on the table!" Roo sings, delighted with her joke. "Do you get it, Mummy? I made up a joke. Pip's peas are on the table but I am pretending it's a wee pea, not a pea pea."

Children are experts at killing a good joke, or a crap one.

"I not pea on the table!!!" Pip shouts. "Mummy, I NOT pea on the table. I pee in toilet. I a good girl. Roo, I NOT talking to you anymore." She turns her back and starts crying, fumbling for her Charlie cloth.

"Okay, okay, no one pea'd on the table, now can we all eat our dinner please," I say, my patience already fraying.

"Do you know, Mummy" says Roo. "All this talking about wee-ing has made me need a wee! Please may I get down from the table and go to the toilet?"

ARGHH! "Fine, but be quick!"

"I need a wee too, Mummy."

"No you don't, Pip. You are just saying it because Roo claims to need one."

"Nooo! I need a wee. It not fair. Roo 'llowed do a wee. I need wee."

"Just go and do a wee then, but be quick. ROO! You must have finished weeing by now," I holler up the stairs.

"I am just wiping my bum, Mummy, like you taught me to."

"I am sure it's wiped now."

"Well, I will just go and wash my hands then"

"Can you please just hurry up before dinner is ruined?"

"MUMMY! I need you wipe my bum," shrieks Pip.

"Shall I do it, Mummy?" asks Roo.

"God no." I storm up the stairs, pick Roo up and plonk her on the landing. "Downstairs!" I point to the dinner table. "NOW!"

I finish sorting Pip out and wash our hands. When we get downstairs, Roo's plate is almost empty.

"Look, Mummy, I've eaten all my dinner!" She beams at me. There is no way she has eaten her dinner. The sausages I served have herbs in them which normally she refuses to eat as she claims they are 'too tickly on my tongue'.

The broccoli has been eaten in its entirety, when normally she only bites 'the top off the tree', and the small bit of mashed potato which is left has not been drowned in ketchup.

I look across the table at Juno. She has a lot of mashed potato round her mouth and she is looking very smug.

"You gave Juno your dinner, didn't you?"

"NO, I did not."

"She did. I saw it. Roo, you a very naughty girl," says Pip, pointing her knife at Roo.

"Don't point your knife," I say, at the same time that Roo starts crying and shouting, "I am NOT a naughty girl. Tell her, Mummy. Tell her I am good girl."

"COULD YOU BOTH JUST EAT SOME BLOODY DINNER?!"

And that is what Jimmy comes home to. His suit hangs off him and he looks like he wants to turn round and leave again at once. I'll beat you to the door, you fucker, I think to myself.

"DADDY!!" the girls all shriek, leaping down from the table, dinner forgotten. While he says hello to them, I clear plates and pick up the peas.

"Alright?" he asks me, as he walks to the sofa with Pip in his arms. I look at his shiny shoes as they pass me, on my knees picking up food off the floor. I think how undignified I look and I hate myself for thinking it. Once Jimmy would have said, "While you're down there …" And I'd have playfully thumped him.

Instead he does not even look at me. The girls cover him like a blanket and they watch pre-bath television in a bubble I am not included in. Jimmy rubs Roo's hair as she snuggles under his arm. Pip is under the other one and Juno is on his chest. There is no place for me in the scene. I wipe down the kitchen sides and then go upstairs to draw curtains and turn on night-lights.

"I'll do the little two," he says as he hoists Juno out the bath.

"Thanks, I'll get Roo down."

"Mummy, can I have big girl's hour tonight, please?" Roo asks as I pull a stripy nightie over her head. "Not tonight, poppet. Mummy has a headache." I smooth down the soft fabric and tuck her hair behind her ear.

"Well can I have big girl's hour with you then please, Daddy?"

Jimmy looks awkward. "Not tonight Roo, I'm sorry. I've got to go back to work in a little while." Roo is too tired for big girls hour anyway and when she gets tired she gets emotional.

"You are always at work! You are never here anymore. You never take me to school and play football. Why don't you want to be my daddy anymore?" Big fat tears fall down her face and her shoulders shake.

"I'll do the little two," I say to Jimmy quietly, scooping Juno up from our bed and taking Pip by the hand. "You talk to Roo."

"Is Daddy still our Daddy?" Pip asks me as we climb up the stairs to her and Juno's room.

"Yes, my darling," I tell her. "He is just working very hard at the minute for us, to get pennies to buy the things we need."

I lay Juno, already half asleep, in her bed and tuck her in.

"I want Fireman Sam helmet, can he get me one of them?"

"I'll see what I can do," I say, pulling back Pip's cover back for her so she can climb into bed. I tuck her favourite Charlie cloth over her before pulling up the quilt. I can hear quiet sobs coming from Roo's room and Jimmy's deep voice whispering, but I can't make out any words.

"What shall I read to you?" I ask Pip, hoping she can't hear her sister's distress.

When Pip is finally asleep I make my way down to the landing, collecting wet towels and discarded socks as I do so, tossing them on the overflowing laundry basket. Jimmy is at the dining table, glued to his iPad. Something on his face tells me he is not watching an episode of Breaking Bad on Netflix. I realise that he is probably gutted about what Roo said to him.

"Are you OK?" I ask, pulling out a chair and sitting beside him. I pull my knees up under my chin and wrap my arms around round them. "Roo is only five, she doesn't understand." Jimmy puts his iPad down and runs both hands through his hair and sighs. I guess now is not the time to tell him that I don't understand either and can he please whisper in my ear that everything will be OK and he loves me very much while I lie in his arms sobbing.

Instead we sit in silence. I'm hoping if I wait it out that Jimmy might start talking, but ten minutes pass and he says nothing. I don't think he has even noticed I am still sitting next to him.

"I think I'll go to bed then," I say finally, dropping my legs down and sliding off the chair. I look at him, hoping for him to say 'it's a bit early', or 'goodnight then', or even 'where's my bloody dinner?' but he just mumbles something and goes back to his iPad.

I pour some water to take up with me, noticing that the glass has not been cleaned properly in the dishwasher. Dried porridge and tea-leaves are crusted to the bottom of it. I can't even be bothered to write 'clean dishwasher' on my to-do list. I never bloody do any of the things on there. I only write them down to get them out my head.

I go to put my phone on charge, but I can't find the lead under the jumble of school letters and bills. Jimmy's phone is under a reminder about the girls' dentist appointments. It's lit up with three messages, all of them are from Meg.

I take a deep breath and pick it up to read them. I'm halfway through the first one: Jimmy, I really wish that you ... when the phone rings in my hand and Meg's number appears on the screen. "Fuck," I say, dropping it and covering it with letters before darting round the breakfast bar and up the stairs.

I'm in the bathroom brushing my teeth when I realise I should have answered the phone. Caught her out, asked her what she wished Jimmy would do, or touch or ..." Yuck. I spit my toothpaste out and turn off the tap. I was so anxious to get away that I did not even hear whether Jimmy answered the call or not. "Stop running away," I tell my exhausted face in the mirror. She looks down and says nothing.

And when the soft knock at the door comes ten minutes later, as I'm half-heartedly rubbing in face cream, I don't even need to look out the window to know who will be standing in the light below.

But this time I am determined to successfully eavesdrop. While he takes her coat for her (bastard) and offers her a drink (creep) I sneak onto the landing, and lie on my front in the dark, before carefully tipping the contents of the laundry bin on top of me. Momentarily, I can't breathe, but I'm well hidden, and feeling rather pleased with myself, until I hear Meg say, "We can't go on like this Jimmy" in a sad quiet voice.

"Can't we just do it for a bit longer?" Jimmy pleads. I lie under a pair of his sweaty boxer shorts and feel sick to my stomach. I can't believe my husband is sat on our sofa begging his assistant to carry on having an affair, while I am asleep upstairs in our bed (in theory).

"I just need a bit more time. I am not quite ready to you know ..." he continues.

Oh my God. He is planning to leave me. All this time that I have been hoping if I ignored our problems they would get better, he has been trying to find the balls to leave me. I pinch myself as hard as I can so I don't cry or scream, or throw up.

"You know it's the right thing to do, Jimmy. It's time we moved forward. You promised."

"I know, I'm being selfish and I'm drawing it out," says Jimmy. He sounds heartbroken and for a ridiculous minute I almost feel sorry for him. A long silence follows. I am just shuffling forward using Roo's wizard cape to disguise me so I can see if they are snogging when I hear Juno stir upstairs. Jimmy looks up. Shit. I need to move. I caterpillar back into our bedroom, pad as lightly as possible across the floorboards and throw myself on the bed, seconds before Jimmy starts coming up the stairs. I leap back off the bed, fling open the door and try and look like I just woke up.

"What?! Yes, I'm awake. Just woke up. I'll go to her!" I say in as normal a voice as possible, which, considering I just heard him promise his assistant he was going to leave me for her, I think I manage quite well.

Then I brush past him with as much force as I can manage.

Juno is half-awake in the half-light of the moon, looking for her milk. I find it under her covers and pass it over, her chubby hand grasps it firmly. I tuck her back in while she sucks away, then sink to the floor next to her. My hands are shaking and tears are falling down my face. I lean over and rest my head on the pillow next to Juno's; her baby breath is warm on my cheek, drying my tears as they fall.

How can this be happening? How can Jimmy be leaving me, leaving us? I look at Juno's face bathed in a sliver of moonlight. How could anyone do anything to hurt this child and her sisters? All the things I used to think were problems were not really problems at all. Apart from Sara dying, I've never had a problem till now. I was just living normal life. I want my old life back so much I can hardly breathe.

Jimmy is up and gone by 6.30 am which makes it easier. It means I don't have to see him. As if sensing there is something wrong, the kids are strangely compliant when I dress them. They push their breakfasts away as normal. My own stomach is in knots but I try and act normally.

"Come on gang, three spoonful's of Cheerios at least please," I say, but it comes out flat and lacking any enthusiasm.

We sit on the sofa together, slumped in front of Ben and Holly's Little Kingdom. I want them all as close to me as possible. There are too many arms and legs for me to hold onto at once, but I try anyway. They don't even tell me to get off when I cling too tightly.

I feel like I am wading through treacle as I carry Juno down to the car. I've never felt so exhausted in my life. I feel like I just gave birth again. My legs don't want to move, my neck does not want to hold my head up. I just want to slip between my bed sheets and sleep the next few months away.

I don't remember who I saw or what I said on the school run. I went onto autopilot, smiling and holding lunch boxes, which I must have packed at some point. I checked and saw apples and marmite sandwiches, cut into fingers. It was all there, even a snack for Roo at break. The girls run off across the playground to the fallen log and the gap behind the bush. I used to tell them not to, in case they got dirty, and wonder if I will ever find anything important again.

Wojtek is still wearing his dressing gown when he comes to the door. "I'm sorry to keep asking," I tell him honestly.

"It's OK, she is very good company for chickens," he sighs, opening the door wider for her to walk past into the living room. He does not sound as sincere as normal. I look at him. His eyes are red and his face is grey. I try and make my mouth form the words, "Are you OK? I'll take Juno back home. Do you need anything?" but I can't. Can't remember the chicken soup recipe

I'd make in times like this. Can't care that my neighbour is ill. I have to start making plans and I cannot have Juno with me to do it.

I hand over a bag of rice cakes, kiss her head and squeeze Wojtek on the arm. It's the best I can do. Once the door is closed behind me I gulp some morning air and march up the steps to Morris' door. I've not even knocked before I hear him say, "Morning. Is that you, Peta?"

"Yes. How did you know?"

"I have a secret spy hole."

"Oh." I pause. "Can I come in please? I need to talk to you."

"Yes, hang on, first, can you just move a half-step to the right?"

I do so and hear the sound of a camera flash.

"Morris, did you just take a photo of me?"

"No," he says defensively. "Sue is Hoovering."

"Right." I'm feeling more unsure by the second. "Can I come in now please?"

"Just a moment. Wait there." I wait while he undoes seven safety chains, bolts and padlocks. When the door finally opens a tiny crack he pokes his head out and he ushers me in quickly. "Hurry, you never know who might be watching."

"You normally," I mutter as I step under his arm and wipe my feet on the mat. Their porch smells of damp shoes and sweaty feet. I wrinkle my nose and walk through into the hall, which smells of sweaty feet and curry. I want to go back out into the summer morning, but I force myself to remember why I am here. If anyone will know what is going on, it's Morris. I am doing this for my children, I tell myself. I am doing this for my children.

He leads me into the kitchen. "Here we are then young, Peta, sit down, sit down, that's right," he says as I gingerly lower myself onto a chair at the dining table. "Now would you like a nice cup of tea?"

"Lovely, thanks." I don't want one but I want to be polite.

"Now, you like the milk in first and one big sugar, is that right?" He whistles as he gets a tea bag out of a canister on the side.

I have never made him tea before or told him how I like my own tea. I look at the door. He's put all the safety chains back on it. It will take me at least ten minutes to get them all open again, and that is if I can find the key.

I turn round and look at the back door. There is no cat flap but the key is in the lock on the handle. If the worst comes to the worst I can run out into their back garden and use the washing line stick to pole vault over their high fence. It will be hard not to catch myself on the barbed wire Morris has put at the top, but it will be worth it.

Having worked out an escape route I relax slightly, then notice the filth of my surroundings. Granules of sugar, old tea bags and dirty spoons litter the draining board. The sink is full of un-rinsed plates. Flies gather round a pungent banana in the fruit bowl. The recycling bin is full of un-rinsed milk bottles and empty tins of baked beans, mouldy at the bottom. Every window is shut tightly, every smell trapped.

Morris makes me tea and himself a coffee then sits down at the table opposite me. Before he sits he pulls his trousers up slightly, just above the knee to stop them from creasing. It's odd in comparison to his surroundings to care so much about creases.

I take a sip of my tea, nervously. It's surprisingly good. I was preparing for out of date milk.

"I need your help," I say as I set the mug down on the sticky table.

"I see, and what do you need my help with?" He brings his hands together in a moment of thought. Would you like to borrow a DIY tool, or ask me for a quote to repair your rotting facia boards? I've had a look and they are not going to last you the winter ..." I can see he is about to carry on so I quickly say, "No, it's none of those things. It's something more, um, delicate."

He leans forward, bitter coffee breath in my face, eyes fixed on mine.

"Is it a matter of a sensitive nature?"

"Yes." I try not to breathe through my nose.

"Will it require stealth, meticulous planning and the use of surveillance cameras to resolve?" He leans in even closer with his death-breath.

"Yes, maybe?" I say through my teeth.

"Then tell me at once, I am all ears." Suddenly there is a loud banging noise. I leap out of my chair alarmed. "What's that?"

"Nothing." He shifts slightly in his seat. "Continue."

I sit back down again. "It's about Jimmy," I start, and then stop. The banging is getting louder and I swear I can hear Sue's muffled voice shouting, "Help, help me!"

"Is that Sue I can hear?"

"Where? No. I can't hear anything. The radio is on in the front room, it's probably that. Now what were you saying?"

"I can't think with that noise. I really think it's Sue, maybe she is in trouble. I think we should check." I get up and try to follow the sound of the noise.

"Oh bloody hell, hang on," Morris snaps then goes over to the utility room and unlocks it.

Sue stumbles out, naked save for an apron with fig leaves on it where her genitals are.

"Hello, lovely," she slurs at me.

"Oh. Hello, Sue"

"Have you come to see me?" She gives me a lavish wink and then trips over the small step up to the kitchen.

Suddenly it does not seem worth it. In that moment I don't care if Jimmy is having an affair. I just want to get the hell out of there, alive. Sue has turned around and her naked bottom is on full view. I notice it's surprisingly toned, then wonder what is wrong with me.

"Look, maybe I should come back at another time," I say, scraping my chair back. "I can see you are, um, busy."

"I'm not busy," says Sue. "He never lets me out you know." I smell wine when she leans into me. If I make it out here I am definitely booking us all into the dentist.

"Uh-huh," I say, sidling along the kitchen table and heading towards the back door. I've not tried pole vaulting since I was at middle school but I think I remember how to do it. I remember the stick having some give in it which might not be the case with the washing line one, but it will have to do. If I vault from the top of the garden I should land on our trampoline. If I shout for Wojtek he will come and help me. I hope. His ill face appears in my mind and I worry about Juno.

"See, this is why I don't let you out!" Morris has hold of Sue's ear and is leading her out of the kitchen. "You are a disgrace. Now go and have a shower, you stink."

"Get off me, you old bastard." She has taken off her apron and is now completely naked. She has a very neat bikini line I notice, then wonder, again, what on earth is wrong with me. She walks into the door frame as she leaves, then turns around to do one final shimmy before disappearing down the corridor to the bathroom.

"Please, sit down again," Morris cajoles.

"I think I'll stand."

"Ok, but please do continue."

"It's about Jimmy," I start again, and then hesitate. Am I really sure I want to get this weirdo involved? I briefly go over my options and realise I have none left.

"What about Jimmy?" he says, getting out a notebook and a pen from his top pocket.

"I think he is having an affair."

"REALLY? With who?"

"You know Cate Blanchet?"

"No."

"Well, she is an actress. The person he is having an affair with looks like her."

"What do you want me to do?"

"I want to know what they are planning to do." I fill him in on the conversation I overheard. He listens, shakes his head sadly and makes lots of notes.

"I don't want to be in the dark about anything anymore. Find out all you can about her, and him and what they are planning to do. I can't sit about and wait to be told."

"Why don't you just confront him?"

"It seems I have no bollocks."

He nods as if I have made a sensible observation. "Right, very good. I'll need a photo of her."

"I don't have a photo of her."

"Well you will have to get me one."

"How?"

"I have a device. You wear it inside your coat."

"But then I would have to go and see her." The thought makes me feel sick. "Can't you just download a photo of Cate Blanchett from the internet?"

"I will for now, but it's not ideal. What else do you know about her?"

"Not a lot."

"I'll have to start her a new file. Come …" He stands abruptly and beckons me into the study across the hall. Lined up neatly on shelves along the wall are dozens and dozens of folders. Each one is labelled with a number and a surname. This rooms smells of body odour. I imagine him in here, sweating in excitement as he spies on people.

"Are those files on everyone in the street?"

"Yes." He is flicking through them, distractedly.

"Is that legal?"

He stops and looks at me.

"I am the Neighbourhood Watch officer. How can I know what is abnormal behaviour from my neighbours if I do not know their normal neighbourly behaviour? … AHA!" He pulls out a file. "Here we go."

I see it has our house number and surname on. I move closer and he raises the folder high and close to his face so I cannot see. It's the kind of thing my brother John would do and I find it incredibly irritating.

"Mm I see, interesting, very very interesting," he says, then shuts the file and tucks it under his arm. "I am going to need to study this closely and then start my tracking."

"Oh, OK. Would you like me to tell you any information? Car registrations or …"

"Please," he interrupts me. "Do you think I am some kind of amateur?" I can see I have offended him and he is very near the door, blocking my exit. I start feeling worried I won't be allowed out again.

"No! Not at all," I cajole. "I am a fool. Forgive me."

He seems to relax. His shoulders drop and I sag with relief.

"Leave this with me. I have three rules. Ask no questions and I will tell you no lies. Tell nobody I am working for you, and please sign my petition to stop my neighbour on the other side of me from getting an extension. It will block my birds-eye view of the street."

"I understand." I sign the petition and shout goodbye to Sue as I walk down the hall to the porch. I can hear her in the bath swearing to herself and splashing water about.

"I would have let her out, you know," he tells me as he undoes the seven locks and bolts and padlocks.

"I know you would have," I say, desperate for the door to open.

"She was not in there all night."

"Of course not," I say, just wanting him to open the door and let me out.

"I'll be in touch," he says, then tries to do a long and complicated secret handshake which I do not know and get all wrong. He tuts at me and then back goes inside and shuts the door. I hear all the padlocks going on again and the camera flash as I walk down the drive.

Once I am on the pavement I stop to compose myself, enjoying the bright sunshine and the smell of cut lawns and hot pavements.

What have I done? I wonder as I walk across the lawn to my drive. Whatever it is, it's too late to stop it now. I wanted answers, and it seems I am going to get them.

There is no answer when I knock on Wojtek's door. I look

through the window and see them asleep on the sofa together, so I decide to go home and make the chicken soup. As I sweat leeks and celery in olive oil I jot down the recipe so I don't forget it again. I love making this meal, the sheen of the orzo rice, the yellow lemons laying like sliced-up suns on the chopping board. There is nothing like the smell of onions softening in butter, or the sizzle of chicken as it browns. Jimmy made me this after I had Roo. Whenever we have it, we call it 'labour soup'.

"Do not think about Jimmy," I tell myself sternly, as I chop up dill, then stop to wipe my eyes on the tea towel.

"Mummy …" Roo asks me when we get back from the school run. "Can we make some cup cakes please?"

She has been quiet since her outburst to Jimmy, and although I could do without the mess and mayhem, I say, "Of course, Pops, do you have anything in mind?" I pull out a child's cookery book and she sits flicking through it looking serious. "Hello, earth to Roo."

"Well I'd like green cupcakes like grass with dogs on top and chocolate buttons as puddles, but Lily-Grace says they sound horrible."

"Well she is not going to be eating them, my love. Why does that matter?" I stroke her hair and watch her worried little face.

"But they are for her mummy. They are to make her want to be my friend again." She carries on turning pages. "These ones. Can we make these ones please?" I look over her shoulder and see she is pointing to some pink cupcakes with purple sprinkles on. "They are Lily-Grace's favourite colours. Those are the cup-cakes she wants."

"What about what you want?"

"I want my friends back, Mummy, and that is all."

I turned my back so she does not see my eyes well up. FUCKING EYES! "NO problemo, baby-face, pink cupcakes with purple sprinkles it is ... PIP, JUNO!!" I holler out the back door, where they are sprinkling chicken food all over the place. "Want to do some baking?" I get out bowls and wooden spoons and hope the mayhem of three kids let loose with icing sugar and food colouring will stop me from thinking about Jimmy.

He does not contact me all day. I want to ring his office to see if he is at work, but I don't want to talk to him and I don't want him to know I have been checking up on him. I want to surprise him with the fact I know all about his affair and plans to leave me. Hurry up Morris, I think, checking my phone for the tenth time.

At Pip's request, we take a bundle of Charlie cloths up the garden and have a picnic on them, shooing away the over-friendly chickens as we do so. Already full of cakes and icing, they pick at their hot dogs and sweet potato fries. I can't eat when I am stressed so I drink lime and sodas and look forward to all the gin I am going to add to it when the kids are in bed, but the sugar has ruined their sleep as well as their appetite and I end up with them all in my bed watching Rainbow Brite.

When they finally sleep, I flit between them and the housework, thinking about Jimmy and Meg non-stop. I can't stop myself. It's like probing a hole where a tooth used to be. Are they together now, making plans? I am just folding up a pile of socks and thinking that there must be something more productive I could be doing when the doorbells goes. I peer out the window and see Morris standing on the porch.

"I have news," he says when I open the door.

"Tell me at once."

"Meet me in the school playing field after midnight tonight," he whispers. I stand back from his breath and say, "I can't. There is no one to sit with the children."

"Fine, I'll come in now then," says Morris in a resigned voice as he steps over the threshold.

"Well?" I ask, trying to grab the folder out of his hands.

"Patience," he tells me. Then, "I'd love a cup of tea." I sigh and go into the kitchen. "And a biscuit," he calls from his seat at the dining table.

I tip some shortbread fingers out onto a plate and carry them through with a pot of tea and the milk carton. I don't even decant it into a jug.

"Now talk."

"Do you always leave that open?" He points to the thinnest window in the world above out patio door.

"What? Yes. Just tell me what you have found out about Jimmy and Meg."

"You could get burgled if you leave that open, you know."

"Only by a ferret, or a snake."

"Not true, you could make a long wire from a clothes hanger and poke it through the window and down to the door to pull the handle up."

"I am sure the noise would alert the chickens, or the birds, or something. Now please, can you tell me what you have found out. Please."

"Fine." He takes a long sip of his tea, then picks up a biscuit and dunks it in his mug a couple of times.

"Seriously?"

He pauses and looks at me. "Jimmy has been going to Eastbourne." He sits back and waits for my reaction.

"Eastbourne. What for? It's full of old people." Why would he go to Eastbourne?

"I don't know that bit yet. All I know is that he goes three times a week, sometimes four and he is not alone in the car."

I know what he is going to say before he says it. He pulls out a picture of Cate Blanchett in lingerie and says, "She's in the car with him," then he adds "not wearing that." I think he thinks it might make me feel better.

"Where do they go in Eastbourne?" I imagine a seedy hotel or a bedsit. I feel sick. I think I am going to be sick. I stand up then sit down again. I don't know what to do with my hands.

"They go to one hundred and thirty-three Seymour Road."

"And what is at one hundred and thirty-three Seymour Road?"

"I don't know. You have to have a special code to get into the gates which I have not managed to crack yet." He looks slightly embarrassed.

"Did you try? Did something happen?"

"No." He brushes away some lint from his trousers.

"Did you try and break in and get in trouble?"

"A bit, the security measures in Eastbourne are significantly advanced to those here."

"I see." I look back at the map he has printed for me. On it, he has highlighted the route they take. I picture Jimmy driving on the M23 while Meg witters on about pop bands and bubble gum, or how she can't wait to show him how she can get her legs round her head. Bile rises in my throat.

"What are these?" I ask, pointing to crosses marked on the route.

"That is where they stop on the journey."

"What are those places?"

"Shops mostly."

"What kind of shops?"

"Clothes shops, home-wares shops, that kind of thing."

Oh my God. It's really happening. Jimmy plans to run away and start a new life with her, Meg. My stomach lurches. I abandon the tea and reach for the Limoncello which is the closest alcohol I have to hand, hoping it will melt the burning in my throat but it just makes it worse.

"I need to go there, now." I go and get my car keys then realise there is no way I am leaving him with the kids.

"I don't think you should be hasty," Morris says. "Let me do some more digging about first, and see what else I can find out."

"What else is there to know? Jimmy is making plans to start a new life in Eastbourne and I am going to be left here on my own with the kids. I am going to be a single mum and the children will hate me and as soon as they are old enough they will leave me to go and live with Jimmy and Meg because Meg is so much younger and cooler than me and lets them wear make-up and buys them Lelly-Kelly sandals."

"Just calm down. We need to be rational and think of a plan. You need to gather all your facts together in case you need them in court."

"Why would I need them in court?"

"Well maybe Jimmy is planning to have custody. Maybe Meg cannot have her own children and has always wanted them?"

"Do you think this is helping me?"

"I am trying to be practical."

A wave of exhaustion hits me. I put down the bottle I am clutching and rest my head on the table. "I don't meant to be rude Morris, but would you mind leaving? I have so much to think about." My voice is muffled.

"Oh."

Morris sounds disappointed. I think he was hoping to stay

up all night talking to me about plans and routes and how to break into places.

"I am very grateful for all your help."

"Say no more," he says, gulping down his tea. "Can I take some more biscuits? Sue is not much of a cook."

"Yes, of course. Take the packet." I force myself to stand up and retrieve it from the kitchen. "I just need a bit of time," I say, handing it over to him.

He looks sad when I shut the door on him. He does not even remind me to do up the lock, which is just as well because it does not work anyway.

I sit looking at the paper print out he has left behind. Why Eastbourne? Why clothes shops? Why all the trips? I need to think of a plan. The thought of thinking makes me feel exhausted again so I drink gin and listen to Radiohead instead.

I wake up when I hear the girls making their way down stairs. I am trying to work out why I am on the sofa and why I feel so bloody terrible when Roo pulls back the cover to put her cold feet on my legs "Where's Daddy? I looked in all the beds but he is not in any of them and his car is not here either."

"What?" I try to sit up but my head feels like it will explode if I do so I lie back down and groan. Fumbling with my eyes shut, I finally locate my phone down the side of the sofa and see it's 5.45 am. Where is he? I drop the phone to clutch my head.

"He must have left early today," I say, praying my stomach stops sloshing about.

Roo wiggles next to me. "Careful poppet," I say, untangling myself, and silently cursing my hangover. I think of all the times my parents told me to be quiet because they had a headache, how I'd tiptoe round my bedroom, trying not to make a noise. Always clumsy when nervous, I remember when I spilt the orange cordial I was pouring. The way Mum shouted at me and called me useless. The promise I made that I would never make my children suffer my weaknesses along with me. "Two secs, get the biscuits out." I slip off the sofa, wait for the room to stop spinning and make my way upstairs.

I shut the bathroom door and peer in the mirror. It's not good. I'm puffy and blotchy and the skin round my eyes and mouth is grey. My hair is lank with inch long roots, and Jimmy did not come home.

I call his phone but it goes straight to answer machine. "Where are you?" I ask his automated message, then text him the same thing.

I splash cold water on my face but everything still feels unreal. I peel off my jeans and t-shirt and turn the shower on as hot as it will go. Before I get in I call down to Roo that I will be down to make her proper breakfast in a bit. She is absorbed in the TV, but the little two will not be so amenable when they wake. I need to pull myself together and fast.

The shower is like a punishment, the force of it almost knocking me over. I reach for the shampoo and hope it can 'wash that man right out of my hair', but all it does is make my scalp hurt. When I finally step out onto the rug, my whole body tingles with pain. I don't know whether it's from my drunken sleep on the sofa, or my broken heart. I imagine it exploding into a million brittle shards inside me, leaving a million scars that will never heal.

I wipe a patch of steam off the mirror with the towel and tell my reflection to "pull it together, the girls need you." She nods but says nothing.

Two Nurofen and three cups of tea later I start to feel more normal and my puffy morning face is going down. My hands have almost stopped shaking enough for me to apply some make up. Not some, a lot.

Try as I can, I can't bring myself to be chatty to the girls.

There is a lump in my throat that I can't seem to speak round, so I let them watch Fireman Sam on the computer and make them *pain perdu* instead. As I go to get the butter out, I see the fridge is more or less empty.

I realise that no one has done any shopping in ages. Jimmy took over the online shopping after I spent £150 on cleaning products and organic vegetables. Since he took over, he orders the same thing each week so it's more or less a matter of repeating the last order and paying, but it's his card, not mine. I don't know his pin number and I don't know how much I have in my bank account, or how I will pay for the shopping we need right now.

I swallow down panic with another Nurofen and make a note on my hand to call Dad about money. He will know what to do.

The children eat their breakfast with gusto, so innocent and oblivious that their world is going to be blown apart. Will I be strong enough to pick up the pieces? How I cope with the break up will shape these girls forever. The weight of responsibility I feel makes my knees buckle as I clear their plates. I stop and clutch the chair that Jimmy should be sitting on and take a breath.

The girls skip down the drive with their light lunch boxes full of stale bread sticks and Frube yoghurts. I promise toad-in-the-road for dinner to make it up to them. I have to run back into the house twice for forgotten sun cream and water bottles and I clutch the steering wheel as I drive.

Everything looks the same out my windscreen. The same mums are walking to school, calling their children to not go so far ahead on scooters and to stop by the roads. The same commuters wait for the bus, the postman nods as he passes me by the traffic lights. But nothing is the same. Jimmy did not come home last night, his phone is switched off and he is leaving me.

I smile benignly at drop off, but hear nothing that is said to me. When I get back home, I do what I do best in times of need. I clean, frantically. I pass Juno a duster and she wanders round waving it about while I empty cupboards, and scrub stains left by hot pans from the wooden work tops. I clean with the single-mindedness of a woman nesting before she goes into labour. I am perched on top of a stool trying to reach a stubborn cobweb on the ceiling when the phone rings. Hoping it will be Jimmy, I jump down, landing awkwardly on my ankle. I'm still rubbing it as I pick up the phone.

"Mrs Newton, you need to come down immediately. There has been an incident involving Rudy."

I clutch the wall to stop me falling. "What incident. Is she OK? What has happened?"

I hear the word fire, then I drop the phone.

I don't even offer an explanation to Wojtek when I take Juno round, still clutching her duster. I am so desperate to get down to the school I can't speak.

As I pull away from the curb I call Jimmy's number on the car phone. It rings, but no one answers. I ring again and again. I am just about to hang up when I hear a soft voice say, "Hello?"

It's Meg. She sounds breathless. I swerve and almost crash into the car in front of me as we pull up to the traffic lights.

"Hello?" She says again. "Peta? Is that you?"

I force words out, chocking on them. "Fire at school. Roo."

"I can't understand you," Meg says. "What did you say?"

I hear the distant sound of an ambulance. Is it for Roo? The traffic is not moving. I abandon the call and my car, and start running.

As I push through the crowds of people and past the cornered off posts that the fire brigade have put up, I scream Roo's name on repeat.

I feel like I will never find her. Everyone is crying and shouting. Teachers are trying to regain a sense of order and failing. Bells ring, whistle blow. The kids are going mad. Parents mill around like flies. I barge through them blindly. A teacher recognises me, grabs my arm and points me towards the reception.

There, through the chaos, I find Roo sitting in the head-teacher's office with an ice-pack over her knuckles.

Rushing to her side, I put my arms round her, crushing her against me.

"Roo, baby," I say feeling her all over to check her injuries. My voice is broken and scratchy. "What happened?"

"There was a fire. Rudy stopped it. She saved Lily-Grace's life," says Mrs Peacock. She goes to continue but Roo butts in, "I will tell you, Mummy." She pulls her head free from my shoulder and sits back to look at me. "See, I saw that Lily-Grace had sneaked into the classroom with Tom and I wanted to check she was OK. Tom is very naughty and I was worried he was going to be mean to her. He makes people do dares." Tears are running down her cheeks, making tracks in the soot on her face.

"So I snucked in to watch. Tom was telling Lily-Grace to climb up and get the Marble Maze down from the top of the cupboard which we are only allowed to play with in Golden Time on Friday, if no one has gone onto amber. I have been gone onto amber lots so no one has been able to play with it." She stops talking and starts sobbing. I hold her tightly and wait till she has calmed down. Finally she carries on.

"Lily-Grace did not want to climb and get it. I know Lily-Grace is scared of being high but Tom does not. Tom said she had to, so she started climbing. She got onto the teacher's desk, and knocked over a big pile of ripped up papers. Then she started climbing up the shelves to try and get on top the cupboard to the Marble Maze. I wanted to tell her to be careful, but I did not want to disturb her in case she felled. Then I smelled the fire. The paper she had knocked over had flames on it. I called to her to get down. I called 'FIRE LILY-GRACE!' and 'RUN'. Tom ran off straight away, but Lily-Grace was too scared to move because of the high. I told her to jump on the cushions in comfy corner, and she tried, but it was too far. She banged her head on the side of the desk. I was worried she was going to get on fire so I shouted her but she was asleep and could not hear me." She is talking faster and faster and wringing her hands.

"Slow down, slow down," I say as she gasps for breath.

She pants a moment then says, "So I ran the tap and poured cold water over her head to make her wake up, like I saw on Fireman Sam then the teacher ran in. She picked up Lily-Grace and smashed a button which made an alarm go off really loudly."

Exhausted from talking for so long, she starts sobbing again. I wrap her inside Sara's cardigan and stroke her hair saying, "It's OK, baby, Mummy is here," over and over until she calms down.

"We had been collecting newspapers for the lucky dip at the Christmas fayre," Mrs Peacock says quietly. "Rudy's class were doing a project on wildlife earlier this week. The magnifying glasses had been left out. The fire officer thinks refracted light from the lens got projected onto the paper when it fell on the floor and that was what caused the fire." She looks pale, the peach lipstick and tidy demeanour long gone.

"Is Lily-Grace OK?" I ask, looking down to see Roo's eyes fluttering.

"Yes, thanks to Roo. She knocked herself out on the table when she jumped, but your daughter's quick thinking saved her from getting badly burned."

"Where is she?"

"She is in the ambulance."

We sit in silence with me trying to take it all in, Roo half asleep in my arms. After ten minutes the door opens and a medic approaches us.

"Is this the heroine?" he asks, crouching down to smile at Roo.

She wakes and pushes her fringe out her eyes to look up at him.

"Would you like to come for a ride in an ambulance, little lady?"

She looks at me unsure.

"We would like to check her along with Lily-Grace, just to make sure she's OK," the medic says.

"Would you like to baby? Lily-Grace will be in the ambulance too. I'm sure she would love to see you."

"She sure would. She has been asking for her best friend Roo. I've been sent here specially to collect you." The medic smiles.

Roo stops crying. "Me?" she asks softly.

"Are you Roo?" the medic asks, winking at me.

When we get to the ambulance we see Wendy sitting next to Lily-Grace's stretcher sobbing. She looks up when she sees me and Roo.

"Rudy, Peta. I … I"

"It's OK." I sit beside her and take her hand, knowing what she wants to say.

Both girls are checked over thoroughly by the doctors and declared to be fine and fit to go home. I realise my car is abandoned miles away, and looking at the time I see pre-school finished an hour ago.

Fuck. Where is Pip? I did not ask anyone to collect her.

Panicking, I reach for my phone, but there is already a message from Faith saying that they know about the fire and that Pip is safe at home with her making butterfly cakes.

Just then Jimmy bursts through the door, panting "ROO!!" He shouts when he sees her, his voice breaking.

"DADDY, I SAVED A FIRE!" she shouts back. He sinks to his knees and buries his face in her hair like I did and tears I did not think I had left in me fall down my cheeks.

"I came as soon as I heard," he says, looking at me over the top of Roo's head.

I nod but say nothing.

We say goodbye to Wendy and Lily-Grace, promising to meet them the next day. The fire was too small to do any real damage but the school is still closed until further notice. The girls discuss where they will go and what they will do as we wait for Roo's cream to be dispatched from the pharmacy.

"My car is this way," says Jimmy as we walk out the dim lighting of the hospital and into the afternoon sunshine. I'm exhausted as I walk across the parking lot to his car. It must show. He peels Roo from my arms onto his shoulders and guides me with his hand on the small of my back.

We drive home in silence, the smell of smoke filling up the car.

I tell Jimmy that Pip is at Faith's house. She comes to the car when she sees us pull up. Pip is covered in icing. She clambers in the back next to her sister. "I made you a butterfly for being a brave," she says to Roo, passing her a tin foil parcel.

I offer Faith a watery smile. She squeezes my arm in return and says to call her later.

It's late by the time we walk through the door. Wojtek is at our house watching TV. I put Juno and Pip straight to bed. They don't protest when I tuck them in, removing shoes and socks and leggings, pulling the covers up to their chins.

I bathe Roo while Jimmy goes to collect my car. She is almost asleep in my arms as I wash her, careful to avoid her sore hands. It's been a long time since I carried her to bed. Her yellow hair fans out on the pillow and she is asleep within in seconds.

I must have fallen asleep with her because when I open my eyes the birds are singing and the sun is glowing behind the curtain. I am hot and disorientated, then yesterday comes flooding back and suddenly I am wide awake. I look down at Roo, still snoring gently next to me.

Pip and Juno are also still out for the count.

It seems there is no avoiding it. I gear myself up to face Jimmy, who did not come home, and was with Meg when I called him, because our daughter had been involved in a fire. With each realisation I get more angry. I throw open our bedroom door, but the bed is empty. No one even slept in it last night.

Feeling sick, I stumble downstairs and see he has left me a note. *I'll be back later. Got some things to sort. Love to Roo x*

I stare at the note, knowing where he has gone. To her, to Meg. Maybe the outcome is different now. Maybe the fire has made him realise he can't leave us, can't leave his children, but I can't sit around and wait for him to come back any longer. After months of feeling exhausted, I am suddenly filled with adrenaline, like I've been shaken awake from a deep sleep.

I'll go and stay with Heather in Wales I decide as I put the kettle on and pull Sara's mug from its hook. I'd planned to take the girls away in the holidays. There is no reason not to. I desperately want to get away for a while, get my head around everything that has been happening.

The Welsh schools break up the week before we do anyway, so her kids will already be off.

YES. LOVE TO HAVE YOU. COME ASAP. I'LL SET UP THE

CARAVAN, she shouts back in capital letters as soon as I text to ask.

Pip and Juno are delirious with excitement when I tell them. Well Pip is, Juno does not really know what is going on. She just runs round the kitchen shouting 'rabbits' as normal. Roo is quiet when I tell her.

"What's up, baby? Don't you want to go?"

"I don't want to leave Lily-Grace, in case when I come back she is not my best friend again."

I ring Wendy who happily passes the phone over to Lily-Grace so she can confirm that her and Roo will be best friends forever. When they have finished speaking, Wendy comes back on the line.

"Peta, I'd like to throw a party for Roo, to thank her. A hero's party. I know that it's her birthday soon." She pauses, tearful. "I'll do it all. I'll make the food and the cake. She likes dogs right? It's nothing, but I want to show Roo how brave I think she is. I want to thank her …" Wendy breaks off and I can tell she is crying.

"I think it's a great idea," I tell her.

"What is a great idea?" Roo asks next to me.

"It's a surprise."

"Are you okay, Peta?" Wendy asks me when I come back on the phone. "It must have been such an awful shock for you." I take a second to compose myself. "Yes fine, just so relieved the girls are OK. What food were you thinking of making?" I steer her back onto the safe topic of food and we chat for ten minutes more until Roo pulls at my arm and begs me to make her some jammy toast.

"Wendy, I've got to go. I'll call you as soon as we are home and we can organise a play date for the girls, oh hang on, Roo wants to say bye to Lily-Grace, again …"

"Can Jake come to the holiday?" Pip asks over breakfast.

I take a sip of orange juice and consider it briefly, but then dismiss the idea. I need to focus on me and the girls. Plus I want to get on the road as soon as possible. I plan to let Jimmy know I am going, but after I am far enough away that he can't stop me. I know he won't come after me. As his note said, he has things to sort out.

"Not this time, poppet, next time, now eat up and go and pack your essential items for the car," I tell them, standing to collect the plates. "Roo, does Spike want these crusts?"

The girls race upstairs to pack, and come back down with backpacks so weighed down with things they don't need, they can hardly stay upright. Roo has even packed a carriage clock in hers.

"But baby, you can't tell the time?"

"Solly can though, Mummy, and I want him to teach me." Solly is Heather's oldest son. He and Roo are great friends. She lets him wear her dressing up clothes and he lets her wear their dog's collar. It's a match made in heaven.

"I've packed Solly the Cinderella dress," she says as I strap her in the car.

"That is very nice of you, how's the hand?" she holds up her thin bandage and waves it at me. "Fine"

"Right then, is everybody ready?" I say in the voice of Daddy Pig.

I text Jimmy from a service station and tell him where we are going. I try and make it sound like a treat for Roo after the fire, time for us to recover.

How long will you be gone for?

I think a week, not sure yet. Let you know.

I'm just about to drive out the forecourt when my phone beeps.

Drive safe. Kiss to the girls.

It's a very long way from Brighton to Wales. Especially when you have to stop at every service station on the way because someone needs a wee. Each time I pull up, get everyone out, to the toilet, then back to the car again, it adds another half hour onto the journey. Juno keeps running off to the cake counter in Starbucks, Roo wants to buy all the fluffy toys in Smiths and Pip wants sweets from the pick 'n' mix.

We finally arrive in Wales, hot, sticky and sick of each other, and the DVD of Kipper, which has been on repeat for five hours.

The girls roll out the car and run off to find Solly, Arlo and Digby.

Heather takes my bag and ushers me into the house where the kettle is whistling on the hob and a plate of homemade millionaire's shortbread is waiting for me.

I sink into the armchair by the Aga and gratefully take the tea she is holding out.

"Welcome."

"Thank you."

"Was it awful?"

"Yes."

"You look battered."

"I look like I fell out a bin."

"You do a bit. Did you?"

"No, but I nearly fell in one after Pip accidentally threw away one of her Monica pocket dolls."

"Well she won't find any Polly Pocket dolls here. This house is full of tanks, Lego and cars."

"I'll toast to that."

We spend the evening preparing dinner together and catching up, taking plates stacked high with food out into her back garden; one of my new favourite places in the whole world. It has a huge pond with an island in the middle that ducks nest on. There is an old fashioned gypsy wagon in the corner, and round the edge of it all, like bunting, is a line full of football shirts and mismatching socks that swing in the breeze and scent the garden with a clean washing smell.

We eat in silence for ten minutes, save for cutlery scraping and the odd appreciative sigh.

"I'm stuffed," I announce, as I eat the last bit of pulled pork. "You are an amazing cook."

"So are you."

"But not like this."

"Pete, you buffoon. This is your recipe. Don't you remember?" Heather chides as she tops up my wine glass.

"No, but then I barely remember my own name these days." I shoo a fly from my wineglass and take a sip. "Things were crazy enough before the fire." I still can't think about it without feeling tearful. I take another gulp and smile weakly at Heather.

"Well they're not going to be crazy this week. What do you want to do tomorrow?"

I put down my glass, stretch my arms languidly above my head and watch birds soar across the sherbet orange sky.

Roo is running round on all fours with the dog collar on. Solly is chasing her dressed up as Cinderella. Pip and Arlo found tadpoles in the pond and are busy transferring them into jars. Juno and Heather's baby Digby are sitting at our feet, playing with daisies in the long grass. I close my eyes tightly and can almost forget all that I ran away from.

"Just lots of this. Lots and lots of this please."

As the week continues I feel the tension loosen from my shoulders. I wake in the morning with the sun across my face and take my morning tea out to the gypsy caravan to drink on the wooden steps. No alarms. No school runs. No packed lunches. No Skype meetings with Michelle and Helen. The kids stay up and sleep in late. We fall into the habit of walking on the beach after a breakfast of croissants and homemade jam. The girls love the white sand. "Why don't we have sand on our beach, Mummy?" Roo asks. I mumble something about the sun and the tide. Solly the smartass says, "That's not right, Roo's mummy. It's because Brighton has flint bedrock so the stones on the beach are flint. Wales has sandstone bedrock, so we get sand. Dover has a chalk bedrock so …"

"I know, we can take your sand back with us!" interrupts Roo, then runs off with a bucket to collect a beach in.

We spend a morning at the Science Museum in Cardiff Bay. Juno is fascinated with the coloured water, while Pip loves the magnets. Heather and I sit watching them explore and marvel at their beauty. We decided long ago that our children are going to get married and spend a happy hour and a half planning cakes and dresses and table settings.

I send Jimmy a photo of the girls every day. I can't bring myself to compose a nice text to him. When Heather asks about him and his work I am vague and quickly change the subject. I want to talk about it but I don't know where to start, so it's somewhat of a relief when on our last evening Heather says casually, "Such a shame you have to go tomorrow, and are you ever going to tell me what's going on with Jimmy?"

"That obvious, huh?" I say, poking at my ice cream.

"You've got 'I ran away' written all over you," Heather says. "Now spill it."

"God, where do I start?"

"At the beginning, hang on… "

She passes me a box of tissues, and re-fills our wine glasses. Then she slings six packets of Skips up the stairs and a bumper sized bag of marshmallows.

"SNACK TIME!" she hollers. Six pairs of feet come charging along the hallway followed by cries of delight and "Midnight feast!"

"Right, that should buy us twenty minutes," she says, coming to sit in the chair opposite me. "Now talk. And DO NOT leave anything out."

And so I do. I talk for half an hour non-stop. I tell her about Jimmy acting weird and losing weight and finding out about Meg. I tell her about how I hoped it was to do with work as I always have to babysit Jake. I tell her about the conversation I overheard between Jimmy and Meg and employing Morris to follow them. "And then there was the fire, and now here I am," I say, picking at a loose thread on the overstuffed chair. "I just don't think I can bear to go home and find out what is coming next. Sorry," I blub, as tears come from nowhere. I wipe my eyes with my sleeve. "So silly."

"Silly? No it isn't. It's not silly at all. It's your life. It's all you've worked for. Don't cry, lovely." She puts her finger under my chin.

"Look at me, Peta. You are a beautiful, funny, amazing wife and mother. Jimmy won the lottery the day he married you. I was there, remember? You should have seen him pacing about while he waited for you to show up. He was a mess."

I offer a watery smile. "I didn't mean to keep him waiting. His sisters were arguing over the hair-spray and ended up squirting me in the eye."

"He was beside himself that you were going to stand him up. When you finally walked through the door, he looked like his knees were going to buckle."

"Oh no, that was just his shoes. They were pinching his feet. I told him to break them in, but he didn't listen."

"SHUT UP! The point is this. You are a catch. He caught you. I really don't think he wants to let you go. He worships you. This is so out of character." She shakes her head.

"Is it?" I remind her about his Lothario ways when he was younger and we are both silent for a moment. "The thing is, you have never actually asked him what is going on," she says slowly.

"Isn't it obvious? If it looks like a duck and it quacks like a duck, what else could it be?"

"I don't know, sweetie. I wish I did. I do know that you are going to have to be strong and face it though. And you are strong. Have faith in yourself, Peta. You are capable of so much; I don't know why you waste your time at that shit online magazine. I can't bear to read your stuff. It's awful. You should be writing your cookery book. Remember the ideas you had? They were brilliant."

"I don't know what happened. I used to have some balance in my life, but then the kids came along and Jimmy's career took off, and now I feel like my life is being the post that everyone else uses to swing off."

"It is your strength and patience which will get you through this. Believe in yourself, Peta. Whatever is going on, you'll cope, and you know you always have me."

I think over her words as I lay in bed on the last evening. "Time to gather up all your strength, Peta," I tell myself in the darkness. "No more hiding, no more running away."

Heather makes us a packed lunch for the journey home. I put it on the passenger seat and turn to say goodbye. There are lots of tears and tantrums as we get the girls into the car. Solly stands sobbing in Roo's dress. "You can keep it. It looks much better on you," she sniffs.

"Thank you, but I still need the dog collar back," he says.

"Don't leave it so long next time, OK," Heather says, pulling me in close for a last hug. "And remember what I said …" She nods at me. "You can do this."

"I love you," I say meaning it.

"I love you too. And your three gorgeous girlies," she says, leaning in through the open windows of the car to give them each a kiss.

"Drive safely!" she shouts as we pull away, my tyres leaving marks in the sand on their drive.

The journey home is uneventful. All three girls cry hysterically for the first ten minutes but are asleep by the time we cross the toll-bridge, worn out from a week of late nights and no rules. I listen to a play on Radio Four and think over Heather's words. It's not just my relationship with Jimmy that needs to change. I need to change too. I want to be a role model for my daughters, more than a mum who turns up late and smoothes things over with Haribo. I want to have a balance between being a mum and being me. Spending time with Heather reminded me of the plans I had. It's time to put them into action. To be the girl who pushed herself forward in her snazziest outfit to take what she wanted.

I text Jimmy to say we'd be home about 5pm. I was expecting to see his black Audi on the drive, but it was empty. I tell myself that I am grateful for the time. I can have a shower, make a cup of tea and settle the girls. I can put my make-up on and my best push up bra. I will say my piece with dignity.

The children shuffle out the car amidst crumbs and crisp wrappers. I gather bags and follow them up to the front door.

The house smells wrong as we enter. It smells of flowery perfume that I do not wear. I walk through the downstairs living room and up the five steps that lead to the open plan kitchen.

It's tidier than I expected. Maybe his mum came down to help him out, I tell myself, trying to stay calm. I dump bags on the floor and go over to the kettle, a Pavlovian response to walking into the house. The instant coffee is on the side and the lid is off. My mother-in-law drinks instant coffee, but she does not leave the lid off. Nor does she wear the bright red lipstick that is coating the rim of Sara's Cath Kidston mug.

Bastard.

Wojtek is delighted to see us and tell us all about the chickens. I let the kids go on the trampoline in the garden for half an hour while I unpack bedtime teddy bears and Charlie cloths, then throw together an easy supper of fish finger sandwiches. Roo discovered mayonnaise in Wales, and mixes it with her tomato ketchup to make 'Rosemary' sauce'.

After we have eaten, and Roo has spoken to Lily-Grace about her holiday, I put them in front of The Aristocats with blankets and bottles of tea. If and when Jimmy comes home, we can go and talk in the garden.

"Mummy, when is Daddy coming home?" Roo asks me as I check my phone for the tenth time in as many minutes. "I don't know, sweetie," I say, stroking her hair out of her eyes. "You are going to need a haircut, little one. All that sunshine has made you grow, like a lovely flower." She won't be distracted so easily. "But we have not seen Daddy for aaaaages. Lola at school has a daddy that she only sees once in a month. Is our daddy going to be like that daddy?" Roo asks. I don't know what to tell her. In all likelihood the answer is yes, but I don't feel ready or equipped to be having this conversation right now. Instead of answering I say, "Lola, is she the one who smells of cheese?"

It works and Roo giggles. "No Mummy, that is Zac."

I force my face to look contrite. "Oh yes, Zac, silly me. Do you think it's his feet, or his hair or what?"

They finally fall asleep in the second showing of Peter Pan and I manage to get them up into bed without them stirring. I'm just turning on the radio for company when Roo comes back downstairs to ask for a drink. Her face falls when she sees mine. "Mummy, you have your cross face on again."

"Sorry Poppet." I try and smile at her, but I seem to have forgotten how to do it. I try a wink instead.

"I liked your pretty face that you had on in Wales. Did you leave it there? Shall we go and get it, Mummy?"

I pour her a beaker of water. "That is very sweet of you baby. Mummy is fine, just a bit tired from all the driving."

She takes a big sip and passes it back to me. "Will you be OK on your own, or shall I stay up and keep you company?" I manage to persuade her that I am fine and it's already very late and she will have no energy for her play date with Lily-Grace if she does not get back to bed.

"Will you come with me please, Mummy?" she asks, holding out her hand. I lie with her until she is asleep and then I drink enough wine to knock myself out.

"Mummy, Mummy, it's the morning. We are not in Wales. Where is Daddy? What's for breakfast? Can we go swimming? Where did you put my sand for the beach?" Roo punctuates each statement with a leap on the bed. My head pounds, my mouth is dry and Jimmy is still not home.

What do I tell them? I have no idea where their father is and I can't keep fobbing them off. This time I tell her he is trying to find a Build-a-Bear wardrobe full of clothes. She leaps off the bed to go and tell her sisters. I go downstairs to leave message after message on his phone: "Jimmy, what is going on? Why aren't you coming home? Me and the kids are worried sick."

I spend £200 on the emergency credit card I promised not to use on a Build-a-Bear wardrobe and outfits to fill it from their website and feel smug at how annoyed Jimmy will be when he sees the receipt. Then I order a massive food shop and 'Blogging for beginners' from Amazon.

Roo goes off to play at Lily-Grace's. Wendy invites me in for a coffee but I tell her I have loads of stuff to sort out. I am feeling too wobbly to be with people. I might start blurting out what is going on with Jimmy.

Pip and I walk along the underpass to Ovingdean Café for an ice lolly and then collect driftwood on the beach. Juno gets in and out the buggy and throws her sun hat on the ground each time I try and put it on her head.

Every ten minutes I try Jimmy's phone and Joe's phone but they are switched off. The office number is engaged every time I try and ring it.

I collect Roo on the way home from the beach and, to stall for time, we walk through Kipling Gardens to look at the flowers. I tell them any that are on the floor can go home into the flower press but picking them is a big no.

When I can draw it out no longer, we make our way along the road and see the drive is still empty.

The phone rings at 4 pm, as Roo and Pip are pressing their flowers and Juno is snoring on the rug in a patch of sun. I snatch it off the hook. "Jimmy?"

"Hi, Peta. It's Jake."

"Oh Jake, hi. Hi, sweetie, how are you?" I'm not as warm as I want to sound, but I need to get him off the phone in case Jimmy rings.

"Can I come and see you please, Peta?"

"Now is not really a good time Jake. I have a lot going on."

"Please, Peta. Dad's not here. He said not to tell you but I'm scared now."

"What do you mean, Joe is not there?"

"He has not been here for weeks and weeks."

"Well who has been looking after you?" I sink onto the sofa confused.

"You have mostly, and when not you, then Auntie Maria. Can I come to you now, please?"

"Of course. If it's okay with Maria, I'll come and pick you up."

"I'll get a taxi, Dad left me money."

"Are you sure? Do you know how to do that? Our address?"

"Yes, see you soon." He is gone before I can ask him anything else.

I put the phone down more confused than ever. Joe has not been home for weeks? Where is he? Why would Jimmy not tell me about this? There must be some connection between Jimmy, Meg and Joe but I can't work out what it is.

I'm still trying to piece it all together when Jake arrives.

He has nothing with him except his bed-time dog. He looks older than when I last saw him. His clothes creased and baggy. He runs into my arms, almost knocking me over.

"I'm scared, Peta. I'm so scared" I hold him against me tightly and stroke the top of his head.

"Why didn't you tell me Joe has not been at home? I could have done more to help you?"

"He told me not to."

"Well, you could have told Jimmy."

"Jimmy knows."

"He knows?"

"Yes, Jimmy knows everything."

Jake starts sobbing and the girls come to find us. "Jake!" Roo shrieks when she sees him. "I saved a fire! Have you brought Spike with you? Did he tell you about Wales?"

"Give us a minute, Pops," I tell her. "Jake is feeling a little bit sad."

"It's OK." He pulls himself from my arms. "I want to see them. I missed them." He lets himself be led away by Pip and Roo. I watch them make their way up the garden and suddenly have a horrible feeling that I am dealing with something worse than an affair.

I don't want to push Jake for more information. He looks exhausted and fragile, but I am desperate to know what is going on.

I prepare some snack bowls for lunch, using breadsticks and cheese to make monster faces and take it up the garden with a jug of banana milkshake.

Jake comes out the tree-house and helps me lay out a blanket on the grass.

"He steals your eggs you know, Wojtek, when you are not here, and eats them in an omelette when his wife is not looking," Jake tells me quietly, pouring himself a drink.

"I knew it!"

"It's because she has put him on a diet."

"How do you know all this?"

"He told me. He thinks I can't speak English because I am so dark skinned."

"Ah. I see." We laugh and then in the silence that follows, I say, "Jake, about your dad …"

"Can we please talk about it later?" he asks, shoving a cracker loaded with cheese and pickle in his mouth.

"Yes, of course," I say, backing off and mentally kicking myself for pushing him. I know his diversion technique only too well.

I go inside to get the ice cream out and check my phone again. I text Jimmy to say that Jake is with me and I know Joe is not well and to please call me and tell me what is going on.

Jake avoids me for the rest of the afternoon, staying up in the tree-house with Roo. Whatever he knows he is not ready, or does not want to share, and I cannot push him.

I make macaroni cheese for dinner and chocolate popcorn to eat in front of a film after. They want to watch Homeward Bound again.

"It's Spike's favourite," Jake explains. Whenever anyone mentions Spike, Pip gets up and goes round the house, doing tai chi moves and patting the air. It makes Jake laugh and his whole face changes. He came to me for this, not to be questioned.

I bathe the girls and offer to run a bath for Jake. "I'll shower later," he tells me in a no nonsense tone. I sit and towel dry the girl's hair on my bed while they bicker over nightdresses. "And I'll read to them," he adds. I smile gratefully and go downstairs to see a blank screen on my phone. No messages and no missed calls.

I sit on the bar stool and start sobbing, then remind myself Jake might see or hear. Me falling to pieces is the last thing he needs right now. He came here for some normality.

I force myself to get up and start tidying up the mess of the day, pegging out washing in the dusky evening light, smiling at Jake's Batman t-shirt on the line next to Roo's sparkly tu-tu and cape. I must go and get him some school uniform from Marks and Spencer if he is going to be here with us after the summer as much as he is now, and I must try to speak to this Spanish aunt of his. Maybe she will have some answers. I will wait till he is asleep and then call her.

Chapter Twelve

"JIMMY?"

"Peta?"

I look at the clock on the wall, its 2 am. "Where the fuck have you been? What is going on?"

"Peta, please. I know you are cross, and I know you are mad but I need you. I need you to calm down and listen to me."

Jimmy looks twenty years older than when I last saw him.

"What has happened?" I take a breath and try to calm down.

"Joe is not well."

"Jake is upstairs," I say in a low voice.

"Good, he got here."

"You knew he was coming?"

"It was all part of the plan."

"What bloody plan? What the fuck is going on?" My voice is getting louder again.

Jimmy sits down on the sofa and takes my hands in his. He looks me in the eye and says slowly, "Peta, Joe has cancer. He is dying."

Things fall into place like a domino rally being knocked over. Joe's absences and shortness of breath. Us having Jake all the time. Jimmy being so stressed about work.

"How long have you known?"

"Since January."

"JANUARY?!" I shout, then remember the kids. "Why didn't you tell me?"

"Him and Jake did not want you to know."

"Why not, and why are you telling me now?"

"Because he does not have very long left."

I think of what it must have taken to keep this secret from me. Of the worry he must have been going through all this time.

"Does Jake know Joe is dying?"

"We've not said that, but we have not said that he is not either. Joe thought if we gave Jake hope that he might get better if he went away alone, that Jake would find it easier to leave him and enjoy spending time with you and the girls."

"Shall we take Jake with us to say goodbye?"

"I don't know. It's going to be so hard."

I think about Sara and the last time she saw her children. I am sure that if she had the choice, her last words would not have been, "Don't slam the door!"

"I think we should," I say. "If we don't he may resent us for it when he is older."

Jimmy looks unsure. "Joe did not say what he wanted. I know he spoke with Jake, but I don't know if that was the last time he planned to see him."

I take his hand. It's trembling. "I'm making this decision for you. Go ask Wojtek to sit with the girls. I'll get Jake." I squeeze his hand and then let it go.

While Jimmy is next door explaining the situation to Wojtek,

I tiptoe into his room and shake Jake gently on the shoulder. He mutters something unintelligible and rolls over.

"Jake sweetie, you need to wake up." I hate this. Waking him up to tell him his dad is dying. Waking him up to tell him his dad is going to sleep.

He opens an eye and mumbles, "Wanna sleep."

"Jake, baby" I sit down on the edge of the bed and put my hand on his shoulder. "Your dad wants you ... we ..." I don't even finish the sentence. Jake jumps up as if he has been stung. I hand him some crumpled cargo shorts from the floor and his Superman t-shirt.

"I wish it would make me a superhero," he said as he slid it on.

I grab his jumper and bedtime dog.

Jimmy is waiting by the door, anxious to get on the road. Jake pauses as he steps outside. "He is not going to get better, is he?"

"No mate, he's not," Jimmy says, then puts his arm round him and they walk down to the car.

As he straps his seatbelt in, Jake says, "I thought if I just did what everyone said and pretended it was not happening, that everything would get better. I was stupid."

I think about how I have been acting for the last few months and say, "No Jake, it was not stupid. It was all you could do."

As we fly through the deserted streets, I think of all the times Jimmy has made this journey without me by his side. How hard it must have been for him, knowing what he was going to have to face, and then having to compose himself to walk through the door at home and face me afterwards.

Tied to a promise to his best friend. I think about Sara and if I could have done this for her. I thought her death was the worst way a death could ever happen, but now I am not so sure. To see someone you love deteriorate before your eyes. To know they are going to die, and that each time you see them they will be a closer to that end, what must that be like?

I've no time to do this now. Jimmy has held it together all year. I just need to hold it together for the last bit, and I will. I look ahead at the tail lights in front, willing them to move quicker.

Jake is silent in the back, and I wonder what he is thinking. I put my hand round the back of the seat and squeeze his knee, then bring it back to rest on top of Jimmy's.

The place we pull up outside does not look like a hospital. It's lit up like a Christmas tree. 133, Seymour Street is a beautiful old building with stained glass windows in the porch and large flagstone tiles on the floor. The front gardens are meticulously maintained. Topiary bushes line the drive, window boxes burst with colour against the sandstone walls.

"Wow."

"Great, isn't it? Joe's room has a sea view."

We talk quietly as we walk up the driveway. Jake lags behind, clutching his bedtime dog. I don't want to rush him. "Has he been here before?" I ask Jimmy, as Jake stops to look at the fountain.

"No."

"How did you find this place?"

"Meg did." Jimmy takes a deep breath and then says, "She's Joe's daughter."

"She's what?"

"He did not know about her until he got a Facebook message from a woman who went on holiday to Spain one summer way back when. They had a bit of a fling and the message said she had something to tell him." Jimmy smiles sadly. "It was when he and Monica were struggling to get pregnant. Joe did not feel it was the right time to meet his daughter, and then after Monica died he was such a mess he did not feel in the right place to welcome her into his life as he would have liked. But then once he was diagnosed with cancer, he asked me to track Meg down. Family for Jake. She came within a week of me contacting her. She has not left his side since," he finishes with a shrug.

"Even with her around to help, I can't believe you have been doing all this on your own. Taking him to chemo, looking after Jake. Trying to sort out all the insurance and stuff at work. Why didn't you tell me, why didn't you share this with me?"

"Joe and Jake did not want me to, and honestly, I don't think you could have handled it, Pete. You're still dealing with Sara. I'm not judging you for that, but seeing Joe go through all this would have been more than you could bear. Lord knows you've enough on your plate. I asked Joe so many times to tell you, but he was adamant."

I think of the conversation we had at the beginning of the year when I ordered him to never die and leave me. Was this Joe's way of trying to protect me?

"He doesn't want Jake to know about Meg yet. She's keen to have a relationship with him, and in time she will tell him, but Jake has got a hard time ahead. It might be too much for him to find out he has a big sister right now, but it will be good for him to know he has some real family left when the time comes to tell him."

"We are his real family now," I say to Jimmy. "We are adopting him, right?"

He stops walking and looks at me.

"Could you cope?" Jimmy's voice is almost a whisper.

"We'll cope," I tell him.

"Are you sure? It's not going to be easy. He's never had a mum, and now he's losing his dad."

"I will be his mum." I pause because Jake is getting within earshot. "Will Meg be here now?"

"Yes, she is with him all the time. Come on this way."

I reach for Jake's hand and give it a squeeze.

"It will be OK, baby" I tell him. He gulps.

Jimmy speaks to the receptionist who clearly knows him well. "Hi Jimmy, good to see you. Go on through, he has been asking for you." She smiles at me. When she sees Jake clutching my hand and his bedtime dog I see her eyes well up with tears.

There is no smell of death in the maze of corridors we follow Jimmy down. I vividly remember going to visit my great-grandmother Tick in a nursing home in Newcastle. The smell of urine and vegetables and decay was so strong you could almost taste it, and you left with an oily slick of it on your hair and clothes. This place is nothing like that.

The pictures that line the walls here are not the generic ones seen in hospitals and care homes. They are paintings done by the patients of the sights they are looking forward to seeing again. Beautiful sunsets and crumbling cottages. Mountains and stormy seas. Faces of friends, family, and pets. There is tapestry too in the richest of colours. This does not seem like a place to die. It seems like a place to come and celebrate life.

Finally we come to Joe's door. It has his name on it in beautiful italic font, with a picture of a sombrero next to it.

"Jean does them. She is the resident comic."

"You know all the people here?"

"Most of them. Are you ready?"

"I think so," I say, but I'm not sure. The last time I was close to death was when Sara was on the floor in front of me. I am petrified to go back there again, but I have no choice and I have to remember however hard it is for me, it's a million times harder for Jake, who stops abruptly just before the door opens.

"I need a wee," he bursts out, looking at me desperately, buying some time.

"I'll take him," Jimmy says.

"You sure?" I look at Jake who nods at me. His eyes are huge in his face. They turn and walk back down the corridor. I take a deep breath and push open the door.

The room is big and white, save for one yellow wall at the back where the headboard rests. Rather than the plastic chairs used in hospitals, this room has overstuffed armchairs for people to sit on. Flowers are everywhere and I recognise lots of furniture from Joe's home. Mugs, side table. Photos of Monica pregnant and then of Jake back in Spain. The room smells of Issi Miyake, of Joe.

I force myself to look at the bed where he is sleeping. He looks half the size he was when I last saw him, almost smaller than Jake. All his beautiful long black hair has gone, his tan too. He is translucent, skin the colour of tracing paper. I stifle a gasp and turn away. My legs wobble and I desperately want to run.

Be brave, I tell myself. Be brave be brave be brave.

Cautiously, I approach the bed. Joe seems peaceful amongst the tubes and wires which are attached to him and the various machines that hum. There is a cannula in his arm, attached to a bag of clear fluid.

Monica's crochet blanket is over his bed. I sit down on the chair next to his pillow and stroke a silky square of her handiwork.

"Hey, Joe," I say, throat burning. Minutes pass before I can speak again. "I can't believe you're in here. That you have been in here all this time and I did not know." I wipe my face on my sleeve, wanting to hold his hand, but scared I will hurt him. "I can't believe you even thought of going without saying goodbye to me. I'm so fucking mad at you," I tell him fiercely. "I thought we had something. I thought we were friends." I'm sobbing openly now. "All this year you've been dying and I never knew. All those times you did not turn up, or cancelled last minute. I didn't know what was going on. The lies you told me. I could have helped." His face remains expressionless. "I could have come here and seen you, massaged your feet, helped you with the crossword. You are terrible at crosswords. Oh why are you fucking dying?" I want to shake him, to make him wake up. I want to rip out all the wires and see his eyes ping open. I'm panting as if I've been running. "Fuck. Sorry, Jake might walk in any second." I pluck a tissue from the box by his bed and blow my nose. "I love that boy, Joe."

I tell Joe about the bond he has made with the girls and all the fun he has and how I am teaching him to cook a roast dinner and he is teaching me to cook Spanish. "I promise you on my life, that I will love him with all the anxiety, passion and partially-poor parenting that I love my girls with. He will never be lonely, he will never be homeless and he will never be without a friend or a pound in his back-pocket." I lean over and touch Joe's tracing-paper cheek.

I don't know what else to say so we sit in silence for a moment. As if he had been listening, the door gently opens and Jimmy walks in holding Jake's hand.

"Hey Jake, come on over, sweetie." I reach out an arm to him, but he won't let go of Jimmy's hand.

"Hey old man," Jimmy says, stooping down to give Joe and kiss on the forehead. "I brought someone to see you." Jimmy is so natural with Joe, he moves with confidence around all the tubes and machines.

Jake approaches the bed slowly. He is biting his lip but he is not crying. I move back and let him have some space.

Jake says nothing for a long time, then asks, "Can I touch him?"

"Of course" says Jimmy, making space. Very carefully, avoiding all the wires, Jake climbs up and slips onto the bed next to his dad, then rolls over on to his side and lays his head on Joe's chest. "Hello, Papi," he whispers quietly. And then the tears come.

I stand watching helplessly, not knowing if I should go and comfort Jake or let him do what he needs to.

"In a film his eyes would open right now." I look up to see Meg in the doorway. I smile at her and she nods at me. This must have been so hard for her too. Her dad finally getting in contact with her, and then finding out he was dying. To be given Joe and then have him snatched away again. What must that feel like?

Meg must have put her whole life on hold all this time. I wonder if she has a family of her own and what she is going to do now.

She looks at Jake lying with Joe and her eyes fill with tears.

"Have you met Jake before?"

"Only at the zoo, and then I was introduced to him as a PA."

"What do you do really?"

"Right now, I'm a nurse. In my other life I work in Tesco." How unglamorous, I think to myself.

"Where is your other life? I mean, where do you live?" I feel like I am interviewing her, but I can't seem to stop.

"In Reading." More and more unglamorous by the second.

"I went to a festival there once," I say inanely.

"Oh yeah, right," Meg says fiddling with the corner of the bed sheet. I see her nails are bitten down to the quick. She is nothing like I thought she would be. Up close her skin is covered in pimples and her breath smells of cigarettes. I hate myself for my relief.

"I'm just going to catch up with Dad's doctor," she says. I almost recoil at her words. It seems so wrong to hear her call Joe that. Jake always calls him Papi, but I guess that would be even more wrong.

When she has left I sink into a chair in the far corner of the room, to give Jake some space.

"How long since he gave up the chemo?" I ask Jimmy quietly. "After the first round. He hated it. His hair came out and he felt so ill all the time. It stopped him from being able to think clearly and he wanted to sort out all his work affairs and enjoy any time with Jake. He said the pain was easier."

"Did you try and change his mind?" I trace patterns in the chair with my finger.

"You know Joe. Once his mind is made up, nothing can stop him. Look how he moved over here and made a new life on the toss of a coin." I look over to the bed where he and Jake are laying together.

"It must have killed him to send Jake to us all the time. Did he not want to cherish every second he had left?"

"Yes, but he knew if he did that, Jake would feel even more alone after. He wanted to know that Jake was happy before he …" Jimmy might have accepted what was going to happen, but he still found it hard to say the words.

"He has been happy," I say. "I just hope he can be happy again."

Meg comes back and joins us. "Doc says he will pop in and see Dad at the end of his round." She flops into a chair opposite me. Jake is whispering quietly in Spanish. Joe has not stirred.

We talk about when he and Jimmy first started working together. How they met in a Starbucks and got chatting. How when they first launched the company they ran it from our front room, and Joe would refuse to do any work until I made him my eggs Benedict.

I used to answer the phone then, to try and make them look busier and bigger than they were. We used to stay up late at night, eating Spanish omelette and working on tenders, faking case studies and client quotes. Joe had a way of winging it which always worked for him.

He used to start work after he had dropped Jake at school, and leave to pick him up at 3 pm, never working an hour over or attending a meeting in his 'Jake time'.

At 3 pm Friday his phone would be off, until 9 am Monday morning. It would drive Jimmy mad when he had a question to ask but Joe was adamant. "This is the Spanish way," Joe would tell him. "Go enjoy your family, Jimmy." But Jimmy could not. He always kept his phone on. I wonder if he regrets it now.

Joe never really liked it when the business got bigger and more corporate, which is inevitable when companies grow. He did not understand it. He never went to London for meetings, and refused to wear a suit. He always wore a floral shirt, open at the neck and beach shorts. Even after all these years of shitty English weather, he never lost his tan, until now.

"Remember the songs he used to make up?" I say from nowhere. When Jimmy was stressing about a deadline or a contract manager who needed impressing, and would push Joe for ideas, Joe would pick up his guitar and sing some old Spanish love song instead.

It used to drive Jimmy mad, but it worked. By taking his mind off it for a minute, Jimmy would always end with the answer he needed.

Joe interviewed all of the original staff, employing them on whether or not he felt a connection with them. Even the ones who spoke next to no English. "I feel them. They are a good person. They will work hard for us." Jimmy would sigh and write up the contracts.

"How are you going to cope at work?"

"Joe and I have it sorted. We have a five year plan and ten year plan in place, and we have recruited internally for people to come and form a board of directors. I'll never have his vision. No one will. It will take five or six people just to try and put in the passion he had for his business. He has picked the people though, which is something. We will not stop, it cannot stop."

Joe's machine beeps, shattering the silence which has fallen over us. "What does that mean? "I ask, alarmed.

"Nothing, it's fine. It's just letting us know his morphine is running low. He may make some movements in a sec. It's time to move, Jake." A nurse comes in just as Jimmy shifts the covers and slides Jake out from the bed.

Joe moans softly and Jake wakes instantly and flies to his side, reaching out to hold his hand.

"Papi?"

Joe does not answer but his hand flickers under Jake's, like a candle going out.

"He is saying goodbye to you," Meg says softly.

The nurse adjusts wires and makes notes, her flat shoes padding softly round the bed.

We stay another hour after she has gone, Jake holding Joe's hand the whole time, in case it moves again, but Joe does not stir.

I don't want to sit and wait for beeping machines to tell us he is no longer in the room. He already left anyway.

Even so, I refuse to say goodbye. Instead I tell him that I love him and I will see him soon.

"Night, old man," Jimmy says, touching the back of his hand. "Sweet dreams." His goodbye is light, but I guess he has had a long time to practise.

Jake walks out as if he is in a trance. I look at Jimmy and he stops to pick him up.

"Hey, you left bedtime bear." I say. "Want me to go get him?"

"No, I left him to look after Papi."

Meg is still there as we leave. She wanted to wait. "I don't want him to be on his own, you know?" Her fingers go to her mouth, gnawing away anxiously. She is no more than a child herself, I realise.

"Well call me anytime, if you need anything," I say, touching her on the arm as I pass.

We walk through the maze of corridors not saying much, all lost in our own private thoughts.

In the car I play Nick Cave and Jimmy keeps his hand on my leg as we drive through darkened streets. It feels warm and safe and strong. All the things I need. Can I be the same for him, the same for Jake?

Going home, all the street-lamps are on. When we get to the seafront road, their yellow light makes the waves look black. I wind down the window and let the breeze fill the car. I turn round to look in the back and Jake has found one of Pip's Charlie Cloths and is sitting underneath it.

Chapter Thirteen

THE next couple of days are hard. Jimmy offers to take Jake back to see Joe again, but Jake clings to me and refuses to go. I thought he might want to see his dad as much as possible while he still can, but when I ask him he says, "That man is not my dad".

So we shut the doors and close in together. To start with Jimmy and I shadow Jake round the house, but when he asks if he can go to the tree-house, we realise he just wants to be alone.

I bake things I think he might eat. Jimmy sorts more paperwork. The girls wander round a bit lost and confused.

Roo comes into the kitchen as I am taking some cherry scones out the oven. "Why is Jake sad?" she asks. I try and explain about Joe being poorly without using words that might scare her. I don't know how much of it Roo understands but once we have finished speaking she asks for her pencils and then spends half an hour at the table deep in concentration. When I walk past I see that she has drawn a picture of me, her, Pip, and Juno. Jake is right in the middle of us all under Jimmy's arm and at the bottom she has written: *To Jake, Yoo can shar my dady, Lov Roo xxx*

"Can I go and give it to him?" she asks.

"Yes, baby, and take him this." I pass her a packed lunch.

Jimmy comes out the study and we watch Roo solemnly make her way up the garden, her drawing balanced on top of the lunchbox. She hesitates before him, her skirt blowing in the breeze. Mouths move in a conversation I cannot hear and then she passes him the drawing.

Jake stares at it for a long time. I can see from the way his head moves that he is crying. Roo looks very worried, but then he shuffles slightly closer so she has room to sit next to him, and takes hold of her hand.

That night Jake pins Roo's picture up on the cork board in his room. Next to it is the letter Joe wrote to him. I don't know what it says, but Jake reads it every night before he goes to sleep. Then he kisses the photo of him and his dad together that we put by his bed.

I am grateful now for the way Joe and Jimmy planned things. If I had known Joe was dying I would not have been able to be easy with Jake. I would have pitied him, and that would have been awful. Without knowing it, I gave Jake normality and no special treatment whatsoever, which is exactly what he needed, and still does.

When the phone rings at 8 am the next morning, we already know it will be to tell us that Joe passed away. Meg was with him and it was very peaceful. The nurse said he never woke again after Jake felt his hand move.

Joe left me a letter too. He said how he saw a lot of Monica in me, and knows I am the perfect mother for his son in place of her since there sadly now must be one. He wrote about friendship and how I was not to feel overwhelmed by the task I was undertaking. "I know you will be worried about raising someone else's child. You will feel the need to protect him that bit more. Don't. Let him get dirty. Let him fall, I know you will be there to pick him up again. Love him with the lioness love you have for your own girls, but never be scared of letting my boy be a boy." As I read it I can hear him saying the words to me.

If he wrote letters to Jimmy, he never said. I think they talked about everything they needed to talk about while Joe was still here. I know the funeral was discussed at great length. Jimmy buried himself in organising everything the second he got off the phone to 133, Seymour Road. I suppose it was his way of coping. Jimmy is a fixer. Give him a problem and he will try and solve it; feelings are a bit harder to repair so easily.

Joe's funeral falls on the last real day of summer. It still dawned bright, but something in the colours of the leaves suggested that the season was fading out.

We arrive early to watch the cars come down the long winding lane to the crematorium. Soon the place is packed out, just like it was for Sara. Another room full of people, full of loss for a life that ended far too soon. I think of all the tears and sorrow the cold crematorium walls have absorbed over the years.

I feel trapped in my pew up at the front, my blue dress tight at my throat all of a sudden. I bend down to get tissues from my bag and try and fight the overwhelming instinct I'm feeling to run away.

For someone who did not know anyone ten years ago here in England, Joe sure made a lot of friends.

It seems everyone who ever knew him is here. The lady who served him his Starbucks coffee is crying as it if was her own husband she was losing. "It might as well have been. He paid me more attention than that miserable bastard indoors ever did."

Clients come in smart office suits and shiny shoes. Suppliers come in their short-sleeved shirts. At the back, mostly in wheelchairs, everyone still well enough to travel from 133 Seymour Road sit together in line holding hands.

The service is short. When Jimmy gets up to speak his hands are shaking. I squeeze his arm as he walks past, but he does not seem to notice. I know Joe must have helped him with the speech because it's full of his humour and stories he loved to tell. In the background as CD of The Eagles play Desperado and people blow discreetly into handkerchiefs.

The wicker coffin is surrounded by flowers. The girls go up to add theirs to it, with no understanding why. Jake's bedtime dog is in the centre and Pip goes to fetch it for him. "No baby, Jake wants to leave it there, my love." She makes a fuss, wanting to reach it. I take her to the back of the room where children's books and wooden toys are heaped in a corner.

As I sit with Juno on my lap reading the story of Jesus and the loaves of bread, I watch Jake thanking people for coming. He was determined to wear his dad's wedding suit, even though it was too big. I was reminded again of Nellie at Sara's funeral. The simplicity of their thoughts; if I dress like a grown up, then I shall be one. As people draw him into their arms, I can see his resolve is weakening; he looks round for me and I immediately stand to go to him, but Jimmy is there first. He lays a comforting hand on Jake's shoulder and takes over the task of thanking people while Jake stands by his side.

People mill about in the car park for ages, talking about what a wonderful service it was and how Joe would have loved it. I remember the same things were said after Sara died. Like then I want to shout. "He would not have loved it! He would have bloody hated it!"

Jimmy hangs back with the stragglers while I drive the kids down to the beach and park up. We have drinks and food laid on at Terraces on the seafront, and once the sun has gone down we go down to the water and light orange sky lanterns. They rise and dance over the waves into the distance beyond. I imagine them travelling all the way back to Spain.

Meg walks over as I am picking up the wrappers from the lanterns. She will be moving away after Christmas. She wants to go to Spain. "He talked about it so much, it feels like home to me already. After all, I was made there."

It's a childish thing to say. I realise again how very young Meg is and how hard this must be for her too.

"What will you do there?"

"Dunno, travel? Work in a bar or be a rep." She shrugs her shoulders. I know Joe left her a bit of money. Jimmy was the executor of the will and made sure she was provided for. "Are you nervous about going on your own? I don't know that I would be brave enough." Meg looks at me scornfully and says, "Of course! Came here on my own, didn't I?"

"Sorry," I say quickly. "I just worry, you know." She smiles slightly and assures me she will be fine. "I'm gonna learn Spanish so maybe I will do some teaching."

I fiddle with the wrapper in my hands, twisting and folding it. The sun is almost in the sea and the air smells of matches and seaweed and chips from the bar.

"Will you come back?" I nod my head in Jake's direction.

"Yes. I will, and he's always welcome to come over and see me." I tell her to get settled first and to let me know if she needs anything from us. I am about to walk back to the restaurant when she says,

"I know you thought Jimmy and me were ... you know ..." She goes red as she says it. I turn away from her embarrassment, and to hide my own. "He never would you know," she says quickly, rushing to get the words out. "Jimmy loves you, he talked about you all the time. You could tell it was killing him to keep it all from you." We stand in silence for a moment, watching the water, letting the words settle between us.

"Thank you," I say finally, turning to face her, but she is already on her way back up to the beach. Jimmy waves at me from the balcony of Terraces and does the sign language for a drink. I nod and hold my finger up to show I'll be there in a minute.

As the day slips into the evening, people start to leave. I ask Jake if he has had enough. "No, I want to stay." He looks done in but I can't force him to leave. "Well come and have something to eat at least." We make our way over to the buffet table and I load him up a plate.

Juno is half asleep as she eats her bread roll. Roo is too distracted by all the lights and chatter. Pip keeps getting up and down from her chair. "What's up?" I ask her. "What are you looking for?" She frowns at me and asks, "Is this a party? I can't find the bouncy castle?" I glance sideways at Jake and am relieved to see he is smiling.

Things have been so busy with him I've not seen Nellie for a while. I don't want her to feel side-lined, but it's hard to juggle everyone and their needs right now. The house is less and less tidy each day. Washing is stacked up all over the place and the sheets all need changing. It does not seem important next to spending time with Jake and the girls, or giving Jimmy my full attention when he talks about the business without Joe.

"What's up?" he asks me one night, as we sit on the deck looking down onto the conservatory. Through it, I can see the kitchen worktops covered in empty plates and bowls. The dining table is hidden under drawing paper and pebbles from the beach. The sofa is covered in army men and Polly Pockets. "Everywhere I look I see a job," I tell him with a sigh. He grins at me in return. "At last," he says. "An easy problem to fix," and goes into the house.

"What are you doing?" I call after him, standing up to see. "I'm getting you a bloody cleaner!" he calls back, tapping away on his iPad. I go to protest, to say I don't need one. To assure him that I can cope, and then I realise that I do need one and I am not coping and actually it would make life a lot easier. When Jimmy comes back out he has a bottle of wine and two glasses with him. I take the opener from between his teeth and tear off the foil. "To Joe," we say as we clink glasses together softly.

"Can I meet Jake?" Nellie asks when get to Sara's bench the next day.

I sit down and think how to word my answer. "If you want to, of course. It might be hard for you though. He is still very raw and I don't want him upset or you upset or …"

"No offence, Peta." She jumps off the bench and stands in front of me with her hands on her hips. "But I *do* know what he is going through. I think I might be able to help."

"Right. Yes, sorry love," I say chastised. "I just don't want to do the wrong thing by either of you."

"You know, Peta, sometimes you need to chill out a bit," she admonishes me. I think how Sara would laugh if she could see and hear Nellie right now, how proud she would be.

"You sure you will be fine with him?"

"Yes fine, bring him here tomorrow."

"To the bench, really?" It's kind of a sacred space for her. I'm surprised she is willing to let someone else here.

"Well he does not have anywhere to go to talk to his dad yet, does he?"

We still have not decided what to do with the ashes. Meg wanted to take them back to Spain, but Jake was not keen. He wanted to throw them out to sea but I thought it might be nice for him to have somewhere to go like Nellie and I do, so at the minute Joe is in a vase on the deck, being toasted by Jimmy and I each night as we drink copious amounts of wine to drown our sorrows.

Now I know he is not having an affair, things are easier, and I know Jimmy was honouring his friend's wishes, but I'm still hurt by the secret he kept from me, and the pain he put me through.

To discuss it now would feel like punishment, and it's not what I want. I know we have things to talk about, but the kids keep us busy all day, and it's so much easier to pour a drink and sit in companionable silence once they are in bed, than to try and undo the knots and kinks in our marriage.

I thank her for sharing her bench and ask, "How is Fleur getting on?"

"She is bloody massive, but she does not look fat anymore, she looks pregnant. The baby really likes it when I talk to him."

"Him?"

"I think it's going to be a him."

"So you talk to him now?"

"Well no, a bit, oh I don't know. Whenever I walk into the room Fleur says he kicks like mad because he likes the sound of my voice. She's probably just making it up."

"Because she's a mean old witch?"

"Nah. She is OK really, quite harmless in fact. I reckon I know more about babies than her. I'm probably going to have to help her out a lot."

"Probably."

"Still think babies are stupid though?"

"Of course, except yours."

"Of course." I pull her under my arm and kiss the top of her head.

Nellie helps Jake more than I ever thought possible, mostly because he fell haplessly in love the second he clapped eyes on her. She is too old for him, but they have a lot in common. Nellie talks about her mum and Jake talks about his dad. They talk about the looks they get at school and how none of their friends know what to say to them. Nellie has moved on a bit from the early stages of grief so she offers Jake great advice on how to handle situations. I see Jake's face light up when she calls or comes to see us.

"Can we go to the bench today?" he asks every morning when he comes downstairs. "Please?"

Chapter Fourteen

"ALL'S well that ends well then," Dad says to me on the phone.

"Not that well, Dad, Joe died, remember."

"Yes, that's a tough row to hoe, but I'd prefer to die on my feet than live on my knees."

"So you think Sara's exit is a better one?"

"I don't know, Peta. I just think that you have spent so long surrounded by death, living in grief and worry. Sara died and it was horrible and now you have lost Joe, but you are still here, Peta, with your life to live. It's always darkest before dawn, and Christ knows you have had your darkness."

It's quite a speech. Dad is almost panting by the end of it. I sigh and pick at a Peppa Pig sticker Pip stuck on the TV. "It's hard. For so long life has been about coping, thinking about other people. Thinking just about me feels wrong and selfish."

"Well it isn't. Stop hiding your light under a bushel. All work and no play."

"Are you calling me dull?"

"No, but speaking of dull, your mother wants a word with you. She wants to know if you are still coming to visit. Please say yes."

Jake loves France. Him, Dad, and Jimmy go out on quad bikes and sea fishing and shoot air rifles while me and Mum and the girls splash in the pool and tend to the horses. The girls are much more confident this time which makes Mum happy.

"I see a lot of potential in Roo. I think she is going to be an excellent show-jumper."

"You do?"

"Yes, look at how she jumped over that log."

"Yes, but she was not on a horse."

"It does not matter, the technique is all there."

"Excellent news." I go inside to get more sun cream. Juno looks a bit pink.

"Shall I cook dinner tonight?" I yell from the kitchen. "NO," everybody yells back. "Have a bloody holiday."

It's odd having time on my hands and nothing to do. I get a pad and pen from the village and sit on the sun lounger, jotting down recipes and the stories behind them.

I must have fallen asleep reading to the girls. Jimmy wakes me with a gentle shake. "Wake up, Peta," he says softly.

We go downstairs and Jimmy unlocks the back door. The pool lights are still on, and flies buzz round the citronella candle he lights. The tiles are still warm from the sun. I sit down on the floor and tip my head back to look at the stars.

"Budge along." I move over as Jimmy sits next to me.

"Ta." I take the beer he is holding and look down at our legs stretched out next to one another.

"You OK?" he asks lightly, but I know what he really means is 'Are we ok? Do you forgive me?' I take a sip from my bottle and watch the pool. The water looks like silk. I imagine it rippling over me.

"I'm OK," I say slowly, nodding in the half light. "A bit bruised maybe."

"I'm sorry," Jimmy butts in. "I never meant to hurt you. At first, it was hard to keep it from you, but then …" He stops and swigs at his drink. "When I saw you thinking that Meg and I were …" He frowns into the top of the bottle. "That you would ever think I would do that to you, to the kids. I was angry with you, and my anger made it easier to keep you in the dark."

"Would you not have suspected the same thing?" I ask, trying not to raise my voice. "I mean, what else was I to think? You lost all that weight and you were never at home and she was answering your phone …" I trail off when he does not respond. "I did not know what else to think, Jimmy." Tears fill my eyes and I swipe them away with the back of my hand. I turn to him and try to explain. "Mostly, I still feel like the same girl you took to the pub that night all those years ago, but you … You've changed so much, Jim. You are so, so grown up," I say, wishing there was a better word for it. "Remember when we used to joke about very important business people? You called them 'Vibls' and laughed at their shiny shoes." I laugh but it comes out as a sob. "And now you *are* a Vibl, and I wonder if you would even look twice at me if we were to meet now."

"Peta, I'd always look twice at you," Jimmy sighs. "My job has changed and I've gotten more responsible. But I did it for you, for our girls. I took on all the boring stuff, the money and the bills, so you don't have to worry about it. I wanted you to be able to stay at home with the girls, to be the mum you wanted to be." He finishes his drink and clinks the bottle down on the steps. "I didn't mean to make you feel inferior. I was just trying to look after you all. I'm still me in here …" He slaps his hand over his heart. I reach for it and pull it into mine. There is silence for a moment and then he says, "You know Joe's finances and stuff were in pretty bad shape. He owed a lot of money, and, well, let's just say, I've had a couple of phone calls from women who thought they might have a mention in his will." He squeezes my hand. "I'd never do that to you. It's not who I am."

Somewhere in the background a dog barks. The tiles are

getting cold below me. "Maybe it was not you I doubted," I say softly. "Maybe it was me. Sometimes I feel like I am in no way qualified to be a mum, or a step mum. I made a pig's ear of Roo's first year at school. Juno is overweight and Pip is so anxious and insecure. I …" Jimmy cuts me off. "Peta, you are an amazing mum. So what if you are not the first bloody person in the playground, wearing a matching fucking twinsets from Boden? It's not about that. Was that really what you wanted from your mum?"

"No."

"What did you want from her?"

"I just wanted her to be interested in me, I suppose." I let go of his hand and pull at a patch of grass awkwardly.

"Well I don't know anyone more interested in their kids than you. You can read them like books. You are the centre of their world and you will be the same for Jake." He pulls my hand back. "Look at me, Peta. You need to believe in yourself. No one can do that for you."

I nod my head, a tear falls onto my lip.

"Do you want to come and work with me? Would that help?"

"Doing what?"

"Well, a space has just opened up for a sexy PA."

I laugh and punch him on the arm. "Seriously though, Joe always praised you and your writing. He would be really happy to have had you on board."

"I was kind of thinking of doing something different." I tell him my plans for my cookery blog 'Baking for a broken heart'. "I want it to be full of comfort recipes for the hard days, recipes for sharing, and recipes for taking your time over. Meals the colours of the season, to remind people that life does go on." I did not realise how passionate I was until I spoke the idea aloud.

"I think it sounds amazing. So you are not going back to Tummy-to-Mummy?"

"No. I told them to shove their contract up their arse."

"Really, when?"

"The day of Joe's funeral. I'd not written my article on making the perfect pea puree and I decided enough was enough. There are some things that are important in life and some things that are not. The perfect pea puree is not one of them."

"It's not going to be one of the recipes in your book then?"

"No."

"How did it feel when you told Michelle to fuck off?

"Amazing."

"How is it going to feel when I throw you in the swimming pool?"

"You'll have to catch me first." I leap up and shriek with delight as Jimmy chases me round the terrace and the garden before finally catching me and tossing me in the pool, then jumping in after me with a huge splash.

The curtains in the bedroom above are opened and Mum pokes her head out the window. "Shut up. You'll wake the whole street," she shouts at us. I hear my dad say, "There is no one else on the bloody street, you mad cow. We live in the arse end of nowhere."

"Shut up, Nigel," she hisses back. "You'll wake the children."

"What about when you just opened the window and howled like a banshee?" he splutters back at her.

I can't hear her answer but I can picture my dad's face.

"So are we OK then?" Jimmy asks again as we float on our backs holding hands.

"Yes, I think we might be," I reply.

The next day Mum takes us to the Tower at Aurignac. It is as boring as it was the time before when she took us, and the time before that.

"Look, look," she squawks at Roo. "If you stand over here at the top you can hear your own echo."

"Just like last time," Jimmy whispers.

I stand in the middle and shout, "THIS IS BORING!" The words echo around and the children laugh. "WHO WANTS AN ICE CREAM?!" Jimmy booms. "Me, me, me, me," say four excited voices.

"Ignorant heathens," my mother says and marches off. To appease her, we go and watch a horse show then take the kids to the local market. There is an old woman giving away puppies. Jake and Roo fall in love with one of them.

"But what about Spike? How would he feel?"

"Spike would not mind. He would love to have another dog to play with when we are at school," Jake insists, stroking the dog's ears.

"I play with Spike when you are at school." I say, pretending to be hurt. "I thought we were friends Spike," I say to the ground next to Roo's shoe. "Mum, Spike is back at Grandma and Grandpa's, silly."

"Oh right. Of course," I say, while Jimmy and Pip look on bemused.

I manage to persuade them that now is not the time or the place to get a dog. My mother does not help at all and goes on about how much she loves Fox and how much fun she is and how she could not live without him and an imaginary dog would never do for her.

"She walks to the beat of a different drummer," I say to Dad as we lead sobbing children back to the car.

"Monkey see, monkey do," he says, watching as Mum tries haggling the price of a cauliflower by shaking her head and hugging it.

I don't want to go home. I have not missed the school run or the housework or the weather. "Let's move to France," I say to Jimmy in bed on the last night.

"You said you never wanted to live in the same postcode as your mum"

"Oh yes," I forgot that bit.

"It won't be so bad going home. I will be around more I promise." Joe made Jimmy swear that he would adopt his old working hours and be at home more. "You have my boy at home now," he told him. "Enjoy him for me."

And I'll make sure we make lots more time for this … he inches my t-shirt up slowly.

"What are you doing?" I whisper. "My parents might hear."

"They are not home," he replies smoothly, sliding it up another inch. "They have gone to the Madman's to get some wild boar." I sit up so he can slide my t-shirt over my head. "it's just you and me …"

"… and four children," I add, my voice muffled from inside my top.

"Oh shut up and get your pants off," he says pulling the cover over our heads.

The journey home is fraught with delays and traffic.

The house is quiet and feels sad when we finally walk into it after a long day of travelling. "It's always been a house that needs filling with children," I say to Jimmy as we lift the sleeping kids from the car to bed. "Just as well," mutters Jimmy as he picks up Juno. "Jesus Christ, she weighs a ton! She's is heavier than Jake."

When they are safely in bed and asleep we unload the car together then Jimmy nips out to get a Nando's takeaway as there is no food in the house.

I run a hot bath and shave my legs, admiring my tan. When I get out I look at myself in the mirror. My white wobbly bits are still white and wobbly. My camel-testicle tummy still looks like a camel-testicle tummy, but Jimmy does not seem to mind. "I want you to see your beauty, Peta," he said in France, tracing his finger over the puckered skin. "These are your battle scars, and you should be proud, but if you really hate them so much, if they make you so unhappy, then maybe we should go and see a cosmetic surgeon?"

I think about it long after he has gone to sleep, feeling my scars in the darkness, remembering my tummy rounded in pregnancy and flat before then. I tug at the skin and think how it stretched for my babies. What message am I giving them if I have it removed? Be perfect or you cannot be loved? Even if I do have the operation, I will always find something to berate myself for. No, I finally decide as the sun sneaks in through the shutters, this skin is mine and it will stay with me.

Wendy hold's Roo's party for the weekend before school starts. When we arrive I see how she has gone all out. She has made cupcakes with marzipan dogs on them, biscuits in the shape of Bonios and a giant cake with a trophy on it. Roo looks overwhelmed when she sees all the banners and balloons, clutching my leg like Pip used to. Pip doesn't do it so much now, I realise suddenly. She tends to clutch Jake's instead. Jake is loving being a big brother. When Nellie is around he pretends he is too cool for the girls, shooing them out his room and closing the door in their little faces, but as soon as she has gone he runs into their room and yells "BUNDLE" before launching himself on the floor so the girls can jump on him.

"Go on, my love." I gently push her forward. "Don't be shy, this is all for you and you deserve it." She takes a couple of steps away from me then pauses. Lily-Grace comes up to us and takes hold of her hand, the one with the burn on, which the doctor's say will scar. She was upset about this until Jake told her how cool scars are. Now she loves it.

"Is this all for me?" she asks, eyes as big as saucers.

"Yes," says Wendy, coming over to put her arm round Roo. "All for the bravest, best friend a girl could ever have."

"Thank you," I mouth at her.

"THANK YOU," she mouths back, pointing at Roo whose shyness is forgotten in moments and she is soon charging round barking like mad and trying to pop balloons.

September arrives far too soon. I forget to get Roo bigger summer dresses. Last year she looked lost and generic in gingham, now she is bursting out of it.

"Mum, I can't wear this, it's too small!" She tugs at the hem and tries to pull it down over her scabby knees.

"It's all we have, my love. I will order you some more on line today."

"Can you cut this label out?" Jake asks, stomping into my bedroom. "It's itching me like mad." Jake is cross, because he's nervous. I'm learning his ticks and how to respond to them. I remind myself it's not easy for him coming from a quiet flat he shared with his dad to a house with four shrieking women in it.

"Yes, lovely, come here and I'll see to it. Are your trousers OK?" I managed to get Jake into the same school as Roo. The uniform is stricter than his last one and he does not like it. He has his father's laid-back attitude to clothes and tugs at his shirt collar as if it's choking him.

"You look so much older in uniform," I say carefully. "Are you seeing Nellie later?"

It works. He immediately straightens up and admires

himself. "Yeah, probably," he says, pushing his hair to one side. It pings back immediately and I smother a grin. "I think I'll get some hair gel." He peers at himself closely.

"Jimmy might have some, hang on." I rummage in the basket next to our bed and produce a pot of wax "Catch".

He goes to unscrew it then turns to me and Roo sat on the bed, then to Pip and Juno who have come to gather by the door. "Do you all have to watch?" he says eventually.

"Oh right, come on gang," I say, picking up Juno and tugging Pip by the hand. "Let's go and make some breakfast."

When Jake comes downstairs fifteen minutes later he has far too much hair wax on. He tries to look cool and casual as he takes his seat and starts attacking his giant bowl of Shreddies but I can tell he feels self-conscious. I take a sip of my tea and text Jimmy surreptitiously at the same time: *Jake looks like he's been in an oil slick. One for you to sort.*

The study door opens a moment later and Jimmy makes his way downstairs. "Good luck," I say as I slip past him into the bathroom with my make-up bag. I need to prepare myself for all the questions I am going to get at school about Jake. "It's no one else's business," I tell myself as I apply eyeliner. "You do not need to explain yourself."

I'm still tanned from France so I skip the bronzer and apply some poppy-tint lip stain instead. A few months ago I felt daunted by all my lotions and potions, now I pluck and brush and sweep with ease.

"You look nice," Jimmy says approvingly, as I gather lunchboxes and reading bags from the kitchen. I'm wearing a khaki green skirt and a white vest top. Instinctively I think 'no I don't', but I make myself say, "Thank you," and smile at him.

"Sure you don't want me to come with you today, Jake?" he asks, inserting a capsule into the espresso machine and checking there is enough water.

"Nah, I'll be fine," Jake replies.

Jimmy managed to persuade him to wash out the hair wax. "Chicks don't really dig grease mate." and his hair is now fluffier than ever. I feel nervous and tearful for him. "Don't," Jimmy says warningly, knowing I was about to go and hug him.

"Right then." I finally locate the car keys under a pile of Peppa Pig pants. "Let's go." I peck Jimmy on the lips as I pass, he cups my bum with one hand and lengthens the kiss, leaning me backwards to finish with a flourish. I'm blushing when he releases me.

"Yuk," Roo says, looking disgusted.

"Is that what chicks dig?" Jake asks Jimmy who says nothing but gives him a wink.

"Juno," Pip says as we wander down the drive, "you have to be a good girl at pre-school and do what Faith tells you." Juno nods happily and clutches onto her lunchbox. She continues to tell Juno all the rules and regulations as we drive along the road. "And you are not allowed to go to the toilet less you ask with your hand up like this." She demonstrates for Juno, who copies. "Yes. That is good, and you have to put your coat on the peg. NO Juno! You are not allowed to eat your lunch yet!"

Faith is waiting at the door for us. "You okay?"

I'm so worried about Jake I've not really considered that my baby is starting pre-school. "I don't know," I say suddenly, my eyes welling up. "Oh bloody hell, forget I asked!" she says, pushing me out the door and mouthing, "She will be fine," through the glass.

I'm grateful we are running late. It means there's no time for Jake to get more nervous as we walk from the pre-school up the lane. The bell rings within two minutes of us being in the playground. "Right." I don't know whether or not to kiss him. Roo is still happy to give me a big smacker but I have no idea what boys do. When Joe left me with him, he did not leave an instruction manual. I decide to go for a high-five. I figure they are always cool. Jake looks at me like I'm mad and then throws his arms around me dramatically "Love you, Guapa," he announces loudly. Some kids near us stop and stare. "Yeah," he tells them. "That's how I roll." They look away awkwardly. I laugh and ruffle his hair. "I'll be here at three twenty to pick you up, OK?"

"And can we go to the park? And you will be in goal? And Jimmy will come and meet us and you will make that chicken noodle thing?"

"Yes, of course." I turn to Roo. "Have you got everything, gorgeous?"

"Yep."

"Sorry I forgot your PE kit. I'll drop it in later."

"Yes, yes, Mummy. Now say goodbye to Spike."

"Roo … " I try to appease her.

She won't be deterred. "Do you want me and Spike to be sad aaaall day?"

"No," I tut.

"Well say goodbye to him then." She puts her hands on her hips and I think of Nellie.

"Goodbye, Spike. Have a nice day. Please don't bark through reading time," I say out the side of my mouth.

"He wants you to stroke him."

"ROO!" I snap

"I don't want you to, Mummy, Spike does."

I wave my fingers lightly up and down in the air. "There."

"Spike is not that big."

Oh sod it. I bend down and do low Tai Chi moves for a long time. I move one arm out and then the other, as if I am trying to get a hand dryer to work.

Roo laughs with delight. "Spike LOVES it, Mummy. He loves it."

She and Jake walk into school laughing. I wave them off feeling pleased with myself for once, and then turn round to face all the nosy mums desperate to know where my new son came from.

Pip is up at 4am the next morning, worried that we will miss the coach for the zoo trip to Drusilla's. She did not believe that it was not leaving for hours, nor that it would not leave without her. I end up getting up with her and letting her watch a marathon session of Peppa Pig while I work on my cookery blog.

As soon as we get out the car she runs over to Faith waiting in the playground, clutching Juno by the hand. "I got mine sister, this mine sister Juno," she says to all her pre-school friends.

"Nice hi-vis," I say to Faith.

"Oh piss off," she says back, then "You OK today?" I pass her the girls packed lunches and change of pants. "No doubt you will need these. Yes, I am okay. Juno is certainly happy enough." I look up to see her and Pip making their way to the back of the coach. "She has no problem with me leaving her," I sigh.

"Which means you are a great mother," Faith tells me, then turns to roar at Ethan and Rowan, "NO STICKS ON THE COACH!"

I laugh, and then see Pamela making her way over and the smile slides from my face. I know what she is going to ask me, and I know what my answer needs to be.

"Ah, Peta, I'm so pleased I caught you." I smile as nicely as I can. "I see you have not put your name down to continue as chairperson this year."

She stops and looks at me expectantly. I take a deep breath and say, "Yes, sorry about that." I'm about to say more when I feel Faith's long fingernail digging in my skin.

"Well," Pamela says, "I don't know what we will do. No one has stepped in as your replacement." I open and close my mouth helplessly.

"Don't do it," Faith hisses behind me. I stand in silence instead while Pamela peers at me with her beady eyes to see if I will crack.

"I do hope we will have enough members to keep running," she says slowly. "Or we may have to close." Neither of us say anything.

Sweat drips down into the crevice of my bra. Faith starts humming tunelessly. Finally, after what seems like an age, the coach driver comes over and tells us he is ready to leave. Pamela gives me one last stare and then turns around on her giant white trainer and stalks over to the coach.

"I did it!" I high-five Faith, then collapse in her arms.

"Really I should be cross with you." she says. "Leaving me with her." I go to apologise and she cuts in. "Don't just bloody ruin all your hard work by saying sorry!" I kiss her on the cheek instead and go and get Jake and Roo out the car, where they are glued to the DVD player.

I spend the morning working on my blog. I'm pretty pleased with it. I make a Twitter account and a Facebook page, then email my old friend at the Argus the link to my site and tell her what I'm up to.

I'm so absorbed in trying to take a decent photo of my banana loaf I almost forget to go and collect the girls.

The coach is late so I have time to park and get in the queue of waiting mums. When the doors open Pip charges off the coach, her plaits pointing sideways out her head. "Mummy,

Mummy," she pants excitedly. "I stroked a German at the zoo!"

"Gerbil, Pip, you stroked a Gerbil in the petting room," says Faith wearily, coming off the coach behind her.

"How was it?" I ask her as she hands out bags and lunchboxes. Her glasses are sticky and her scarf has lots of tomato ketchup on it.

"The same as it is every year. Bloody awful."

"Did the kids enjoy it?" I say, accepting the bag of soiled pants she hands over. "The ones who didn't get lost and cry for their mummies did. Pamela forgot her glasses and thought the sloth was a giant bat. She took lots of photos of it."

"I'd love to have seen that." I fumble in my bag for my beeping phone. Heather and I have been texting this morning.

"Mummmeee …" Pip tugs my hand, interrupting. "I want to goooo."

"Alright, hang on. How was she?" I ask Joy, angling my head towards Pip.

"She liked the giant millipede because it looked like a giant poo." I nod. "Did she do a poo?"

Oh yes." Faith waves off a child to her mum while I stand waiting.

"In the toilet?" I ask hopefully.

"No."

"Oh God." I wince "Where?"

"Don't worry. It was in the petting farm near the pig-sty."

I breathe a sigh of relief and hoist Juno up onto my hip. "Not too bad. Did anyone see?"

"Only a cow," Joy says. "And she was not wearing her glasses."

We laugh and nudge each other.

"How was Juno?" I stroke her sticky head. "Loud, boisterous, excitable. Pig-headed. A true Newton."

I feel my heart swell with pride, meanwhile, Pip is very bored by my side, desperate to get away. "I want a cuppa tea NOW, Mummy!"

"OK, OK, let's go. Love you." I drop a kiss on Faith's cheek.

"Love you too, hon. Well done on standing up for yourself today."

We bump fists then Pip, Juno and I skip back to the car singing about the zoo. "What was your favourite animal?" I ask them. "The giant poo!" they chant together.

Jimmy cooks dinner that night. "I do love all the recipes you have been making recently for the blog," he says apologetically. "But I really want to stay this weight." He busies himself chopping veg for the stir fry and does not look at me as he says, "When Joe told me he had cancer, I went for a full medical at the Nuffield private hospital. I had everything that can possibly be checked, checked."

He winces at the memory of the prostate gland bit.

"And they found nothing?" I ask, immediately anxious.

"Nothing at all." He throws me a quick reassuring smile. "Except my weight. They said I was too heavy. It was horrible," he confesses to the broccoli in front of him. "I felt so ashamed."

I feel ashamed as I listen to him speaking. There I was thinking he was trying to lose weight to impress his PA and really he was doing all he could to make sure he was around for his family.

I've done nothing to support Jimmy's diet. Sure, I substituted some meals with fish for him occasionally, but on the whole I was so cross with him all the time I just cooked what I normally cooked, with extra butter.

"I'll research this protein diet and make him some delicious meals for you," I promise him. "It will look good on the blog." My mind is already on turkey wraps with Papadew peppers when he says, "I want you to go for a full medical as well, Pete."

"Really?"

"I could not cope …" he says to the chopping board. "With you know …"

I walk over and rest my cheek in the dip between his shoulder blades. "I know, baby, I know".

Jimmy's grief swoops upon him like the starlings that fly round the pier. One minute he is fine, and the next he is swamped by pain. I know this because I still feel it too on the days I wake up and for just one second I forget that Sara is not here. It's a pain that beats like a thousand tiny wings.

The next day Roo comes out of school dragging her feet and looking like she has far too much on her mind for a five-year-old.

"What's up, Poppet?"

Is God cross with me, Mummy?"

"Of course he is not, my sweetheart. Why would he be cross?" I feel my shoulders droop. I thought we had got everything sorted.

"Because I got him confused with a donkey last year," she says mournfully.

"No, he did not mind at all. He thought it was, um, funny," I say, desperate to nip this in the bud.

"How do you know?"

I say the first thing I can think of, "He called me."

"How?" she shoots back immediately suspicious.

"On the er, whisper-ma-phone." My palms sweat slightly as I think about this story going round the school.

"The one in the Lorax?" Roo asks, still looking unsure.

"Yep," I say lightly, hoping it's the end of the conversation, but Roo won't let the matter rest.

"Wow. I didn't know we had a whisper-ma-phone." She goes on and on about it all the way home and all evening over a dinner of Sara's Pie, which is what I have decided to call my chicken pie.

Jimmy is not home to save me. He is having to meet with all his clients to assure him that they can expect business as usual. I'm not expecting him back till much later.

I look at Jake for help but he just laughs at me and replies to Nellie's texts on my phone. I distract Roo with some angel cake, but it does not last long.

"I love God, Mummy," she says in the bath, making patterns on the wet tiles with her finger.

"Uh-huh, me too! Would you like some nice warm milk?" I collect up the wet sponges and fish round for the plug.

"No thank you, I want to talk to God on the whisper-ma-phone to check he is not cross with me." I hear Jake laugh softly from his room.

"I think God is busy right now, poppet" I say through gritted teeth.

"But Mrs Peacock said God is never too busy for us." My loathing for Mrs Peacock comes back with a vengeance.

"I think God is going to bed now." I wrap her in a towel and carry her into the bedroom, where her sisters are arguing over who gets to wear the yellow nightdress.

"God never sleeps though," she persists as I wrestle a pair of night pants onto Juno.

"Oh fine, can I just get the little two into bed first please?" I wipe a film of sweat from my brow.

"Just sit STILL, Juno. Pip, get off my make-up bag. JAKE! get off the phone!"

The little two are asleep in seconds, but Roo is unsettled. I run down the stairs and hiss, "FIND ME A WHISPER-MA-PHONE," at Jake.

"OK, OK, chill out, Guapa." He sounds so much like Joe that tears come from nowhere. I squeeze them away. No time for any of that. I need to fashion a whisper-ma-phone and find a way to talk to God.

I go back up and read in my most soothing, and boring voice, hoping Roo will fall asleep. I chose the Famous Five, thinking it will be boring, which it is, but it's also full of sentences like "Hurry up, Dick" and "My Aunt Fanny will be cross with you" which I can't help but laugh at.

"Have you got the whisper-ma-phone?" she says, just as I am inching my way out her room, thinking she is asleep. Fuck.

"Yes, it's downstairs, I'll just go and get it"

When I get downstairs Jake is holding the garden hosepipe with the spray gun attachment on the end of it and grinning.

"Are you being serious?"

He is enjoying this. I snatch it from him.

"This is never going to work," I say, as I go back upstairs with it.

"That is not a whisper-ma-phone, that's Daddy's hosepipe with the spray gun on the end," Roo says immediately.

"No it is not. It's a whisper-ma-phone *disguised* as Daddy's hosepipe."

Roo looks at me for a long moment, deciding whether or not she is going to buy it. "OK then, Mummy, get him to say something down it." Bugger. I had not thought of that bit.

"Um, hello. Hello? Are you there, God?" I look at the hose pipe hopefully then say, "Oh, it's his answer machine, Pops. He must be out." I try to look disappointed. "He's probably at Starbucks with the angels and his donkey."

"Probably." I put down the hose and tuck her in.

"Just leave him a message then to call me back," she says.

I sigh and pick up the hose again. "Hello, God, this is Roo Newton's mummy. We were hoping to have a quick chat with you but you are obviously busy. Maybe you will call us back on the landline."

"Will he have our number, Mummy?"

"I am sure of it, Pops. Now try and get some sleep." She rolls over and reaches for her rabbit teddy.

I go downstairs and tell Jake it's time for his bed. He sighs and tuts.

"I wanted to stay up and watch the football with Jimmy." I waver, but then remember Joe's words about not treating him differently because I feel sorry for him.

"Maybe tomorrow night, eh?"

"Fine." He stomps off, then stops and comes back over to me, resting his chin on my shoulder. Then he says, "Sorry, Guapa."

"No problem." I pat the top of his silky head and wait.

"Did you um …"

"Yes, Jake, I spoke to Nellie today. Yes, she mentioned you. She said do you want to go trainer shopping with her on Saturday?"

"Can I?" He looks at me and his eyes are shining.

"Only if I can come." His face falls at this condition. "I will stay well back, and I won't bring the girls in case Pip poo's or

Juno steals from the pick 'n' mix. I'll just be around and I'll buy you both milkshakes from Shakeaway in the Lanes."

"DEAL!" He high-fives me and then walks upstairs.

"Come Spike," he says to the rug on the landing.

Jimmy gets home at 9.30 pm and we are just sitting down to dinner when Roo reappears. I notice her little bare legs dangling through the gap in the stairs.

"You OK, Pops?" I ask, reaching through the open riser to stroke her soft heel.

"He never called me back, Mummy. He is cross with me, isn't he?"

"No, my lovely, of course not. He is just very, very busy. Try not to worry about it. Come on, back to bed."

It takes another half hour to settle her. When I come downstairs Jimmy is outside feeding the chickens.

"You want me to what now?"

"I need you to whisper into Roo's ear while she is asleep. Tell her, "Hello, Roo, it's God here. I am not at all cross with you. I loved the donkey story, and I love you."

"Are you in your right mind?" he says, stroking his favourite hen.

"Probably not" I say, sitting back on my heels.

"How did this come about?"

"I don't know," I sigh. "I just wanted to make her feel better."

"I don't think she is going to feel too good when she realises that her mother lied to her."

"But she is not going to find out, because you are going to help me, aren't you?"

"It won't work, she will recognise my voice."

"We'll disguise it."

"How?"

Ten minutes later Jimmy whispers, "This is ridiculous. I don't know how you get yourself into these messes."

"Just shut up and get on with it." I poke him in the shoulder, and he tuts. "Is that any way to speak to his holiness?"

I poke him again. He sighs, then picks up the wrapping paper tube, places it over Roo's ear and whispers, "Hello, my child, it's God."

"What's that accent?" I whisper.

"Morgan Freeman from Bruce Almighty," he says over his shoulder to me.

"Oh, quite good." I pat him on the arm.

"Thank you, I've not even practised."

Next to us, Roo stirs.

"Quick, get on with it!"

"Don't wake up or open your eyes," he coos. "You must not see me. I am so, um, sparkly, I will burn your retinas. I just wanted to let you know that I love you very much. Especially when you help find snails." I dig him in the ribs again and make a cutting action under my chin.

"That is all. Er, peace be with you and Ahmen." He bows his head.

As soon as we get out her room I smack him over the head with the tube.

"Why did you add that bit about the snails? What if she works it out?"

"She won't. Now get your kit off. You owe me."

"Is that an order, God?"

Roo seems happier when she skips into school the next morning. "Come on Spike!" she shouts as she runs across the playground. The dying summer sun sends light through the leaves and throws patterns on the playground. I never normally notice these things and realise I am quite relaxed, then I realise why. The-Iron-Curtain is not here. She has not been here all term.

"Where is The ... um, Regina?" I ask Zac's mum.

"They have moved back to Russia."

"REALLY?"

"Yes. It was all very sudden. She bought the snails back in on the last day of term, told the teacher they were dead and that she was leaving."

"Oh. Wow." I almost feel bad about the garden snails masquerading as giant African land snails. Then I remember how much I hated her and I don't.

"She also said she was sick of this country, the competitive mums and all the reading practise."

"What?" I splutter. "She was the worst one for all that stuff!"

"I know! Just as well she has gone eh, snail killer." She smiles at me conspiratorially.

"Mmm." A confession is burning on my tongue but I swallow it. The school hates me enough as it is. No good will come from telling her that Pip fed them to the chickens. Pip will be starting in September. I desperately want her first year at school to go better than Roo's has.

I drive home, say "bollocks" to the empty cereal bowls, piles of washing and dead flowers that Roo has been collecting to make perfume with. I put on my running gear instead and make my way down the drive.

"Hello, bird." I pant when I get to her bench. "Sorry, I'm very sweaty."

I take out my water bottle and take a long swig, then I tell her about The-Iron-Curtain leaving and Juno starting pre-school. I tell her about the whisper-ma-phone and how much Jake is in love with Nellie.

When I have run out of news to tell her I curl up in the corner of the bench and watch dog walkers and other morning joggers for half an hour before making my way back home.

I am trying to write an explanation for Joe's Spanish omelette when the patio door opens and Jimmy appears with a pile of paperwork.

"Why are you at home?"

"Lisa in accounts is having ladies' problems. She keeps talking about them really loudly with the door open and I can't concentrate. I am going to work here."

"Oh."

He looks hurt. "Don't you want me here?"

"No, it's not that. I was just planning on cracking on with some recipes."

"Well I won't disturb you."

He disturbs me. He sucks two fingers in his mouth when he is concentrating. It sounds like a welly being pulled out of mud. He taps his pen against his teeth and spins his wedding ring on the table.

"Jesus, Jimmy! Could you make a bit more noise?"

"Sorry. I am finding you very distracting covered in flour with a pinny on. Please may you go upstairs and let me do rude things to you."

I think of all the reasons why I should not, then think sod it and say, "OK then, but hurry up. I have a flan in my oven."

"I can't wait to see that," he says winking at me.

Epilogue

OF course Roo wanted a real dog for her birthday. Initially, Jimmy was adamant she was not having one. "She just got a new brother. She does not need a dog."

But then there was the fire, and everything changed.

"Promise it won't upset my chickens and poo on my lawn?"

"Promise. Think about how happy it will make her."

"What about how unhappy it will make me? And who will walk it?"

"We all will."

"Where will it sleep?"

"Outside in the playhouse."

"What kind of bloody dog does she want anyway?" he asks, but he is only pretending to be grumpy now.

"I think Spike is a brown Labrador."

"Well, she does not need one of them then."

I don't answer. I just look at him.

"Jake would love a dog too you know. And it would be good for him. It would give him a sense of responsibility. I know he is desperate to prove himself as a man in the family.

"Where do you get one of these Labradors then?"

"The rescue home?"

"I don't want an old one with one leg. It will just die on us, like everyone else does." I know this is Jimmy's way of dealing with Joe's death so I don't admonish him.

"A puppy it is then."

"Oh God. It's going to piss everywhere, chew my work shoes and poo on the rug, isn't it?

"Yep."

"It will be just like having Pip all over again."

"At least we can shut it in the garden when it drives us too mad."

"True."

"I …"

"Shut up. I have not said yes yet. I am thinking about it, and that is all. No more and no less. Do not push me, I will not be swayed. Not even if you take all your clothes off and try and seduce me."

"Ok, I won't bother then."

"Well you might as well try. It might work I suppose."

A week later he comes home with a giant grin on his face.

"Go and look in the car," he tells me. I slip on the green crocs he bought on our honeymoon and make my way down the drive.

In the back of the car is a box. Inside the box, smelling of milk and fur and babies is a tiny brown Labrador puppy, curled up and fast asleep.

"Oh, wow." I reach out a finger and trace it down his silky little back.

"Hello, boy. Aren't you a beauty."

Jimmy appears behind me. "No stupid names. He is going to have a proper name. "

"OK."

"And don't buy him a wussy dog collar with diamantes on. He won't like that either."

"Got it."

"And don't pretend he is a baby. He is not, he is a dog."

"Absolutely."

I go to pick him up.

"No, not like that, like this." He scoops a hand under him and brings him to his chest. "He likes to be near you, where it is warm, see."

"How do you know all this stuff?"

"I read about it. You can't go buying dog without reading about what to do with them."

The puppy looks so tiny in his arms.

"I think I am having one of those naff Athena poster moments," I tell him. "There is something ridiculously attractive about you holding that puppy." I go to stroke him.

"Get off! I might drop him. We will have to keep him in here till the kids are in bed, then we can set up his bed and bowls."

"Have you got all of that stuff?"

He gestures to a bulging bag on the front seat inside a furry basket.

"I thought he was going to sleep in the porch?"

"Well, maybe when he is a bit older. It will be cold in the porch right now."

"I see."

The puppy stirs and opens a brown eye to look at me, then yawns sleepily and nods off again.

"Oh my God. I lush him."

Christmas eve is perfect. We spend the morning finding the perfect tree and decorating it. Then we go back and buy another one. One for us and one which we take to Stanmer Park and place in the middle of Sara's and Joe's benches. We can not string lights on it so we hang red ribbons all over it instead.

We cram into the pew for the crib service. Jake seems to know everyone already. The church is awash with brightly knitted scarves and excited children. I open Tupperware pots full of snacks to keep the little two quiet and settle myself in for the nativity.

Father Matthew approaches the microphone and fiddles with the settings. Finally his voice booms out.

"Good evening, everyone. Thank you so much for coming. I hope you don't mind, but I would like to do something a little bit different this year before we start. There is a very clever little girl amongst us. She saved her whole school from burning down with her quick thinking, and she rescued her best friend. She is also very good at writing stories. I am going to read my favourite one of hers to you right now. Rudy Newton, would you please come and stand next to me as I do so?"

Roo stood up shyly and took her place next to Father Matthew. The lights on the giant tree twinkled and the little wooden Jesus in his little wooden crib on his little bed of hay dreamed on as Father Matthew read: "Once upon a time, there was a tired donkey ..."

We are a motley bunch round the dining table the next day. Roo, Pip, Juno, Jake, Jimmy, Wojtek, Faith and Morris. He has even bought Sue with him. When I told Jimmy about her being locked in the cupboard he was horrified.

"I think he just needs more things to do," I said. "Have you not got anything for him?"

"Well I suppose he could look after the tracking devices on the vans," Jimmy said. "They are always breaking down."

It's Morris' dream job. He loves it, and works twelve hour day. Checking the tracking devices only takes about an hour; he spends the rest of the time setting up video cameras and installing locks.

Sue is drinking far less now he is not at home with her all day. She still refuses to wear clothes however.

"I just feel more comfortable naked," she says simply.

"You might feel comfortable," I say kindly, "but no one else does."

She is more or less decent for Christmas lunch, so at least she won't be putting anyone off the turkey that I have spent weeks trying to perfect. The recipe was a hit on my blog. I got an email from Sainsbury's asking if I would like to meet up in the New Year to discuss how we could work together.

I lie in bed once everyone has gone to sleep and think about the year we have had. I started out with one husband and three children, and I thought that was hard enough. Now I have one husband, four children, one dog and three chickens, and I have Nellie.

She did attend the birth in the end. Fleur went into labour in the middle of the night and there was no time to get to the hospital. "It was amazing," Nellie gushed, "seeing him come out. I am definitely going to be a midwife when I grow up." She is besotted with the baby. It's hard not to be. He is beautiful. As promised, Nellie was allowed to pick his name and called him Joe.

"For Jake?"

"A bit, and a bit because I feel like I knew him from all you said, and I feel like he is with Mum now looking after her ..." She trails off.

"I think it's beautiful."

Jimmy is sticking to his promise to Joe and working less, although I know it's hard for him and I know how much he is missing his business partner. I never tried to work again after Sara, but he has no choice.

Mickey's girlfriend Jen is pregnant. They went over to France for Christmas and broke the news during the toasts. Mickey thought that Mum would be happy but he was very wrong. She threw the turkey on the floor, kicked Dad and stormed upstairs to write posts about betrayal on Facebook.

"Why did she kick you?" I asked him when he Skyped me on boxing day.

"I have no idea. She is crazy."

"Walk softly, and carry a big stick."

"She is coming round a bit now anyway. Demanding to be at the birth and all that stuff."

"Jesus."

"I know."

"She wants to move back to England but I have said no."

"I wish you would."

"Ah, you don't really. You have your own family and your own life."

"I know but I still wish you were closer."

"Hey, the road to a friend's house is never long."

"Urgh."

"Can you all just sit next to each other please? I've been trying to take this photo for half an hour."

I sigh with frustration. "Pip, stop chasing seagulls. Roo, stop covering yourself in leaves. Jake, get OFF my iPhone!! Juno, get out my handbag, there is no food in there. Jimmy, no one is going to steal your bike and I don't want it in the photo. Move it and hold the dog!"

I finally get them to sit all together on the bench; it's a squash. "Now I just need to work out how to set the flash and I will come and join you." I fiddle with the buttons and adjust the settings then run to the bench and sit on Jimmy's knee. Pip and Juno immediately try and climb on my lap. Jake and Roo call Smike (what else would they call him?) to come in the photo. Jimmy looks the other way to check no one has stolen his bike, even though he is holding onto it. I am the only one looking at the camera. My eyes are half-shut but I'm laughing.

I run back to the bench while Jimmy is loading the kids into the car.

"Next year who knows if anyone else will be in the photo with us. It seems the doctor was more worried about setting up a play date than checking my coil properly. It's too soon to tell Jimmy. Don't want to get him excited and let him down. It's too soon to tell anyone apart from you."

I lay the stick down on the bench. "Sorry bird, I think a bit of wee went on you."

THE END

About the Author

I am a single mum to three small children (age not size). Once, BC (Before children, not Christ) I worked in PR and journalism. My blog, Mum In The South, describes my life as a mother and occasional person in her own right. When I am not writing or wrestling with my children, I can be found walking the dog, bidding for retro furniture on eBay or hiding in the bath with a book.

ENJOYED THIS BOOK? WE'VE GOT LOTS MORE!

Britain's Next **BESTSELLER**

DISCOVER NEW INDEPENDENT BOOKS & HELP AUTHORS GET A PUBLISHING DEAL.

DECIDE WHAT BOOKS WE PUBLISH NEXT & MAKE AN AUTHOR'S DREAM COME TRUE.

Visit **www.britainsnextbestseller.co.uk** to view book trailers, read book extracts, pre-order new titles and get exclusive Britain's Next Bestseller Supporter perks.

FOLLOW US:

BNBSbooks   @bnbsbooks   bnbsbooks

BRITAINSNEXTBESTSELLER.CO.UK